"GLOVES ARE OFF, BABY. GET READY TO HAVE YOUR ASS KICKED."

Tingles spread through her abdomen. He moved with the deadly grace she'd seen in a panther once years ago, his steps sure, his stance aggressive. Tace and aggressive with a woman? They didn't go together. "What is wrong with you?" she asked, keeping him squarely in her sights.

He chuckled, the sound both pissed and frustrated. "We don't have that kind of time, darlin'."

Darlin'. She swallowed and tried to ignore that sexy accent. Oh, he'd called her endearments before when they'd trained, but there had always been a brotherly fondness to his tone, so she'd been able to keep him in that safe slot. This was different. This tone caught her breath in her throat and shot lava through her veins, which was all sorts of bad. Her penchant for bad boys had ruined her life more than once, but never again. They had to remain colleagues if not friends. "You've lost your mind," she muttered.

"No doubt about that." He feinted in and back out.

Her head lifted, and she set her feet on the mat. "I guess the good ole boy needs a lesson." She used the falsest Texas accent she could muster, fighting to remain in control.

His upper lip lifted just enough for her to notice. "One of us is learning a lesson tonight."

JUSTICE ASCENDING

REBECCA ZANETTI

ZEBRA BOOKS
KENSINGTON PUBLISHING CORP.
http://www.kensingtonbooks.com

ZEBRA BOOKS are published by

Kensington Publishing Corp.
119 West 40th Street
New York, NY 10018

All Kensington titles, imprints, and distributed lines are available at special quantity discounts for bulk purchases for sales promotion, premiums, fund-raising, educational, or institutional use.

Special book excerpts or customized printings can also be created to fit specific needs. For details, write or phone the office of the Kensington Sales Manager: Attn.: Sales Department. Kensington Publishing Corp., 119 West 40th Street, New York, NY 10018. Phone: 1-800-221-2647.

Zebra and the Z logo Reg. U.S. Pat. & TM Off.

First Printing: February 2017
ISBN-13: 978-1-4201-3798-9
ISBN-10: 1-4201-3798-0

eISBN-13: 978-1-4201-3799-6
eISBN-10: 1-4201-3799-9

10 9 8 7 6 5 4 3 2 1

Printed in the United States of America

ACKNOWLEDGMENTS

I have many people to thank for help in getting this book to readers. I sincerely apologize to anyone I've forgotten.

Thank you to Big Tone for taking the kids to basketball and football and volleyball and lacrosse (our kids are seriously busy) while I wrote this book, and while also working so hard with your architecture firm. I honestly don't know how you do it all, and I'm grateful that you do.

Thanks to our amazing kids, Gabe and Karlina. I'm so very proud of you both.

Thank you to my talented agents, Caitlin Blasdell and Liza Dawson, who have been with me from the first book and who have supported, guided, and protected me in this wild industry.

Thank you to the Kensington gang: Alicia Condon, Alexandra Nicolajsen, Vida Engstrand, Jane Nutter, Michelle Forde, Lynn Cully, Janice Rossi, Ross Plotkin, Lauren Jernigan, Gary Sunshine, Arthur Maisel, Steven Zacharius, and Adam Zacharius.

And thanks also to my constant support system: Gail and Jim English, Debbie and Travis Smith, Stephanie and Don West, Brandie and Mike Chapman, Jessica and Jonah Namson, and Kathy and Herb Zanetti.

Chapter One

The Darkness doesn't just stare back . . . it moves forward, opens its mouth, and swallows you whole.

—Tace Justice

Tace Justice read the last depressing line on the page and growled, tossing the journal across the room. When it landed, the cover slapped back into place with Hello Kitty smiling at him. Jesus. Paper was scarce, but doc could've found a different notebook when she'd ordered him to start journaling. Like his descent into madness really needed to be recorded by a happy cat.

He glanced around his dismal apartment in Vanguard headquarters. Worn beige bedspread, tan couch, ripped brown linoleum that smelled like, well, nothing. Hell, it probably smelled bad, but he'd lost his sense of smell. If he wasn't crazy already, the entire room would have depressed the shit out of him. The walls had been painted white decades ago and even now stood bare and dingy. Should he get some art to brighten the place up?

Why bother? He stood and stretched, wincing as new bruises ached to life.

They'd returned mere hours before from a full-out battle

up north where they'd rescued two of their own. His adrenaline had ebbed, yet his mind still spun. No way could he sleep.

A tremor started in his right foot, and he paused, taking note. It vibrated up past his knee, and he had to balance on his other leg as weakness assailed his entire limb.

Not another tremor.

He sighed and waited, breathing in and out evenly until his strength returned. Damn it. What was wrong with him? He lacked the emotion to be truly concerned, but this was certainly annoying.

His bed was empty of company, and he needed to burn off some energy. At the midnight hour, the gym downstairs would be free, so he deserted the crappy apartment, leaving the door unlocked. If anybody wanted to steal his ugly bedspread, they could take it with his blessing.

He turned down the quiet hallway where the elite Vanguard soldiers slept. All was quiet. Apparently, anybody getting some had already done so, and folks were now recuperating from the fight earlier.

Reaching the landing, he hustled down a flight of stairs to the vestibule of the brick building, tuning in to the soup kitchen to the right. No breathing. The place was deserted. Pivoting sharply, he took two stairs at a time to reach the basement, which housed their makeshift gym.

"What are you doing up?" A female voice caught him unaware.

He stopped cold at the sight of Sami Steel stretching out on the blue gym mat, her dark hair piled on top of her head, her fit body in tight yoga pants and a tank top. Bruises marred her slim jaw from the fight earlier, and a purpling lump showed on her right wrist. "Couldn't sleep," he said, his body awakening completely. Hell, he hadn't realized his body had been slumbering. "You?" he asked.

She breathed in, raising very nice tits. "Too keyed up from the fight earlier."

"I'm with you." After the fight, it had taken hours to return to Vanguard territory, so they should both have been fine by now. "We're strange."

She grinned, and cute lines crinkled by her soft brown eyes. "Anybody who has survived Scorpius is weird, if you ask me."

He nodded. The Scorpius bacterium had spread through the human population like a biblical plague, killing more than 99 percent of those infected. Since the bacteria localized in the brain, it altered everyone who'd survived it. Some were faster, some meaner, some crazier, and some evil. He was still figuring out where he was landing on that spectrum, and all indications pointed to sociopathic. "You fought well earlier."

She lifted a dark eyebrow. "Thanks, although I did notice you covering my back more than was necessary. I can kick your ass, remember?"

True. She'd been kicking his ass for months in training. The woman had been raised by a father who owned a karate studio and an uncle who owned a street fighting organization, so she'd been fighting since birth. Yet lately . . . Tace had been holding back, not wanting to hurt her. Or to take away the confidence she seemed to need. "You are tough, now, aren't you?"

Something in his tone must've alerted her, because her chin lowered. "You wanna go a round?" she murmured.

His cock perked up. Damn it. He should've gone looking for the woman he'd been sleeping with lately, but the gym had interested him as much as sex, which was a bad sign. Lately he kept seeing Sami's face, even with Barbara moving naked beneath him, and that could never happen. For as tough as Sami was physically, she had a delicacy of spirit he'd destroy. Right now, before he completely succumbed to his darker side, he needed to make sure they stayed colleagues. "Nah," he said, letting his natural Texas twang free. "I don't wanna fight."

"Chicken," Sami taunted, standing and pulling one arm across her chest.

His mouth went dry, but he couldn't look away. "I, ah, was trying to write in a journal and got frustrated." Why was he sharing?

Sami rolled her eyes and worked on the other arm. "The doc told me to start journaling, too. Said it would be good for my brain as well as a proper recording of us rebuilding civilization."

Tace snorted. "You've been keeping a diary?"

"No," Sami shot back.

Lie. Interesting. While Tace couldn't smell things any longer, he could sure as shit make out a lie. His chest heated. Oh, he was fine with her calling him a chicken, but lying to him? The darkness inside him rose up to battle with his good intentions. "Why the hell are you so secretive?" he snapped.

Her eyes widened and then narrowed right on him. "I'm not."

Another fucking lie. The woman had more secrets than a CIA agent he'd met once while working as a medic in the army. "I'm not the only one who can read a lie these days, sweetheart. Many of us survivors have extra abilities, it seems. You might want to watch yourself."

Her upper lip curled. "The day I need advice from you, Justice, I'll be sure to ask nicely."

Oh, he wanted to sink his teeth into that pretty pink lip. He took a step back, shaking his head free of the image. This was Sami, for Pete's sake. They were both lieutenants to Jax Mercury, the leader of Vanguard, and they needed to keep it professional. Hell, at some point, if he turned crazier, she might be present when somebody had to put him down.

"You sure you don't wanna go a round?" she asked again, her stance wide.

His chin lowered. "I don't think you want my hands on you right now."

She blinked. "Oh, you are asking for a beating."

The challenge, arrogant and annoying, barreled right through him. The beast growing in him won. He moved without thinking, grabbing her and putting her ass against the wall.

She gasped as he held her a foot or so off the ground.

He leaned into her face and smiled. "You should watch your mou—"

She chopped to his neck, and he saw stars. Two seconds later, she'd knocked him on his back, planted her ass on his abdomen, and angled her hands around his throat. "Tap out," she snarled, straddling him.

A day ago, he would've tapped out. But something new and dark rose in him, hard and fast. "No." Sweeping her arms away from his trachea, he grabbed her hip and shoved, rolling them both over. "I'm done tapping out."

Sami's shoulders hit the mat a second before her butt landed. Going on instinct and a lifetime of training, she struck out, nailing Tace in the throat. His head jerked back, and she rolled away, leaping to her feet. "What the fuck?" Her breath puffed out in bursts. How had he gotten to her so fast?

He angled to the left, his movements agile, his gaze on her legs. "Gloves are off, baby. Get ready to have *your* ass kicked."

Tingles spread through her abdomen. He moved with the deadly grace she'd seen in a panther once years ago, his steps sure, his stance aggressive. Tace and aggressive with a woman? They didn't go together. "What is wrong with you?" she asked, keeping him squarely in her sights.

He chuckled, the sound both pissed and frustrated. "We don't have that kind of time, darlin'."

Darlin'. She swallowed and tried to ignore that sexy drawl. Oh, he'd called her endearments before when they'd trained, but there had always been a brotherly fondness to his tone, so she'd been able to keep him in that safe slot. This was different. This tone caught her breath in her throat and shot lava through her veins, which was all sorts of bad. Her penchant for bad boys had ruined her life more than once, but never again. They had to remain colleagues if not friends. "You've lost your mind," she muttered.

"No doubt about that." He feinted in and back out.

Her head lifted, and she set her feet on the mat. "I guess the good ole boy needs a lesson." She used the falsest Texas accent she could muster, fighting to remain in control.

His upper lip quirked just enough for her to notice. "One of us is learning a lesson tonight."

All right. He'd asked for it. She inventoried him quickly. Clear eyes, fluid movements, absolute focus. The fight earlier hadn't seemed to weaken him. At six foot four inches tall or so, he towered over her. Add in cut muscles and raw strength, and she'd need to take him to the mat to win. She also had her mouth and brain to use against him. "If you're feeling so frisky, why didn't you call on the doctor you were screwing? Or the second-squad soldier? The one you've been banging this last week." If he just moved an inch to the left . . .

He angled to the right, his hands loose, his body relaxed. "Those were both casual and aren't gonna work out."

"Oh?" Keeping her peripheral gaze on his feet, Sami slid to the left, trying not to care about his relationships ending. When he was with somebody else, she didn't see him as a possibility, which he could not be. "Why isn't it going to work out with the inner-city doctor?"

He lifted a broad shoulder. "We agreed on just fuckin', and I'm getting bored. Angie wants more."

An ankle shot would take him down, but she couldn't put him out of commission. "Love, huh?"

"No. A good beating."

Sami stilled. "What?"

Tace shrugged. "She likes it rough. I've enjoyed smacking the hell out of her ass, but I can't bring myself to use a whip. She wants a whip, and she wants it to cut deep."

Sami shook her head and took a step back, mentally erasing the image of Tace delivering a sexual spanking. Her chest heated. "She's a masochist?"

"I guess."

"But you're not a sadist." This conversation had taken a serious detour. Why were they talking about sex?

"Guess not." He rubbed his chin, his gaze traveling across her body. "Though the right woman could probably talk me into it."

Sami held up a hand, her skin tingling where his gaze had landed. "Whoa. I do not want to be whipped."

Triumph filled his gaze. "Who said I was talking about you?"

Her mouth snapped shut. She drew a breath in. "Fine. Then how about Barbara? She's a great soldier, and you've seemed happy with her this last week."

He shrugged. "We agreed to no commitments." His eyebrows rose. "I'd ask about your love life, but you haven't been seeing anybody. Don't you miss sex?"

"Who says I haven't been having sex?" Time to put him in his place, damn it. She moved then, punching him hard in the gut and sweeping left. He bent over with a muffled *oof*, and she kicked out, aiming for his shoulder.

"You've been celibate. I've watched." His torso pivoted, and he grabbed her foot before it connected with his flesh.

What the hell? She hopped back, her entire body going into a fight-or-flight mode. He'd never moved that quickly before. Her breath sped up, and only part of her reaction was from the fight.

Giving a low laugh, he shoved her foot up into the air, knocking her off balance.

She landed on her back with a loud slap against the mat, the air whooshed from her lungs, and he was on her.

Her mouth gaped open.

He straddled her and manacled his powerful hands around her biceps, pressing her upper body to the mat. He leaned down, his eyes right above hers.

She blinked several times. From day one, his eyes had fascinated her. Deep and blue, they looked what she'd imagined the Texas sky looked like. But as she focused, awareness struck. Dark blue rims, nearly black, encircled his irises. Those were new.

"Tap out," he whispered, his voice gritty.

Oh, he really didn't know her at all. She went limp as if giving up. His lips started to curve into a smile. Using her butt as a fulcrum, she rolled her hips, pushed off from her shoulders, and yanked her knees up beneath his arms. Putting all her strength into her legs, she kicked him squarely where his arms met his shoulders. The shock of the impact ricocheted up to her hips.

He fell back, releasing her.

She rolled into a backward somersault and leaped to her feet, her gaze tracking him. Awareness clacked through her, igniting nerves to life. Her blood stirred, and her body went on full alert, reacting to the raw maleness suddenly challenging her.

He stood and stretched his right shoulder, smiling. The

smile wasn't amused and held more than a hint of warning. "That's relief in your pretty eyes, Samantha," he whispered.

"Ha. That's boredom," she shot back, keeping track of his hands, her heart thundering. She'd spent her whole life courting danger, and she wasn't changing now. If he moved in fast, she'd need to kick.

"Hmm." He rubbed his other shoulder. "I originally just wanted to let off some steam, you know." He moved forward, just a foot, already in a fighting stance but way too calm.

"Is that so?" She kept on her toes, her body on alert for his move.

"Yeah. Then I kind of wanted to win and make you tap out. But this isn't about just tapping out anymore, now is it?" His chin lowered, and he focused on her knees, a different look in his eyes than she'd ever seen there.

The look stole her breath away.

She couldn't transmit her intention with her legs, so she shook out her hands, trying to draw his attention. His concentration didn't move. Her entire body felt sensitized and primed—hyperaware of him. "What more is there than tapping out?" Her voice lowered to a whisper.

His nostrils flared like a wolf's catching a scent. "You're wondering what it'd be like. You and me—just once."

She stiffened and then quickly loosened her muscles in case of attack. How did he know that? Her legs trembled, and she settled her stance again. "Not even close."

His grin was full-on this time. "Liar."

She swallowed. All right. The guy had blue eyes, chiseled features, ripped abs, and a Texan drawl. Plus, she'd always had a thing for blonds. "Wait a second." She cocked her head to the side. "Is your hair getting darker?" He'd cut it, but now that it was growing out a little, she could see burnished auburn instead of blond.

"Yes, ma'am. Apparently hair and eyes can change color

after Scorpius." He moved his head, his gaze on her feet now. "The eyes of some early Ebola survivors changed color, so it's not a huge surprise."

She lowered her shoulders. Okay, this was good. They had returned to talking about Scorpius. "I see."

"Back to the point. You're attracted to me, and I think I'm finally seeing how you've managed to hide that so well." Regret twisted his lip even as he spoke.

Heat climbed into her face. *Focus. Don't get angry. Keep calm to fight.* Her father's mantra rippled through her head. "Maybe you're just crazy now."

"Could be." He moved then, and she countered, shocked when he took her down with one arm around her waist.

She struck out, and he once again straddled her, his groin firm against her abdomen. His hands pinned her arms to the mat, and this time, he kept his elbows in so she couldn't use her legs.

Tace had always been a fast learner.

He leaned down, his face once again above hers. Heat bracketed her from all sides. "The fact that you could kick my ass kept you feeling all nice and safe and superior, now didn't it?"

Warning pricked through her abdomen at his words. His hold was absolute, so she didn't try to fight it. A pulse pounded between her legs. He'd move, and then she'd find an opening. "That's ridiculous."

"Is it?" He leaned down, and his breath warmed her mouth. "I'm thinkin' an old-fashioned girl like you would not want a guy she could beat. It's a biological issue, especially now that civilization has died."

"Old-fashioned?" She snorted even as she fought a shiver.

"Oh, Samantha. Little girl, big Hispanic family, raised by street fighters? Yeah, you're old-fashioned."

She rolled her eyes. "My mama was Hispanic, but a name like Steel? I'm descended from Scots as well, buddy."

"No wonder that temper is so glorious." He kept her easily in place, and she had to try hard to banish images of him over her in another way that involved multiple orgasms. He smiled. "I appreciate the old-fashioned side, but you know what? I like the wildness in you even more." His voice lowered to a deep rasp.

Her nipples peaked, and finally, anger won. Fury against them both as well as her traitorous body. A fellow soldier shouldn't affect her like this. "Do you, now?"

"Oh yeah. I just hadn't realized it needed to be tamed." He leaned down farther, and his lips brushed hers. "The old me? The pre-Scorpius Texan good ole boy? The one you could handle?"

"Yeah?" Finally, she let her temper free. The man had no clue whom he was messing with. She met his challenge and sank her teeth into his bottom lip.

His head jerked back. "He's almost gone." The growl that rumbled from him sounded much more animalistic than human. Keeping her in his sights, he slowly licked a dot of blood off the small wound. "Stop challenging me, because I'm what's left."

Her heartbeat sped up until her chest ached. "Meaning?"

"Tap out." He leaned down again, his gaze so intense she could feel it through her entire body. "And remember one more thing."

She couldn't breathe, and it wasn't from his weight, because he was balanced on his knees. "What's that?"

He nipped her lip. "I bite back."

Desire speared through her, this time edged with a sharp blade. So for the first time since Scorpius had hit, for the first time since she'd arrived at Vanguard, Sami Steel tapped out.

Chapter Two

If Scorpius turns off emotions like a fountain, what happens when the spigot turns back on?

—Tace Justice

Morning sun illuminated the stairwell without artificial light—it was going to be another hot day. Tace tugged a dark blue T-shirt into place as he hustled down the stairs in headquarters, his flak boots clunking on the steps. Reaching the vestibule, he turned left into the war rooms, running into Barbara Bradley.

She grabbed his arms to keep from falling. "Tace." Pink blossomed into her pretty face.

He stepped back, his thoughts swirling. They'd hooked up a couple of times, but now his mind was on Sami. "Ah, sorry."

The tall brunette nodded and stepped away. "I was hoping we could talk later today after my shift." She leaned back, her blue eyes clear and soft. A bulletproof vest covered her stacked chest, and a gun was tucked into her waist. "I'm on duty in a minute."

He nodded, the saliva in his mouth drying up. It was hard to imagine he'd been smooth with the ladies at one time. Though he needed to end things, he didn't want to hurt her. "Later would be good."

She smiled, flashing a dimple in her left cheek. "Jax put me in charge of B-squad."

"Congrats." Tace nodded. He'd helped to train her, and she was a good choice.

She passed him and patted his arm. "Later."

Tace took a deep breath. "Later," he repeated, moving into the war rooms.

Jax Mercury was waiting for him in the back room, feet up on a monstrous coffee table. "You're late," he said.

"Sorry." Tace dropped into a plush leather chair they'd scavenged from a law office near Malibu. "Couldn't sleep and then finally dropped off an hour ago." To have a fucking wet dream about Sami Steel. Hell. He hadn't had a wet dream since he was fourteen years old and discovered how much girls liked a Texas accent. He admired her, enjoyed working with her, and needed to stop the nonsense now. He was way too volatile to be around a woman like Sami, but he had to break things off with Barbara, too. It wasn't fair to her. "Where is everyone?"

Jax eyed the sun streaming through the window. "I've changed the time for our status meeting. You and I are taking a different meeting now."

"Copy that." Tace leaned back in the chair and studied the man known far and wide for creating the seven full blocks of Vanguard territory. An ex-Delta Force member, Jax had returned to East Central Los Angeles where he'd grown up in a gang to create a haven for survivors after Scorpius had descended upon them all. "Am I supposed to be the good ole boy or the badass enforcer for this one?"

Jax reached for a chipped mug in front of him. "Neither. I just want you to watch and listen."

"All right." Tace rubbed the scruff along his jaw, not really giving a damn about a meeting. There was a time he'd been a curious person, but he couldn't remember why. Even so, he could manage small talk and pretend to be normal. "You still mad at Raze?"

"Yep."

Wonderful. Jax had been furious upon discovering that Raze Shadow, one of his top soldiers, had been working with the Mercenaries, a group of dangerous vigilantes in control of the Santa Barbara area. Of course, they had kidnapped Raze's sister and were blackmailing him. Even though Jax had been angry, he'd put himself in danger to rescue the woman.

Apparently, Jax didn't forgive quickly.

Heavy boot steps sounded outside, and Damon Winter strode into the room, a steaming mug in his hand.

Tace straightened in his chair. He hadn't been expecting this meeting.

Damon nodded over the mug. "Thanks for directing me toward the kitchen while we waited for Tace. This is my third cup. We're out of coffee in Merc territory."

"Now that's a shame," Jax drawled, dropping his feet to the floor. His brown eyes narrowed. "Didn't know you were roughing it."

Damon settled into a chair. "It has been a trial."

Tace cataloged the man. He was about thirty years old, long and lanky, with dark brown eyes and skin. He'd flashed an LAPD badge the last time they'd met, so he no doubt had some decent training. Unfortunately, he'd also aligned himself with the Mercenaries. "You're fairly brave to just show up in our territory," Tace observed.

Damon shrugged. "You didn't kill me the last time I was here, and if there's a chance for Vanguard and the Mercenaries to form an alliance, that'd be good for both groups."

"Then the Mercs probably shouldn't kidnap women," Tace drawled, letting his accent free.

Damon sighed. "Maureen Shadow is currently safe at

Vanguard, so let's just let bygones be bygones. She was treated well with us. In fact—"

"No." Jax crossed his arms.

Tace remained stoic.

"Listen. Maureen's specialty is food development, and we control all of the research facilities and greenhouses," Damon said. "Greyson would've come himself to request her being stationed in our territory, but you've banned our leader from Vanguard."

"If I let Greyson Storm set one foot in Vanguard territory, Raze Shadow will rip off his head and reach down to remove his heart." Jax spoke evenly, but his Hispanic accent slipped out at the end. "Then Raze would most likely shove it up Storm's ass."

Now that was quite an image. Tace bit back a snort. "Besides, we don't *station* civilians anywhere."

"Maureen Shadow is more than a civilian. She's probably the best food developer in the remaining world," Damon said. "Shouldn't we ask her if she'd like to continue her work?"

"No," Jax said.

Tace didn't react. While Jax might be pissed at Raze, he was willing to protect the soldier's sister. Jax had been shot full of vitamin B when he'd contracted the bacteria, thus retaining his humanity because the injection counteracted the effects of Scorpius somehow. They'd been out of B when Tace had gotten sick. Or maybe he'd always had sociopathic tendencies, and now they were finally free. Who knew?

"Damon, are you here just to ask about Maureen?" Jax asked, pushing away from the table.

"No." Damon lost the smile. "We'd like to borrow one of your doctors for the next couple of days. Ours was killed in the attack yesterday, and we need help."

The Merc territory had been attacked by the Elite Force, the president's military group. Unfortunately, the president of the former United States was one of the worst sociopaths out there. "I can help," Tace said. Getting away from headquarters and Sami was a good idea at the moment.

Jax frowned.

"We can't afford to send one of the doctors from inner territory," Tace said, standing. "I'm a combat medic, anyway, and that's what the Mercs need right now."

"We'd take it as a sign of good faith," Winter said.

Jax pushed away from the table and stood. "I don't give a shit how you take it. Wait outside for a minute."

Winter glanced at Tace and then nodded, turning on a work boot and exiting the war rooms.

"What?" Tace asked.

"This could be a trap." Jax turned and paced the length of the room. "You know everything about Vanguard. If they want to kidnap somebody and extract information, you'd be a top target."

Tace nodded. "I know. We were there during the attack, Jax. If their doctor was hit, then they need help. You saw the damage." Hell. The entire headquarters had been blown to hell and back.

"You want to help them?" Jax narrowed his gaze.

Tace lifted a shoulder. "Sure. I mean, why not go in, take notes, help out, and report back about the inner workings of the Mercenary camp? As a medic, I'll be granted access, right?"

Jax eyed him. "An undercover op?"

"Yeah. It's the perfect in."

Jax shook his head. "Since when are you the strategist without a heart?"

Tace paused. "Since Scorpius."

Jax's head lifted, and emotion smoldered for a second in his gaze. "Fair enough. Well, we do need intel on the Mercs. It's a risk, but you're right. Detail their weapons, their facilities, and their resources. Find out how many vials of vitamin B they have and where they're weak."

"You got it."

"Good. I'm not sending you in alone," Jax said.

Tace stalked to the lockers holding weapons along the back wall and quickly inserted a knife in his boot. "Raze can't come. He'll start a war."

"No, and I need to stay here to deal with internal matters. I'm sending Sami. She's our best fighter, anyway." Jax waited until Tace turned around with guns in his hands, already scowling. "You disagree?"

Tace breathed out and shoved a Sig into his waistband. "I don't think Sami should come."

Jax's eyebrow arched. "Why not?"

Because Tace kept picturing himself riding her like a prized pony. "She's a woman, and we don't know how the Mercs deal with women, even though they didn't harm Shadow's sister. If it's a trap, we can't risk Sami like that."

Jax's gaze narrowed. "She's a soldier, and we've always treated her as one of us. That hasn't changed."

No, but the way Tace looked at her had. "That's true." He didn't have a better argument, damn it.

"Also, I wouldn't mind having you watch her interaction with Damon Winter." Jax crossed his arms. "It's interesting that they don't know each other."

"Maybe." Tace instantly had the raging urge to defend the little soldier. Sami had stated from the beginning that she'd been a rookie with the LAPD, and yet, she and Winter hadn't recognized each other. "LAPD was a large organization. Huge, really. It's not unheard of for people to work there and not know each other."

"Yeah, but she acted odd when we brought it up. Was twitchy."

That was true, yet Tace kept defending her. "Perhaps they just never crossed paths."

"Or?" Jax asked.

Tace sighed. "Or one of them is lying."

"If that's the case, figure out which one." Jax picked a bandage over his right arm that covered a recent bullet wound.

"Leave your injury alone," Tace ordered.

Jax slapped the bandage back into place. "I know you and Sami are friends, but if she's been lying to us, you need to tell me." He moved toward the door. "After Raze's lies, I'm having trouble accepting secrets from any of you."

"I've been an open book, pard." Well, except for the recent tremors and numbness attacking his limbs. But that was temporary and probably yet another side effect of the bacterial infection. "You can trust me."

"I do." Jax slapped him on the arm. "More than anybody."

Man, if Tace really went dark, it would suck if Jax had to kill him. "I'm sure Winter is the one lying, if anybody is. There's no reason Sami would lie to us, right?" Tace asked, his gut churning.

Jax walked with him through the room. "Hell if I know. But it's now your job to find out."

Sami finished drinking some type of broth-based soup from a cup and glanced around the mishmash of tables in the headquarters eating area, once a soup kitchen. Folks, mainly soldiers, were scattered throughout, drinking the unappetizing soup; it smelled like feet. She nodded at a couple, and they nodded back. Home. This odd, dangerous, frightening place was her home, and for the first time in her life, she felt whole. Needed . . . and part of the group.

She'd never been part of any group before. God, she had to hold on to that feeling.

Barbara Bradley tipped back some soup and headed

across the room, stopping at her table. "Hey. Do you want to practice sparring later tonight? I'm having trouble with the grappling hold you taught us last week."

Sami swallowed and quickly nodded. She'd liked Barbara from the beginning, but the thought of Tace's mouth on hers the night before forced heat to climb into her cheeks. Even though he'd said it was casual, it still had happened, and Barbara deserved better than to be lied to by anybody. "Sure. You heading out now?"

"Yeah." Barbara smiled, transforming her face into the perfect girl-next-door look. "We're scouting on the east side for supplies. Found a bunch of kids' toys the other day, and it was like Christmas inner territory."

Sami grinned, catching the excitement. "That's awesome. Jax didn't get cranky, you guys spending time and resources to bring back toys?"

Barbara chortled. "He tried, but when he saw how happy the kids were, I swear, he actually smiled."

"A real smile?" Sami lowered her voice to a hushed tone, fighting another grin.

Barbara nodded, her eyes sparkling. "I wouldn't have believed it if I hadn't seen it. Maybe I'll try to bring back some board games for adults later."

"Don't push your luck," Sami said.

"Good point. So, training?"

Sami sipped her soup. "Sounds good. I'll meet up with you tonight."

"Perfect." Barbara turned and headed for the outer door. "You're the best," she called out, shoving the door open to the sunny day.

Yeah, right. The best. Sami shook her head. What had she been thinking to even daydream about Tace? Barbara was her friend, damn it.

Jax bellowed her name from the war rooms.

She rolled her eyes and pushed away from the round

barrel serving as her table. "Coming," she screamed back. Dropping her cup in the bucket on the counter, she strolled out of the soup kitchen and into the vestibule, where Jax, Tace, and Damon Winter waited.

"What the hell are you doing here?" she snapped at Winter. The Merc soldier was an enemy as far as she was concerned.

"Man, you can yell," Damon said, slapping a hand against his ear.

"Sami," Jax said. "Damon arrived an hour ago to request assistance. I'm sending Tace into Merc territory to help with the wounded from the attack yesterday, and I'd like you to provide backup."

Merc territory? Eesh. Although it would be advantageous to catalog their weak points. "Got it." She kept her face stoic and strode past the men and into the war room. After she'd tapped out the night before, Tace had let her up, and she'd all but run for her quarters. A sleepless night later, and she still couldn't forget his lips so close to hers. No way was she getting involved with a brilliant bad boy who freely admitted he was about to go dark—especially since he was smart enough to figure out everything she was fighting so hard to keep hidden.

Tace followed her. "You shouldn't come with me," he whispered, keeping pace past the table to the lockers.

What was happening with him? "Why not?" she whispered back, yanking open a locker to outfit herself.

He didn't answer.

She fit a gun holster over her shoulder, pushing her green sweater out of the way. A knife went in her jeans pocket, and a couple more went beside her calf and in her boot. She looked up. "Well?"

Tace's jaw flexed, and he stepped into her space. "It's Merc territory."

"No shit." Heat flared through her at the nearness of his hard body. Man, she was off-center. "Would you move back?"

"No." He tugged on her shoulder holster. "This isn't secure enough."

She slapped his hands. "Stop it."

He yanked on the strap, and she smacked his wrist, engaging in a clumsy struggle. He leaned in. "You need to listen to me. Last night I dreamed of you beneath me, naked in bed, and coming hard. We need distance from each other."

She didn't back down even as her libido sprang right up into awareness. "What about Barbara?"

"It's over," Tace said flatly.

"That's your problem and not mine." Sami drew out a knife.

"Yeah, except you're the one haunting my dreams," he said, his voice gravelly.

She shook her head. "You're just having more brain issues from the illness. It'll go away once you heal. Nothing can happen between us because of our jobs." And the fact that she was lying to everybody about her past. Oh yeah. That.

His jaw clenched. "I know that, which is why we could use distance."

"I'm not neglecting my job because you're horny, Justice." She shoved him.

He tugged on the strap again, and she slapped his hand. Again. They engaged in a struggle for control, and she shoved his arm.

"What the hell?" Jax snapped from the doorway.

Her head swiveled the same time Tace's did. Heat climbed into her face.

Jax frowned and looked from Tace to Sami and back. "Is something going on between you two?"

"No," Sami burst out just as Tace snarled, "Hell, no."

Jax rocked back on his heels, his face harder than usual. "All right. Keep it that way."

Sami brushed by Tace. "No worries there." When she reached Jax, he stopped her by the arm. She lifted one eyebrow and stared up into his sharply cut face.

He dropped his hand. "This isn't an order. If you don't want to go into Merc territory, you don't have to."

Sami stiffened. The men had never treated her differently because of her sex. Her abdomen cramped. "Did you give Tace the out if he didn't want to go?"

Jax paused and then frowned again. "Actually, yeah. I did."

"Oh." She settled. "All right then. I'm fine on the mission."

"Copy that." Jax released her. "Learn everything about the Mercs that you can—I'm interested in their holdings and provisions. Well, and security. If we decide to take out Greyson Storm, who steps up?"

Sami paused. Sometimes she forgot what a cold strategist Jax could be. He'd mellowed a little since falling in love . . . but only a little. "You're thinking of taking the leader of the Mercs out?"

"Maybe." Jax turned toward Tace. "Are you focused enough for this?"

"Yep." Tace grabbed a black cowboy hat off a rack near the door.

Sami shook her head. "Do not let him wear the hat. We'll look like idiots."

Tace ran his finger along the brim of the hat. "This is my natural look."

It might have been at one time, but the new Tace Justice? She took a good look at him. The brim hung low over his blue eyes and cast part of his face in shadow. Fine lines and rugged features were visible and yet his expression remained veiled. Tingles exploded in her abdomen. He did look good in the hat. "Maybe it will fit our purposes for them to think you're a moron." She pivoted on her heel and headed for the vestibule, using every ounce of her strength to sound normal.

He chuckled low behind her, and the sound shivered down her spine. Her temper stirred, and she wanted nothing more than to get in his face and tell him to knock it off. But Jax was already frowning, and the last thing she needed was to be treated like somebody's woman instead of a fellow soldier. Both Jax and Raze were committed to women, and they had turned all alpha protective over them.

Sami refused to be hidden safely behind Vanguard walls. She had a job to do, and she was damn good at it. Finally, she kind of belonged, even though she'd never use her true skills again.

Damon waited by the door, his gaze curious.

Shit. She'd almost forgotten about the whole LAPD issue. She should've figured she'd one day meet up with a real former LAPD member. "Damon," she said.

He nodded. "You didn't tell me your name last time I was here."

When they'd tied him to a chair and threatened to torture him. She smiled. "Sami."

"Nice to meet you." He cocked his head to the side as if trying to force himself to remember her. "LAPD, right?"

"I was." She kept her voice pleasant, her mind scrambling. What if he asked her a specific question?

A little blond girl ran in from the soup kitchen.

"Lena," Sami said, crouching so they were eye to eye, relief filling her at the interruption. "How are you?"

The girl smiled, and her pretty black eyes sparkled. Yet once again, she didn't talk. Instead, she reached into her pocket and drew out a cracked *S* key from a keyboard to drop into Sami's palm.

Sami smiled. "*S* for Sami."

Lena grabbed three more letters, *X*, *U*, and *G*, to hand over. Sami's lips trembled, and she formed them into a line.

"What do the *X*, *U*, and *G* stand for?" Damon asked, craning his neck.

"Dunno." Sami forced a smile for the girl, who had been giving gifts with odd meanings to Vanguard members for months. The computer keys were a clue Sami couldn't let anybody in on.

Lena nodded and moved toward Damon.

He smiled. "Do you have a letter for me?"

The girl shook her head and reached in her jumper pocket to hand over half of a shiny toy sheriff's star.

Damon paused and took the gift. "How did you know I was a cop?"

"Lena, there you are." April Snyder, the girl's pseudo-guardian, rushed to the doorway. "You have to stop taking off like that." She pushed curly brown hair away from her classically lovely face.

"Well, hello," Damon said, straightening, his gaze sharpening.

"Um, hi." April reached to tuck Lena against her, her eyes wide on Damon. "Jax? We need to talk about, ah, my mission."

Damon's head jerked back. "You have a mission, pretty thing?"

April's mouth gaped, and then her posture straightened. She met his gaze directly. "I surely do."

Damon's grin was slow and somehow nearly sweet.

Jax nodded. "Sami, Tace? I want you back in forty-eight hours, no matter what." He leaned in to Damon's face. "If they're not back, I'm waging war."

"Got it." Damon took one last look at April and then shoved open the door.

Sami waved at Lena and turned to face the rapidly heating day.

"It's odd that Lena gave Damon the star and not you, right?" Tace said quietly, walking right on by her.

Odd? Not really. Lena knew things she shouldn't, and

Sami had never been a member of the LAPD. "She's a kid, Tace. Who knows why she gives certain gifts."

He turned and pierced her with his blue gaze. "Someday you're gonna be honest with me, darlin'. And it's gonna be sooner rather than later."

Chapter Three

The dinosaurs probably thought they'd live forever, too.

—Dr. Frank X. Harmony, *Philosophies*

Tace scouted the old parking lot outside of headquarters and led the way toward the fence, which surrounded the entire seven-block Vanguard territory with metal and wrapped barbed wire. He gave a whistle, and two of the guards opened the gate. Downed trucks, vans, and industrial barrels provided another layer of protection along with tons and tons of discarded tires.

The piles of tires were uneven, and he had to fight a strong urge to go even out the stacks. Damn Scorpius had given him OCD. He maneuvered beyond them, his hands shaking with the need to organize, and stopped short at an ancient yellow Datsun truck. "Nice."

"We aim to please," Damon said, striding around the grille. Tension cut lines into his face.

Tace turned and waved at the guards pointing weapons at them. Good ole Damon had a reason to be stressed. Most of the guards were itching to take him out and steal the truck. Tace opened the door. "Get in, Sami."

She faltered. "You get in."

Oh, he wasn't sitting in the middle. While the woman could fight like a demon, she shot like a debutante—a fact she hadn't quite explained, considering she had been LAPD. "The day you learn to shoot straight, you can take point in a vehicle." He whispered the words so Damon couldn't hear.

Sami glared but slid into the truck and moved over.

Tace settled against the ripped seat in the weathered truck. Sami should stay at Vanguard where it was somewhat safe, damn it.

"Why do I have to straddle the damn gear shift?" she muttered as she set her gun on her jean-clad leg.

The words shot images through his head that shuddered right down to his dick. He cleared his throat. "Why use our gas when the Mercs have supplied us with transport?" Although Tace would've preferred that he was driving. When had he become such a control freak? Oh yeah. When Scorpius had ripped through his brain and tore him into a new being.

"We set?" Damon shut his door and ignited the engine, which clunked rather than purred.

"Oh, no Rippers will hear us trying to get through town in this piece of crap," Sami muttered.

Tace leaned over and put his lips near her ear. "The more sarcastic you get, the more I want to strip you naked and make sure you stop talking."

She stilled and then turned her head until their noses brushed. "Sexual harassment these days doesn't go to HR, Tace."

"Oh?" He lifted an eyebrow. If he moved a millimeter, his mouth would be on hers. He swallowed. What the hell was wrong with him? He had to get control of himself and now.

"Yeah. These days you get your dick cut off and shoved in your ear."

Amusement burst through his chest. He coughed and leaned back. Was that an actual human reaction? A normal one? It had been so long. "I'm sorry."

She blinked. "Huh?"

He winced. Had he been that much of a jerk lately? "I'm sorry for the harassment. It's wrong." The words were correct, but he wasn't quite sure about the line between right and wrong any longer. Apparently, he'd crossed it, though. If a guy had treated one of his sisters like that, Tace would've maimed him. "I'll do better." If he thought to appease her with his very nice apology, he'd apparently missed the mark.

Sparks flew through her pretty brown eyes. "Don't even think of charming me, Texas. I'll make you pee blood for weeks."

"You're an intriguing woman." The words slipped out of him before he could call them back. Harass her, and she was all fire. Be nice to her, and even though she'd spit venom, vulnerability would darken those stunning eyes.

She turned toward the dirty windshield. "Whatever."

Damon glanced across the seat. "You guys done with the foreplay? I'd like to get on the road."

Tace leveled him with a look.

Damon grinned. "All righty, then."

"Stick to back roads as much as possible," Tace said. "Gangs have set up traps on the freeways, and they're armed."

"Yep." Damon drove around a pile of what looked like milk jugs in the crumbling street. "I have to ask, why would Jax set up Vanguard in the middle of the poorest area in LA?"

"It's where he grew up," Sami said. "He was familiar with the area, and it contained an old food-distribution center, medical offices, and a school."

Tace watched shattered storefronts go by out the window. Were they walking right into a trap by voluntarily heading into Merc territory? "It was an easy area to fence and protect, just like a military base."

Sami cleared her throat. "Why did the Mercs settle in Santa Barbara? Seems not so tough."

Damon barked out a laugh. "We have the ocean, multiple

greenhouses, and all of the resources built into UC Santa Barbara. In other words, we have more food and water than you do."

Tace kept silent and let Sami press the Merc for information. She was a natural at it. Had she been lying to them all? Once again, a pit opened up in his gut.

Was he starting to feel things again? Sure, he'd had plenty of sex since he'd recovered, but the enjoyment had been an act. Was sex turning into something else? What would sex be like with Sami? Probably explosive. He shifted in his seat to ease some of the raging pressure suddenly in his groin. Man, he had to get a grip.

"Right, Tace?" Sami asked.

Shit. What had she been saying? He grunted in response. She turned back to Damon. "So that's why."

"I see." Damon slowed down to turn west.

"How many Mercenary members are there?" Sami asked.

Tace tuned back into the conversation.

"About seventy men." Damon winced. "Maybe sixty after the attacks yesterday."

"Just men?" Sami asked.

Damon nodded. "All male soldiers like in the old days of the military."

Sami didn't react. "Ratio of soldiers to civilians?" she asked smoothly, playing her part perfectly.

Damon turned the wheel to avoid what looked like a human leg in the road. "All soldiers."

Sami cut Tace a look. "What happens to civilians?"

Now Damon grinned again. "We drop them off in Vanguard territory."

Well, at least they didn't eat civilians. "Who came up with that plan?" Tace asked.

"Greyson did. We're a military vigilante group, and we don't want to train or protect civilians. You Vanguard folks do, so we either direct them to or sometimes drop them off for you to coddle."

"What about, you know, sex?" Sami asked.

Damon glanced her way. "You offering?"

Tace sat forward just enough to make his point.

Damon turned back to the road.

"What is up with everyone these days?" Sami snapped. "You're all just horny dogs."

Tace bit his lip.

"Sorry," Damon said. "Um, to answer your question, if any soldier wants to keep a, well, companion, then they can. But Mercs are soldiers, all male, and anybody keeping somebody is fully responsible for them."

"Keeping?" Sami asked slowly.

Damon held up a hand. "All consensual and all voluntary. Greyson double checks with anybody living in the territory, especially women, to make sure they want to be there. Period."

Good. "So you're hoarding resources and pawning civilians off on us," Tace said, watching a couple of shadows move near the street corner. He tensed and lifted his gun to the open window.

Sami lifted herself to see better and brushed her breast against his arm.

Electricity jolted through him. He kept perfectly still and tracked two women digging through rubble. "Slow down."

Damon sighed but slowed to nearly a stop.

Both women looked up, their bodies tensed to flee. They were in ripped jeans and heavy jackets, both with long hair already formed into dreadlocks. Dirt marred their faces, and scratches showed down their arms.

"Rippers?" Sami whispered.

"Not sure." Tace leaned out the window. "Do you ladies need help?" He let his twang free.

The first woman, rail thin and about fifty, shook her head.

The other one, a twentysomething, didn't move.

"All right." Tace pointed back the way they'd come. "If you go about a mile east, you'll enter Vanguard territory. Scouts will find you and take you to food and shelter, if you want."

The younger woman shook her head. "We're fine on our own."

"We have vitamin B," Tace said.

The women looked at each other.

"Your choice," Damon called out, shifting the gear into DRIVE. "Good luck." He drove away from the corner and around an abandoned library that had books scattered all over the front steps. "That's why you're almost out of provisions."

"Maybe we'll just take yours," Tace said evenly.

"You can sure try," Damon said agreeably. He sped up as the road cleared. "So, tell me about that April chick. She with anybody?"

Tace slowly turned his head toward the Mercenary soldier. "Yes."

Sami started. "No, she isn't."

"As far as the Mercs are concerned, she is," Tace countered. Protectiveness for the young widow who'd lost so much rose in him so quickly, he nearly gasped. The last time he'd felt this way had been for his two sisters back in Texas. Neither had survived Scorpius. "Listen, Damon. I don't like you, I don't like the Mercs, and I'm going to help today because I'm a medic and that's what I do." Not entirely true. "If we do form some sort of alliance, which I doubt will truly happen, then we're still not gonna be friends. You all got rid of the civilians, so you don't get to come cherry-pickin' for a good lay now."

Sami's eyes widened. "That's the longest conversation I've heard from you since you were infected with Scorpius."

Had he been that laconic? Maybe. "Humph."

"Sorry, buddy," Damon said, speeding up even more. "Didn't know I was stepping on your toes."

"You ask about Vanguard at all, and you're past my toes to my feet," Tace returned. "At which point I shove my foot up your ass."

Damon lost the grin, and he turned toward Tace, his brown eyes darkening. "You're not the only one who can fight, Texas. Might want to keep that in mind."

Tace flashed his teeth. "Is that an invitation?"

"Whoa." Sami held up both hands. "Boys, we're working together right now, so there's no need to pull 'em out and measure them. You're both big dicks, so don't worry about it."

Damon snorted. "Don't you mean that we both have big dicks?"

"I said exactly what I meant," Sami said, flattening her hand over her gun again.

Tace couldn't help the chuckle, surprised when his chest warmed. "I like you, Sami." He genuinely liked her. He'd forgotten that fact in the last few weeks as he'd recuperated from the fever.

"Man, you're smooth," Damon murmured.

"Shut up," Tace said.

"Both of you shut the hell up," Sami snapped. "I feel like I'm in a bad chick flick all of a sudden." She lifted her gun toward the windshield. "Next guy who speaks in the coming hour gets shot in the face."

Fair enough.

Tace sat back to watch crumbling buildings and deserted alleyways rush by. Nature had quickly begun to reclaim the earth, poking through concrete and climbing up brick. What was once a perfectly gray and concrete area was rapidly turning green again. Seemed like the earth always won the battle, didn't it?

The ninety-mile drive took nearly three hours as they

tried to avoid roving gangs and Rippers. Soon the smell of the ocean salted the air.

Tace shifted his sweaty back against the seat and glared at the sun. For weeks they'd enjoyed an odd and strong rainy season, but it appeared to be over. Air-conditioning was a thing of the past . . . a luxury already fading from reality. "We in Merc territory?" He broke the heated silence.

"Yep. We're relocating headquarters to the mansion next to the one the president blew up," Damon said. He glanced at Sami. "How would you like fresh fish for dinner?"

She lifted a shoulder, but Tace could see anticipation in the curve of her lip. Man, he had to stop focusing on her mouth. "We're not here for a social hour," he drawled.

Sami nodded and focused outside the truck, no doubt taking mental notes.

Tace did the same. They drove beyond two fences guarded with guns and into a high-end suburban area full of mansions. He whistled.

"You wouldn't believe some of the stuff we found in these places," Damon said. "Drugs, guns, prepper provisions. And lots of dirty homemade videos with fortysomething-year-old women with fake tits and Botox faces. When did home sex tapes become a thing?"

"Dunno," Tace said, counting soldiers on the way. They patrolled in packs of three, all wearing black T-shirts with different pants. "The black shirt mandatory?"

"On patrol for soldiers, yeah," Damon said.

Loud pops punctuated the quiet day.

Tace went on full alert. "Was that gunfire?"

More pops echoed, and he partially turned to cover Sami.

Damon swiveled his head. "From the beach." He yanked the wheel and ripped through the empty streets, driving past a house and right onto the beach. The wheels churned up sand, and the ocean rolled in not far from the truck.

An explosion ripped apart the world, throwing debris into the air.

Tace moved his body between Sami and the fight.

Damon jumped out. "Status?" he barked to a group of men fronting a fence that faced another mansion.

A redheaded guy turned around, blood dripping from his chin, his eyes a wild blue. "Noise yesterday brought them all out—Rippers and rogue scavengers. Third attack of the day . . . and this one has explosives." His buddies fired over the fence.

Tace quickly scanned the area, his blood boiling. They weren't familiar with the area, and he didn't see a safe zone. The truck was too visible. He leaped from the vehicle and yanked Sami out by the arm. "Stay behind me."

"No." She pushed past him, her gun already out.

He paused. A tingle spread from his foot up to his knee. God, not now. His vision hazed. That was new. His knee weakened. Shit. He was gonna fall.

"Tace, get down!" Sami tackled him, and sand erupted all around them. Blackness caught him a second later.

Chapter Four

Hit and then think.

—Sami Steel

Sami scrambled over Tace, frantically searching his torso while staying low. Nothing. She ran her fingers through his hair. "You're okay," she said, feeling along his ears and ducking as sand whipped around them. Should she try to shove him under the truck? What if a round hit the engine and it blew? "Tace?" she yelled.

He blinked, and his eyes opened. "What the hell?" Without waiting for an answer, he rolled them both and flattened her in the sand, looking up and toward the fence. "We gotta move." He dodged to his knees, grabbed her shoulders, and crab-walked them behind the men furiously firing.

She shook him off the second she regained her bearings. Sand poured down her arm. "Are you all right?" There was no blood. "Have you been hit somewhere?" Panic whipped through her.

"No." He crept up behind one of the shooters, manacling her wrist to keep her shielded. "Status?"

The soldier in front of him lobbed a grenade. "Duck."

"Shit." Tace turned in time to wrap himself around Sami.

She ducked low and slapped her hands over her ears. Warmth and a whole lot of muscle surrounded her. Tace had always been fit, but since Scorpius, he had new rips in new muscles.

A boom echoed through the day.

Then silence.

She slowly lifted her head, her shoulders shaking.

Gunfire rattled against the other side of the fence again.

"Damn it." Tace glared at Damon over Sami's head. "This is the shitstorm you dragged us into?"

Damon leaned up and fired over the fence. "They're two houses over. We can hit them by the beach."

Sami shook her head and concentrated on the problem. "If the beach side is fenced, you'll be walking ducks."

Tace nodded and glanced up. "I have another idea."

"Roofs are booby-trapped," Damon said, crouching. "We catch at least one Ripper a week trying for the roofs."

Sami winced. So body parts just flew around Merc territory. That was nice. She glanced to her left at the sprawling stucco mansion facing the beach. Bullet holes marred the peach-colored stucco, and half of the chimney bricks had fallen along the angled roof. "What about from the street?"

"Probably covered," Tace said. "But we can't just wait here."

"We have men coming from the other side, I'm sure," Damon snapped. "You two just sit tight and wait it out."

Tace cut her a look.

She shook her head. Neither one of them was a "sit tight and wait" person. They had to do something before one of them got blown up or before Tace passed out again. What was up with him? *Through the house?* she mouthed.

He looked toward the house, his gaze intense. "Keep on my six." His whisper was a warm breath against her ear.

She shivered. "Copy that." They'd been fighting together for months, and this was only one more battle. But he'd just been unconscious. Had he somehow been hit in the head by flying debris? "You sure you're okay?"

"Yeah. Keep up." He turned in a fluid motion and launched himself across the yard, keeping low and beneath the fence line.

"Tace!" Damon growled.

Sami moved to follow him, but one of the soldiers grabbed her arm. Without missing a step, she pivoted and kicked out, knocking him on his ass, and turned to run after Tace.

The sand turned to stone tiles, and she hustled around an oval swimming pool and across a wide deck into the much cooler house. Tan hues, stunning oil paintings, and crystal everywhere. Tace moved gracefully as if he was back in control, but she hadn't seen any weakness in him before he passed out.

What had happened?

She'd have to find out later, because he ripped through the living room and to the front door, gingerly opening it and looking out. He held up a hand to stop her.

She halted, leaning over to breathe, her gun clutched in her hand. Point and squeeze. No pulling the trigger. Aim and squeeze. Tace's lessons rippled through her mind. She could do this.

He slid the door open more and stepped outside.

Sunlight cascaded inside.

She moved behind him, staying low.

Several quiet fountains shaped like cherubs were visible in the front, which was also gated. An empty driveway made of oval pavers led to an intricate gate facing the quiet street. Tace jogged silently across the driveway to the rock wall serving as a property division. He leaned against it as gunfire continued in the rear of the house.

Sami moved toward him, reaching him, blinking against the blinding sun. The wall was about six feet tall, and she couldn't see over it. A wide maple tree provided some shade from the other side. "Well?" she whispered.

Tace slowly lifted himself up and looked over the fence. He was quiet for a moment and then ducked down, his back against the wall. "Big house, empty circular driveway, another rock wall on the other side. I think the shooters are one over."

She calculated the distance and remembered a similar scene in the newest *Bloody Hell Suburban Fight* game that had come out right before Scorpius had hit. She'd solved the game in less than a week by not taking the easiest route. "We go over the fence?"

His eyebrows drew down. "They could be in the next house. We don't know."

"Then we sweep and go fast," she returned, adrenaline flowing through her veins.

He studied her. "You been studying shooting more than just what I taught you?"

A man screamed in the distance, the shriek full of pain.

She gulped. "Yeah. I can hit somebody." Although she'd never actually shot anybody. Her talents lay in strategy and not true action, like any good street fighter. Oh, the punch mattered, but placing it just right mattered more. "LAPD, remember?"

His gaze narrowed. "Right."

"What happened to you back there?" she asked, checking his eyes. Clear and focused.

He shook his head.

Another explosion boomed from the beach area.

"Let's go." Sami tucked her gun in her waist. "You need to boost me."

He grimaced but set his gun down. Grabbing her hips, he breathed out. "Stay behind the tree."

She nodded.

He lifted her as if she weighed nothing, giving her a girly moment she quickly banished. She slapped both hands on the top of the wall, pivoted, and dropped silently to the other side. A second later he'd landed next to her, his big body in a crouch.

She peered around the maple tree. Gunfire continued in the back. "I think they're concentrated near the beach."

"Maybe." Tace eyed the silent windows of the newest mansion.

Sami angled her neck. The sun reflected off the windows, so she couldn't see inside. The massive wooden door was closed, and the place actually felt abandoned. Smoke and debris drifted down, and her eyes stung. "I'll go first. Stay low and watch those windows."

Tace nodded and pointed across the rather plush front lawn to a garden area with a multitude of flowers and weeds. "Go right over the hydrangeas and straight for the fence. Aim for next to the garage, because the windows face away."

"Hydrangeas?" she asked.

"The big purple ones."

She lifted an eyebrow and curved her lip.

He shrugged. "My mama liked to garden. Now go."

She sucked in air, centered herself, and then ran full bore for the purple flowers. She cleared them, ran across the driveway, and plastered herself to the edge of the garage. Tace was right on her heels. It took her a second to realize that he'd covered her back the entire time. If anybody had shot from the windows, a bullet would've gone through him before piercing her.

Once again, a large stone wall was too high for her to see over. These rich people sure had liked their privacy, hadn't they? Maybe because they were all making sex tapes, like Damon had said. "Look over the fence," she whispered, trying not to cough from the smoke.

He leaned up and glanced over. Then he turned and crouched down. "Nothing. The front door is open, though."

Sami wiped smoke from her eyes. "What if we go past

that house to the other side? I mean, come up behind them on the beach side."

Tace glanced at her and at the closed iron gate at the end of this driveway. "If we do that, we should go out on the street and run past this house to the next."

"No." She shook her head, strategy coming easier now. "They're too well equipped and organized not to have somebody on the street. They won't be expecting us to use the front lawn of the mansion they've infiltrated." She bit her lip. "Probably. I mean, there could be somebody watching the front lawn, but if they have the street covered, they may not have the manpower to cover the lawn."

"That's a lot of could-be's and mays," Tace muttered.

The battle continued by the beach, and another grenade went off.

"You know, this isn't really our fight," Tace drawled, his body beyond tense. "We could just hang low and see what happens."

She rocked back. Months ago, Tace would've been the first one through the door to fight for justice and right, but they didn't really know who was *just* in this fight, did they? "That's true, but we have a tentative alliance or agreement with the Mercs, and we don't know who this roving band is. The Mercs are probably stronger with much better numbers, thus making them better allies." Her legs twitched with the need to move.

"True."

A shuffle sounded on the other side of the fence, and Tace stiffened. He motioned her down.

She sidled to him at a crouch, her gaze at the top of a fence. Without warning, a body bounded over, landing easily on the pavement.

Tace shot forward faster than she could and tackled the guy onto his back, one hand over his mouth.

The guy struggled, fists pounding against Tace's ribs.

Sami rushed toward them, stood, and aimed a kick beneath the guy's jaw. His head snapped back, and his eyes closed as he fell unconscious.

Tace rolled off him and breathed out several times.

Sami studied the guy. Black pants, yellow shirt, buzz-cut hair. She leaned over and tugged down his shirt to see a couple of tattoos winding down his chest. One had a skull and some weird numbers.

"Prison tats," Tace said, sitting up.

"Oh. I mean, yeah." Shouldn't she be familiar with prison tats if she'd been in the LAPD? "You okay?"

"Affirmative." Tace stood and dragged the guy over toward the garage. "My guess is the attackers wanted to infiltrate Merc headquarters the same way we want to get to them—through the front of a house. Let's go through the yard now while they think this guy is gone."

Sami nodded. "With the prison tats—do you think there's a new player in town?"

"A new player?" Tace's eyebrows rose. "I don't even know what that means."

"Fine." She moved toward the wall. They had enough enemies to worry about, and she should stop sounding like the gamer she'd been. This was real life. "Boost me over."

"Wait a sec." He leaned up and scouted the area. "All right." This time he held out his hands, and she stepped into them. He lifted, and she shot right over, rolled, and landed on her feet. This place looked like all the others, with a gated driveway, bunch of grass and flowers, and stucco sides. Gray this time.

Tace heaved himself over and landed next to her, gun already sweeping. "I'm point."

She followed him along the fence to the front of the house. This one had a wide bay window looking out, and again, the sun shimmered off it. "Go in high," she whispered.

He ducked and ran along the window. She kept to his six, holding her breath. They reached the open doorway.

Slowly, Tace slipped inside, leading with his gun. Sami went low. Nothing. They crept through a large gathering room with red leather furniture and toward an open balcony at the back.

Two shots were fired, and then a scream of pain chilled right through her.

Tace sped up and stepped outside on the deck before straightening. "Holy shit."

Sami followed, her gun pointing, and moved to his side.

A huge guy in a black T-shirt dumped one man on his head and then turned, knife out, and sliced the jugular of another. Three other downed men lay at his feet. Bullet holes marred the wall behind them, while guns lay on the ground around them.

"Is that a Merc shirt?" Sami asked, steadying her aim.

The guy looked up and raised his arm, gun pointed at them.

Tace edged in front of her.

Panic heated her throat as she recognized the fighter. "Greyson Storm. Remember us?" she called out breathlessly.

Slowly, the guy nodded, his bluish-green eyes furious. His black hair had been slicked back from a sharply cut face. Rugged and strong. Blood was splattered across his faded jeans and still dripped from his knife. "Yep. Don't remember your names, though."

They hadn't given their names, she was pretty sure.

"I'm Sami, and this is Tace from Vanguard? Tace stitched you up yesterday after the fight with the president." Sami slowly lowered her gun. Greyson Storm could seriously fight. She hadn't had a chance to watch him while they'd rescued Maureen and Vinnie the previous day, but wowza. If the Mercs were all trained like him, they definitely would be necessary allies. The Vanguard soldiers were good, but they had civilians to worry about, too.

Damon Winter jumped over the fence leading to the beach. "Holy shit, Grey. You said to give you five minutes."

Grey looked down at the dead men. "I guess I only needed three."

Sami's knees weakened, and she sidled a little closer to Tace. He remained unerringly still as if waiting for an attack.

Damon jerked his head toward them. "Sami and Tace? I'm sure you remember Grey, the leader of the Mercs."

Grey looked them both over, a veil drawing down over his eyes. "Where's Maureen Shadow?" Although rich and deep, his voice held a hint of violence. The promise of such anyway.

"She's not here," Tace said, moving another couple of inches in front of Sami, his back muscles visibly tightening.

Greyson's head went back. "That's unfortunate. I guess we should get started, then."

Chapter Five

A sociopath is the hero in his own twisted story.

—Dr. Vinnie Wellington, *Sociopaths*

Tace stepped completely in front of Sami, facing what could only be considered a threat in the form of Greyson Storm. The man was dangerous, and for the first time, Tace felt a sharpness to his need to shield Sami. If he was gonna make a mistake in defending her, it would be to shoot first and reason later. "What do you want to get started, Greyson?" He kept his hands loose, but his finger tightened on the trigger.

Greyson pointed toward the headquarters, and blood splattered from his hand to turn the grass red. "We have wounded. That's why you're here."

"Yes." Tace slowly relaxed.

"I gave my word you wouldn't be harmed," Greyson said, wiping his knife on his jeans and leaving a red streak while stepping over the bodies.

"Yes, you did." Tace didn't put away his gun.

Grey turned toward Damon. "Let's take down any fences between the beach and all of the houses, and then let's look at the walls between houses. Maybe we'll blow them apart. This can't happen again."

Damon nodded. "On it." He turned back for the beach, his movements fluid and graceful.

Grey motioned to them. "If you'd follow me."

Tace glanced over his shoulder and waited for Sami's nod before striding down the tile stairs and across scrub grass to the fence opening. Men were already arriving with tools and sledgehammers, and several paused to give Sami the once-over.

Tace's lips peeled back at two of them.

Sami shoved him in the ribs.

He kept following Grey, his boots flicking up sand. "How many wounded in the attack yesterday?"

Grey didn't turn. "Too many. I haven't counted."

Tace frowned and glanced at Sami, who shook her head.

"You've counted," Sami said. "How many?"

"Ten serious and about twelve nonserious." Grey turned back, and his eyes had changed to all green in the afternoon sun. "It was a bad hit."

"How many did you lose?" Sami asked softly.

"Four." Grey turned back around. His T-shirt covered the top of his arm, but a bandage peeked out.

Tace wanted a few minutes with the leader. "I'd like to check your stitches." Grey had been shot twice the previous day, and Tace had sewn him up on-site without anesthesia. The Merc leader hadn't even twitched, but he had kept a close eye on the needle. Trust didn't come easy to any of them these days. Oh, they'd worked together against the president's men in order to rescue Maureen Shadow and profiler Vinnie Wellington from the president, but it had been a temporary alliance. "After that fight a minute ago, you might've pulled stitches."

"I'm fine." Grey turned at the first house and led the way past the pool.

Tace glanced at the blown-up mansion next to it that had served as the Mercenary headquarters. The president's explosives had been deadly and well delivered. Rubble and still-smoldering materials choked what had been a swimming pool. It was a miracle only four people had died.

Greyson continued into the adjacent house and through the cooler living room. "The makeshift hospital is right across the street."

Tace paused at seeing several research books on the counter. "*Sociopaths* by Vinnie Wellington?" The doc, a former profiler, was a Vanguard member currently dating Raze Shadow.

Grey nodded. "Since the president of the United States was infected with Scorpius and has become a sociopathic Ripper, I'm trying to figure out the Rippers and how they think. Found this book in one of the mansions, and I've been reading it. That doc knows her stuff." He turned. "And she kind of owes us one since we helped to rescue her yesterday, right?"

Tace winced. "She's with Raze Shadow, and considering you kidnapped his sister and thus necessitated the rescue of both Vinnie and Maureen, I don't think the doc will be visiting you anytime soon." Hell. Raze would blow up the entire Santa Barbara area before he'd allow Vinnie within a mile of the Mercenaries.

"Pity. I would've liked to have talked to the shrink. Although I won't get that pleasure, we need food, and so do you. After you've finished for the day, I'd like to speak with you about Maureen Shadow returning to her work at the facility," Grey said, his face implacable.

Sami's quiet snort behind Tace said it all.

Greyson continued through and led them past the fence to what appeared to be a former workout facility for the subdivision. They'd replaced the machines with beds. Men lay on them, some breathing poorly, some groaning.

The room smelled like blood and dirt.

Tace glanced around and appreciated the even layout of beds and neatly stocked countertops. "Give me the status."

"We patched up everyone we could, but I wouldn't mind you checking for problems. Two guys need bullets removed, while a few have contusions or bruises. I wanted somebody with medical expertise especially for the bullet removal so we didn't cut out anything important." Grey turned and faced them. "We have generators we can use for extra light in the next room, which we've cleansed as a surgical area."

Tace slid his gun into the back of his jeans. "Drugs?"

"Raided the nearest hospital right when Scorpius got bad. We have anything you could possibly need." Grey rubbed blood off his chin. "Not a lot of anything, but enough for now."

Tace swallowed. "All right. Here's the deal. I'll work on your men, but I need Sami to assist."

"Understood. Many of my men have been without a woman for too long, and I'd rather she stayed here with you." Grey looked her over. "No offense. I saw you fight yesterday, and I'd prefer you didn't knock a bunch of my men out this afternoon. I need them to focus."

"Let's get to work," Tace said, not liking the appraising look or the compliment.

Grey leaned in. "It goes without saying . . ."

Tace held up a hand. "I'm here to help and not harm. I'll do my best with your men."

"Okay. The drugs are locked up. What do you need?" Grey asked.

"I'll come look at what's available," Tace said easily. What kind of resources did Grey really have?

Grey smiled a quick flash of teeth. "Not a chance. Tell me what you need, and I'll bring it to you."

So much for that thought. He'd get another chance. Tace gave him a quick list and then turned toward Sami after

Greyson had left. "Let's check patient by patient and see what kind of information you can get from them."

Her eyes widened. "What about help and not harm?"

"That too." Truth be told, they were on a mission. "We can multitask. Are you okay in a surgical situation?"

She blanched. "No. I can handle you stitching people up after a fight, but going into an operating room and seeing you dig for bullets? I might puke."

Somehow, he'd figured that. "Don't worry about it. You stay in here and interview the patients with our primary objective in mind. Keep your gun close and your wits about you." He'd hear her if anything went wrong.

"No kidding." She shoved him.

"In the middle of the first surgery, I'm going to lean out and have you go get a drug immediately from Greyson. I'll know which one once I see what he brings." Tace leaned in to whisper. "Follow up, kind of upset, and see what kind of stockpile they have. We need to know."

She shuffled her feet. "Will the guy really need the drug?"

"No. It's just to give you access to the stockpile."

"All right." A man groaned over to her right, and she turned, moving toward him. "You okay?" Her voice softened.

He groaned again. She leaned down and felt his forehead. "You're not hot."

"Broken leg," the guy said. He looked about nineteen with thick dark hair and brown eyes. "Already set but don't want to waste pain pills."

Sami stroked his arm. "You're very brave."

The kid closed his eyes. "You have a nice voice."

She smiled and then sat, leaning down to whisper to the kid.

Tace watched her, his heart warming. Oh, he'd seen her feed stray animals many a time when she thought nobody was looking. Now she whispered what sounded like a poem.

The kid's breathing evened out. She straightened and turned toward Tace, giving him a glimpse of the sweet heart that lived in Sami.

Why did she try so hard to hide it? "What was that poem?"

"Longfellow. 'The Day Is Done,'" she said, hunching her shoulders.

Tace smiled. "That was nice of you."

She rolled her eyes. "Whatever."

He moved a stray curl away from her cheek. "Why don't you want me to see you being kind?" He truly didn't get it.

"Don't be ridiculous." She backed away from him. "I'm the tough one, you know? My sister was sweet, and I was tough."

Tace narrowed his gaze. "Ah. Who were you so tough for?"

She lifted a shoulder. "My dad, I guess. I caught on quickly, and he liked to train me."

"Your dad trained you, and the tougher you got, the more he liked you?"

She smiled. "He liked me anyway, but it's what we had in common, and it meant something. He didn't understand much about me or my life, but we had that." Her voice sobered. "For a while, anyway. He was into rules and right, you know?"

"You weren't?" Tace peered closer. He'd give anything to unwrap the many layers of Sami Steel.

"Not even close." She sighed. "I miss him. I could've been better and fixed things—I know I could have."

Oh, Tace wanted to dig into that statement, but now wasn't the time. Hell. Never was the right time. "I miss feeling good things." He blinked. Why had he said that?

"You will again," she murmured. "It takes a while to heal."

She wasn't getting it. "Oh, I feel, but not good, you know? It's dark and dangerous and . . ." He should be scared but he wasn't, and that should scare him, too. "I'm different."

"We all are." She appraised him. "I haven't forgotten about your little fainting spell, you know."

He turned and faced her fully, knowing he needed to leave her alone but unable to just walk away. "I'll tell all my secrets if you'll tell yours."

Her mouth opened and closed.

"That's what I figured." He straightened as Grey reentered the room with a basket of drugs in his hands. Time to get started.

Jax Mercury paced from his war rooms and into the soup kitchen, pausing at seeing Barbara Bradley cleaning a weapon on an old wine barrel serving as a table. "Hey." He moved toward her, noting her careful movements. "Do that in the war room next time."

She looked up, her eyes bloodshot. "I didn't want to disturb you."

"That's all right." When he looked at her, he still saw the young paralegal she had been before Scorpius. "Nice job on the raid earlier." The woman had taken down a crazed Ripper all by herself, saving her entire squad.

She smiled. "Thanks. I can't believe I'm a soldier these days."

"You're a good one." Though damn, she looked much younger than her twenty-five years. "Why are you still up?" He was trying to mellow out and get to know his people, but it was harder than he'd thought.

She lifted a shoulder. "Boy troubles."

Ah, shit. Jax took a step back.

She chuckled. "I don't want to talk about it."

"Thank God," he muttered, shoving a hand through his hair. "Though Tace will be back soon."

"Not about Tace," she whispered, her eyes softening.

Jax blinked. "Ah. Well then." Truth be told, they hadn't fit in his mind, and he hadn't liked working the schedule around their romance, if it could be called that. "Good."

She rolled her eyes. "Thanks for the shoulder."

"Anytime." Jax had handled that perfectly. He was getting this whole relate-to-people thing down.

"Oh, we stapled pictures of your missing brother around the east side, mainly on trees, and asked for info on him. Said that the Vanguard soldiers wanted to find him and help him." She grimaced. "I don't think it'll bring too many Rippers out."

"It might, but we'll just deal with them." Jax believed his brother was still alive, but he fought images of his younger brother becoming a Ripper. Marcus had to be all right and just holed up somewhere. "Thank you."

She smiled. "No problem. Thanks for the talk."

Enough emotion. Jax gave a curt nod. "You're on duty tomorrow. Get some damn sleep."

"Yes, sir," she murmured, the sarcasm barely discernible.

He grinned and crossed the room into what was now the medical wing of Vanguard headquarters. The area had once been a free clinic for the destitute and desperate, and technically it still was, while the main infirmary was located inner territory and well protected. He headed beyond the reception area, past two empty examination rooms, and to the room serving as a pathetic lab.

Lynne Harmony hunched over a microscope at a cracked yellow table, muttering to herself.

"Blue? You haven't slept in two days, and I'm done with that." Jax leaned against the doorjamb, his patience wearing thinner than his worn jeans.

She looked up, and her pretty green eyes focused. Well, they were usually pretty. At the moment, red marred the white parts, and dark circles slashed beneath them. "I'm not tired." Even her words slurred together.

"I'm not asking."

She thrummed her fingers on a leather-bound journal next to the microscope. Her father's journal and one she had read often to relax herself. "Unless you have another former head of the CDC infectious disease unit in your pocket, I'm it for us, buddy. Which means I need to keep working."

Did she just call him "buddy"? Jax flashed a smile as his temper stirred. "Baby, move your ass, or I'm gonna do it for you."

She sat back in her chair, and her telltale blue heart glowed through her white T-shirt. He wanted to take a little credit for the fact that she was more comfortable with the blue since they'd gotten together. Her heart had been changed when she'd been injected with a possible cure for Scorpius that hadn't quite worked. Now she was a target for way too many bad guys, and he often lost sleep worrying about how to protect her. "You're awfully bossy tonight. What has you tied up?" she asked.

He blinked slowly. "I'm not here to chat."

"Why are you here?" She pushed back her soft blond hair and lowered her chin.

Temper tickled the base of his neck. "To tell you to get some sleep. You keep going like this, and you're gonna get sick." They were out of most antibiotics, and the idea of her falling ill made his chest hurt. He might not be able to control much in this new world, but he could at the very least make sure his woman got some sleep. While he never would've thought God would give him a brilliant, spirited, kind woman like Lynne, He had, and Jax wasn't going to lose her now. "Did you even eat dinner?"

She squinted and leaned to the side to peer beyond him at the darkened back door. "What time is it?"

That's what he'd figured. He breathed in and out slowly

like the doc had told him to do when he was about to explode.

Lynne arched one light eyebrow. "Seriously? You're using calming breathing techniques?"

"Better than beating your ass," he returned.

She snorted. "What is wrong with you tonight?"

"Why are you killing yourself with this research?" With the crappy lab, even if she figured out a cure for Scorpius, they didn't have the resources to do anything but talk about possibilities.

Her eyes darkened. "Time is ticking, Mercury. Not one live birth has occurred since Scorpius infected the world, and we have to change that."

He lifted a hand. "No live births from Scorpius survivors, you mean." Any woman who hadn't been infected could still have babies.

She nodded. "Yeah, but we have more survivors than non-infected, and since the bacteria lives on surfaces and will probably always be around, someday perhaps everyone will have been infected. We have to do something, and preferably soon, since we have a pregnant teenager here. One who survived Scorpius."

"Jill Sanderson." Jax wiped a hand across his eyes. "I can't believe those kids."

"Right." Lynne coughed. "Like we never forgot condoms."

Oh, he was well aware of his limits. "You didn't get pregnant."

"No, but it was a possibility." She frowned. "Even using condoms, it's possible. They're only 97 percent effective, and someday we'll be out of stock."

The idea of a little girl with Lynne's intelligent eyes both tempted and scared the shit out of him. The world wasn't safe for anybody, and he was holding on as tight as he could as it was. He swallowed. "That's a worry for another day. Tonight my concern is all on you."

"Fantastic although not quite true." She twirled a pencil across the table. "You're worrying about Tace and Sami." She looked up. "As well as everyone else in Vanguard."

Yeah, he was. "Tace and Sami are well trained, and they have each other's backs. Greyson gave his word that they'd be safe."

"Do you believe him? Or rather, did you believe Damon Winter?" Lynne asked.

Jax moved toward her. "Yes, or I wouldn't have sent two of my top lieutenants into his territory." He hoped the risk had been worth it.

She straightened in her chair. "Did you send drawings of Marcus with them?"

Jax nodded. "Sami always has a drawing of my brother with her when scouting." He was losing hope that his younger brother was still alive, even though an old enemy had hinted at that possibility before dying. "She'll ask if anybody has seen him." The chances were slim.

"I think we'll find him. I really do." Lynne tilted her head and focused on the outside door again. "I hadn't noticed but the rain has stopped completely. How long will we have water resources?"

He shook his head. "I'm having that calculated right now. Soon we'll have to head north for both food and fresh water. I'm not ready to leave Vanguard, but we may not have a choice."

She winced. "Moving more than five hundred people? That's going to be difficult."

"I know." He leaned over her and pushed the microscope out of the way, his gaze catching on some of her neatly printed notes. "Any news on the Bunker?"

She looked up into his face as her gaze dropped to his lips. A pretty pink blush bloomed across her high cheekbones. "Um, Tace and I sifted through more documents yesterday, and we think it's on the coast somewhere. It exists, Jax. There are too many references to it."

Yeah, he believed the mysterious government facility existed as well. The government had to have had something in place in case of a plague, especially after the wakeup call of Ebola. The question was whether or not the Bunker scientists had found a cure for Scorpius. "We'll find the Bunker." He wasn't placing much stock in a cure, though.

"I know," she said softly, stretching and knocking over an empty cup. Man, his woman was a klutz.

He swooped down and lifted her against his chest, quickly straightening.

She yelped. "What are you doing?"

He nuzzled her neck, calming himself with her sweet scent. "I need you." True words.

She softened in his arms. "Are you just manipulating me to get me to sleep?"

"Yep." He turned and strode through the clinic and toward the other side of headquarters. "But if manipulation comes with a few orgasms, who can complain?"

"A few?" She nipped at his chin.

"I'll see what I can do." He held her easily. Had she lost more weight? Man, the woman needed a keeper. For now, at least he could focus on her and not on his absent lieutenants.

He hoped he'd done the right thing sending them into Merc territory. If Greyson Storm harmed either one of them, Jax would wage war in an instant. Vanguard was big enough to take down the Mercs, God help them all.

Chapter Six

I only make mistakes that are catastrophic.

—Sami Steel

Exhaustion wore on Sami as she finished taking a very quick shower with rose-scented shampoo. All she had at Vanguard territory was dish soap, so she took a precious moment to appreciate the luxury. The shower was outside under a barrel of cold rainwater, but even so, it was heavenly. The smell of the world after Scorpius hadn't returned to nature as of yet. It would, though.

The water stopped pouring, so she figured her ration was up. Good thing she'd gotten rid of the suds. She glanced at the heavy tarps surrounding her and then poked her head out. "Towel?"

Tace, his hair slicked back from his own shower, handed over a towel. He was basically keeping guard outside. Oh, she could fight naked as well as dressed, but she was happy nobody had interrupted her few moments of rose-smelling bliss. She toweled off her thick hair and then her body before wrapping the towel around herself.

She stepped out and onto a small basketball court set next to the new Mercenary headquarters. Had the kids who'd lived there survived? Maybe they'd headed up north with their parents. Or maybe not. She tried not to think about them or of her many cousins who had perished. While she'd always considered herself fortunate to have a large family, now that they'd all passed on, she felt the void every day.

Leaning down, she rummaged in her duffel bag for clothes and quickly stepped back inside the tarps to throw on yoga pants and a clean shirt.

Stepping out again, she finger-combed her hair. She and Tace had finished dealing with the wounded long after the sun had deserted the sky, and after a quick meal, they'd both showered with the other one guarding the door. It was the first time they'd had privacy all day. "Grey wouldn't let me follow him to the medicine stockpile."

Tace sighed. "He's crafty." Then the medic straightened. Greyson Storm was moving their way from the beach.

"Thanks for the shampoo," Sami said.

He nodded. "Figured you'd like the girly stuff more than Tace. How are my men?"

Tace rubbed his eyes. "Everyone will live. The last guy had a bullet a little close to the spine, but I think he'll be okay. When he awakens, we'll need to make sure he can move his legs. I did my best."

"I appreciate it." Grey eyed the rolling ocean beneath the full moon. "I wanted to thank you both. The men in the infirmary are singing your praises, Sami."

She shrugged and heat climbed into her face. "I just talked to them."

"And told poems, jokes, and sang songs," Greyson said with a smile. "You went above and beyond, and the soft touch made a difference. I'm in your debt."

"She's a sucker for a wounded animal," Tace said, his gaze inscrutable. "Apparently, wounded soldiers as well."

Grey nodded. "You guys must need sleep. I'll show you to your quarters while we're here."

Sami's eyes were gritty, and the idea of a few hours' relaxation was too appealing to resist. She fell into step after him as he led the way back into headquarters and through the east wing of the house, using an industrial-sized flashlight to show the way.

"One room or two?" Grey asked.

"Two," Sami said just as Tace answered, "One."

Grey sighed, and he turned by a large white door. "All right. I'm in the master bedroom, which is the farthest doorway at the end. Damon is in the one we just passed. There's an empty bedroom here for one of you that is decorated in butterflies and tiaras." He turned and pointed down the hallway and toward his bedroom. "There's another one there that has green carpet and NASCAR decorations. The house is patrolled by armed guards, and I have sentries at each entryway."

Tace leaned against the wall and crossed his arms. "One room. Butterflies or cars?"

"Not a chance," Sami snapped.

Greyson rolled his eyes. "This is a Vanguard fight, and I'm too tired to give a shit. Sami, if you kill him, toss his ass outside and one of the guards will dispose of the body." Greyson handed the flashlight to Tace, and without another word, he strode down the hallway and shut a door none too gently.

She was exhausted, her defenses were down, and she couldn't go a round with the Texan hottie. "I'm tired, Tace. Let's get some sleep and figure things out tomorrow."

"We can sleep all you want, but we're bunking in the same room." He glanced down the hallway of the quiet house. "You want to be treated like one of the soldiers, and that's fine, but if Jax was here, we'd bunk together. We're in hostile territory, and one room is better defended than two."

She lifted her chin. "You and Jax would not share a room." Yet would they? It did seem a lot safer just in case.

"Sure we would. So the question is why you wouldn't want to share with me? You'll sleep better."

That was probably true. Or maybe not. Things had been off between them since the other night, and she didn't like being confused. She had to remain apart to protect herself. "I don't know."

"Why, darlin'?" The Texas twang drawled out in full force. "You don't trust yourself?"

That stupid accent spread warmth through her entire abdomen. She never could resist a challenge. "Fine. We're taking butterflies." She stole the flashlight from him and shoved open the door, only to stop cold. The bed was in the center, all white with flimsy netting wrapped around it. Pink and blue butterfly pillows decorated it and matched the huge butterfly rug on the floor. The walls were a soft yellow with a pink border full of tiaras.

"Sami?" Tace's warmth heated her back.

"My sister had a girly room like this years ago. I'd forgotten," she whispered, tears instantly filling her eyes. Jackie hadn't survived Scorpius. The pain struck so suddenly, Sami sucked in air and tried not to fall.

His breath brushed her hair, and he wrapped an arm around her waist from behind. "Take a moment, baby."

She nodded and let the feelings soar through her, remembering Jackie, grieving as a good sister should. "I'm okay."

He gave her several moments, heating her from behind, just supporting her weight. She could feel his heart beating against her shoulder, and she allowed herself one moment of weakness to sink into his strength. "Jackie was so girly." Sami breathed out, her body settling.

Tace held her tighter, his forearm comforting across her abdomen. "What was your room like?" His breath brushed her ear.

She blinked. "Um, blue and yellow with pictures of fighters." She shrugged. While she could've gone with butterflies, she had liked her room. "I was a tomboy." It hurt to look at the pretty things. "My sister was all girl. God, I loved her. She was one year younger than me, but we were best friends. When she made cheerleader, I created a huge collage for her room that she had until the day she died." The last word ended on a sob.

Tace tugged her backward and leaned around her to shut the door. "Let's sleep with cars." Gently taking her hand, he led her down the hallway.

She held on to him, allowing him to lead, feeling not so alone. Oh, she couldn't be vulnerable like this, and yet, she couldn't stop.

Tace pushed open the door. "Ah, shit."

A chuckle bubbled through her and sounded like a sob as she swung the light. "Neither one of us will fit in that." The car-shaped bed would probably fit a toddler. Even the furniture was pint-sized and shaped like cars. "It's okay." She swallowed and turned back toward the girly bedroom. "Sometimes it just hits you out of the blue, you know? I can handle the butterflies now."

He glanced around. "We could sleep on the floor."

"No. We're tired. The bed was a queen-size and will fit us both." Plus, now that the shock had ebbed, it'd be nice to be surrounded by butterflies and tiaras for a night. When was the last time she'd been close to the innocence of the pre-Scorpius days? "Come on." She kept his hand and pulled him along, entering the room.

Her breath quickened. She was leading Tace Justice into a bedroom, for goodness' sake. Friends. They were just friends. Although, if she truly felt that way, would she be lying to him like this?

Tace entered and then engaged the lock. After a quick look around, he shoved the creamy white dresser in front of the door. "Just in case we really drop off." He moved toward the window and made sure it was locked. The man looked as out of place in the sweet room as a wild lion.

Sami faltered by the bed. "Um, what side do you want?" Okay, this was getting weird.

"Right side." He moved toward the side by the window.

She nodded and slid into the other side, turning off the flashlight. The room was plunged into darkness. Soft sheets caressed her skin. "Tace?" she whispered.

"Yeah?"

"Do you really sleep on the right?"

He rolled to his side to face her. With her eyes adjusting, she could barely make out his strong features. "I wanted to be closer to the window in case it was breached," he murmured.

That's what she'd figured. "You know, it occurs to me that you've always done stuff like that, and I'm just questioning why now." She moved onto her side.

"You're a girl."

She opened her mouth to snap at him, but he tapped a finger against her lips. Shock and the electric heat suddenly sparking through her kept her silent.

"I know you're a dangerous and well-trained soldier, and I respect that. But I'm still a guy who was raised with a strong mama and two little sisters, and I'm always gonna try to shield you. It's who I am. I like you, Sami. Even if I didn't, I'd still try to protect you as much as I could. But I do like you."

He sounded almost confused about the last.

"What's wrong with liking me?" she whispered, her toes freezing. Maybe if she moved them just a little toward him, they'd get warm. The guy was like a heater.

"I only seem to like you." He rubbed his face. "I mean, I think I like the other Vanguard soldiers, but I really like you, and that's not good right now. I'm not the guy I was—though that guy would've tried to charm you."

She chuckled. "You come from Texas guys who wore white cowboy hats, don't you?"

He shifted in the bed. "Yeah. The men in my family were all Texas Rangers, and before that, sheriffs. I always thought I'd finish in the service and go back and be a lawman. With our last name, there was never much of a choice." He breathed out. "I've let them down."

She paused. "How?"

"By losing myself to Scorpius," he whispered, emotion clouding his eyes. "The darkness was always there inside me, so it's my fault it even exists for Scorpius to let free. I know that deep down."

She shook her head. "That's crazy. Plus, truth be told, I think anybody who ever settled Texas probably had a dark side. It was necessary." How could he not see that he was every bit the hero he'd always been . . . just with a darker edge?

"That's sweet." He ran his knuckles across her cheek.

She blinked and tried to remain perfectly still. "Tace."

He nodded. "I know."

Her throat clogged, and her body rioted. Okay. She had to get control. "Um . . ."

Tension spiraled from him, surrounding her in a hungry heat. His lips started to move, and she had to force herself to concentrate on what he was saying. "I want to proposition you, just for the night, even though it'd be a colossal mistake. But we're in bed together, and . . ."

Man, when Tace opened up, he sure did it with a vengeance. "We're friends." She scrambled to find a reason why they couldn't.

"Is that all?" he rumbled.

"Yes." She liked him, too, and having him this close was a dangerous temptation. Anything more than a friendship would be a mistake, especially if her past caught up to her, which it always did. At that point, if Tace tried to shield her, he'd be demolished—and that was only if he understood. But how could he? He was a good guy from a long line of law-enforcing good guys. She didn't know how to separate sex and feelings, damn it. "Friends is all we can be."

"All right, friend." He caressed the side of her face. "Tell me about your sister."

Sami leaned into his touch, warming to her memories. "Jackie was a year younger than me, and she was the good one. Straight A's, sweet, pretty. Studied teaching in college and taught kindergarten for two years before she died."

"Scorpius?"

"Yeah. She didn't survive. I reached home in time to say good-bye, though." Sami's chest ached. If she kept talking, she'd reveal too much. "I was the rebel."

His thumb ran along her jawline, his touch soft. "I can see that. Just how did you rebel, baby?"

She blinked. "Ah, I usually chose the wrong boys."

Tace chuckled. "How so?"

"I fell for my first Dice Monkey when I was fourteen, and I never looked back," she whispered, knowing she was saying too much but wanting to share something real with him.

"Dice Monkey?" He grinned, his fingers fanning out to her neck.

"Gamer," she whispered, her pulse spiking at his soft touch.

"Like computer games?" he asked, watching his fingers run down her neck.

She swallowed, her clothes suddenly too tight. "Yeah." Time to change the subject. Her thighs trembled and she pressed them together. "Tell me about your sisters."

He leaned slightly to the side, watching his hand flatten over her collarbone. "Melanie and Juniper." His voice deepened with affection. "Mel was a smoke jumper, and Junie was studying to become a thoracic surgeon. Was in her residency when Scorpius took her, and I was half a world away." The pain in his voice echoed through the quiet room.

Sami cupped his whiskered jaw, her heart aching for them

both, unable to refrain from touching him. "There wasn't anything you could've done, even if you had been right beside her. Trust me. I know." She'd held Jackie for her last moments.

"I know." He turned his face into her palm and gave her a soft kiss.

Her body trembled. "That's interesting, though."

"What is?" he whispered.

"Your sisters—two such different career tracks but each related to what you do." How she would've loved to have met his family and seen where he'd come from. "I bet you were a protective older brother."

"I was terrible." He chuckled and somehow scooted closer to her. "If death threats were truly illegal, I'd be in prison."

"They are illegal," Sami shot back.

He grinned and slid his hand through her hair. "Only if you get turned in."

His touch was driving her crazy, and the man knew it. Sami cleared her throat. "Tace."

"Do you trust me?" he asked.

She removed her hand from his hard jaw. "Yes."

"Then let me help you. Whatever has you so scared and has forced you to keep secrets can be beat. Trust me." His dark plea hinted at more than just the moment.

She didn't bother to ask how he knew she kept secrets. Tace didn't miss a thing. "Why do you want to help me so badly?" she murmured.

His gaze swept her face. "Because of this." Leaning in, he brushed his mouth over hers.

She murmured against him, sucking in her breath. One kiss wouldn't change anything. She was curious, and she was tired of wondering. "Tace."

"I love how you say my name." He threaded his hand through her hair and drew her toward him. His lips hovered over hers for the briefest of moments before he pressed against her. Firm and strong, he kissed her, exploring at his leisure.

She'd known. Oh, she'd known Tace Justice would take his time with a kiss.

Her eyes fluttered shut, and she moved into him. Just one kiss. He rolled her onto her back, kissing her in that unhurried way, levering his body above her. His groin pressed against hers, and man, he was hard. Rock-solid hard.

She might have whimpered into his mouth.

He licked the corners of her lips, nibbling softly. The gentle kiss was such a contrast to the incredibly hard body bracketing her that her lungs just seized. Her thighs widened on their own, and her eyes rolled back when he pressed against her clit. God, it was too much. She should stop him, but it felt too damn good. Just another minute, maybe.

His broad hand held her jaw, and he pressed in with his thumb, forcing her mouth open. His tongue explored inside, bringing delicious tingles and coaxing her to explore on her own.

She'd never, in her entire wild life, been kissed with such complete focus. His warmth drugged her, and his taste of mint, promise, and man seduced her more completely than any words of love. The kiss was all Tace. Everything she'd wanted and everything she'd feared.

Yet she couldn't help but kiss him back, pulled into his slow movements and deliberate gentleness.

A growl rumbled up from his chest and into her mouth, sending electricity through her. She moved against him, her body becoming restless. His pressed her into the bed, holding her still, as he continued playing.

Finally, he lifted his head to let her breathe. His eyes had darkened, and his nostrils flared. Desire was stamped hard across his face. "If you don't want this to happen, now's the time to put a halt to things." The drawl deepened with his need. His strong hand still cupped her jaw, and he swept his thumb across her tingling mouth. "I want to taste every inch of you."

She shivered. He'd take his time about it, too. Her mind fuzzed and her body yearned. "This is a mistake."

"Yeah. Wanna make it?" His gaze dropped to her mouth again.

God, she wanted him. It seemed as if her penchant for bad boys and huge mistakes hadn't ebbed. Maybe it was impossible to truly change. Right now, with her body on fire, she didn't care. She needed relief. "Yes, but just one night."

"Darlin'? I could take a whole night just with your breasts."

Her nipples hardened to rock. Traitorous little bastards. She thought rapidly but not too deeply. "Okay, two nights. These two nights in Merc territory, and then we go back to normal. This can't be a thing." Her voice came out breathy and low. If he knew her story, her criminal past, he wouldn't like her. Even now, at his darkest, Justice was all about law and order.

"Hmm." He licked along her jawline, and she arched against him, caressing down his flanks.

She'd said yes, and now she could touch him. Really touch him. Firm muscle and unreal strength filled her palms. Even his lower back was muscled. She hesitated upon reaching his very fine butt.

"Don't stop now," he whispered, his breath heating her ear right before he nipped.

She jerked and then laughed. "All right." While he licked the shell of her ear, she ran her hands over his taut ass. Firm and hard . . . just like the rest of him. He finished with her ear and lifted up to settle his mouth over hers, more firmly this time.

She caressed up his torso and under his shirt. They had too many clothes on. She opened her mouth to tell him, and he dove in, kissing her hard. She lost herself in the moment, her palms on his warm skin.

A hard knock on the door had him off her in a second and standing between the bed and the door. "What the fuck?" he snapped.

"Tace?" Greyson knocked again. "We need a medic."

Sami sat up and fumbled for the flashlight. She flipped it on and tried to control her breathing somehow. Then she yanked the sheet to her throat like a damsel from the fifties would have.

Tace stomped forward and shoved the dresser out of the way. "If you're fuckin' with me, I'm killin' you." He yanked open the door.

Sami pointed the flashlight at Grey. He stood bare chested with unbuttoned jeans it appeared he'd hurriedly yanked into place. Bruises, cuts, and ripped muscle showed both the strength and danger he exuded. His dark hair was ruffled and his eyes cloudy.

He winced and held up a hand to protect his eyes. "We had a Ripper attack on our south border, and one of my guys needs stitching up. The other is still knocked out, and I don't know how bad it is. Would you take a look?"

Tace's shoulders went down.

Sami tried to calm herself. Oh God. What had she almost done? Heat flared into her face. Thank goodness it was dark in the room. Five minutes more, and she would've been naked with Tace Justice.

Tace glanced her way and then back at Greyson.

Oh. Sami slid from the bed. "I'll come assist."

Tace shook his head. "If you put the dresser in front of the door, then you can sleep. Don't let anybody in but me." He glanced at Grey. "I expect you to guarantee her safety if you want my help."

"I give you my word." Grey eyed them. "I'll meet you in

the kitchen." He turned and disappeared down the darkened hallway.

Tace grabbed her hand and tugged her toward the door. "I'll wait until I hear the dresser in place. I'll be back in a few hours, so you get some sleep." He turned and pressed a hard kiss to her mouth. "We're not done with this."

He moved into the hallway and shut the door.

She swallowed several times.

"Dresser," he barked from the other side.

She rushed for the dresser and shoved it in front of the door.

"Better. Get some sleep, darlin'. I'll be back."

Chapter Seven

I fuckin' hate this bacterium.

—Tace Justice

Several hours after he'd had to leave a willing woman in his bed, the woman he'd been dreaming about for far too long, Tace leaned against the wall and stretched his back, his gaze on his silent patient. The guy had been bitten by a Ripper and thus had been infected with Scorpius. The damn bacteria lived in saliva and other bodily fluids, and for some reason, the really crazy Rippers liked to bite. Nobody confused them with zombies, though.

They were just insane humans. Poor bastards.

He'd sewn one guy up with about a hundred stitches, and now he slept peacefully against the south wall. The two guys he'd operated on were in the other room, and now he just had to worry about this poor soul.

At about fifty years old, the guy had gray hair and loose skin. His nose was a bit bulbous. Had probably been a drinker.

Tace eyed the dawn breaking outside the room, tapping his fingers against his belt three times. It was always three times. Soon the sun would be bright enough to dispense with the light created by the generators. He wondered how much fuel the Mercs had stockpiled. It'd be worth a look to find out.

His body had rioted all night, while his head had remained calm. Sami in his bed . . . saying yes. It would've been a mistake he would have enjoyed. Would she give him another chance? If he finally got inside her, maybe he could stop dreaming about her and return to normal. Well, normal for these days.

Greyson Storm strode into the room, fatigue lining his face and a cup of coffee balanced in his hand. He gave it to Tace.

The strong-smelling brew nearly made him groan. Tace took several drinks and allowed warmth to settle in his gut. Someday the world would be out of such delights, and he didn't even want to think about how quickly that would happen. "I thought you guys were out of coffee?"

"Raid last night. Have enough for the rest of the week now." Greyson had found an old Metallica T-shirt to throw on somewhere. He stretched his neck and glanced toward the ex-drunk fighting the fever. "How is he?"

"Hopped up on vitamin B and Darvocet at the moment." Tace angled his head to double check the restraints holding the guy to the bed. "He had a restless phase, and his fever is up to 105. We've tried medication and somewhat cold compresses to cool him down. It's not looking good."

"Damn it." Greyson breathed out. "I figured Vanguard was lying low until Scorpius finished spreading before moving north, but is it ever going to finish spreading and creating Rippers?"

"Dunno. So long as there are uninfected people, I guess it could keep spreading." Tace grimaced. "Frankly, we don't know that all of us will remain sane. Vitamin B keeps some of us from going crazy for a while, but it could be a temporary fix, you know? Maybe we'll all just go nuts and turn into serial killers."

"You're a fucking ray of sunshine in the morning," Grey said slowly.

"You're not the first to say so." There had been a time when he was the cheerful one in his unit every morning—when he had the land of his fathers to return home to. Scorpius had changed more than his brain. "Sami and I are leaving tomorrow. That plan remains the same, no matter what new disaster occurs here."

"Understood." Greyson glanced toward the doorway. "Where is your pretty weapon?"

Tace frowned. "Weapon?" He'd thought of Sami in many terms but not that one.

Greyson arched an eyebrow. "Oh, I saw her fight the other day. She's definitely a weapon."

"Humph." Tace nodded. He liked that description of her. "She's still sleeping and definitely needs rest. We haven't had enough in too long."

"Yeah. I get that." Grey ground a palm into his left eye. "I'm too tired and pissed to be smooth about this, but I want Maureen Shadow back here working on the food supply. I'm willing to trade for her."

Tace cocked his head to the side, reading the Merc leader's body language. He was angry and exhausted . . . and trying to sound nonchalant. "We don't trade people."

"Then I'm willing to hire her. Pay for her services. Exchange some of my goods or people for her services. I don't give a meager fuck how we define the situation. But Moe needs to be back here and working on food development in those damn greenhouses, or we all starve, including Vanguard."

Tace stilled. "So it's Moe, is it? What exactly happened between you two when you kept her captive?" Did Maureen have a story to tell that would put Vanguard and the Mercs at war? If so, he needed to get Sami the hell out of there.

Greyson's arms dropped, and he gave Tace a look. "Seriously? Nothing happened. The closest we came to anything happening was she rushed me with a knife, and I took it away. Without bruising her, by the way." He rubbed his jaw. "Well, she also knocked two of my guards out one night trying to escape." Amusement lowered his tone.

Tace lifted back. Whoa. "You like her."

"Sure." Greyson rolled his eyes. "I kidnapped her, and she tried to cut me. Strong and feisty. Plus, she's probably the foremost expert in food development still living on earth. What's not to like?"

Tace shook his head, a part of him he disliked wondering how to use that information against the Mercs. "Listen. I know we're not pals, and at some point, we may be enemies. But no matter what, Raze Shadow is a killer, and a good one. You kidnapped his sister and blackmailed him to turn over the woman he was falling in love with."

"So?" Grey asked, focusing.

Tace lowered his chin. "Raze is going to kill you. I don't know when, and I'm not sure how—he prefers a knife— but he will be coming for you."

"He's not the only one who can use a blade," Grey said softly.

"I know. So either you're gonna die, or Raze is gonna die, and no way will Maureen want anything to do with you either way. Especially if you're dead." Numbness attacked Tace's right hand, and he stretched his fingers, trying not to wince or show weakness. "It's my job to make sure Raze succeeds, by the way." He had no problem killing these days, felt more distance than ever from his proud heritage.

"So you're saying there's no hope of an alliance between Vanguard and the Mercenaries."

Tace frowned. "I'm not saying that, actually. Jax Mercury is a brilliant strategist, and right now, Vanguard has the most dangerous force in the country gunning for us. Hell, the president apparently is gunning for you, too."

"The enemy of my enemy is my friend," Greyson murmured, fatigue fanning out from his blue-green eyes.

"Exactly." Tace lifted a shoulder. "At least for now."

"We do live in interesting times." Greyson glanced at the sun streaming through the window. "So. Have we given your little weapon enough time to scout around?"

Everything inside Tace stilled. "Excuse me?"

"Did you really think I'd fall for our little chat here? I knew the second Sami slid out your bedroom window, as did Damon. She's not going to find a thing except for trouble as she tries to catalog my resources."

What the hell? He'd told her to get some sleep and stay put until he returned. Of course she'd hadn't listened. Tace moved for the doorway, and instantly three men blocked his way, guns pointed at his chest.

"Keep him here," Grey ordered them, striding beyond them and out the door. "Continue doing your job, medic. I'll make sure Sami is well taken care of."

Tace growled low in a sound he'd never heard from himself. From anybody else, either. He could take down the first guy, maybe the second, but the third would get off a shot. If he was injured or dead, he might not be able to help Sami. "You harm her, and I'll rip you apart piece by piece." His voice dropped to a hoarse rasp that made him cringe.

Grey turned from beyond his men. "It'd be an interesting contest, to be sure. Keep my men alive, Justice. Unlike your leader, I do believe in an eye for an eye."

"You've misjudged both Jax and me. We're fine with cutting out eyes and adding them to the soup," Tace ground out.

Greyson's low chuckle wafted in his wake.

The numbness in Tace's hand turned to trembling and

vibrated up his arm. Dots swam across his left eye. The back of his head heated and then went numb. God, not now.

He leaned against the wall to keep from falling on his ass in front of the Merc soldiers. What the hell was wrong with him? He had to regain control and go after Sami. The instant one of the Mercs gave him an opening, he was taking it.

Sami crept low along buildings in Merc territory. The sun beat down, hotter than it should be this early in the morning. She'd been scouting for nearly an hour, going through nicely kept mansions. The Mercs had gotten rid of any bodies or rotting food, so the search thus far had been pleasant, unlike many of her scouting missions.

Damon Winter was following her, and she'd lost him twice, but he'd caught her scent. The guy was part bloodhound. Probably had been a good cop.

For now, she let him tail her as she went through another mansion. Like the others, the cupboards were bare. The Mercs' food had to be stored in a central location, and so far, she hadn't found it. Or the medicine and weapons.

Think, damn it.

While neither man would appreciate the comparison, Greyson Storm and Jax Mercury were similar. So, where had Jax located his stores? Some of the Vanguard's weapons, medicine, and food were kept at headquarters. Sami needed to get back in the main house and check for a basement.

Yet many of Vanguard's provisions were under guard at various warehouses throughout the territory. Merc territory was a hell of a lot larger than Vanguard, so those storage areas could be anywhere. But they'd have to be close enough for Greyson to get to quickly. She sighed and dodged out the back door of the house, stopping when she spotted Damon leaning against a fountain of a massive fairy with wings. A quiet fountain since water no longer flowed.

"I'm tired of the cat and mouse," he said, crossing muscled arms. Today he'd worn a Merc black T-shirt, dark jeans, and a gun at his hip. "It's getting hot."

"Then go back inside and fan yourself." The cat and mouse had brought back some bad memories of hiding from cops in the past, and she was almost relieved he'd stopped the game. Cops had made her nervous since her first illegal hack, and she had to control her expression as she faced Damon squarely.

He watched her like a hawk seeing a mouse on the ground. "How about I tell you that you're not gonna find our stockpiles, you tell me to go to hell, and then we actually talk about why you're lying to everyone about being an LAPD rookie?"

She swallowed and tried to appear bored. "Did anybody ever tell you that you look a little like Shemar Moore?"

He lifted his chin. "No, but I did have a girlfriend tell me I looked like Taye Diggs once."

She studied him. "Humph."

"I didn't think so, either." No. There was a hardness to Damon that came from real life and not television. "Why, Sami?"

"I wasn't lying. Maybe you are, or perhaps you didn't know every single cop in LA. I mean, ten thousand people worked for the LAPD before Scorpius." She'd learned to speak slower and almost in a drawl when lying.

He nodded. "You're right, but I also can discern a lie, and you're definitely not being truthful. Who was your deputy chief? Your commander? Your captain?"

"I'm not doing this." She brushed by him toward a large garden shed beyond an overgrown lawn.

"That's why I don't believe you. Hell, that's why nobody

believes you," Damon continued from behind her. "Of course there's a chance I wouldn't know you—there were tons of cops. But you don't move like a cop, Sami."

She pivoted. "You've seen me fight."

"Oh, you can fight, but you don't move like a cop. You don't scout the area like a cop, and you sure as shit don't hold yourself like one." He shook his head. "It's something learned on the job, and you have never been on that job."

She crossed her arms, bluffing for all she had. "I guess we'll have to agree to disagree."

"No. I can cause trouble for you within Vanguard if I push this, lady." He moved toward her, all muscled grace.

Heat ignited down her back. "What are you saying?"

He narrowed his gaze as if thinking. "I'll keep quiet, maybe even remember you as a rookie, but you owe me."

She stepped back, more than ready to kick his ass. But from the way he moved, she knew he could fight. What was he saying? She shivered. How long had it been since the ex-cop had had a woman? "Excuse me? What exactly do you want in trade, asshole?"

His head jerked. "Geez. Not that. Give me a break."

She glared and the world seemed to close in on her. "Right."

"I look like Shemar, remember? I don't need to blackmail women for sex. Ever." He did appear a little affronted.

Sami studied him. "You don't really look like him. I take it back."

"Okay." Damon sighed. "Listen. Just give me schematics of Vanguard territory, locations of provisions, a breakdown of the fighting forces, and we'll call it even. I'll back your story up with Tace, and nobody will ever be the wiser about your lying."

She reared back. "You want to blackmail me to betray Vanguard?"

He shrugged. "Same information you've been trying to

get on us the whole time you've been here. Give me the information, and I won't turn you in to your own people."

She crossed her arms. "You Mercs all use blackmail. That's weak and pathetic."

"Answer the questions."

"No." She didn't even need to stop and think.

"You'd sacrifice your position there to protect them?" he asked.

For so long, she'd been running and hiding. Now she'd found a place of safety, and giving Damon the information he wanted would keep her there. But she thought of Tace, Jax, and Raze. Her fellow soldiers. She thought of Lynne Harmony with her blue heart, and Vinnie Wellington, who'd shown Raze he had a heart. And she thought of little blond Lena, who might already know her secret. There was really only one answer. "Yeah. So turn me in and do your worst. I'm not giving you shit about Vanguard."

Damon's chin lowered. "Fine. Then turn back, and let's go talk with Greyson about your scouting activities here today."

"No." She settled her stance, wanting nothing more than to kick Damon's butt.

He stilled. "You don't want to fight me, little warrior. The guys you've been training with are on your side and make sure not to harm you. I'm not on your side."

"Oh, buddy. Let's go." She clenched her hands into fists, her entire body lighting with anticipation. The previous night with Tace had left her confused and emotional; this would be an excellent way to focus and deal. Making the ex-cop bleed was just a bonus. "You make a move."

"I don't think so." Greyson Storm loped out of the house, long and lean and looking a bit more than mean. His black-T-shirt stretched tight across his muscled torso, and his torn jeans hugged tight hips. Those odd eyes appeared all blue in the morning light. Alert and dangerous.

Damon stepped back. "Would've been a good fight."

Sami scoffed. "I doubt it."

Grey eyed her head to toe. "I like that you wouldn't sacrifice Vanguard for yourself."

"Gee, thanks." The thought occurred to her to take on both men, but she'd seen Grey fight, and she'd need to handle him by himself to even have a chance. He was skilled enough that she'd have to really hurt him to win.

"The question is, what would you sacrifice for Tace Justice?" Grey asked calmly.

She stilled, her focus narrowing. "Excuse me?"

"At the moment, he's surrounded by guns. Tell me what I want to know, and I'll make sure nobody fires." Greyson smiled, and his eyes lost all expression. "Stay silent and stubborn, and we'll see if your boy likes the taste of lead."

Chapter Eight

The aftermath of the apocalypse is when life will get interesting.

—Dr. Frank X. Harmony, *Philosophies*

Tace eyed the three guys holding guns on him and worked out the math yet again. Take the gun from the first guy, use him as a shield, and then shoot the other two guys. His odds sucked. "We seem to have an issue here."

"What's that?" the first guy on the right asked, showing a large gap between his front two teeth.

"If I shoot any of you, I'm the medic. Do you really want to fire on the one guy who can patch you up if you're injured?" He leaned to look around them at the Scorpius patient now thrashing on the bed. "He might be upset with you if he awakens."

The soldiers angled to the side.

"Help him," Bad Teeth ordered.

"Nope." Tace crossed his arms. The feeling was rapidly returning to his head and limbs, and his vision had cleared. Whatever these attacks were, they ended quickly. So far. His mind tried to rush to Sami, and he held tight, keeping calm. The woman could fight; she'd be all right. Yet everything in him wanted to run through the guns to reach her.

"You're a doctor. You have to help," said the second soldier, a blond kid still fighting pimples.

Tace shook his head, relieved when dizziness didn't bombard him again. "I'm not a doctor. I'm a field medic from the army. Drop the guns, or your buddy there dies."

"If you're a medic, you've taken an oath to save lives," Blond Guy muttered.

"The old rules and oaths are dead, kid. Drop the guns," Tace said, truly meaning the words. Less than a month ago, he would've felt obligated to help the sick man. Now most of him didn't care. He was broken, and that thought alone should keep him the hell away from Sami. Except to protect her, of course.

The guy on the stretcher moaned and kicked out, finishing with a high-pitched scream.

Tension filled the air, and Tace moved off the wall and into a fighting stance. "Boys?"

"Jesus. Put the guns down." Greyson stalked into the room, wiping blood off his lip. "Help the man, Justice." The soldiers lowered their guns and backed out of the room. Greyson half turned. "Go patrol the beach." Bootsteps answered his order.

Tace lifted his head, his body going into overdrive. "What happened to your mouth?" The Merc leader's lip was already swelling nice and fat.

"Your woman kicked me in the face," Greyson growled, gingerly touching his mouth.

Anger, the real kind, sped through Tace so quickly his ears burned. "What did you do?" He advanced.

Grey held up a hand. "Just threatened to shoot you. We didn't touch her."

Tace paused. A smile tickled his mouth, and warmth bloomed in his chest. "She was defending me?"

"Apparently." Greyson frowned. "She didn't need to kick me in the mouth though." He shook his head as Tace started to ask the question. "Of course I didn't retaliate. Even though it'd be a fun contest, I don't hit women. Even mean ones who kick a guy in the lips just for making an ordinary threat against somebody not even present. God."

"Tace?" Sami called out.

Tace hustled to the door to see her stomping inside, her hair in twin braids, irritation marring her smooth skin. Without any makeup on, she looked like an angry teenager. "You okay?" he asked, watching her entire body settle into calmness.

"Fine. You?" She looked beyond him to glare at Grey. "You're a shitty bluffer, Storm."

Grey shrugged and then winced as the guy behind him screeched.

Tace turned and headed for the counter and another syringe. "He can't have another sedative for an hour, but he's due vitamin B." The needle went in smoothly, and Tace plunged the contents through him. The patient continued to thrash, his face a bright red. Tace felt his cheeks. "He's burning up. Do you have anything resembling ice around here?"

"No, but I can get more cool cloths," Greyson said.

"I have cloths," Tace muttered. They were going to lose another one, and there wasn't anything he could do about it.

The patient seized.

"Shit. What's his name?" Tace asked.

"Goes by Bucknell," Grey said. "Think it was his last name, but he's never said."

Tace noted the guy's labored breathing. The next progression would be—

The guy jerked up, his body shuddering.

"Damn it." Tace immediately started CPR. "You been infected?" he asked Grey.

"Yeah."

"Good. Breathe into his mouth when I tell you to." Tace counted out his thumps and told Greyson to breathe. Even though Sami had been infected, he didn't want her near a thrashing man.

They worked on Bucknell for nearly twenty minutes. Tace continued to perform CPR. Finally, Greyson leaned back and clapped Tace on the arm. Lines cut into the sides of the Mercenary leader's now-swollen mouth. "He's gone."

Tace leaned back and wiped his brow. "Call it. He's your man."

"He was," Grey said, his eyes a somber green through the blue. "Damn it."

"I'm sorry," Tace said, seeing Sami position herself to his left.

Greyson nodded and then his gaze focused on Sami. "No need, lady. I'm not blaming Justice for this."

"Just making sure," she said, her voice soft.

Tace cut her a look. She'd immediately taken his back just in case. Somehow, that thought banished some of the darkness surrounding him. But she kept her gaze on Grey and didn't meet Tace's eyes. Wonderful. They'd almost gone horizontal and nude the night before. Now things were going to be awkward. Tace sighed.

Greyson straightened. "We'll bury him this afternoon and celebrate his life tonight. I promised you guys fresh fish, and you didn't get it last night. We also have some good booze from these rich homes."

Sami rubbed her nose. "I'm sorry for your loss, Greyson."

A groan came from the other room.

Greyson turned and jogged into the post-op area. A second later, he called out. "Ah, Justice? Should this guy be bleeding all over?"

Damn it. "No." Tace pivoted and ran to find one of his earlier patients spitting blood. "Ah, crap. Okay. I need brighter lights and a surgical kit. Now." It was going to be a long afternoon.

* * *

Sami paced outside the surgical room as weird squishy sounds emerged along with an occasional grunt and order from Tace for Greyson to do something. To tie something off or hand over an implement.

"I need more hyoscyamine as well as another saline pack," Tace snapped.

Sami edged closer to the door, her stomach cramping. The desperate smell of blood was everywhere. "Tace?"

"Now, Greyson," Tace said, his voice cracking. "We're gonna lose him."

"I can't take my hands out of his chest right now," Greyson hissed.

Sami poked her head in, relieved that Greyson's broad back blocked her view of the guy with his chest apparently open. The metallic smell of blood nearly dropped her to her knees. "I can get it."

Grey turned and pinned her with a hard look. Dots of sweat collected across his forehead. "Call one of my men."

"There's not time," Tace said, edging to the side.

Sami took a step back. Blood had splattered across his neck. "Trust us, Greyson."

The Merc leader gave a low growl. "Fine. The nearest storage area is across the back street in the house with blue shutters. Go down to the basement, find the utility closet to the left, and shove a hidden panel out of the way. It was a panic room for the rich people. The medicine is on the far right."

Sami turned and launched herself into motion, running through the building and out the back door. A quiet street fronted by overgrown lawns and huge houses surrounded her. The sun beat down, making her shield her eyes. The blue shutters caught her attention at a three-story house with red roses along the front.

She ran across the already cracking driveway and up the stairs, pushing open the door. Cool, stale air slapped her. She shut the door in case any of Greyson's guys came by. An unlit but still sparkly chandelier hung down from two stories up; a staircase went up to the right and down to the left, the stairs alternating between black and white tiles. She hustled down into darkness. Shit. A table sat at the bottom, and as she neared, she could make out several flashlights. Smart.

Flipping one on, she turned left and ran down the hallway, pushing open a closet door. Empty shelves lined the walls. Reaching the end, she tapped the beige-painted wall and then pushed to the side.

It rolled open to reveal a room probably half the length of the house. Guns were tacked to the west wall, water was stacked to the north, and medicine, tons and tons of it, took up all the shelves on the east wall. She ran forward and cataloged the vitamin B vials. At least three hundred vials were there.

She tried to memorize the different drugs while searching for the right one. Finding it, she grabbed a vial, a couple of syringes, and a saline bag. They had at least fifty saline bags. For good measure, she grabbed a bunch of gauze and several large bandages.

Greyson must've been one of the first to scavenge the local hospital.

Turning, she noted a large number seven tacked to the door. Seven? Were there at least six other depots like this?

She wanted to take more medicine, but she didn't have a pack. So she hurried up the stairs and into the glaring heat, running across the road to the former workout facility.

Reaching the surgical room, she paused. "I have the stuff."

"Over here," Tace muttered, his hands in the guy's chest.

Sami kept her gaze averted and moved his way, dropping the materials on a table. "Do you, ah, need me to do anything?" She tried to breathe out, but nausea rolled up her throat.

"Yes. Fill the syringe to the second line," Tace said.

Sami did so, her hand shaking.

"Leave it on the table and go outside. I can't have you puking," he said, his voice not unkind.

She turned and bolted, taking several deep breaths outside. If it had been such an emergency, why did she leave the syringe on the table? Maybe Tace was using it right now.

Just how calculated had he become? Had he faked something so important during surgery just so they could find the resources? Was Greyson even needed in there?

Sami shook her head and slid down to sit on the ground. No. Tace wasn't that cold—no way.

Yet she couldn't help but shudder. The surgery went on for another hour, punctuated by terse comments and low expletives. Finally, Greyson caught her attention. "Call it, Justice. He's done."

"Fuck." Tace stormed out of the room and yanked off blue surgical gloves. "Damn it. Fuck."

Sami pushed to her feet.

He leaned over and breathed out several times.

Greyson strode into the room, his gaze somber. "I was there. You did everything you could in shitty conditions."

Tace stood and put his back to the wall, tapping his head several times pretty hard. "I should've saved him." He shook his head, his eyes tracking nothing as he probably replayed the surgery.

"You tried," Sami said, wanting to approach him but not sure if he'd snap her head off. "I know you did."

Greyson sighed. "I'll go round up a couple of guys to bury him. We're getting drunk tonight, friends." He smacked

Tace on the arm as he walked by, his movements slow and weary.

Silence pounded around the small room with death just a doorway apart. "I'm sorry, Tace," Sami murmured.

He lowered his chin, his eyes inscrutable. "What did you find in the storage area?"

She blinked, and warning ticked through her abdomen. He'd gone from pissed to calculating in a nanosecond. "Medicine, water, and guns."

"A lot?" he asked.

"Yes," she whispered, chills suddenly attacking her. "Did the medicine I brought help?"

"Didn't need it." Tace wiped a hand across his eyes. "I lost that guy an hour before he died. There wasn't a way to save him."

Sami took a step back. "But you tried."

"Of course I tried." His eyes darkened. "Feel like shit that I couldn't save him."

Yet the medic had still used the situation for them to gain information. "I, ah—"

"We're at war, Samantha." His voice lowered with a matter-of-fact tone that cut right through her. "We had to go home with some sort of intel, and I figured out a way to get it."

She nodded. "I know. Man, you've changed."

"That's the truth." He scratched at the now-dried blood on his face. "You're smart to stay the hell away from me. I'm sliding fast, and there's no light at the end of the fall. Let's help bury their dead and then commiserate and celebrate life with a lot of liquor."

"You wanna get drunk?" she asked, the world tilting. Where had her compass gone?

"Why not? At the very least, maybe we can get information out of them when they're drinking." He looked down at his hands. "I need to clean up. There's still blood on my hands."

Chills clacked down her spine.

Chapter Nine

Fighting just to fight doesn't last. Everyone needs
somebody to fight for.

—Sami Steel

Sami kicked her legs out and settled her boots on the antique
coffee table, her head swimming and her belly nice and
mellow. The chenille couch cupped her butt, and the fire
from the massive stone fireplace flickered soft light around
the darkened living room. Even though they'd finished hours
ago, she was still pleasantly full. "That was the best dinner
I've had in a year," she murmured. Nothing compared to her
grandma Juliana's chicken casserole, however.

Tace grunted in agreement next to her, swirling bourbon
in a fancy crystal glass.

"I'm glad you liked the fish," Greyson said, his head back
on a matching chair, his face in profile with the fire on the
other side of him. "I hope it was good enough you'll both
come back. In fact, we could use a medic, Tace."

"No," Tace said, tipping back his drink. "I belong at Vanguard."

"We need a doctor." After nearly two bottles of bourbon
between the three of them, Grey's voice had mellowed and
lost the hard-cut glass sound it usually had.

"Yeah," Tace agreed, leaning over to pour more alcohol

in his glass. "Somebody better than me. I lost two of your guys today."

Sami blinked several times and then patted his hard thigh, her heart hurting for him. Even though he said he didn't feel emotions any longer, there had been a lost look in his blue eyes after the second guy had died. Lost and desperate. "Nobody else could've saved either one of them. You did your best." She tipped a little on the couch. How many glasses of the potent brew had she knocked back? Not that it really mattered.

Tace drank his glass and poured another.

"You have quite the tol-er-um, tolerance." She blinked rapidly when his face wavered.

"Texas, baby." His words slurred a little, but he flattened his hand over hers, trapping it on his warm leg.

She gave a weak struggle but failed to dislodge him. When he'd left her the previous night, she'd spent many restless moments replaying the entire kiss. Tace Justice could kiss, that was for sure. But they couldn't happen. No matter how badly her body wanted to be naked against his. She had enough problems without trying to save him, too. She'd always fallen for the ones who needed saving, and it had always ended badly.

At the mere thought, she shivered.

"You cold?" Tace asked, releasing her hand to tug her into his side, his arm around her shoulders.

"No." She tried to push away and ended up nearly on his lap.

"Settle," he murmured, tugging gently on her hair.

Greyson's eyes opened, and he studied the two of them. "That's why I don't have women around here."

Sami breathed out. "You can't keep going under your current organizational structure." Whoa. Even three sheets to the wind, she could sound smart. Who knew? Maybe she should drink the good stuff more often. "You have to know that."

"Nope." Greyson shook his head. "Soldiers have always carried out wars far away from home, without entanglements or spouses."

"Yeah," Sami said softly, "but those soldiers had a home to return to. Yours don't. This is their home. Once survival isn't the only goal, people need something or someone to fight for. You're not giving them that." The booze was making her too verbal, and she needed to knock it off. "Or whatever."

Tace turned his head. "What or who do you fight for, Samantha?"

When he used her full name in that slow Texan drawl, she felt like a Samantha. All feminine and powerful. "We're still in the survival mode, Texas."

"Uh-huh." His dark gaze roamed her face.

She bit her lip. "And Vanguard. I guess we both fight for Vanguard."

Greyson cleared his throat. "Is Vanguard any closer to finding the Bunker?"

Sami partially swiveled toward him. "You believe the Bunker exists?"

"Yeah. Enough people know about it that I believe the place exists." Grey leaned over and poured himself another glass, noted Sami's empty one, and filled hers, too. "Don't you?"

She shook her head and tried to keep her expression clear. "Nope. I think it's a wild tale whispered about to give hope. If the government had created some secret underground lab to study Scorpius or other diseases, we'd know about it by now. When Scorpius got bad, all secrets were let loose." Was she saying too much? Trying too hard to convince him?

She reached for her glass to take a couple of sips. The bourbon warmed her throat and heated her stomach.

"That's our Sami," Tace rumbled, dragging her up on his lap. "Always the realist."

She struggled and ended up with her butt between his legs and her feet on the couch as he cradled her.

Greyson sighed. "Just so you guys know, the stockpiles you found earlier are all we have left. Attack us for them, and we'll take you out."

"We have more people than you do," Sami returned.

"We have sixty or so trained soldiers, and so do you. The rest of your group are either newly trained or civilians, and my guys shoot to kill," Greyson said. He cleared his throat. "Speaking of fighting, where did you learn so well, Sami?"

"My dad and uncle," she said, trying not to sink into Tace's heat.

"Ah. Your dad wanted a boy, huh?" Grey asked.

"No." She frowned. "Why?"

Grey grinned. "No reason. That's awesome, by the way."

She smiled. "My dad and I understood each other usually. Well, until I discovered boys."

Tace chuckled. "I can imagine that was tough for him. Did you go for street fighters?"

"No." She breathed out. "I went for lost souls and the brilliant nerdy ones. Always turned bad."

"I'm not brilliant." Tace leaned in and nuzzled Sami's neck. "But I'm definitely lost."

Fire lanced through her, and she turned to shove him away. "Knock it off."

Greyson stretched to his feet. "Tell Jax that I've asked everyone in Merc territory about his brother, and nobody has seen Marcus. I showed them all the drawing of the man."

Sami nodded. "We'll let him know. Thanks for trying." God, she hoped her friend found his brother.

Greyson nodded. "It's about midnight, and you two need to leave in a couple of hours to reach Vanguard while it's still dark. Sleep off the booze. I have a thank-you box of provisions to send with you when you go. For good faith and all of that shit." He loped by them and disappeared toward the bedrooms.

"'Night, Grey," Sami called out and then snorted. "And I thought Jax was grumpy."

"Jax is grumpy." Tace tugged her so she straddled him, moving her easily. "So."

Sometimes she forgot his strength. His thighs heated hers, and this close, his unique scent of man combined with the rich smell of good bourbon. If she moved any closer, the obvious bulge in his jeans would be right where her body wanted it. "No," she whispered softly.

His chest shuddered. "I don't need to ask why." Yet his big hand flattened against her collarbone and swept her shirt down her arm. "So pretty and soft." The pads of his fingers slid across her bare skin. "I dream about you," he murmured.

She stilled. "You do?"

"Yes. Every night. Sometimes during the day. Always you, always sighing my name." He shook his head. "Sometimes I think you're haunting me."

Those were sweet words that should be a little creepy but weren't. Gone was the cold and calculating man from earlier, and in his place was the sweet Texan she thought she'd known. "What do you want from me?" she asked, her question pouring out of her before she could stop it.

"I don't know." He traced a path up her jugular and beneath her jaw as if memorizing her shape.

She wobbled on his legs and pressed against his chest for support. "We're drunk."

"Yep. How easy would it be to, uh, use that as an excuse?" He tilted his head to the side and watched his hand spread out over her chest. "Isn't that why we both kept drinking? Really?"

If he moved any lower, her aching breasts would finally get some attention. "You don't want to use booze as an excuse?" she whispered.

"I do want to," he murmured, moving his hand down and over her breasts. "Fuck, baby, I'd use anything for an excuse."

She gasped. Pleasure, too hot to be real, streaked from her nipples to her core. "Tace." She closed her eyes as heat swept her in nearly painful tingles. How was it possible to want this badly?

"The world sucks." He leaned in to let his mouth wander across her neck and gently clasped one aching mound. "Shouldn't we take pleasure when we can?"

As a line, it was a damn good one. She wanted to laugh at them both, but she ached too much to find true humor. He palmed her, his big hand enclosing her entire breast. "Tace?"

He lifted his head, his gaze square to hers. "I could talk you into this, but I'm not gonna. I don't want that."

She blinked.

He drew his fingers along her breast to caress her nipple, pulling just hard enough to steal her breath away. "You're all in with your eyes open, or we're done. One night, Sami. A couple of hours here in Merc territory and away from home."

She swallowed and couldn't help pushing into his hand. They could die on the way home from a Ripper attack. Shouldn't she take this one moment of pleasure? "Then it's back to normal."

"It has to be." He leaned in and licked across her collarbone.

God. She couldn't take it. She trembled. One time. Just a couple of stolen hours? This new, grown-up, desolate world did call for pleasure when possible since it was so rare. She knew one taste of him wouldn't be enough, but once back at Vanguard, she couldn't be somebody's girlfriend. Not with the past coming close, and not if she wanted to continue to fight. And if he ever found out the truth, he wouldn't want her anyway.

He lifted his head and nipped beneath her jaw. "Samantha?"

"This night—what's left of it. Eyes open. Just one." She could barely get the words out.

He stood suddenly, his hands cupping her ass, and moved beyond the couch and through the house, somehow maneuvering perfectly fine in the darkness. One foot nudged open their door, and he stepped inside, letting her slide down his body. "Hold on." He turned and blocked the door with the dresser.

Moonlight poured in the window, making the butterflies all sparkle. She backed away and tugged off her shirt. A quick shimmy, and her yoga pants and boots hit the floor. They only had a couple of hours, and she didn't want to miss a second.

He stalked her, a hard-cut shadow, and tossed off his shirt. Weak light danced along the hard ridges of his abdomen and chest. His Vanguard tattoo—a shield, sword, and Scorpius with VANGUARD through the middle—was right above his heart. Hers was on her left shoulder blade with much more delicate lines. Her throat went dry. "Um."

"Um what?" he asked, shucking his jeans and boots.

God. Tace Justice was naked with her. And he was all man. She swallowed and tried not to cough. "There's just a lot to you." Holy cow, he was big.

He reached her and ran both palms down her bare arms. "Don't worry, darlin'. I'll make sure you're more than ready." Then he kissed her. Slow and deep, taking his time, his hand somehow finding the small of her back and pulling her into his strength. Hard muscle and heat instantly warmed every inch of her.

"I, ah, it's been a while." Reality tried to intrude.

"I know." He backed her to the bed and bent her over, sweeping a hand down her front. "So pretty, Sami."

She scooted up, crossways on the bed, and he crawled up her to kiss her again. There was so much to him. He leaned down and sucked a nipple into his mouth.

Hot. God, his mouth was hot. She arched into him, needing more. It had been too long for her.

He nipped and sucked her, moving to the other nipple, his fingers tapping down her abdomen and finding her folds. She moaned and thrashed against him. He lifted up. "That sound. Make it again."

She tried to focus.

He grinned then, his chin between her breasts, his hand between her legs. One thumb brushed across her clit.

She moaned again.

"Yeah, that."

"I know you like to take your time," she ground out, moving against his fingers. "How about fast first and slow later?" If she didn't get him inside her and now, she was going to implode.

He blinked slowly. "You wanna take over this time?"

"Yes." She shoved his shoulders, almost crying in relief when he rolled to his back. She was wet and hot and nearly desperate. The bourbon in her blood was no competition for the desire he'd ignited. She grasped the base of his shaft, running her fingers up and then back down.

He bucked against her, and a quick glance at his eyes confirmed they'd darkened. "Keep going, darlin'."

She smiled and straddled him, lifting herself up with her knees and positioning him at her entrance.

"Whoa." He handed her a condom he'd tossed on the bed.

She ripped open the foil and unrolled the rubber, feeling powerful as he arched against her. Then she grasped him and tried to lower herself on his thick cock. He reached for her breasts, caressing them, sending sparks of need right to her clit. Now, damn it. She tried to take him in, but pain instantly assailed her. She drew out air and tried again. Pain. "You're too big."

"No." He grasped her hip and rolled them both over. "Leverage helps." Then he kissed her again, his mouth firm, his tongue sweeping inside hers. She tangled with him, shoving both hands through his hair. Her thighs widened. He deepened the kiss and started to penetrate her.

She gasped, and he nipped her lips, taking her under again.

Slowly, keeping her drugged with kisses, he worked his way inside her, taking his time, letting her adjust. She ran her hands down his flanks, over new scars and old battle wounds, her fingers wandering over all that taut skin. Nothing mattered but his body over hers. She reached his butt and squeezed. Nice and firm and oh so many muscles.

He lifted his head.

She blinked. He was fully inside her, pulsing. "Tace," she whispered.

"Fast this time, slow later." He caught her face, his mouth working hers as he began to thrust. Hard and full, taking her deep, he started to pound. Each movement awoke nerves she hadn't realized she had. Soon she was panting, her nails raking his back.

Everything in the world focused on Tace Justice and how well he was using her body. She shut her eyes to just feel.

"Samantha," he said. "Open your eyes."

She opened her eyes to see the most primal male she could ever imagine. Determination and lust were stamped hard across his rugged face, but his gaze remained gentle. Concentrated.

"Now, baby. Come for me," he whispered. He thrust into her, filling her completely.

The world disintegrated and she called his name, coming apart as pleasure took her over. She tightened and held on, her eyes shutting, and let the ecstasy take her away. When she came down with a soft sob, he dropped his head to her neck and shoved hard, coming with a shudder.

She went limp.

He took care of the condom and dragged the covers over them, turning her into his arms. "Rest for a couple of minutes. Then we're going again."

She murmured against him, tucked in, warm and full of bourbon. "We have about an hour."

A sharp rap on the door pierced the silence. "The moon is full, but there are clouds now. It's time you folks went home," Greyson rumbled.

Sami sighed and moved away from the warmth. "So much for going slow next time."

Chapter Ten

*The world doesn't create darkness. I've found that true
darkness, the real kind, comes from within.*

—Tace Justice

The tension gripping Tace finally abated as they reached
Vanguard territory in the same crappy truck they'd used
before. Damon drove, which explained why the guy hadn't
been lifting his glass and cheering with everyone the night
before.

The drive had taken three hours, but they hadn't seen
another soul. No Rippers, no rogue gang members, no lost
civilians. It was as if the world had taken the night off.

Dawn had yet to break, but the moon poked through the
clouds enough to provide plenty of illumination. Sami had
fallen asleep curled into his side like a little kitten. That'd
make a great nickname for her, but he knew the first time he
used it, he'd get a fist to the face. The pain might be worth it
to have a special name between them. Man, he was losing it.

She shifted against him, and he settled an arm around her.

"No," she breathed.

He stiffened, ready to back off, and then realized she was
dreaming. "Sami."

She bolted upright with a scream that had Damon jerking

the wheel to the left. He corrected and slowed down. "What the hell?"

Tace grabbed Sami's arms and turned her toward him. "Wake up. It's just a nightmare."

She blinked and reality returned to her eyes. Several deep and shuddering breaths wracked her small body, and then she relaxed. "I'm fine."

"Now that was a nightmare," Damon murmured, driving around a pile of shoe boxes.

Tace frowned. "Are you all right?"

She nodded, her face pale. "Fine. Just a bad dream."

"What about?" Tace asked.

She shook her head. "Nothing." Then she looked around and brightened. "We're home."

Damon drove up to the first barrier, and the guards let them pass after seeing Tace.

"You comin' in?" Tace asked Damon when the truck rolled to a stop outside the large gate.

"No." The ex-cop craned his neck to look up at the cloudy sky. "I think I can make it back before it's too light." He left the engine running but jumped out of the truck.

Sami smiled, looking about sixteen years old. Her hair was mussed around her face, and her skin was nearly translucent in the moonlight. "Sorry I fell asleep."

"You were tired." Tace gave an "all okay" wave to the guards nearest the wide gate.

She blinked, and roses filled her cheeks. "Yeah, but still."

"We were also tipsy." And they hadn't had a chance to sleep. "I kept point. It's good to sleep." Every time he'd closed his eyes, he'd seen visions of Sami being torn apart by Rippers, so he'd concentrated on the darkness outside. He'd deal with the darkness *inside* once they were safe. Fucking her had been a mistake, because all he wanted was to have her under him again. Now. "Let's go inside."

She nodded and pushed away from him.

He fought every urge he owned not to yank her back into his side. Instead, he stretched from the vehicle, did a quick inventory of any threats, and then extended his hand.

She faltered and then slid her palm against his.

His hand easily enclosed hers. Sometimes he forgot how damn tiny she really was. He helped her from the truck, wanting to get her inside the fence. Wanting? Hell, needing. Every nerve he owned screamed for him to put her into safety. The nightmare seemed to have shaken her, and a part of him, deep down, wished she'd share. The other part knew she was probably smart to keep her distance.

What the hell was going on with him? He tapped his free hand three times against his hip.

As her feet touched the ground, he pivoted to keep the outside world away from her. Every instinct in his body went on full alert to protect her.

Damon strode around the truck and reached in for a wide box. "Stuff from Greyson. We'll be in touch."

Tace took the box and led Sami toward the now-opening fence. He couldn't exactly blame Damon for making a fast exit. Jax would probably torture him for information about the Mercenary territory if he stayed. Or perhaps hold him hostage to be exchanged for medicine and guns.

Sami shook her head in the cool air.

Yeah, his brain was a little muddled, too. "We drank too much," he murmured.

"I thought that was your grand plan to gain info?" She tripped and he steadied her with a hand at her waist, the box in his other arm.

"It was my plan, but then the bourbon went down so smoothly." He nodded at a couple of guards, and then his chest eased as they passed through the opening in the fence. Good. That was good. The headquarters building rose high and silent in front of them on the other side of the crumbling parking lot. Well, what used to be a parking lot.

"Was it your plan to get me drunk?" she asked.

It took him a second to interpret her words, and when he did, fire shot down his spine. He pivoted her to face him. Moonlight caressed the delicate angles of her face and made her look like an angel. Yet her words cut deep. "Are you kidding me?"

She shrugged, her gaze dropping to his chest. "You seem awful strategic all of a sudden, Tace."

He breathed in sharply and grasped her chin with two fingers. No way was he letting her hide from what had happened between them. Yeah, they'd fucked up, but it was both of them. "I didn't plan to get you drunk, no. Last night happened and we let it. I own my part in it."

"So do I." That chin firmed beneath his fingers. "Just wanted to ask, that's all."

"Well, you did." Why that made his chest feel like she'd hit him with a hammer, he wasn't sure. He released her and strode toward headquarters, holding the door open.

She swept inside where Jax Mercury waited, surrounded by candlelight. The Vanguard leader wore ripped jeans, combat boots, a dark T-shirt, and a scowl across his face. His eyes were the exact color of the bourbon they'd been drinking without the welcoming warmth.

Tace handed over the box. "Shit from Grey."

Jax set the box down on an old table that had always sat in the building's entryway. He ripped it open.

Tace peered over his shoulder. Two bottles of bourbon, twenty vials of B, various antibiotics, and a letter with Maureen Shadow's name on it. He whistled. "That does look like a good-faith gesture." His vision went black.

"We'll see. Is there anything we need to discuss immediately?" Jax asked.

Sami answered when Tace kept silent. "No. We found one of the storage depots, and they're well stocked."

"All right. I want a report from the two of you tomorrow

morning that includes estimates of Merc holdings, provisions, and soldiers. Then I want an infiltration plan," Jax said. "Get some shut-eye before you do that."

Tace stepped back, trying to picture the vestibule in his mind. Two more steps back, and he put himself against the wall. The darkness over his vision dug deep and pierced his brain with pain. "Not a problem," he managed to say.

Weakness attacked his left arm. He drew in a breath.

"You okay?" Jax asked, his voice sounding far away.

"Yep. Just had too much bourbon." Tace forced a grin. The world lightened, and he could see again. What the hell was going on? A residual pounding remained in his temples, and he tried not to wince. Or cry like a baby. "I'm not tired. Maybe I'll hit the lab and get some work done."

"Tell Lynne she has about fifteen minutes to get her butt to bed, or I'm coming for her." Jax turned and carried the box up the stairs.

Sami swallowed. "I'll, ah, talk to you tomorrow." She pivoted and all but ran for the stairway.

"Yeah, you will," Tace murmured. He wanted to stop her, to make her face him, but he could barely see. All right. He could figure this out. He hustled through the vacant soup kitchen and into his domain, the former free clinic. Light flickered down the hallway, so he skirted the reception area and high-tailed it to Lynne's makeshift lab. "Harmony?" he asked.

She looked up from a stack of papers, her green eyes tired, her lips pursed. The halogen lantern next to her cast an eerie blue glow over her face that matched the one from her T-shirt. "You're back." She smiled. "How did it go?"

He glanced behind him and then stepped inside. "I need help with a patient."

She straightened. "You're the doctor here. What's going on?"

"You've studied Scorpius longer than any of us have." He yanked out a plastic chair and dropped into it. "I'm not sure what's going on. During your initial research, before communications went down, had any Scorpius survivors gotten episodes?"

"Episodes?" Lynne shoved blond hair out of her face and leaned toward him. "What does that entail?"

"Weakness in limbs, blurry vision, possible unconsciousness." He swallowed.

She frowned. "I don't think so, but everyone had different symptoms with the fever. How long has your patient been infected?"

"A few weeks," he said.

She lifted her chin, her intelligent gaze narrowing. "Ah."

"Isn't me," he countered quickly. There was no question her loyalty was to Jax, and she'd tell him if one of his top lieutenants was having episodes. But Tace couldn't let Sami out on missions without him. All of a sudden, more than ever, he needed to cover her back. "It's a scavenger, one of the best, and I'm worried what will happen to him if we send him out." Tace purposely made the patient a male in case sex became relevant.

Lynne gestured toward the series of boxes in the corner. "There are old patient studies over there, if you want to scour through them. Everything happened so quickly with Scorpius that we just don't know much. It's not impossible that there will be long-term repercussions with a bacteria like this. But I haven't heard of anybody in Vanguard dealing with symptoms like that. Just the headaches."

"Yeah." The headaches were a killer. Migraines to the nth power, and they didn't seem to abate after time. "I'll go through the patient records tomorrow." He was too far away from Sami. What if she needed help? He stood and held out a hand. "I promised Jax I'd bring you with me."

Lynne scrunched up her face. "How late is it?"

"It's beyond late to early," Tace said.

Lynne winced and stood, grasping the lantern. "I guess I could sleep. What did you learn in Merc territory?"

He escorted her out of the clinic and through the soup kitchen to the stairs. She only tripped twice, which was a record for her. "They have a lot of supplies, I think. But they're also all soldiers prepared to fight. If Jax orders a hit, we're going to lose a lot of people." Sami couldn't go. He just couldn't let her put herself in danger like that.

What was wrong with him?

He'd been fighting by her side for months. Hell, until the other night, she'd kicked his butt every time. Had things shifted when he'd made her tap out? Or had they changed because they'd had sex? Or was it him? Was he becoming obsessed?

They climbed the stairs, and he left Lynne at her quarters. The light disappeared when she shut her door. His eyes adjusted, and he continued down the dismal hallway, pausing in front of Sami's door. Was it locked? It had better be locked.

He flattened his hand on the rough metal and leaned in, listening.

Nothing.

She was probably asleep. So close, though. He could open the door and be inside with her, surrounded by her.

No.

He was starting to freak himself the hell out. Turning, he headed down three doorways to the room at the end and shoved inside. Moonlight poured in the window at the far end of the apartment, more than lighting his way. His ugly beige bedspread was still in place. Bummer.

Stomping inside, he set his jacket on a broken chair and continued to drop onto the perfectly made bed. His head ached at the base, and the pain radiated down his back.

But at least he wasn't numb anywhere. Yet.

He breathed in and out slowly, counting balloons. Then

dogs. Then cats. Then Sami's different expressions. There were hundreds. After about an hour, he rolled from the bed, smoothed out all the lines, and moved to the couch, extending his legs to the coffee table.

What was Sami doing?

Sleeping, damn it. Which was exactly what he should be doing.

He reached down and flicked on the lantern. The Hello Kitty journal lay next to it. Sighing, he reached for a pencil and the journal to write something. Anything.

Sami. Samantha. Sami Samantha Steel. Samantha Steel. Did Sami have a middle name? He should find out. Maybe Susanna? Lynne? Florence? God, he was totally losing it.

Flipping the page, he sketched her face in long, broad strokes. Her expression was languorous and satisfied with a spark in her eyes. The look she'd had right after she'd reached orgasm. Pink cheeks, parted lips, relaxed face. So much contentment in those eyes that he could've drowned.

His entire body tightened. Whoa, boy. Down.

His damn cock didn't listen.

He turned the page and sketched her in full tactical gear out on a raid with her hair up and intense concentration in her expression. Then another sketch with her talking to little Lena.

The night wore on, and he lost himself, forgetting consciousness for a while.

The moon turned to a soft sun. Blinking, he looked toward the window. It was maybe midmorning. Where had the entire night gone? What the hell?

He slowly turned his head and looked around the couch.

Sketch after sketch after sketch of Sami Steel lay all around him. On the sofa, on the chair, all over the table. He glanced down to see a myriad of sketches littering the floor.

He flipped the journal closed. His obsession had switched from organizing things to something else. Somebody.

Sami.

Chapter Eleven

Every murderer has a good reason in his own mind to kill.

—Dr. Vinnie Wellington, *Perceptions*

Sami had had another nightmare where white walls and danger surrounded her, so she'd almost hunted Tace down the night before to make her forget the past. Morning had finally arrived, and she'd headed to work. She took a big drink of her coffee and settled at the monstrous conference table in the Vanguard war rooms. Her body had been on fire all night, and Tace Justice had promised her another round before they'd been interrupted by Greyson.

But they'd said only those hours.

Now it was back to business and she needed to calm her raging hormones. Maybe her body was like a valve. She'd been so content to concentrate just on work, and now after having had good sex, she wanted it again. By that logic, she'd be fine in a couple of days and then move straight to spinsterhood. Yeah. That would work.

Tace strode into the room wearing worn jeans and a blue T-shirt that stretched across his packed upper body.

Her mouth went dry.

His eyes sizzled like the sky over the ocean on a heated day, deep and blue. A shadow covered his square jaw, drawing attention to his full lips. Or maybe that's just where her gaze wanted to go. For the rest of her life she'd remember the feeling of his mouth, firm and busy.

She shifted in her seat.

He took the chair across from her and didn't look her way.

Um, okay. She kept her face expressionless. So he didn't give her a look or smile. So what? She needed things to be normal. Even so, maybe a little bit of reassurance wasn't out of line. Was she just a quick lay? A pit opened up in her stomach. Maybe he was just a quick lay. Yeah, that was it. She'd used him. Tears pricked the back of her eyes. What in the world? She batted them away and took a long drink of her coffee.

Jax finished taping an old map of Santa Barbara up on a whiteboard. He glanced at the full wall of windows. "We have enough light with the sun that I'd like to conserve the lanterns. Let's get this done during daylight."

Raze Shadow stalked silently into the room and took a seat next to Sami. The guy exuded danger. He'd pulled his dark hair back at the nape, drawing attention to his sharp Native American features. He had a gun at his hip and at least two knives strapped to his thigh. His light blue eyes cut her way. "Welcome back."

"Thanks." She took another sip of the coffee, the tears gone. "Is it just the four of us?" It had been a while since it was just the four lieutenants in a team meeting.

As if on cue, Maureen Shadow hustled into the room. "Am I late?"

"No. I just wanted to give you this." Jax slid the letter from Greyson across the table.

"What the hell?" Raze asked, reaching for the envelope.

Moe beat him to it, snatching it against her chest. "My name is on it, dumbass."

Sami bit back a smile. She hadn't had a chance to get to know Maureen yet, but so far, what she saw, she liked. The woman was in her twenties, had black hair, and the same odd blue eyes as her brother. She was some sort of food development expert, whatever that meant. Something about creating food sources for underdeveloped countries . . . which now included home.

"Read it," Jax said, and then added, "Please."

Maureen shoved back curly hair and gingerly opened the envelope to read.

"Dear Maureen,

I trust that you're safely back with your brother, and I'm glad you're all right after being kidnapped by the president," Maureen read, and then snorted, looking up.

Sami smiled. "He doesn't mention that he kidnapped you, too, or the blackmail plot?"

"No." Maureen shook her head.

"Asshole," Raze breathed.

Maureen cut him a look and focused back on the paper again.

"We've gone through all the nurseries and greenhouses in the area, and things are dismal. The water and electricity cut off before we took over the area, so I'm afraid many of the specimens are lost forever. However, there are seeds, sprouts, and even bulbs that I have no clue what to do with. I'd like to ask for you to temporarily stay in Merc territory and go through this stuff. The world needs food. I will personally guarantee your safety.

Yours, Grey."

She looked up.

"No," Raze said shortly.

"Bulbs and seeds," Maureen said thoughtfully. "We need those."

"Can you get the greenhouses going again?" Jax asked.

She shook her head. "I don't know, but I'm not sure that's the wisest course, anyway. We should find fertile land with freshwater resources and start planting. It'll be back to the basics for civilization for centuries, I think."

"You're not going to Merc territory again," Raze said.

"He didn't hurt me." She pivoted to face her brother. "Not once did anybody even threaten me while I was in Merc territory." Maureen rubbed her chin. "I wonder if that was the plan all along. To go through the greenhouses and then see what we could use."

"Do you want to go?" Jax asked.

She eyed her brother and then nodded. "I do. If there's a chance to salvage any bulbs or sprouts, then I definitely want the chance to do so."

Jax nodded. "All right. We'll discuss it and get back to you."

Maureen's eyebrows rose. "I wasn't asking your permission, Jax."

Sami nodded. Attagirl.

Raze leaned forward. "You don't have mine, either, little sister."

Moe's chin lowered. "You're about to get punched in the face."

Jax sighed. "Family stuff later. Work now. Maureen, please go back to work inventorying the packets of seeds the scavengers found in that drugstore on the Westside."

"I'll let you know when I'm ready to go." Maureen quickly exited the room.

"Get your family shit together, Shadow," Jax said, turning back toward the map.

Sami smiled at Raze. "You're lucky, Shadow. So lucky to have your sister here." The room went quiet for a moment, and Sami flashed to memories of her sweet sister and the good times they'd had together. Man, Sami had gotten Jackie drunk when she'd turned twenty-one.

Jax cleared his throat, bringing her back to the present. "Where is Grey's current headquarters?"

Sami shook off the past, stood, and grabbed a marker off the table to circle the location of the current headquarters. "Here's where he and Damon stay, and here's the head-quarters trauma area, and here's where we found the supplies. There was a seven on the door." She made notations.

Jax took another marker and drew a rough square over acres. "We think this is the entire Merc territory. So if they have at least six depots like the one you found, where would they be?"

"Probably spaced evenly, just in case," Sami said, glancing around.

"What?" Jax asked.

"Pencil," she said, just seeing markers.

Jax reached in his back pocket and drew out a stubby, well-chewed pencil. "Here. I didn't bite it."

She winced and carefully took the pencil to draw wider circles spaced evenly throughout the Merc territory. "Say there are ten, then here's an even spacing of them." Of course, she was just guessing. She retook her seat.

Jax planted both hands on the table. "I'm figuring we'd need a full-out assault to get the provisions?"

Tace nodded. "I think so. An infiltration would be another way, but those places are usually well guarded. The one nearest headquarters is the most open, but that's because it's the farthest from the borders, and the guards and scouts circle out."

"Give me a pro list for waging an attack," Jax ordered.

"They have a lot more medicine and water than we do," Sami said slowly. "If every depot has the number of guns I saw in the headquarters depot, they have plenty of weapons and ammunition. And they have vitamin B. A lot of it."

Jax breathed out. "Cons?"

"They're trained and well prepared," Tace said. "If we take fifty soldiers, we'd be man on man, but then we'd be leaving Vanguard vulnerable. And Jax, we're gonna lose people in a fight. Greyson won't fuck around."

Sami nodded. "Agreed. I'm not a profiler like the doc, but Greyson seems like a good guy to have on your side. Loyal. But cross him, and I think he'd slice your neck and not lose a minute's sleep."

"Good point." Jax turned and eyed the map. "Both of you meet with the doc today and give her your impressions. I want an actual profile from her." He tapped the map at several places. "Raze? If we decided to go in and take resources, what's the best infiltration point?"

Raze studied the map. "They're vulnerable from the north. I think they've protected the area south because of the university holdings. They only have so many guards to rotate, so they have to concentrate on the most valuable area. If we go in, we go in from the north and west."

"From the beach?" Sami asked. "Won't they be expecting that since that's how the president attacked?"

"Yeah, but there's a reason that's how the president infiltrated," Jax murmured. "So attack first from the north, draw the guards, and then a secondary hit from the beach."

Tace nodded. "Looks good to me."

Sami shook her head. "We're not really considering attacking the Mercs, are we? I mean, we still have the president and his Elite guard on our butts, and if we're allies with the Mercs, that gives us more fighting strength."

"Agreed." Jax drew out a chair and sat. "But we're running out of B, medicine, water, food, and ammo. All the allies in the world don't help us if we can't feed our people."

"What if we brokered a deal?" Tace asked slowly. "A trade of services, so to speak?"

Raze lifted his head. "I hope you're not saying what I think you are."

Tace blew out air. "If they have food resources, and your sister can get those or develop those or grow those or whatever the fuck a food production expert does, then why wouldn't we do that? Especially if she wants to go and check out the holdings."

"No." Raze crossed his arms.

"Your call. Then how about medical expertise for hire?" Tace asked. "I'm fine going back periodically and helping out if they give us medicine and so on."

Jax studied him. "That's not a bad idea."

Sami's breath quickened. She didn't like the calculating gleam in Tace's eyes.

Tace nodded. "At the very least, if we have this above-board exchange a few times, I might be able to discover the locations of the other storage depots so we know exactly where to hit them."

"Man, we're assholes," she muttered.

"Survival, baby," Tace said, turning that intense gaze on her.

Jax stilled.

Raze's chin dropped. "Did you just call her *baby*? Sami?"

Sami's legs trembled, and pure panic swept through her. She opened her mouth but nothing came out.

Tace blinked. "I have a Texas drawl. We call everybody 'baby.'"

Sami glared and regained her voice. "Fine. Call Raze and Jax that next time we're in a skirmish."

"Gladly." Tace tipped his head toward Jax. "Though he's more of a sweetcakes."

Jax pressed his index fingers into the corners of his eyes.

"Where did I lose control here? I mean, we're planning death and destruction, and all of a sudden, I'm a pastry."

Raze narrowed his gaze and looked from Tace to Sami and back again. "If you guys are fuckin', you can't go on patrol together."

Sami gasped, and her entire face exploded in heat. "Raze!" Geez. He could've kept quiet. Jax had already moved on to another topic. Kind of.

"Sorry," Raze said, not looking apologetic in the slightest. "But if there's personal shit going on, I don't want either one of you covering my back with the other one there. It's not smart, and it's not safe."

Jax dropped his hands to the table. "Are you guys fuckin'?"

"No," Sami exploded. They'd agreed on two hours, and those two hours were long up. "I can't believe you guys. Seriously. I have to stuff cotton in my ears on a nightly basis because of you two and your doctors banging beds against walls, but not once have I said a word. Not one word. And for the love of all that is holy, there is a *g* on the end of fucking. Fuck*eeeeng*. You two need grammar school."

Jax held up a hand. "Whoa. Let me make this perfectly clear. I'm fine if you two are going horizontal, but I need to know because it will change the rotation of our schedules. That's all."

Sami swung her gaze to Tace.

He was looking directly at Jax. "We are not going horizontal. We are not fucking . . . with a *g* or any other letter. We are soldiers, colleagues, and hopefully friends. That's all."

Jax turned toward Sami. "If that changes, you have to let me know."

"It won't change," Tace said.

Sami's chest ached. She hadn't figured Tace would be so glad to keep them just friends. Had she sucked in bed? Of course she hadn't. She was there the whole time. But maybe he wanted more kinky stuff like he'd been getting with that inner-territory doctor. No way did Sami want to get whipped deep. Not a chance. Nor did she want a boyfriend. Man.

"Sami?" Jax asked, scowling.

"Okay, Jax." She rolled her eyes. "I didn't know you needed confirmation of the obvious."

"I guess I'm just slow." Jax cut her a hard look.

Barbara poked her head in while wearing combat gear. "Jax? We have a problem."

Oh yeah. Sami had forgotten all about Tace's other lover. Heat flamed into her face.

Jax stood. "Of course we do. What is it, Barb?"

"Scouts found the yellow truck driven by that Merc guy at the western edge of our territory all shot up. There was blood on the front seat, but no body anywhere. They came back in to report," Barbara said.

Sami pushed away from the table, her heart thundering, her mind clicking into place. "The Mercs will blame us if Damon doesn't make it back to them." Then there would be a war whether they wanted one or not.

"Copy that." Jax turned for the weapons lockers. "The four of us will go. Dead or alive, we need to find that cop."

Chapter Twelve

My study of this bacterium shows the window closing on humanity's short time of overcoming illnesses with drugs. We are rapidly returning to an era where a minor scratch can kill a man.

—Dr. Lynne Harmony, *Notes on Scorpius*

Tace kept to the storefronts, his gun sweeping the area. Glass crunched under his boots, and he tried to step lightly, but combat and weeds were tearing up the concrete of the former sidewalks. Being out in bright sunlight was a seriously bad idea. Sami kept to his six, while Raze and Jax covered the other side of the now silent street. Not too long ago, the road would've been jam-packed with people honking and getting pissed during congested traffic.

Traffic jams were a thing of the past.

As was safely walking down a sidewalk in the middle of the day.

He tapped the knife at his hip three times.

At some point, the crazy Rippers would kill themselves off. But the ingenious ones would last a while. A yelp echoed across the street, and he dropped into a fighting crouch, half in front of Sami.

An orange cat screeched and barreled past Raze, who flinched away.

"Sorry," Raze mouthed.

Tace shook his head. "How can such a badass be afraid of cats?"

Sami snorted. "Speaking of nicknames, you need to stop calling me 'baby,'" she whispered, pointing her gun into a former jewelry store. Empty velvet boxes were scattered across the floor, and all of the glass display cases had been smashed. Nothing sparkly could be seen.

"I know," he said. What kind of jewelry did Sami like? Probably turquoise. She seemed like a turquoise girl. "We're just colleagues, and I won't call you 'baby' again." He didn't feel like a colleague. He felt like a guy who wanted to strip her nude and bend her over the nearest table. Wow. He actually felt something. Maybe his feelings were coming back. "Although I'm thinking we were shorted an entire hour last night, you know?"

"I didn't think you noticed," she said.

He frowned. Was she pouting? "I noticed."

"Humph."

He tried to focus and figure her out. Nope. He held up a hand to halt her at the corner, angled himself around, and surveyed an empty alley that stank like old death. Giving her hand signals, he hustled across the alley to the next sidewalk and pointed his gun into a defunct Laundromat. Vacant with dented washing machines. "Listen, Sami. You're sending mixed signals, and my new and improved brain can't read subtext. Do you want to fuck again or not?"

"Not," she snapped.

"That's what I thought." Okay. She'd been clear as day. 'Good, then."

"Yeah. Good, then." Her voice lowered.

Was she pissed? He shook his head. None of this was making any sense. They reached Luke's Bar on the corner, and he peered in to see an old jukebox against the far wall. It had probably been too heavy for early looters to take.

They reached the end of the corner, and he spotted the yellow truck in the alley. A quick whistle from him had Jax and Raze crossing the street.

Jax signaled, and Tace nodded, taking the right side with Sami. Jax and Raze took the left side.

They reached the vehicle and saw the scouts had gotten it right. Bullet holes along the passenger side and blood on the driver's seat. Not a lot. "He could be okay," Tace said, his focus narrowing.

Jax bent down to study the ground. "Blood trail."

Tace hustled to the front. "Yep." He followed the dots of blood deeper into the alley, which the building cast in shadow. The coolness felt good, but a chill swept down his back.

Steps led down to a basement entrance outside what used to be a flower shop. Something rustled. Garbage cans clashed.

Jax motioned, and Tace and Raze moved in unison, covering the steps.

"Damon?" Jax called out.

Silence.

Then a shriek, and a man ran up the stairs, fur in his mouth. White and black fur. Was that a skunk?

"Whoa, buddy," Tace said, trying to see his eyes. "You okay?"

The guy wore a black suit jacket with bell bottom jeans. Sparkles decorated down one side. His hair might have been brown at one time but was now a dirty black. Dirt and blood covered his face. He spit out the fur and screamed.

"Shit," Raze said. "Shut him up before every Ripper in the vicinity comes running."

Tace swallowed. "Buddy, be quiet. Okay?"

The guy shrieked louder. He was definitely insane and definitely a Ripper.

"Shut up," Jax snapped. "I don't want to just blow away an unarmed guy, so stop screaming."

The guy quieted. Then he sucked in air and wailed.

Tace squeezed the trigger. The bullet impacted the Ripper between the eyes. He stilled and then fell backward down the stairs.

Jax turned to look at Tace.

Tace shrugged, his heart rate remaining calm and steady. Okay. That was a bad sign—shouldn't he feel slightly bad about killing the guy? "He was going to get us killed."

"Probably did the bastard a favor," Raze said, moving forward to look down the stairwell, his steps sure and graceful. "He was alone."

Jax motioned them forward, and Raze fell into line next to him.

Tace turned to see Sami staring at him, her face white. "What?" he asked.

"Only a month ago, you would've been the last one to shoot that guy," she said. Standing in the dirty alley with her hair in twin braids and freckles across her nose, she looked more out of place than the sparkles had.

"You don't belong in darkness," Tace said. Then he shook his head. Focus, Justice. "I mean, you're right. I wouldn't have taken the shot." Yet he wasn't the same guy, was he? "Sorry."

She blinked. "Why are you apologizing?"

Because he wasn't the guy she probably could've liked. The darkness in him was too strong and apparently getting stronger. He motioned her forward, where he could cover her back.

She ducked her head, hurrying behind Jax and Raze, her steps making no sound on the cracked concrete.

He followed her, trying not to notice how nicely her ass fit in those worn jeans. They were so old the fabric on the bottom of her butt was white instead of blue. Man, her butt was tight.

His body hardened at the thought of the night before.

He really wanted another night with her, but after spending hours zoned out drawing her face over and over again, he had to keep away from her. What if he went really dark and lost any sense of humanity? Would he actually hurt her? How could he think about her, about sex, three seconds after he'd taken a life? Yeah, he was fucked up.

Gunfire pattered ahead, and all four of them froze.

Jax half turned and gave hand signals for them to take each side.

Tace nodded and kept to the right, following Sami to the back of what had been a bank. Another shot echoed from inside.

Tace glanced down to see the blood trail end at the back door to the bank. The door was green and metal . . . and slightly open. He hustled up to the side. "Plan?"

Jax eyed the overhead sun. "Raze and I will go in the front. Wait until the count of twenty, and you two go in the back."

"Copy that," Sami said.

Jax and Raze ran along the building and past two more stores before turning at the corner and disappearing from sight.

Tace counted in his head. Dizziness smashed him in the face. He dropped to one knee. His right arm shook and trembled, and his forehead went numb. That was fast.

"Tace!" Sami grabbed his vest and shoved him against the wall. "What's wrong?"

He couldn't see her. He blinked several times, and she slowly came into focus. "I'm okay."

She leaned into his face and studied his eyes. "What's wrong?"

"I don't know. Bad headache." Which was the absolute truth. His head felt like she'd kicked him right in the temple. Slowly, the strength returned to his arm. "We have to go in."

She frowned and looked like she was going to argue.

"Now, Sami."

She shoved him. "You guard the door. I'll go in."

"No." In a surge of power, he stood, grabbed her arm, and shoved her behind him. Then he opened the door and went in high, knowing she'd go low. They were in a long corridor with career notices and schedules tacked to the length of the wall.

"Son of a bitch, get out here," came a male bellow.

Tace paused. He didn't recognize the voice.

"Come in and get me, asshole," shouted another man. Damon. It was Damon, and his voice was low and in pain.

Tace ducked and ran through the corridor, stopped at a door, and turned to see what must've been the employee lunch area. A useless microwave sat on a counter next to a quiet fridge. The room was empty. He motioned for Sami and crept along the rest of the hallway to a slightly open metal door—an incredibly thick one.

He nudged it ajar with his toe. Sunlight cascaded in through the windows and illuminated the wide cashier's counter, the square-shaped offices to the right, and the center area of the bank with its tables.

Two men dressed in black faced the center office, their guns pointed at a desk. One guy shot, and shards of wood from the desk popped into the air.

"Missed me, dickhead," bellowed Damon.

Tace angled back to see Jax and Raze edge in the front door. Another two seconds, and they'd have the guys surrounded.

"Come out now, buddy. You're outnumbered." The shooter reached in his cargo pants and drew out a grenade. "I'm getting a little tired of playing with you."

Sami sucked in air next to Tace.

"Then stop playing," Tace said, his gun pointed at the guy's head, irritation clawing through him that Sami had been scared. Yeah, that was nuts.

The guy swiveled to face him, pointing an assault rifle.

"Drop it," Jax said, coming from the other side.

The second soldier put his back to his buddy's and aimed at Jax.

"You boys are now the ones outnumbered," Jax said easily. "Drop the guns, or we'll drop you."

A grunt echoed, and Damon Winter poked his head up from behind a desk. "It's the fuckin' cavalry."

"Another missing *g*," Sami muttered, shaking her head.

Tace moved in front of her.

She shoved him in the hip. "You have got to stop doing that."

He couldn't. "Guard the rear exit," he ordered.

She hissed but did as he said, turning to aim toward the hallway. That was trust, whether she liked it or not. The woman was letting him protect her from two guys with guns and grenades.

"I'm getting bored here, boys," Tace said, using his drawl. "How about I just shoot one of them?" he asked.

"Which one?" Jax responded.

The two guys in the middle didn't flinch.

Tace cocked his head to the side and read the insignia across their left breasts. "E.L., huh? I'm thinking the president's Elite Force got some new shirts. How nice to get new shirts during the apocalypse. Jax? How come we don't get shirts?"

"We get tats," Jax said easily, his gun trained center mass.

"Yeah. Tats are better than shirts." Tace motioned for Damon. "You okay, Winter?"

Damon used both hands on the desk to pull himself up and then wobbled around the heavy maple to the door. "No. I got shot."

He reached the doorway and went down.

"Shit," Tace said, trying to see the impact wound. Damon

was wearing a black shirt, so his entire chest might be bloody, and Tace wouldn't be able to tell. "We gotta move, Jax."

"All right. We only want one of you. Who dies?" Jax said pleasantly.

Then everything happened at once. Time slowed. "Alley is clear," came a deep voice from behind Tace.

"Drop it," Sami yelled.

Tace pivoted in time to see a guy in black take a shot. "Sami," he yelled, leaping for her.

The bullet hit her center mass, throwing her head back and her body into Tace. He grabbed her with one arm and fired with the other, hitting the Elite soldier between the eyes. The guy flew back into the hall and bounced twice upon landing.

"Sami." Tace set her down. "Sami?" She was out cold, and all color had deserted her face. He yanked open her shirt and tore the Velcro straps on her vest open. His heartbeat thundered through his ears, and his hands shook. "You're okay, baby. You're okay."

Two shots popped behind him, and he half turned, shielding her with his body.

"Fuck." Jax grabbed his shoulder, and blood welled through his fingers.

One of the Elite guys was down and bleeding profusely. The other dropped his gun and put his hands in the air.

Tace turned back toward Sami and gently lifted the vest over her head. He ripped open her undershirt. "Okay. You're okay." The bullet hadn't made it through, but her entire sternum was turning purple.

"She okay?" Raze called, pressing a hand over Jax's on the bleeding wound.

Tace nodded, his throat choking. He cleared it. "Yeah. She's bruised pretty bad, and she's out cold, but the bullet didn't tear into her." The idea of a bullet ripping into her soft skin made his teeth clench. He felt along her sternum and down her ribs to make sure nothing was broken. Man, she was going to hurt when she came to.

He lifted her and carried her over to a table still holding pens and deposit slips. "How bad, Jax?"

"Dunno. Hurts like a bitch," Jax said through clenched teeth.

Raze moved out of the way. "Damon? I'll be right there." He took zip ties from his back pocket, grabbed the Elite soldier's arm, and kicked him behind the knee. The soldier went down and Raze secured his hands behind his back. "Stay." Raze kicked the guy's gun across the room and then turned to go for Damon.

Tace moved Jax's hand and tugged the material away from the wound. He peered around to the other side. "Through and through. Doesn't look like it hit anything important, but you'll need stitches." He tore off his shirt and tied it around Jax's upper arm. "Keep pressure on it."

"Copy that." Jax moved into position to cover Sami, pain etching lines into his face. "Check on Damon."

Tace hurried over to the fallen Merc soldier and bent down on one knee to do a quick survey. Blood covered Damon's entire abdomen, and his shirt was dripping with it. "Ah, shit. He has a bullet to the gut, Jax. I need to do surgery." Tace glanced around, his mind returning to the day they'd lost Wyatt, another soldier, from a gut wound.

Raze breathed out. "I'll go get the truck. We'll get home faster."

Tace felt Damon's pulse. "Hurry."

Chapter Thirteen

This blue heart led me to Jax Mercury.

—Dr. Lynne Harmony, *Notes on Scorpius*

Lynne Harmony stretched her back in her lab and eyed the newest evidence she'd found that the Bunker existed. This was detailed lists of medicines sent there. Finally. She clapped her hands together once and stood to do a quick shimmy dance she'd made up on the spot. She could prove the place existed. Now all she had to do was track down the right file and find the damn place.

Her quick adrenaline rush ebbed from lack of sleep and carbs. Yawning, she poked her head outside to see Jax pacing the hallway like a caged animal outside of the trauma surgery room, accidentally bumping her hip on the doorknob. "Why don't you come sit down?"

He scowled but did as she suggested. His broad body overwhelmed the plastic orange chair. "How's the research?" he asked.

"I'm getting closer but don't have a location yet. I will, though." She let her excitement show for a moment and then ran her fingers over his battered knuckles.

A bandage covered his right arm, and he hadn't bothered to put a shirt back on after being stitched up. His powerful torso beckoned her, but the blood across his jeans made her think twice. Tension still rode her hard at the thought that somebody had shot at Jax, but he seemed at ease with the entire situation. If she lost him, she'd lose everything that mattered in this new world. She'd lose her odd blue heart. "I think you should've waited for Tace to sew up the bullet hole."

"Raze did fine. He's got a good hand," Jax said, poking at the bandage, his tension palpable. "He doesn't swear as much, either."

Lynne eyed his wide chest and ripped abs. It was hard to imagine sometimes that he was not only real but hers. The man owned her heart, without question. Maybe her soul, too. "Well, one more scar won't detract from your rugged looks."

He grinned, his honey-brown eyes sparkling. "Are you flirting with me, Dr. Harmony?"

"Maybe a little." It was nice to see him smile. Jax had a killer smile, but he didn't get the chance to use it often. "How is Sami?"

Jax frowned. "She's hurting but will be fine."

"Then why are you growling?" Lynne asked.

He licked his lips. "Tace won't let her out of his sight. She's on the bed in the examination room, just a few feet away from surgery."

"Oh." Lynne sat back, wondering how to diffuse the situation for Sami's sake. The woman needed a chance at something good, and the men would screw that up. Lynne changed the subject. "How is surgery going?"

"Tace was swearing up a storm, and Raze was handing him instruments on cue. I guess it's going okay," Jax said.

Lynne pushed an empty water bottle out of the way. "I hope Damon survives."

"Me too." Jax scrubbed both hands down his face. "If anything happens to Damon, Greyson will declare war, and I'm not sure we're ready for war on another front. We need to up the training of soldiers, so the last thing I have time to worry about is two of my lieutenants. Tace is definitely acting over the top right now. Kind of crazy, if you ask me."

Back to Sami and Tace. Lynne had thought it could happen. There had been more than one time she'd caught Sami watching Tace when he didn't realize it. Since they were now the topic, maybe Lynne could help them out a little. "About your lieutenants—that's an interesting development. Is Tace acting so protective just because they're partners on patrol?"

"Gut feeling? No. It's more than that. But there's something about Tace that's setting me on edge." Jax reached for her hand and flipped it over, smoothing the pad of his index finger over her love line.

Lynne's abdomen jumped. Just from one little touch. "Is Tace being over-the-top possessive and protective?"

"Exactly." Relief soothed out the lines on Jax's face. "That's the problem."

Lynne couldn't help but wrinkle her nose. If a medal existed for male over-the-top possessiveness and protectiveness, it would hold Jax Mercury's name at the top in shiny gold letters.

"That's different. You and I are different," Jax said, his gaze roaming to her blue heart beneath her T-shirt. "We don't go on patrol together, and even if you were a soldier, we wouldn't be scouting partners. There's a reason cops can't date their partners and that soldiers can't fraternize. It's a good reason, and it keeps people alive."

She chose not to argue the point of whether or not he'd be comfortable with her taking on Rippers, because she wasn't trained and it would never happen. "So what's the problem? If Sami and Tace are dating, then they can stop patrolling together." If they'd found happiness with each other, it was a good thing for everybody.

Jax nodded. "Yeah, except they both lied to me earlier and said they weren't fucking."

"Maybe they aren't," Lynne said softly. "Maybe there are feelings between them and neither one of them knows how to deal with them. But if they said they weren't, ah, you know, then I think you can believe they spoke the truth at the time."

"Fucking." He leaned in and tangled his hand in her hair, taking control of her head. "Say it, Harmony."

Why did he always push her out of her comfort zone? "No," she murmured against his lips.

He kissed her, deep and hard, driving her head back against his broad palm. Holding her in place, he explored her, tasting of bourbon and man. Finally, he let her breathe. "Say it, Blue."

"Nope." She nipped his lip, butterflies zinging from her breasts to her sex. "Maybe you can get me to say it later in our apartment." As a dare, it lacked creativity but would probably still get the job done.

"It's a date." He released her and sat back, making the chair creak. "And now you're going to have to use it in a sentence that sounds more like begging."

She smiled, her body lighting on fire. "We'll see who begs."

"Yeah, we will." His answering smile held a hint of warning.

She needed to get him back on point or they'd end up naked in her office. "I'm sure they didn't lie to you."

"The essence of lies is in deception, not in words." At her raised eyebrows, he confirmed it was one of the many quotes he'd memorized while reading between military missions. "John Ruskin—art critic and philosopher."

"Ah. I'd give them the benefit of the doubt anyway."

He shrugged. "My other problem with Tace is that I'm not sure he's okay with Sami going on patrol with anybody but him. It will turn into a battle between them, and I can't have my top lieutenants fighting. Especially since the president's Elite Force has now sent scouts into Vanguard territory."

"They have?" Lynne asked, her voice catching. The president was making another move? God, she hated Bret Atherton. "That's who attacked you guys?"

"Yes." He drummed his fingers on the counter. "We took out two of them but have one guy downstairs in the boiler room."

She paled and sat back, knocking some pencils to the floor. "You're going to question him."

"Yes." He met her gaze without flinching, no expression on his hard face.

"We've talked about this," she said, her hands fluttering on the table. "We're trying to rebuild civilization, and we can't do that by employing methods that were against the rules before." Why wouldn't he listen to her about this?

His gaze darkened. "If you think torture wasn't employed before Scorpius, you're way too naïve. Torture has always been used in times of war—in times of peace—against our enemies, like it or not. This guy has information we need to survive, and he's going to tell me all of it."

A shudder wound down her back. She'd arrived in Vanguard territory because she'd needed help, and she'd found love. The world was so much more dangerous than she'd ever imagined. Even so, she had to at least state a case for mercy. "That's not who we are."

He reached across the table and ran a knuckle along her jaw. "It's not who you are, sweetheart, and I'm happy about that. But you need to know, it's exactly who I am." He pushed back from the table and strode toward the doorway. "I understand you think things will change and we'll start this whole creation of a new civilization. But Lynne, it ain't gonna happen in our lifetime. We'll be fighting to survive the entire time."

She coughed. "Do you mean that?"

He faced her. "Yeah. I like that you're dreaming big, but the world is only changing for the worse for quite a while. I'll protect you, but none of it's gonna be pretty." He turned away. "And you're in for the long haul. There's no out."

"I don't want an out, Jax. No matter what," she whispered at his broad back.

His body stood straighter, and he nodded. Then he disappeared around the corner.

Tace ran his hand through his wet hair, slicking it back. It was growing out again, and he should probably find somebody to cut it. Could Sami cut hair? Shit, he had to stop thinking about her. He tapped his belt buckle three times.

"Doc?" he asked, loping into Vinnie Wellington's office at the rear of his clinic, not surprised to see the woman working well after midnight.

Vinnie looked up from a stack of papers on her small desk. Her blond hair was piled on her head, and her stunning eyes were clear and focused. Moonlight came in from the back doors, and she had a lantern glowing as well. "Tace. How is Damon Winter?"

"Good. Got the bullet out with minimal bleeding, and I think he's going to be all right." Tace had become more methodical during surgery, which had been advantageous in dealing with the gut wound. He'd performed surgery most of the morning, had double-checked everyone's wounds, and then had assisted at the inner-territory hospital for hours. Now it was dark again, and he couldn't remember if he had eaten or not.

Vinnie smiled. "Jax said you'd be popping by so I could profile Greyson Storm." She stood and crossed to an area with a couple of chairs. "Shouldn't you be sleeping?"

"Can't sleep." He dropped into a stuffed chair they'd

found in a tea parlor on the southern end of Watts. It had been days since he'd slept.

"Ah. Scorpius symptom number three." Vinnie crossed her legs beneath a pink pencil skirt.

Tace watched the movement and lifted an eyebrow.

She chuckled. "I met with a lot of patients today and thought I'd look the part of a real shrink."

Tace nodded. The woman had been an FBI profiler before Scorpius descended and had the education to be a shrink. "It's nice."

She blushed. "Well, Raze found the skirt the other day on a mission."

So she was wearing the skirt for Raze Shadow. That was sweet. What would Sami look like in a skirt? Probably fabulous and mouthwatering. He shook his head. "I'm obsessing."

Vinnie reached for a notepad to take notes. "Still being compulsive and organizing your surroundings?"

"Yeah."

"Now you're obsessing. It does seem as if Scorpius altered your brain and gave you OCD." She shrugged. "As far as I know." She leaned to the side and scowled toward the doorway. "Go away."

Tace blinked. "You're still seeing your dead stepmother?"

"Yes, and today she's dressed as a hula dancer."

"I don't think I'm the nuttiest person in this room," Tace said quietly.

"Not even close, although hallucinations are associated with the Scorpius infection, so maybe I'm normal," Vinnie said agreeably. "What are you obsessing about?"

Tace frowned and stared at the profiler.

She stared back. "We have patient-doctor confidentiality here."

Yeah, but she worked for Jax and had a duty to inform him if anybody wasn't up to mission. He couldn't be prevented from going on missions. "Just about my job," he said.

She nodded. "So not about Sami?"

He blinked. "Huh?"

"I might be psychic because I get images from other people, and you're all but broadcasting Sami all the time." Vinnie scribbled on her notepad. "Plus, Lynne said something is up between you and Sami. That you wouldn't let her leave the surgical area until you were finished with Damon."

"Lynne has a big mouth," Tace said, not wanting to discuss new possible psychic abilities, which he did not believe in.

"Yes." Vinnie looked up, and her eyes focused on him. "We all like to gossip. Jax is worried you and Sami lied to him about a physical relationship."

A rock dropped into Tace's gut. "We didn't lie. We don't have a physical relationship."

"Do you want one?"

He opened his mouth but couldn't find the right words. They'd already gone down that path, but it was supposed to be a onetime deal and didn't constitute a relationship. Did he want one? "I don't know. But I think about her all the time."

"Well, it might be obsession." Vinnie rubbed out a crease in her skirt. "But the beginning of any crush, of any relationship, involves some sort of obsession."

He sat straighter. "Really?"

"Sure. That's why they're called crushes. We build up imaginary connections and then get smashed by reality." She smiled.

He frowned. "I'm not sure that's helpful."

"I'm not really a shrink," she whispered, her eyes twinkling. "Seriously, do you want to harm Sami in any way?"

"No."

"Then why not explore your feelings? Relax a little and stop fighting them, and perhaps you'll stop obsessing."

As advice went, it wasn't horrible, but the doc had a definite romantic streak that was showing. "What if it changes?

I mean, I'm getting darker each day, and what if I end up wanting to wear her skin as a suit?"

Vinnie laughed, the sound high and almost tinkly. "That's funny."

His frown deepened until he felt it down his neck. "No, it isn't."

She sighed. "Listen. You're definitely a darker guy than you were, but the world is a darker place than it was. If you don't want to harm Sami, you won't. Stop worrying about that."

"I can't hurt her. I can't let her down." His chest thumped hard.

"Ah." Vinnie pressed her lips together.

He stiffened. "'Ah,' what? What does 'ah' mean?"

"You've never let anybody down, Tace."

He nearly exploded. "Of course I have."

"How?"

"By, I mean, by failing everyone. My sisters, my family. I didn't live up to their expectations." Hell, he came from Texas Rangers, for God's sake. And now, here he was, a day after killing a man he'd never met.

"I hate to tell you this, but the survival guilt is in us all." Vinnie's eyes sobered. "Living when others didn't isn't your fault. You couldn't have saved them, and you're doing the best you can do under unimaginable circumstances. Keep writing in your journal. I insist upon it."

He was so tired of that damn journal. His ankle tingled, and he stilled.

"What's wrong?" Vinnie asked.

Man, the woman was observant. "Every muscle I have is exhausted," he said. Not now. He didn't need an attack right now. She would definitely have to tell Jax. The tingling went away, and he relaxed. "So, I'm here to talk about Greyson and not myself. He's a good fighter, is methodical, and seems fair."

"Would he kill?" Vinnie asked, smoothly letting Tace off the hook.

"Without hesitation," Tace said, losing the frown as he warmed to a subject that didn't involve him. "Just like the rest of us."

Vinnie cocked her head to the side. "You liked him?"

Tace leaned back. "He's a potential target and a possible ally. That's how I saw him the entire time."

"Yes, with your brain. But feeling-wise, you liked the guy." Her eyes focused on him.

Was there a difference? "Okay."

"Give me specific examples of his behavior, please." She poised her pen over the paper.

Tace nodded and ran through the entire two days in Merc territory, minus those last few hours. He wasn't going to kiss and tell—and he wanted to kiss again. Interesting. His blood started to thrum.

Vinnie finished writing. "Perfect."

A shadow crossed the doorway, and then Shadow poked his head in, his odd blue eyes nearly glowing in the dark. "Doc? It's gotta be close to midnight, and you need sleep." Raze nodded at Tace. "You crazy?"

"Probably," Tace said.

"We all are," Vinnie said cheerfully, setting her notepad down. "Thanks for coming in, Tace."

Tace knew a dismissal when he heard one. He stood and then paused. "Shadow? I thought you were scouting inner territory tonight?"

Raze shrugged. "Sami took my place with Jax. Said she needed to get some air."

"She was shot less than sixteen hours ago and needs to rest." Fury roared through Tace, and he stalked by Raze. "Damn it."

He heard Raze behind him but barely comprehended the words.

"Should we stop him?" Raze asked Vinnie.

"Nah, let it happen," she responded.

Yeah, like they could stop him. He stormed out of the clinic to the back of the building and a wide street. Where was Shadow supposed to have scouted? Oh yeah. The western corner, where there was some weird church for people who hadn't been infected by Scorpius. A place that had seen gunfire and where Lynne Harmony had been taken hostage just a few days ago.

That wasn't exactly where Sami needed to recuperate from a bullet to the chest.

Damn it. His fingers closed into fists, and he launched himself down the quiet street toward the west, knowing he was being unreasonable but unable to stop himself.

He and Sami were about to come to an understanding neither of them was ready for.

So be it.

Chapter Fourteen

I've found that a punch to the face works better than reason more often than not.

—Sami Steel

Sami noted the quiet apartment building surrounded by more crumbling apartment buildings. The moon glittered down and made the scouting job easy, for once showing that the Pure church had finally listened to reason. "They took the fence down," she murmured. Her chest ached like she'd been kicked by a horse, and her voice was still weak.

"*We* took the fence down," Jax said, turning and facing the silent brick structure. "Well now. That makes me unhappy."

Sami crooked her head to see a guard at the front door holding an automatic weapon. Moonlight glinted off the polished barrel. "Me too." She straightened, and pain shot through her breastbone. The Pure church had fenced the western blocks inside Vanguard territory, and their leader had taken Lynne hostage the previous week after fencing their perimeter. He was dead, but a new leader had stepped up. "I thought the new guy was more reasonable than the first one."

"Reasonable doesn't include a guy with a gun at the front door," Jax said. "Stay here."

Sami drew her weapon.

"Put that back." Jax eyed her. "We're not having a shootout."

"You're not walking right up to a guy holding a gun without backup behind you and pointed at the asshole," Sami wheezed.

Jax grasped her shoulder. "Are you all right?"

"Fuck no, she's not all right." Tace Justice stomped into sight. "Are you fucking kidding me? Your entire chest is probably the color of shit-pukin' purple goblins right now."

Jax slowly turned his head. "That's quite an image, Texas."

"You both should know better." Tace crossed his arms and glanced beyond them. He stood taller. "Why is there an armed guard at that door?"

"I was just going to find out," Jax said.

Tace flashed his teeth. "I'll come with you. Sami, get your bruised self back to bed."

Her mouth gaped open. Oh, he did not. She bit back a stream of raw heat before it could bellow forth in curse words way more creative than his goblin image. She swallowed several times and tried to look like her body wasn't about to collapse into itself. "I am perfectly capable of being here, Medic. In fact, if I remember right, I'm the fucking soldier between the two of us." Her very strong words might've been abated a little since she wheezed the last sentence. But she remained standing.

His stance widened. "If you were anybody else in the world, you stubborn little shit, I'd tap you in the upper chest right now and say prove it."

If he tried it, she'd freaking pass out. Even the thought of somebody smacking her bruise made her ribs ache all the way down to her waist. "My chest is fine."

His eyes gleamed, and she took a step back.

Jax crossed his arms. "What in the hell is going on between you two?"

"Nothing," Sami snapped.

"Excuse me, men." Joe Bentley, the new leader of the Pure, strode past the armed guard and out of the building while shoving his glasses up his nose. The church leader wore khaki pants and a white golf shirt. He stepped across the cracked parking area. "Oh, I'm sorry. I mean men and miss." He smiled with even teeth as he approached.

"Bentley. Why the fuck is there a guy with a gun at the doorway?" Jax wasn't one to mince words.

Bentley's glasses reflected the moon. "Master-Sergeant Mercury, please be courteous." He wiped thin-boned hands down his trim hips. "Our congregation sleeps better knowing there's protection at the doors. Surely you can understand."

Jax towered over Bentley, his hard body one long line of danger. "The armed guards are all around the perimeter of Vanguard. I do not like armed guards covering buildings against other Vanguard citizens. It is unacceptable."

"We have uninfected children and pregnant women inside, Jax." Bentley took a step back. "We must assure their safety."

Another man strode out of the apartment building. "Joe? Is there a problem?"

"No." Bentley waved the guy back. "I'm just speaking with Vanguard soldiers."

The guy tipped his head, and highlights in his brown hair shone beneath the moon. Light eyes, probably green, studied them. "One of them is a woman."

Sami lowered her chin. "Good guess, buddy. Want to come closer?"

"Sure." He put his hands in his jeans pockets and walked over the uneven ground. The new guy was about six foot two and maybe thirty years old. He nodded. "Pastor Zachary King."

"Pastor?" Sami studied him. "I thought you were in charge, Bentley."

Bentley cleared his throat. "Ah, no. I'm in charge of the

clerical work, but the pastor gives sermons. I'm more of an organizational leader, and he leads the church."

Yeah, she could see that. Bentley lacked charisma, and Zachary had it in spades. He smiled and she almost smiled back.

What sounded like a growl came from Tace, and she stiffened. It was probably her job to diffuse the situation because Tace had something mental going on and Jax was just pissed off, but her chest hurt, her head hurt, and parts of her tingled from Tace's being near. "What are the guard's orders if we approach the building?" Might as well get the facts.

Zachary rocked back on his heels. "His orders are to keep anybody from entering the building."

"Even by using lethal force?" Sami asked quietly. Just talking was beginning to create pain.

Bentley shook his head. "No."

"Yes," Zachary countered with a smile.

Jax's chin lowered.

Zachary held up a hand. "We're happy to negotiate the entire situation."

"'Negotiate' is the wrong word," Jax said softly.

Sami winced. When Jax got really quiet, things were about to blow up. "How's the scheduling for interviews going?" Maybe she could turn the topic. Vinnie was supposed to interview and thus profile all the Pure members to make sure they were living together voluntarily.

"Still working on it," Zachary said. "Many of our members think it's unfair for them to have to explain their actions or plans to anybody. We still live in a free society."

"You live in my society," Jax said.

Tace stepped closer to Sami, somehow taking over. "We just want to make sure everyone is on board with your plans. From what we've seen, we have doubts people are acting out of free will instead of coercion." He tapped the knife at his belt three times. "You also have children who aren't yours in your little flock."

"It isn't safe for us in Vanguard," Bentley said.

"I'm fine with you all leaving, after I speak with each member," Jax returned. "Yet I gotta tell you, you definitely won't be safe outside these walls."

Zachary chuckled. "God spared us from being infected by the most deadly pathogen ever to infect humans. I think He will make sure we're all right once we move on."

"You were spared through dumb sheer luck," Tace returned, his body vibrating.

"He shall cover thee with His feathers, and under His wings shalt thou trust: His truth shield and buckler," Zachary said.

Jax breathed out. "You're quoting Psalms to me while posting an armed guard at your door? I don't think so."

Next to Sami, Tace stilled in a way that made her stiffen. She focused on him through her peripheral vision. Moonlight caressed his suddenly pale features. Instinctively, she angled her body closer to his. "I'll check with Vinnie to see how the scheduling is going. Once everyone is interviewed, and Vinnie is assured that nobody is being forced to join the church or leave Vanguard, you're free to go wherever you wish, Pastor." Tace moved next to her.

She couldn't let Jax see Tace lose control. Yeah, she'd wonder why later.

Jax was already staring at his lieutenant. "Tace?"

Tace dropped to one knee.

Sami went for him just as Jax swept his gun out, looking for threats. "What's going on?" Jax snapped.

"Tace?" Sami put a hand on his shoulder. "You okay?"

He nodded, his gaze down as he took several deep breaths. "Just lost my balance for a minute."

It wasn't the first time—not by a long shot. "When was the last time you slept?" Sami asked.

"Dunno. Been days." Tace's jaw firmed, and he slowly stood.

A thought occurred to her, and she almost fell right next to him. "You're not experiencing numbness, are you?"

He blinked. "No." Then he looked up at her. "Why?"

"Just asking," she whispered. It couldn't be. He couldn't be having a reaction to the vitamin B concoction. It was so rare. But if he wasn't going numb, he was fine.

Zachary backed away. "Scorpius is still affecting people even after months of recuperation, isn't it?"

"Yeah, but Tace fought the fever just a couple of weeks ago," Jax said, his gaze inscrutable. "He's still healing. Sami? Get him to bed, please."

She nodded and tucked her gun in her waistband before sliding a shoulder beneath Tace's. Her head buzzed, and her chest ached from more than the bullet earlier. She had a duty to tell Jax about Tace's health, but it was true the guy hadn't slept in way too long. Maybe sleep would take care of the problem. It couldn't be anything else. His problem had to do with lack of sleep. "Let's go, Texas."

It was a sign of how bad he felt that he didn't argue with her but instead let her shoulder some of his weight.

By the time they'd tromped through the blocks of Vanguard territory, he was standing on his own and walking easily. "Sorry about that," he said, rubbing his eyes. "Damn it. How's your chest feeling?"

"Sore but okay. You need sleep." She cleared her throat. "Are you sure you haven't had any weird numbness or tingling?"

He paused. "Why?"

"Just answer." She held her breath.

"Nope." He ran a hand through his thick hair. "Just a little bit of dizziness once in a while. I'm sure it's a sleep issue."

She smiled and breathed out, her body relaxing. "That's what I figured. Okay. That's good."

They reached headquarters and trudged up the stairs to his apartment. He shoved open the door. "You gonna tuck me in?"

She started to answer when she noticed a lantern on inside. Then she craned her neck to see a stunning brunette sitting on the sofa, legs kicked out, looking more than comfortable to be there. "Oh. Hi, Barbara." Her stomach clenched like she'd been kicked, and she quickly backed away. "Uh, I'll see you at tomorrow's meeting, Tace." Heat filled her face, and she turned toward her own door.

"Sami, wait—" Tace started, but she'd yanked open her door and quickly shut it, leaning against it.

She'd forgotten—totally forgotten—about Barbara. God, she was so stupid. Tace Justice had been a good ole boy charmer before getting Scorpius, and now he was a bad boy with a gun who liked women.

She had been just one of many.

Tace sighed and shut his door. "Hi, Barbara."

Gray yoga pants covered the soldier's fit legs, and a blue tank top showed off high breasts and nice arm muscles. Her pretty eyes sparkled. "I am so sorry about that."

"Nothing to be sorry about." Tace strode into the room and dropped into the chair across from the couch. His head still pounded, and cramps gripped his sides. All he wanted to do was turn around and go erase that hurt look on Sami's face that she'd tried so hard to hide, but he had to do this first.

Barbara reached behind her back and drew out a tiny kitten with white and black tuxedo markings. "I brought you a friend."

He blinked. "You brought me a cat."

"Yeah." She grinned and pointed to cat food and water in

the corner. "There's a litter in warehouse number eight, so I took him for you."

Tace shook his head, trying to get his bearings. "Um."

She held up a hand. "I know cat food is scarce and he'll have to eat something else soon, but a pet would be nice, right? You're always so alone." She let the kitten go on the tile, and he licked her foot. Her bare feet were small and perfectly adorable, and Tace had spent a good part of an hour a while ago torturing her by tickling them. Now they were the wrong feet. "What do you say?" she whispered.

He shook his head. "I, ah, can't keep a cat. But I appreciate the offer." His gaze narrowed on her face. Soft eyes, turned-down lips, pink cheeks. "Ah, why did you bring me a cat?"

"I . . . I wanted to, well . . ." She looked away.

He caught his breath and stilled. "Are you dumping me?"

She grimaced. "We're not dating, remember?"

Amusement tickled his mouth. "Barbara."

She turned her gaze back to him, her head still down. "I'm sorry."

He chuckled, feeling better than he had all day. Man, she was adorable, and a good friend. "You brought me a kitten to make up for the fact that you're breaking up with me. Or rather, that we're no longer going to engage in casual sex." How sweet was that?

She slowly nodded, her eyes glistening.

"Shit, Barb. It's fine. We were casual." He leaned toward her. "Why, though?"

She bit her lip.

Ah. "You've found somebody. Something real." Tace smiled. "That's good. Who?"

"Derek Diamond," she said.

Tace ran through names and faces. "The mechanic. The one who has fixed every machine or vehicle we have."

She nodded. "He's funny, and I like that he isn't a soldier, since I am. You know?"

"I totally get that." Tace smiled. "He's a good guy, Barb. I hope you two are happy, and I admire the hell out of you."

The soldier lifted an eyebrow. "You do?"

"Yeah," he said, meaning every word. "This world is crappy, and it's really brave of you to take a chance on something real. I'm happy for you."

Finally, she smiled. "I'm so relieved. I don't want to lose you as a friend."

"You won't, and if Derek hurts you, I'll gut him."

"That's so sweet."

Yep. That was him. Sweet. He glanced at his closed journal, where he'd put all of his Sami sketches. "If you say so."

She blinked. "What about you? You've been distracted lately. I was thinking that maybe you'd found somebody?"

He winced. "I'm not sure."

Barbara chuckled. "What about Sami?"

He sighed. "It's that obvious?"

"Yeah, but I wonder, you know? You guys are shooting buddies. She can kick your ass three ways to Sunday, and a guy like you can't deal with that. Neither can she, probably."

Enough truth existed in the statement that anger tried to catch hold of him. He shoved it down. "That's not true. I'd like to think we're both more evolved than that." Yet were they? He hadn't made a move until he'd forced her to tap out on the mat. Was he that much of an asshole? Probably. "I like that she can fight." Hell, that was true. She was hotter than hell when she grappled. His groin hardened.

"That's good, then. I think you two make a really great couple. A power couple." Barbara chuckled.

Tace lifted a shoulder. "I'm not sure, but I'll keep you informed."

Barbara stood, grabbed the kitten and food. "Good. Still friends?" Vulnerability lowered her tone.

"Yeah." He followed her to the door and drew her in for a hug. "Always friends."

"Good." She headed into the hall. The kitten howled. "Sorry." She laughed and hustled toward the landing.

He winced. That would've awakened pretty much everybody. He heard doors quickly opening down the hallway. Damn it. The first gaze he saw was Raze's. The soldier had a knife in his hand. "Sorry. Angry kitten."

Raze snorted and shut his door. There were grumbles, but all the other doors soon closed.

Tace noted with a sigh that Sami hadn't opened hers at all.

Well, guess it was time they had a discussion. Straightening his shoulders, he moved toward her room and gingerly tried the knob. The last thing he wanted was to awaken everyone again by pounding on the door.

It opened easily. *Go back, go back, go back.* What was he doing? He needed to leave her the hell alone.

He shoved open the door anyway.

Chapter Fifteen

I should never have tapped out.

—Sami Steel, *Journal*

Sami sat up in the bed the second her door opened, knowing exactly who was there. Oh, she'd heard the howl of a cat but hadn't wanted to poke her head outside and see Tace, since no doubt he'd heard it, too. "Get out."

He slipped inside, filling the entryway. "We need to talk." The door shut behind him, and he strode inside as if he had every right to be in her private domain. "I'm really sorry about you walking in and seeing Barbara. To be honest, we've been so busy, I forgot to break up with Barbara earlier. I mean, we weren't really going out, but still."

Sami pulled the covers over her bare legs. She'd thrown on an old tank top and panties to sleep in. Her hand fumbled, and she ignited the lantern on her bedside table. "You broke up with her?" Not that it mattered.

He paused. "She broke up with me, softening the blow with a kitten."

Sami's eyebrows rose. "A kitten?"

He grinned. "Yeah."

"Are you, I mean, sad?" She tucked the blankets around her thighs.

"No. Barbara and I were just friends with a couple of

benefits, and you know it." He eyed her chest. "How's the bruise?"

"Fine. Took some aspirin I'd been hoarding." Her mouth went dry. "We can talk tomorrow."

He lifted his head, looking dangerous in dark jeans and a shirt that showed off his predator's body. "Why is your door unlocked?"

"Lock doesn't work." If he wasn't leaving, she was getting dressed. She reached for a pair of yoga pants off the floor and quickly shimmied into them, wincing as her chest ached in response.

He crossed muscled arms, overwhelming her space with the sense of masculine power. "Why would you choose a room where the lock doesn't work?"

"It's nicer than the rest of the rooms." If he got any closer, they'd be back in the bed. Her thighs softened at the thought.

He glanced around at the living room with fifties-style furniture and the extra-large sitting area complete with a small office. A beautiful Persian rug covered most of the floor. "Where'd you get the rug?"

"Mansion near Malibu." She shrugged, trying to keep the conversation casual when all she wanted was to tackle him to that pretty rug. "Thought it was classy."

"It is classy." He frowned.

She had the oddest urge to rub the frown lines away, so she tucked her hands at her hips. "What?"

"It's different than I expected. Your place, I mean."

It was odd he'd never been inside her apartment, considering they worked together every day. "In what way?" Defensiveness rose in her.

He eyed the row of decorative glass bottles along the worn kitchen countertop. "I don't know. I figured there would be a wall of weapons and a sparring dummy in the center of the room."

"The sparring dummy is under the bed," she shot back.

"All right." He moved then, closer to her, and she fought the urge to sit back down. "I think it's time you and I had a little talk."

"About what?" She rubbed her chest and then made herself stop.

Heat swelled from him. "I'm tired of you trying to prove yourself all the time. Nobody else would've gone out on a scouting mission after being hit with a bullet."

"In the vest," she countered, not liking the direction of the discussion. "It wasn't like I'd been shot. In fact, Jax was shot badly enough that he had to be stitched up, and he went on the scouting mission." Why the hell was she explaining herself to him?

"Jax had a through and through. You were hit center mass and have serious contusions." Determination, the hard and male kind, darkened Tace's eyes.

Sami rolled her eyes, finally fed up with his over-the-top male attitude. "Listen, Tace. You've been edging toward being an ass the last few weeks, and then we made the mistake of having a quickie. This caveman routine you've got going on has to end."

"Was that all it was? Just a quickie?" A muscle ticked in his strong jaw.

She opened her mouth to agree and pretty much lie, but the glint in his eye stopped her. Tace was becoming a master at discerning lies. Sure, the night meant something to her, but that didn't matter right now. It couldn't. "Let it go."

"I can't." His gaze hardened, and he stepped forward to manacle her upper arms. "I know I should, but I can't."

The strength in his hold stole her breath away. She lifted up on her toes, heart galloping. "Let go."

"I don't want to." Frustration curled his lip. "Believe me, letting go would be an out I'd take in an instant. But here's the rub, Samantha. Nothing in me, not one little atom or molecule, wants to let go. Fuck. You're in my head all the time, in my chest, in my damn skin. I breathe you, damn it."

Her breath heated and caught, her entire body flaring alive. Maybe for the first time . . . sensing danger and something more. Something she couldn't quite identify, and that intrigued her in ways she'd never admit. "What about all your other women?" It was the only thing she could think to say.

"They were all relegated to the past from the first time I touched you." Tace leaned in, overtaking her space. "We weren't anything anyway, and that's the way they all wanted it."

"Was that the way you wanted it?" What was happening? This was crazy. *They* were crazy.

"It was the way everything had to be. Nothing serious and nothing with emotion." His grip tightened, holding her too easily in place.

"And now?" Her voice wavered, but she forced the words out.

His eyes darkened, and his lids lowered to half-mast. "Enough emotion we should both be scared shitless. I don't know what's happening, Sami. I really don't. But you're at the center of me, and I'm not sure it's healthy or right."

Scorpius. The bacteria that created sociopaths. Sami swallowed. "Are you turning dark?"

He barked out a laugh, his breath heating her face. "I've been dark since the first day of recovery. I don't know what this is. I can't explain or analyze it."

"Okay." Her rational mind tried to take over even as her nipples hardened to sharp points. "You're still in the recuperation phase of Scorpius. The return of emotion now is probably normal for you with your genetic makeup. Everyone reacts differently to the bacteria."

"I've been attracted to you since the first day we met—right after I joined Vanguard and Jax decided he wanted a medic at headquarters." Tace released one of her arms and smoothed her hair back from her face. "I walked into that first meeting, and I swear, my heart just stopped."

"Yeah, but—"

"That was before I was infected, Sami. Way before. I was still me then." His head dipped toward hers. "The old me, that is."

"But you never said a thing." She was quickly becoming overwhelmed by him, and her body rioted for more.

His jaw clenched. "Of course not. Jax and Vanguard need us to be clearheaded and focused. Plus, you kept kicking my ass."

She lifted her head. "And now?"

"And now you're not."

"I still could." There were moves she hadn't taught him yet, but even as she said the words, she had doubts. Could she still take him? He was stronger and faster than before . . . and more devious. Even worse, he wanted into her head, into her thoughts, and she couldn't allow him there. "It matters to you? Who wins in grappling?"

"No." He frowned and ran a hand from her bicep down to her wrist. "But having you beneath me, soft and pliant, matters. I don't know why, but I want you there again right now."

The look in his eyes—the sheer determination coupled with a heat he'd never shown before—weakened her knees. She'd always been a rebel of sorts, and she'd always pushed boundaries. Instinct whispered not to push with him . . . not right now.

Yet sometimes, true nature couldn't be denied. "Not a chance, Justice," she whispered.

"Try me," he challenged.

The air changed, became heavy with the sense of an upcoming storm. The atmosphere swelled and heated . . . all with the sense of male. With the sense of Tace Justice.

Without even consciously thinking about it, she hooked a leg around his knee and pushed him off balance. He kept hold of her arm as he fell back, landing solidly on the rug. She scrambled, but the man and gravity won, and she found herself sprawled across a body harder than stone.

"Hey." She tried to get off him, but he smoothly rolled, putting her beneath him, body to body.

"Now, this is what I was talking about," he murmured, his mouth right above hers.

"Oh yeah?" As always, challenge rose in her. She clapped both hands to his ears and raised her hips to buck him off.

He growled and grasped her wrists, pinning both hands above her head and pressing her lower half into the floor with his strong body. Even grappling, he protected her aching chest by keeping his torso off her.

She couldn't get leverage from this position to shove him off, but he couldn't exactly move, either. So they lay, both suddenly panting, groin to groin. Her nipples ached in need, and her entire body flushed. But no way in hell could she be considered pliant. She'd make sure of it, damn it. "There's not much you can do from this position, Tex."

"I don't like that." He pressed against her, his erection barely contained within his worn jeans.

Her clit throbbed. "Like what?" Her voice emerged hoarse.

"The nickname Tex or even Texas . . . from you." His forehead dropped to hers in a moment of intimacy she couldn't hide from. "You use it not as an endearment but as a way to distance yourself from me. I don't like it."

"Distance between us might be a good idea." Even as she spoke, she arched just enough to scrape her nipples against his hard chest and provide some relief for her aching breasts, even though it made her bruised skin smart. "Don't you think?"

"No. I want to be inside you so deeply I can never get free. Forget distance." He leaned enough to press a kiss to her nose. Pausing for a moment, he took her measure and then moved down, brushing his lips across hers.

She sucked in air. "For now," she breathed against his mouth.

He chuckled then, the sound regretful. "Now is all any of us has."

It was hard to argue with his logic, especially when her body pulsed beneath his. Suddenly, she was tired of fighting, and she was beyond tired of hiding. At some point, her past was going to catch up to her, so why not enjoy the moment?

She leaned up and pressed her mouth against his, everything inside her softening when he took over the kiss, his mouth firm and masterful. He released her lips, kissing along her jaw and down her neck.

"I fuckin' love your neck," he said, licking down her jugular. "It's so delicate and strong all at once."

She arched against him, her hands struggling beneath his.

"Oh." He let go of her hands and reached down to gently lift her shirt over her head. "Are you sure?" he rumbled, his mouth returning to her skin.

"Yes."

"Good." He kissed across her breasts, taking one nipple into his heated mouth.

She moaned and tunneled both hands into his hair. Had his mouth always been so hot? He rolled her nipple with his tongue and then moved on to the other one. Desire flashed through her, sharp and burning.

He chuckled and kissed down her abdomen, pausing to tear off her yoga pants and panties. "If your chest starts to hurt too much, tell me."

She gurgled a response.

Then his beyond-hot mouth was on her, nipping, and licking. The man was a master at playing the female body, or maybe he just knew her too well. While the thought should give her pause, her brain had stopped working. Completely.

He nipped her thigh, made her jump, and then pressed his tongue against her clit.

White-hot shards of electricity rippled through her nerves, and she whimpered, her thighs tight against his broad shoulders. He slid one finger inside her and explored, finding her G-spot with unerring accuracy.

Sparks flew from her nipples to her clit. "Tace," she whispered.

He moved to her other thigh and sucked hard.

She yelped and smacked his head. "Don't even think of it."

"Too late." His voice was rough and hoarse . . . like he'd swallowed rocks. "You're wearing my mark for at least a week."

She wanted to hit him again, but she was so close to going over the edge. The orgasm hinted through her, promising bliss. "I haven't had a hickey since high school," she groaned. And then it had been on her neck, not her inner thigh.

His finger brushed her G-spot again, and he went at her clit with a fast rhythm.

She exploded into a million pieces, hissing his name, her arms dropping to the worn tile. The climax rippled through her in waves, and she shut her eyes to enjoy the ride. So much pleasure it almost hurt.

Finally, she came down and went limp.

He rolled to his knees and then stood, his hands going to remove his shirt. Broad muscles, cut hard and sharp, came into focus. Along with a series of bruises and old scars and his tattoo.

Her mouth watered. If there was a more masculine man alive, she hadn't met him.

He dropped his jeans and boots to the side after grabbing a foil package from his pocket. He was firm and fully erect.

She started to sit up, and he leaned to lift her, falling backward on the bed.

"I don't want to hurt your chest." He lay down with her straddling his hips. "You're ready this time."

His words wound through her brain and down to her heart. Even now, fully aroused, he was careful with her.

She took the condom and quickly rolled it down his impressive girth. Carefully balancing herself on his ripped abdomen with both hands, she lifted up and then lowered herself. Several times she had to stop and breathe out to let her body adjust.

His fingers curled into the bedspread, and dots of perspiration broke out on his forehead. Tension cut lines into his face, and his entire body seemed to vibrate.

The firm leash he kept on his self-control broke hers completely, and she shoved down as hard as she could, taking all of him in.

Pain lanced through her and she stilled, her butt flush against his groin.

"Take your time, baby," he groaned, his muscles reverberating beneath her. "God, you feel good. So hot and wet."

Pleasure followed on the heels of pain and filled her. She lifted up and then slid back down. "Ah," she sighed, throwing her head back. "I'm all right now, Tace. You can—"

He grabbed her hips and lifted her, slamming her back down and setting up an out-of-control rhythm she could do nothing but follow.

Her nerves flared and contracted. A thrill deeper than she could've dreamed of ticked through her, igniting pleasure centers she'd never found before. He was so much, he was everything. She clutched his abdominal muscles, trying to keep tethered to something, anything.

His unrelenting grip kept her moving.

Energy uncoiled inside her, flashing out, exploding the room white. She cried out, her eyes shutting. The orgasm rolled through her, flooding her energy with so much raw pleasure she could only open her mouth in a silent scream.

His grip tightened, and his body shuddered.

Finally, she came down and fell, her face landing in the crook of his neck. Her eyes closed, and her body went limp in satisfaction.

He ran a big hand down her back to her butt.

She sighed. What now?

Chapter Sixteen

Love and obsession are just different sides of the same coin.

—Tace Justice

Tace stepped out of the outdoor shower in the early morning hour and almost walked right into the towel held out by Raze. He took it, his body going on alert. "Either you have a crush on me all of a sudden, or you wanted to talk privately."

The soldier rolled his blue eyes and stepped back in the alley. Makeshift showers were set up with rainwater in barrels, and all of the debris and glass had been swept away to leave the concrete smooth. "You were loud last night, and while I don't think Jax heard you, those of us with rooms close to Sami's did."

Tace winced. "Somebody will tell Jax."

Raze shrugged. "Or Lynne. This place runs on gossip."

Tace measured the former sniper. "What about you?"

"I mind my own business, but if we're on a mission together, where your focus is becomes my business." Raze turned on a combat boot toward the building.

"What the hell does that mean?" Tace called out to his friend's back and rubbed the towel through his hair.

Raze partially turned. "I'll partner with either you or

Sami—you're both good. But one of you needs to inform Jax and make the change." He shoved open the back door of the soup kitchen and disappeared inside.

"Good talk," Tace called out, striding for shelves against the building where he'd left clean clothes. He'd awakened in Sami's bed and she'd all but shoved him out of the room before somebody saw him.

It was time to stop hiding and start figuring out who they were and what they both wanted. Time to explore a little— and let people know they were together.

Were they together?

He jumped into worn jeans and a faded Grateful Dead T-shirt before leaning down to secure his socks and boots. He dropped the towel into a bin near the door for the laundry brigade—the group taxed with cleaning clothing when they ran out. So far they kept raiding malls or homes and getting fresh clothing more often than not. Shoving his hair back, he followed Raze's path inside and through the eating area to the war rooms, grabbing what looked like fresh bagels on the way.

He munched on one as he entered the conference war room, where Jax, Sami, Raze, and Pastor Zachary King already sat. "Real bagels?" he asked Jax, his body instantly attuned to Sami, although he couldn't quite read her mood.

Though by the way she was munching on her bagel, she seemed rather content.

Jax finished chewing. "Scouting team found flour and yeast at an old bakery near Pacific Palisades yesterday. Can you believe it?"

"No." Tace drew out a chair next to Sami to sit in, noting how happy carbs were making everyone. It really was the simple pleasures they missed most. "What's going on?" Why the hell was Zachary King in headquarters? He took a moment to give the pastor a measured look, momentarily surprised at how much the unexpected meeting bugged him. He liked things orderly and planned out these days. "Zachary."

"Pastor King," Zachary corrected gently. His brown hair waved back from a clean-cut face, and those green eyes showed intelligence and cunning. "I asked for a meeting."

Jax smiled without even a hint of amusement. "Zachary? What did you want to say?"

Zachary turned his attention to Jax. "Many of my people are afraid to meet with you."

Sami lifted her head, her eye on the uneaten portion of bagel in Tace's hand. "Why?"

"Because you're all carriers, of course." Zachary clasped his bare hands together on the table. No gloves and no concern, apparently.

Tace arched an eyebrow. "You're not afraid?"

"God won't let me catch the plague. I'm here for a reason." He flattened his hands on the table. "I have nothing to fear."

All righty, then. Tace sat back in his chair and fought the totally absurd urge to block Zachary's view to Sami. "I'm thinking we should have the doc here for this little meeting." Vinnie could profile the guy for them all.

"Agreed, but she's in the middle of something," Jax returned. "I'm sure this is one of many meetings."

Tace shoved the rest of his bagel into his mouth and bit back a grin as Sami's lower lip pouted out.

Zachary smiled. "I have no problem being profiled. Most of us called to preach the Word think we've been chosen by God. If you have any faith at all, you have to be open to that possibility. I'm not narcissistic or deluded."

Sami tilted her head to the side. "I do most of the take-ins here at Vanguard, and I don't remember you."

"I think a guy named Wyatt did my take-in," Zachary said.

Sami sucked in air, and Tace could almost feel her pain.

Wyatt had been one of them, and he'd been the heart and soul of the place. They'd lost him in battle just a couple of weeks ago.

Zachary nodded. "I'm so very sorry for your loss. I didn't get a chance to know Wyatt beyond that first meeting, but everyone speaks about him so highly."

"What did you do before you were, ah, called?" Sami asked.

Irritation sizzled through Zachary's eyes before he smiled. "Does it really matter what any of us did before Scorpius?"

"No, but I'd like to know," Sami returned.

Tace bit back a smile. Smart woman. She'd taken over the questioning naturally, somehow noticing that Zachary didn't want to speak with either an underling or with a woman. He kept trying to focus his comments to Jax, and Sami kept drawing his attention.

Jax remained silent, as did Raze, no doubt having already caught on to the tension.

Zachary tried to ignore Sami and turned toward Jax. "We need to discuss the Pure's plans for either remaining in Vanguard or moving out on our own."

Jax tilted his head very slightly toward Sami.

She leaned forward. "You didn't answer my question, Zach."

Zachary leaned back and sighed. "I think this meeting would be better served if just you and I spoke, Master-Sergeant Mercury. Leader to leader, as it were."

A ruckus started up outside the war rooms, and a man's raised voice bellowed through. "I will not stay here where I can get Scorpius. Let me out of here and now."

Tace pushed back from the table, his body going on full alert. "Is that Damon?"

"Sounds like it," Jax said, standing, a scowl marring his smooth features.

Damon Winter limped into the room, his face pale, an arm banded across the bandages protecting his abdomen. He wore loose sweats, and his feet were bare. "Mercury? Get me the hell out of here."

Tace stood and partially put his body between Sami and Damon. "Why are you out of bed?"

Damon all but fell against the doorframe. "I haven't been infected and I need to get out of here. In Merc territory, we have separate facilities. If you've infected me, I'm gonna kill you." His brown eyes darkened with fury, and his breath panted out almost painfully.

Tace took in his rigid stance. "I didn't work all day yesterday patching you up for you to bleed out now." He moved toward the soldier and paused when Damon held out a hand to stop him.

"Don't touch me," Damon groaned, closing his eyes.

Jax sighed and strode past Damon, disappearing into the vestibule while bellowing for April Snyder. They both returned seconds later, with the young widow wringing her hands together. She often worked in the soup kitchen in headquarters.

"What's going on?" she asked, her voice soft and her blue eyes wide.

Tace narrowed his gaze. The pretty brunette seemed even more fragile than last time he'd seen her. She'd lost her husband to Scorpius months ago, and she'd lost her only daughter a couple of weeks ago. It was amazing she was still standing. "It's okay, April." He couldn't help but try to soothe her.

Jax jerked his head toward Damon. "Would you help get this asshole back to his bed before he bleeds all over my floor?"

April wiped her hands down her jeans.

Jax cleared his throat. "Damon? This is April, and she

hasn't been infected by Scorpius. Let her help you, or I'm gonna grab you and bite your damn shoulder, you ungrateful shit."

Damon tried to glare, but his face contorted in agony instead.

April rushed for him and gently slid her shoulder beneath his arm. "It's okay. I'll get you back to the infirmary."

Damon nodded and leaned heavily on the small woman, turning and almost meekly allowing her to lead him out of the room.

"Dick," Jax muttered, returning to his place at the head of the table.

"Why don't we just send him back to the Mercs?" Sami muttered.

Tace shook his head. "He needs to heal first, or he'll bleed out. The bullet was tough to remove." If they sent him back dead, there'd be a war. Though right now Tace was feeling okay with that, considering Damon was being such an ungrateful prick.

Pastor Zachary leaned forward. "This is why we need two separate territories within Vanguard for those who've been infected and those who have not. I don't need to remind you that only the unaffected can procreate."

"We think," Sami shot back.

Tace nodded and retook his seat. "We don't yet know if Scorpius survivors can carry a baby to full term. It's too early to tell."

Zachary shook his head. "So far, not one has done so, therefore it doesn't look good. That one little fact should make all of you want to protect our women. All of us want humans to survive, right?"

Sami drummed her fingertips on the table. "It occurs to me that you never answered my question, Zach."

The pastor's nostrils flared. "I chose not to, woman.

Now stop harassing me with silly questions, and let me conduct some business with your leader."

Heat filled Tace's ears, and fury crawled down his back. Without a second's thought, he half stood and reached across the table, manacling Zachary's neck. A quick pull, and he jerked the pastor across the table and took him to the floor.

Zachary yelped and grabbed Tace's hand, trying to dislodge the hold.

"Tace!" Sami jumped up, and her chair flew back.

Tace punched Zachary in the nose, and blood sprayed up. Anger poured through him so quickly he could barely see, so he kept striking, trying to find a release for the fury consuming him.

Jax and Raze reached him, each grabbing an arm and yanking him away from the profusely bleeding pastor.

He fought them, elbowing Jax in the gut and dropping another punch to Zachary's cheekbone.

Jax and Raze dragged him away again, and he struck out, fighting them.

"Jesus," Raze said, yanking Tace to the side and manacling his arms over Tace's chest from behind. "What the hell is wrong with you?" He finished the capture hold, and Tace fought against it, making unintelligible sounds of fury.

Jax dropped to one knee. "Zach? You dead?"

The pastor groaned and rolled over. "Get away from me."

"No problem." Jax stood and turned, his gaze not even remotely friendly. "Tace? Go take a fuckin' walk."

"Not if Sami stays here," Tace ground out before he could stop himself.

"You have got to be kidding me." Jax's head snapped up, and then his chin lowered. "Fine. Everyone sit down."

Zachary managed to get to his feet and held his bleeding nose. "This is unacceptable." His words were a little slurred.

Jax nodded. "Agreed. Pastor? Why don't you head back to your flock, and we'll meet again tomorrow morning same time. However, bring a list of your church members with you like you were supposed to do today."

Zachary tipped his head back and somehow still skirted the table and headed for the vestibule. "That crazy bastard had better not be here," he muttered as he disappeared.

Sami got right into Tace's face, her cheeks blazing. "What the hell is wrong with you?"

"I don't know." Tace stopped struggling against Raze's hold, and his vision cleared. "The guy insulted you, and it felt like a threat. I just reacted." What was wrong with him? If the guys hadn't stopped him, he would've killed the pastor.

His vision wavered. The right side of his body went numb. God, not now. He tried to flex his right hand, and nothing happened. His knee gave out, and he sagged.

"Whoa." Raze altered his hold and held Tace up beneath the armpits. "What's happening?"

Darkness flashed fast in front of Tace's eyes, so he closed them, and the world spun around. His left leg trembled and then went numb. He started to go down.

Raze helped him to the ground and laid him flat on his back. "Tace?" Raze smacked his face.

"Tace?" Sami touched his forehead, her knee hitting his shoulder right before it trembled.

"Get a doctor from inner territory," Jax barked into the vestibule.

Running feet echoed through Tace's mind, and then everything went blank. He could feel his body spasming, and his head hit the ground a couple of times before Sami pressed her hand flat against his forehead to keep him still.

His body seized.

"What the hell is going on?" Raze muttered from above him somewhere.

Movement sounded, and soon soft fingers pressed to his inner wrist. Hell. He could feel his wrist; that was good.

"His pulse is erratic," Lynne Harmony said softly. She pushed up his shirt. "Whoa. Was that rash here yesterday?"

"No," Sami murmured.

Tace stopped shaking and tried to open his eyes. "I can't see."

"Close your eyes," Lynne ordered. "He's been taking vitamin B, but the rash is a sign of a vitamin B6 deficiency."

"Isn't there B6 in the shots we all take?" Jax asked, his voice sounding far away.

"Yes. The shot is a combination of all the vitamin Bs, but there's a stronger percentage of B6 and B12," Lynne said. "I don't understand the rash."

Tace opened his eyes, and the world came into focus. His head hurt, and his chest pounded. "Ouch."

"How long has this been going on?" Jax asked, standing over him.

Tace winced. "Weakness in limbs for about a week. This on-the-ground situation is new."

"He passed out the other day," Sami said quietly. "In Merc territory."

Jax scowled. "You're just telling me this now?"

"Scorpius is a bitch," Sami countered, concern filling her pretty brown eyes. "Nobody knows why or how it'll affect each person. I figured he'd be fine."

"He's not," Jax said curtly.

Tingles and then weakness swept down Tace's legs. "It's gonna happen again," he ground out. "I lied. I have been going numb. All the time."

"Oh God." Sami swayed. "Get salt. Hurry. Get him some salt."

He tried to focus on her, but her face wavered in and out. "What?" he grunted. Heat and then sweat swept over his skin.

Jax ran out of the room and then returned with a salt shaker.

Sami reached out. "My hand."

Jax poured some in her hand, and she fed it to Tace.

He grimaced but swallowed the salt. Slowly, the tremors subsided. He took several deep breaths and then tried to sit up. Raze grabbed his upper arm and assisted him. "Thanks."

Lynne looked at Sami. "Salt sometimes helps with seizures in people who are vitamin B6–deficient. How did you know?"

Sami paled and sat back on her knees. "He's not deficient. His body is rejecting the vitamin B concoction."

Lynne frowned. "How do you know?"

"I've seen it before," she murmured, her shoulders slumping. She swallowed, and Tace could swear her lips formed the words *I'm sorry*. She took a deep breath. "It was one of the things they studied."

"Studied?" Jax dusted salt off his hands. "Who are *they*? Where did they study this?"

She kept her gaze on Tace. Her entire body shuddered, and her eyes lost all expression. "At the Bunker. It's one of the things the scientists studied at the nearest Bunker."

Chapter Seventeen

The sum of all mistakes can be wrapped up into one decision made in one moment.

—Sami Steel

Sami waited outside the conference room, sitting on th steps leading to the apartments. Everyone would gather in five minutes, and she'd have to tell the truth. She droppe her chin onto her hand, unable to stop the flashback.

She'd been in North Dakota with her soon-to-be ex boyfriend, the smartest man she'd ever met. They were alon in the basement of a three-story office building he'd pur chased with money stolen from a hotel magnate. "What hav you done?" she whispered, her hands shaking.

Spiral had looked up, his soft blue eyes now gleamin and somehow darker. "This has to end. Everything we'v done, everything that has happened, is all retribution. Don you get it? God is mad."

Sami swallowed. Servers lined one wall, console another. "What are you talking about?" She'd joined hir in his crusade to track down Internet predators and peopl working in the slave trade, and she'd known many of thei methods were illegal. Hacking into secured federal govern ment databases had been a necessary evil.

That had put their names on FBI wanted lists.

She could live with that, but as the code for a new computer virus flashed across the bigger wall screen, her heart stopped. "Spiral. You didn't."

"I did." At twenty-six, Spiral Samuelson looked much younger with his pale skin, blue eyes, and clean-shaven face. He was tall and wiry, and he had read multiple books on how to please a woman.

They'd been dating four months when he'd contracted the fever but protected her from getting ill. Most of their friends had died, and it appeared that the infection was running rampant across the country.

Two weeks after Spiral had survived Scorpius, Sami began to notice a change in her boyfriend. He'd started memorizing the Bible, and he'd begun chatting with people on the Net about Armageddon. At first, she'd thought he was just reacting to the impossible world they were about to face, but now? Now she could see madness in his programming.

A line of code caught her eye, and she fell back, her heart almost stopping. "Oh my God."

Spiral nodded and gleefully jumped up and down. "It's a computer virus, Sam. See it? See what it can do? Not just bacteria are dangerous to us . . . look what I made."

She shook her head. "No," she whispered. He'd created a bug that attacked software and changed the routing to null. "This won't work long-term." She could come up with a software fix if she had enough time.

"Yes, it will." He lifted his chin. "I've hit all thirteen root servers, and the key is . . . there aren't enough people working to fix them. Scorpius has either killed or is currently attacking most of the people who maintain those servers."

She coughed. It was possible. "Stop it. You have to stop it."

Spiral cackled like a crazy witch. "The Internet is going down, baby. Say good-bye to technology. God wants us back to basics."

"No." She grabbed her keyboard and started furiously typing, trying to delete the code. The barrel of a gun pressed against her temple. She stilled and turned slightly. "Spiral?"

He pressed harder. "Don't deny God."

"God doesn't want this," she croaked out. "God likes the Internet. You can't do this."

"I just did." His grip on the gun remained steady, and he leaned forward to be closer to the screen. "Oh, look. Six of the servers have already been infected. I also created a secondary attack with several automatic software updates. The Internet is about to be gone."

"The Internet is like a worm. Take out some of it, and the rest will survive." Tears clogged her eyes.

"Only with proper maintenance and fixes," he said happily. "We don't have those any longer."

Bile rose in her throat.

An explosion sounded from upstairs, rocking the entire basement.

"Shit." Spiral pointed his gun at the computers and started firing. "I think the Brigade is here."

Sami screamed and shoved herself out of the way, running for the stairs.

Instantly her way was blocked by soldiers wearing combat gear, even their faces covered by masks. One grabbed her and took her down, zip-tying her wrists before she thought to fight back.

Spiral fired at them, and two soldiers fired back, killing the computer expert.

One guy yanked Sami to her feet while ripping off his mask. He had dark brown skin and even darker eyes. "Sami Steel?"

She gulped and nodded.

He gestured at the equipment. "Get everything you can." After issuing the order, he dragged her up the stairs and out side into the empty, rainy street.

She struggled, seeing a transport van. "Where are we going?"

The soldier paused. "You're going to the Bunker to fix this mess. Our orders were to take Spiral and kill you, but since he fired, you're on." He all but shoved her into the back of the van.

She struggled against the restraints. "Where is the Bunker?"

"California." He slammed the doors shut.

Vinnie touched Sami's shoulder and pulled her out of the past. "Let's go sit down."

Sami nodded and followed her into the war room, where everyone quickly entered and sat. She needed to throw up. Her legs wobbled, even while sitting.

She tried to keep from panicking and running from the conference room as she sat at the sprawling table with Lynne, Jax, Vinnie, Raze, and Tace. The entire elite force of Vanguard looked at her, all waiting for some sort of explanation.

Many times during her formative years, she'd been called to the principal's office, so this was a feeling she remembered well. That was before she'd been arrested, of course. It was too late to turn back since she'd dropped the bomb about the Bunker, but what if they didn't believe her? Even if they did, she already knew the outcome of this meeting.

Jax sat at the head of the table, directly across from her. The Vanguard leader's expression had gone to watchful, which was never a good sign.

Yet the man at her right held her attention. Tace was still pale, but a hardness had entered his blue eyes the second he'd realized what she'd said.

"Explain." It was Tace who'd given the order.

She nodded. "All right. First, you all need to know that the Bunker isn't this great place where we'll all be saved."

"No. Start at the beginning." Jax's voice was clipped.

She sighed. "Fine. I'm not LAPD."

"No shit," Tace muttered. "Who the fuck are you?"

The Texan rarely swore at women, and never at her. This was so not good. "I'd say out of everyone here, you know exactly who I am," she snapped back at him.

"I don't think so," he returned, his rugged face a hard mask of stone. "Get to it."

"Fine. I, ah, am a hacker." She kept her voice level when all she wanted to do was beg them to still like her. "A computer hacker. One of the best, actually."

"The fighting skills?" Jax asked.

"Truth. Dad owned a karate studio, my uncle a street-fighting gym, and they started us young. I had fun, learned a lot, and bonded with my dad over grappling. Then I learned a few more tricks from the US military when I worked for the government."

"As a hacker," Tace drawled.

"No. I was a hacker in high school, got arrested with my boyfriend Cricket because we hacked into a secured court-house document center to get his uncle out of jail. We got caught, and it led to a job offer and free education from Uncle Sam if I agreed to keep working for the government after school. Cricket died the next year in a car accident." Man, she'd missed that lost boy. He'd come from a bad family and had been angry . . . and brilliant. "I, ah, got tired of working for the government and went out on my own."

"So you were wanted by the law?" Jax asked.

Sami nodded. "Yeah, but I hooked up with a group that used, ah, unlawful methods to take down sex traders and pedophiles, so I don't think the law really wanted us until Scorpius hit."

"Why didn't you tell us?" Jax snapped.

She winced. "Seriously? You, Raze, and Tace are all former military, Lynne worked for the CDC, and Vinnie worked for the FBI. The FBI wanted me, damn it. I couldn't tell all of you guys that I was a criminal and not a good government person like you all were."

"That's why you pretended to be LAPD," Lynne said softly.

"Yeah. I wanted to belong here, and that did it." It was the first time in her life she'd felt complete and like she was doing something good that other people couldn't do. She was special, and she worked hard. Very hard.

"Did you take down the Internet when Scorpius got bad?" Tace drawled.

She sucked in air. "No, but I was with the guy who did. I tried to stop him, failing, by the way. Soldiers showed up and there was a firefight."

Lynne gasped. "You saw the Brigade?"

Sami shrugged. "Spiral thought they were the Brigade, but they were just soldiers from the Bunker, who brought me to Los Angeles and the Bunker there." The Brigade was the country's first line of defense when Scorpius had taken over, but Sami wondered if they really existed any longer.

Jax sat forward. "There are more Bunkers?"

"Yeah." She drummed her fingers on the table, her nerves short-circuiting. "The Bunker is actually a series of underground facilities spread across the country, all with resources and unique purposes."

Lynne gasped. "How many are there?"

Sami shook her head. "I honestly don't know. Based on the infrastructure and data I worked on, I'd say about ten, but I could be off a couple in either direction." Even though everyone was angry at her, the relief she felt in telling the truth made her constant jaw ache stop. Finally.

Jax shook his head. "You said LA. The Bunker is in Los Angeles?"

"Yes. It's located beneath the Maritime Plaza building in

Century City," she said, forcing herself to face them all. Her legs itched with the need to run hard and fast.

Lynne's jaw dropped open. "Are you serious?"

"Yes. There are several floors beneath the lobby, all cement, and all owned secretly by the government," she said. "None of the businesses in the building had any clue about the Bunker."

"Unbelievable," Tace muttered. "The entire time it has been right here, and you haven't said a word."

"Why is that?" Vinnie asked almost gently.

Sami focused on the ex-profiler. "I escaped the Bunker and I don't want to go back. Ever."

"Escaped?" Raze asked. "You had safety from Scorpius underground, and you escaped that?"

"Yes. My family became infected, and I wanted to go home to be with them, and we were on lockdown. At that point, we already knew about the vitamin B concoction, so I'd been taking supplements, which helped when I contracted the disease after I'd escaped." She'd arrived home to find most of her family already gone, but her sister had hung on—for a short while.

"Why didn't you go back afterward?" Lynne asked.

"I didn't want to go back at that point," Sami said, her voice quavering. She cleared her throat. "The Bunker became hell, I'm telling you. All of a sudden we went from a computer center to an experimentation hellhole. It was horrible."

"Experimentation?" Tace asked.

"Yes. The computer center was just part of the underground bunker, and there was a whole other side I was unaware of until right before I left. It was a myriad of cells and genetic labs that was largely unused until Scorpius Then it became a place to not only create and store the vitamin B concoction but a place to conduct experiments or survivors—cruel ones."

Jax reared back. "You're kidding."

"No," she whispered. "So a couple of us figured out how to override the system—it was still on its own generators—and open all the cell doors. Then we ran. I've probably committed treason at the very least."

"Again," Tace muttered.

She shivered from his furious tone. "Huh?"

His chin lowered, and his gaze remained hard. "You committed treason *again*."

"Yeah," she said softly. There was no way he'd forgive her.

"The experiments—did they lead to a cure for Scorpius?" Lynne asked, her face pale.

"I don't know," Sami said, her stomach churning. "All research from all over the world was centralized there in the LA Bunker, so if a cure was discovered, they'd have it."

"Why didn't they come forward then?" Jax asked. "I mean the doctors or scientists or whoever."

"They didn't have a cure when I escaped," Sami said. "Maybe they have one now, but there's no way to get the word out. Or maybe they're waiting for most of the world to die off and then plan on taking over. I truly have no clue."

"So you lied to me about being a cop," Jax said quietly.

"There were rumors about you, Jax. That you were put in place here by the leaders of the Bunker." Now she could see they had been untrue, but it had kept people in the Bunker from reaching out to Mercury for help. "I figured if you thought I was LAPD, you'd let me into the inner circle, and I could see how dangerous you were."

"Have you?" Jax asked quietly.

She shivered at the low tone. "Yes." The man was beyond dangerous, but he wasn't part of the Bunker. "I know you don't work for them."

"What about me?" Tace asked. "You said you knew what was happening to me earlier when I went into convulsions."

She nodded, her throat closing. "Yeah. I compiled the

data on one subset of the vitamin B concoction, and there's a very small percentage of Scorpius survivors, incredibly small, actually, who reject the B therapy after a couple of weeks. The seizures, rash, and numbness are indicators."

"So what happened to them?" Tace asked.

"The first dozen died, but then they discovered a cure. Some enzyme that allowed the recipient to accept the B concoction," she said, grinding her palm into her eye. "I just did data input and didn't pay attention to the actual cure. I'm sorry."

Lynne turned to Jax. "We have to get the data. Not only for Tace, but if the researchers were on top of Scorpius, maybe they've found a cure. Or at least a way for women to reach full-term pregnancies."

Sami shook her head. "The soldiers at the Bunker are armed and fanatical—they definitely are not the Brigade soldiers. I'm sorry. Infiltrating the Bunker would be nearly impossible."

Jax pushed away from the table and dragged over a whiteboard. "Then I guess you'd better get busy giving us the layout of the entire facility, Sami. Afterward we'll decide what to do with you."

Sami blinked, and her stomach cramped. Would Jax kick her out of Vanguard? While that should be her foremost concern, she couldn't help but concentrate on the silent Texan next to her.

Would Tace ever forgive her?

Chapter Eighteen

One little lie, and I felt the monster inside me break his chains.

—Tace Justice

Sami curled into her side, facing her window. She wanted to sleep, but memories kept attacking her. With a sigh, she forced herself to count sheep, and soon she was dreaming again.

The nightmare, inevitable as it was, slid right into another dream.

Two months after being taken to the Bunker in California, she continued fighting Spiral's computer virus, which had taken longer than he'd no doubt planned to infiltrate so much software. She knew she wouldn't be able to stop the shutdown, but she had to try. And all the while, the files she'd found earlier were burning through her brain.

Just what was this place?

Dr. Ramirez stalked into the room, his eyes tired, a white lab coat over his thinning frame. "Anything?"

She shook her head. "No. The Internet will go down." She cleared her throat and concentrated on the man in charge of the Los Angeles facility. "I did find a couple of files on the laboratory area."

His thin lips pursed. "None of your business."

Her stomach ached. "The bodies you've burned . . . there are so many. How can—"

"Enough." He glanced down at his watch. "Keep working." Then he turned on his heel and exited the room.

She glanced back at the screen. "Apparently, you've forgotten what I do," she whispered, typing furiously and finding the code within minutes. She stood and left the room, walking through sterile white hallways to the medical lab. A keypad was on the door.

"Sami?" George Bankel asked, looking up from a computer. "What's up?"

She smiled at the former Harvard computer programming professor. "Just stretching my legs. You?"

The man glanced at his clock. "Ah. Time to pray. I'll be back."

She'd known it was his time to face Mecca, and she waited until he'd left her alone in the center. Many people had succumbed to Scorpius, so the hustle and bustle of the computer center had ebbed. She ran past the refrigerators holding icky-looking vials of dangerous stuff and to the keyboard, typing in the code she'd uncovered.

The wall opened.

A long hallway stretched before her, the floor concrete, the walls a stark white. Blue doors with windows were set every few yards.

Her legs trembled, but she moved forward and looked inside the first one. It was a room that looked like a jail cell with a cot, toilet, and sink. A woman sat against the far wall, her arm in a cast, bleeding pustules all over her face. She looked up, her brown eyes already dead. "Kill me," she whispered.

Sami stumbled back. Voices roared around her, all from different cells. Several faces pressed against the small windows, bruised and bloody. Oh God. There were so many test subjects.

*"Sami!" Greg Valentin ran for her, his gun in his pants.
He was a guard in the center, and he'd become her friend.
"What the hell?" He glanced quickly around, grabbed her
arm, and dragged her back into the computer room before
shutting the door. "Are you crazy? They'll kill you for going
in there."*

She gaped. "You knew?"

*He blanched, his dark skin flushing. "The doctors are
trying to cure and understand the infection, and they need
test subjects. Only people who've been infected already."*

*Sami backed away from him. "That's inhumane. We can't
do that."*

*Greg leaned in. "There's no choice. Go back to work, and
don't tell anybody what you just saw."*

*She turned, bile rising in her throat. Oh, she was going to
open those cells and let those poor people out . . . and then
she was running like hell to get home to her family. If any of
them had survived, she needed to find them. They were all
she had left.*

Months in the future, she woke up with a gasp, her heart
thundering. Oh God. What were they thinking to consider
going to the Bunker? The place was closer to hell than she
ever wanted to get.

Yet did they have a choice? She'd do anything to save
Tace, and this might be his only chance. Her body trembled.
There had to be some way to shore up their defenses first. If
not, then they wouldn't stand a chance against the Bunker
soldiers and their weapons.

In her worst nightmares, she'd known she would die back
at the Bunker.

Was that just her imagination or was it a premonition?

Tace kicked back in his chair and studied the rough drawing of the Bunker on the whiteboard. Raze sat on his left,

Jax on his right, and they all swirled crystal tumblers of Scotch. The good kind they'd found in a doctor's office in Westwood. The three women had disappeared to try to get some much needed sleep. "Human experimentation. I guess we shouldn't be surprised," Tace murmured.

Jax winced. "I can't imagine what they tried. I mean, if you think about how we've changed, how many brains did they cut into?"

"Gross." Tace scrubbed both hands down his face. Sami had told them about a couple of files she'd found, and it was ugly. Everything from trying deadly cures to seeing how quickly a survivor could heal from different injuries—even snakebites. He focused on the physical layout of the Bunker and tried to banish the nauseating thoughts. "Looks tight," he muttered, pointing to the center of the building.

Raze nodded. "If they have enough soldiers to guard each point, then it'll be next to impossible to infiltrate with our current resources."

"We need explosives," Jax said, tipping back his drink. "Otherwise we have no chance."

"Copy that." Tace crossed his legs at the ankle and viewed the schematics of the elevators. "The entry point concerns me."

"There has to be another way via stairs or a tunnel," Raze agreed. "Sami said the workers only used the elevators to get underground, but once electricity went down, no way would the Bunker use generators in such a wasteful manner. Especially if they kept people prisoner there."

"Or she's right that the elevator shafts are the only way up or down," Tace said thoughtfully. "That's how she got out—by climbing the ladders set into the walls."

Jax glanced toward his medic. "You okay with all of this?"

"No." Tace cocked his head to the side to memorize the layout. "You?"

"Well, I'm fuckin' tired of my closest lieutenants lying to me," Jax snapped.

Raze shifted in his chair. "I said I was sorry, and then we punched each other. Now we move forward." He looked at Tace. "You and Sami gonna break up?"

"I thought I'd send her a note ending it in gym class," Tace returned, keeping his focus on the board and his temper in check.

Jax snorted.

"Don't be a dick," Raze said agreeably. "So she lied while trying to survive in a world that has gone dead. It isn't impossible to understand."

Yeah, but she'd continued lying even after they'd become close and trusted each other. After they'd had sex. "You don't know what you're saying," Tace muttered.

"Sure, I do. Vinnie forgave me even though I'd planned to turn her over to the enemy. If she can do that, why can't you? I mean, the world has changed for the worse after Scorpius, and we're all doing our best," Raze said.

"Fuck, that's the longest sentence you've ever said," Jax muttered.

"Vinnie forgave you because she's much nicer than I am," Tace said.

Raze nodded. "Well, that's true."

Jax reached over his shoulder for the bottle and poured himself another glass, waiting until the other two held theirs out for refills. He set it back with a thump. "While your delicate feelings are of great concern to me, Tace, I'm more worried that we still don't know the full truth."

Tace paused. His nape tickled, and irritation swelled. "What do you mean?"

"What if this is the plan? What if Sami has been working for the Bunker the entire time, checking us out, and is now sending us right into an ambush? What if the science part is true, and those assholes need new test subjects?" Jax scowled and took a healthy drink of his Scotch.

"She wouldn't do that," Tace shot back, straightening in his chair. His chest filled with air, and his testosterone surged.

"How the hell do you know?" Jax returned. "We've been looking for the Bunker for months. Hell, you and Lynne have been poring over data every day trying to find a lead on the damn place, and Sami has known its location the entire time. To think of the time we wasted."

"She wouldn't set us up to be harmed," Tace said. Why the hell was he defending her against reasonable questions? "She lied because she was scared. I don't think she's devious enough to send us to our deaths."

"You're thinking with your dick," Jax said.

Tace clenched his free hand into a fist.

"An hour ago you were on your back having convulsions," Jax said easily. "You might want to think twice about hitting me."

"Then keep your mind off my dick," Tace snapped.

Raze chortled and drank down his entire glass of Scotch. "While I hate to be the voice of reason, we need to get the personal shit ironed out before the next mission. I'm talking to both of you."

"Sami's off mission," Jax said.

"She gets to stay in Vanguard?" Tace asked, his jaw tightening so much his neck hurt.

"For the time being but she's confined to base," Jax said.

"That's fair," Tace said, his shoulders loosening. Truth be told, he liked her confined somewhere safe at the moment.

Jax cleared his throat. "So are you."

"No." Tace rubbed a bruise beneath his jaw. "My weird attacks have been going on for a while, and I've been fine or mission. I can tell when they're coming." Not exactly the truth.

Raze nodded. "Jax, you're needed here to deal with the Pure church—they're about to make a move, and we have to protect any kids involved. Tace and I can go scouting for explosives inner city like we'd planned. He'll be fine."

Tace's chest warmed at the support.

"Or I'll just shoot him in the head, and we won't have to worry about it any longer," Raze finished. "It could go either way."

Tace studied the former sniper. "Are you joking?"

"Eh." Raze lifted a shoulder.

"Works for me," Jax said, his gaze returning to the board. "Just make sure he's dead if you shoot him. Don't leave him for Rippers to finish off."

Tace finished his drink. "You're both all heart."

"You're off mission except to go with Raze or me," Jax said, shaking his head. "We can cover you, but other than that, you're here until the passing out ends."

Tace grimaced. "Fine." Yeah, that was fair.

"You should've told us you were having issues," Jax said.

"Yep," Raze agreed.

Well. If nothing else, it appeared as if Jax and Raze had buried the hatchet—right in Tace's back. "I thought it was just another aspect of Scorpius that would go away."

"Why didn't you say anything anyway?" Raze asked.

"We have enough going on, so I thought I'd just hold tight and be strong." Tace rubbed both hands down his face. "I'm sorry. I should've said something."

"You're forgiven," Jax said.

"Ditto," Raze echoed.

Tace settled, and the world righted. Circumstances had forced them to bond quickly, but even in a different world, he would've trusted these men. Now they all wore the mark of Vanguard, and that meant something. They truly were brothers, and he needed them. He thanked God he'd found them. "Thank you for understanding. Are the two of you all right now?"

"Yeah," Jax said as Raze nodded.

"Good." Tace shoved to his feet. "See you guys tomorrow." He needed to go sleep it off before facing Sami.

Leaving the war rooms, he headed up to bed. Feeling a thousand years old, he trudged up the steps and turned at the landing.

Sami waited for him by his door.

That quickly, he went from tired to full alert. His heart slammed against his ribs, and every nerve in his body perked up to full attention. And he hadn't even touched her yet.

Ah, hell. This was bad. She had her fighting stance already in place, and it was all he could do not to take her down in the hallway and teach her a lesson. A lesson that lying to a guy like him, the guy he'd become, was a seriously bad idea. He reached her in long strides. "Now is not a good time."

She crossed her arms, her gaze tumultuous. "We need to talk."

Anger roared through him, and he shoved the door open behind her, backing her into his room. "You asked for it."

Chapter Nineteen

Whoever said that truth sets you free was a moron.

—Sami Steel

Sami knew in an instant that she'd miscalculated. Not in keeping secrets or finally confessing . . . but in forcing her way into Tace's night. She should've given him time to work out his thoughts and dealt with her nightmares on her own. Waiting at his doorway close to midnight had been a colossal mistake. "Um, maybe I should—"

"Too late." He used his big body to maneuver her into the room, giving her no choice but to walk backward. The door closed with an audible click that sent a shiver down her spine.

She blinked, and her breath heated. "You're angry."

A swell of vibrating heat rolled through the room, and she actually took another step back.

"Angry? No." He crossed his arms and leaned against the door, very effectively blocking the only exit. "Angry brings to mind a slight argument or bad day. What I am is fuckin' pissed."

"Well now, that does sound worse than angry." She gave up any pretense of facing him head-on and backed farther away and into the apartment, keeping him in her sights. She'd learned long ago to keep a threat in view, and there was no doubt Tace was all threat at the moment. "I'm thinking we should talk about it tomorrow."

"I'm thinking you showed up here to fight it out, which is exactly what's going to happen." His voice remained too low and soft, which was all the more frightening for the fury behind it.

She swallowed.

The good ole Texas boy was long gone. She'd seen him disappearing the last few weeks, but now, facing the deadly furious soldier, she knew it was for good. Oh, Tace would always carry part of his former self, but this guy was harder and deadlier. Yet this form of him, the impenetrable strategist, was the one who softened her thighs and quickened her breath.

Right at the moment, however, she wasn't sure she could handle him. "What do you want from me?" she whispered.

His eyelashes swept up in a curiously dangerous way, and his focus narrowed. "I want to break you, Samantha. Completely."

Her mouth gaped open. Warning ticked through her, but so did spirit. "Not a chance."

He was on her then. Faster than she could track, he had her up against the wall, one hand fisted in her hair.

She gasped and sucked in air.

Heat poured off him, surrounding her. Slowly, deliberately, he rolled his wrist, forcing her face to lift to his.

Weakness swept through her legs. Worse yet, her nipples hardened to diamonds at the show of dominance. What was wrong with her? "I don't play these kinds of games," she whispered, her voice hoarse.

"I'm not playing."

Her body did a head-to-toe tremble.

His answering smile held a darkness way out of her experience.

Her breath quickened, and she panted quietly as she tried

to keep her chest from exploding. This was too real. She had to create some sort of distance. "Listen, Texa—"

He jerked her head, and a slight pain rippled along her scalp. "What did you call me?" His heated breath brushed her face.

She opened her mouth, but the look in his eyes stopped the words in her throat. "Um."

He leaned into her. "What's my name, Sami?"

"Tace," she breathed, her instincts taking over.

"Good. Don't do it again."

He knew. He totally knew she'd been trying to put him off. She wanted to challenge him, to fight whatever he was doing, but she felt as if she were balancing at the edge of a jagged cliff and trying not to fall. Her entire body shot into overdrive, nerves firing, breath catching. Tears pricked the back of her eyes.

"No. No tears," he ordered.

She batted them away, and her vision cleared.

"I've been inside you, and you've cried out my name. What did you think would happen when you came clean about the lies?" he asked, a liquid curiosity in his tone.

"Not this," she whispered.

"What is this?" His upper lip barely curved.

She swallowed. "I don't know."

"You will." He nipped her bottom lip none too gently.

She jerked, and raw heat clambered down her body, zinged a few times, and landed between her legs with a fierceness that scared her. She reacted, shoving a leg toward his ribs and shooting her arms up in a defensive move.

He flattened her against the wall with one step forward, swiping her leg back. "Hands down," he growled, the hand in her hair tightening in warning. "Palms flat against the wall. Now." He pressed his thigh up and between her legs against her aching clit.

She bit her lip to keep from crying out. "Please, Tace—"

"No. If I decide you need to beg, I'll fuckin' tell you. Hands. Now."

Her brain fuzzed. Think. She needed time to think. So she flattened her hands against the wall, a dangerous curiosity filling her. How far would he take whatever this was? "Don't forget I can kick your ass," she muttered, not even remotely sure she could any longer.

"It occurs to me that I've misread you from day one," he murmured thoughtfully, his gaze on her upturned face.

"How's that?" she asked.

"It all makes so much more sense now. An LAPD rookie with fighting skills would be an idealist motivated by saving people, unlike you," he said.

She narrowed her gaze. "And me?"

"You're a brat motivated by the challenge of the hack. Of beating the next guy," he said.

There was enough truth in the statement that she had to keep herself from wincing. "Not anymore."

"It's about the game, right? You love to play the game." His voice darkened and warmed.

"Life stopped being a game a long time ago," she snapped, briefly shutting her eyes.

"I don't think so. You like games so much? Oh, baby, we're gonna play a game, and only one of us is gonna win." His thigh ground against her, and mini-orgasms vibrated through her lower half.

She opened her eyes to face his directly, determination lancing through her. "You want to play, Justice? Fine, we can play all you want." He'd lifted his thigh just enough to give her an opening. She clapped both hands beneath his knee and lifted, throwing him off balance.

His fist flattened on the back of her head and he took her with him, falling backward onto the cracked linoleum.

She cried out, shooting an elbow beneath his chin even as he dragged her down.

The second he hit, he rolled, his foot kicking a kitchen chair over. It splintered, and wood clacked across the floor.

She kicked and struggled, knocking the lantern off the table. Plexiglas cracked, and he swept the pieces out of the way with one arm. She punched him in the throat, and he choked, his face turning red.

Following up with her nails, she tried to grab onto his larynx.

He levered up, grabbed her hips, and tossed her over and onto her stomach. She landed with a muffled *oof*, and the breath swooshed from her lungs. She struggled furiously, but he dropped a leg across her lower back just as a large hand manacled her wrists together beneath her shoulder blades.

She bucked and writhed, shoving her shirt up, but she couldn't dislodge him. The old linoleum smelled like mold and scratched her chin. Her kicking feet connected with the stuffed chair, sending it spinning into the coffee table.

He kept silent, letting her fight like a fish on a dock. Finally, she subsided. "You are such a dick," she muttered.

"The first game we're going to play is truth or lie," he said agreeably. "And stop beating your chest against the floor. That has to hurt."

"I'm fine. The bruise is healing fast." She turned her head and tried to tilt her head to see his expression. Determination completely lacking in humor or fun. This was still dark Tace. "You have no right to do this," she hissed.

He paused. "I disagree. We've been scouting partners for months, we've been friends, and now we're lovers. If anybody has a right to an explanation from you, it's me. So get ready to play, baby."

She glared but probably didn't look too scary flattened to the floor and unable to move.

"Game starts now. Did you give us the correct schematics for the Bunker?" he asked.

The man wanted to talk about the damn Bunker? She bit back a scream. "Yes."

He patted her ass. "Truth."

She stilled. "Wait a minute, Tace."

SMACK. He didn't hold back as his free hand descended on her butt. "Did I forget to mention the rules? You don't speak unless it's to answer a question."

"You fucking—"

SMACK. SMACK. SMACK.

"And swear words get it threefold," he said easily.

Oh, she was going to kill him. "The second I get up, you're a dead man."

Five hard—very hard—smacks descended before she could cry out. "Death threats get you five," he murmured, his voice guttural.

Pain ratcheted through her lower half, and she fought a whimper. Even so, her body was on full alert, and more than a little turned on. It was official. She'd completely lost her fucking mind. Ignoring her body's needs, she carefully began to plot his murder.

"Have you told us the full truth about the Bunker?" he asked.

She pressed her lips and her thighs together.

He ran a gentle hand across her smarting ass, and she tried not to arch into his touch. "Did I mention that the silent treatment gets a count of ten—on your bare ass?" he asked conversationally.

She stiffened.

"Not gonna say it again, Sami."

She'd cut him into pieces and fry him up for the wild lion roaming around Los Angeles to eat. "I told you everything," she ground out.

He patted her. "Good girl."

Forget cutting him up. She'd fry him whole.

"Did you tell me the truth about your upbringing and the government work?"

"Yes," she muttered.

"Are you still working for the government or the Bunker facility?" he asked.

She coughed, and a shocking hurt billowed in her chest. It was a fair question, but how could he believe that? "No."

"You're not leading us into an ambush?"

"No," she whispered, her voice shaking. "Let me up, dickhead."

Three hard smacks impacted her upper butt. She tried to arch into the floor and away from the punishing blows.

"Rules, Sami. They haven't changed," he said, his voice a low growl.

Her sex throbbed, and her breasts ached for more. She bit back a death threat, sure she couldn't handle five more, even as she settled back down.

He cleared his throat. "You and me the other night. Was it part of some grand plan?"

"No," she burst out, struggling uselessly against his almost easy hold. Man, he'd gotten even stronger. Poor Marvin the lion would probably choke trying to eat Tace's hard muscles.

"Do you want to be at Vanguard?" Tace asked.

"Yes." That one was easy.

"Do you want to be with me?"

She paused. "I'd rather strip your skin from your body right now."

He barked out a laugh. "I guess death threats are okay when given as an honest answer."

She snarled.

"You've told us about the schematics and a little bit about the Bunker, but you know you're going to have to tell us all of it, right?" he asked.

"Yes, but some of it's hard to explain unless you understand the computer systems," she said.

"Understood." He patted her butt, and she hissed. "One more question. Are you turned on right now?"

Her body ached, and she wanted to rip his clothes off and jump his bones. Yet she was beyond furious, and a good part of her wanted to kick his ass into the next county and back . . . twice. "I don't know what I am."

"Fair enough." He lifted his leg and released her arms, hauling her to her feet.

Her butt stung, and her ego smarted. She wobbled and then regained her balance. Without even thinking, she hauled off and punched him square in the face.

His head jerked back.

She moved her leg into an attack position.

He held up a hand. "I gave you one because that was fair. Hit or kick me again, and I'll stop playing."

She fought the urge to rub her sore ass. "That was you playing?"

"Yeah." He crossed his arms across his chest. "Now the power and decisions are yours. You gonna stay and see where this takes us, or you gonna be a scared little brat and run away?"

So much confusion rolled through her, she couldn't think of an appropriate answer. But her body was primed and ready. She wasn't even sure she could walk, and it wasn't from his silly spanking. How was it possible to ache this badly? "I don't want words or promises or any of your slow shit, Texas."

His nostrils flared at the nickname, and his body seemed to vibrate in place. "Spell it out for me. What do you want?"

"Fast and hard."

She'd barely gotten the last word out before she found herself on her back on the bed, her yoga pants spinning across the room. She barked out a startled laugh as he shucked his jeans, and then he was on her.

He ripped off his shirt, exposing all of those hard muscles. She shimmied out of her top.

"You sure?" he asked, poised at her entrance.

"Yes." She bent her knees.

In record time, he rolled on a condom. Where the hell had the condom come from? She barely had time to register the thought before he moved again. He shoved inside her hard, stealing her breath away. He set a fast rhythm, and she came instantly, crying out his name.

Her nails dug into his back, and she clasped her feet together, holding on with all of her strength. He hammered inside her, stroking deep, one hand flattening across her butt and half lifting her from the bed.

He squeezed fresh bruises, sending erotic pain through her erogenous zones.

She gasped, and he chuckled, doing it again.

"More," she murmured against his damp shoulder.

He increased his pace, and the strength of his thrusts shoved the mattress hard against the wall.

"I'm still mad at you," she ground out, shutting her eyes to just feel.

"We have all night for you to forgive me." He leaned down and bit her shoulder with enough strength to give her pause.

Her nails raked his back. "We'll see."

He angled up, brushed her clit, and she detonated. Waves pummeled through her, sparking raw nerves, taking everything she was. She opened her mouth in a silent scream.

His body shuddered, and he came hard.

Still inside her, he lifted his head, the black rim around his blue iris more pronounced. "You still mad?"

"Yes," she murmured.

He grinned, looking like the old Tace for a moment. "Well, the night is young." Then he leaned down and kissed her, going deep.

Chapter Twenty

The darkness inside me was always there, lurking, waiting to be freed by Scorpius.

—Tace Justice

It felt natural scouting the territory with Raze, yet Tace missed Sami. He'd gotten accustomed to her humor as they faced the dregs of life, and Raze didn't talk much, if at all.

Tace drove the truck around a mound of old paint cans in the center of what was once a busy street just outside of Vanguard territory. Raze kept watch out the passenger-side window, his gun out, his gaze tracking a series of shadows in an old thrift store. "I see several Rippers or survivors, but they're not coming out to investigate."

"Good." Tace reached the open road and pressed the gas. "I always get twitchy scouting in the daylight."

"Ditto, but we're running out of batteries for flashlights and fuel for lanterns," Raze said. "Daylight it has to be."

"I know." Tace kept his focus out the front and side, ready for any threat during the dawn hour. They were heading inner city to some former home construction businesses, hoping to find explosives to use at the Bunker. The large, well-known construction areas had been wiped clean of anything useful months ago.

"You guys were really loud last night." Raze turned and

eyed Tace's aching face. "She nailed you with a good one. It's purple now and will end up quite the shiner by the end of the day."

Tace nodded. "Yeah." It wasn't like he'd had ice or a steak to put on it, even if he hadn't been otherwise occupied with making Sami scream his name. "Sorry about the noise." Not really, considering Raze and Vinnie had kept him awake more than once. The doc was a screamer.

"No worries." Raze turned back to scan for danger. "You and Sami all made up?"

"I don't think so," Tace said. "She was sleeping when I left, and we never really got a chance to talk, you know?"

"I think so." Raze tensed. "There's something going on in the old McDonald's to the right."

"Slow down?"

Raze craned his neck. "Yeah." He stilled. "I see two small kids throwing bricks at people."

"Shit." Tace pulled around back and away from the windows. "Kids can be Rippers, too."

"Yeah." Raze leaped from the truck and ran up the sidewalk. "Give me the count of five and then come in through the back. I'll take front."

"Wait." Tace moved beyond an overflowing Dumpster to test the back door. It opened easily. "Let's go in and scope."

Raze nodded. "Your call."

Tace slipped inside and swept both ways. Packaged straws littered the way along with what looked like finger bones. He moved quietly, feeling Raze at his back but not hearing a sound.

A kid screamed from the other room, and he stiffened, breaking into a fast jog.

"What do we have here?" a low voice asked.

"Let us go. We won't tell anybody you're squatting here." This voice belonged to a girl—a young one?

Tace slid out from behind the wall to get a better look.

Two men wearing purple gang colors had cornered a couple of kids, one boy and one girl, both around seven. The girl had long, wild black hair with mocha-colored skin, and the boy was a towhead with blue eyes.

"Oh, I think we're gonna take you with us." The guy speaking half turned, showing a series of tattooed tears up his neck and face. He was about thirty, and if the tats told the truth, he'd been an enforcer for Twenty, the local gang.

The boy pushed in front of the girl, who was already crying. "Take me and not her."

Brave little kid.

The other gang member scratched his scarred chin. "I say we use them first—before we take them back. Then they can meet everyone else and start earning their keep."

Tace's gut rolled.

The girl whimpered.

The boy set his stance, his eyes blazing. "You touch her, and I'll kill you."

"Learn to shut up now, kid." The first guy backhanded the boy, and he flew into the counter. Instantly, the kid shot up, hands in fists, body in front of the girl.

"Hit him again, and I'll blow your head off," Tace said, moving around the wall and pointing his gun at the guy's head.

The boy covered the girl, whispering something and shielding her with his small body.

Raze stepped gracefully around the counter, his gun trained on the second guy. "On your knees. Now."

The second guy looked at his buddy.

"I'm happy to shoot you," Tace drawled. "In fact, it'd make the rest of my day a lot better if you were just dead. So make a move, and let's get on with this."

The guy looked at Raze, who didn't so much as twitch. He was silent and deadly . . . and it showed.

The gang members dropped to their knees, both clasping

their hands behind their heads. Obviously, they'd been arrested more than once and knew the drill. Knives and a gun were visible in their waistbands.

Tace sighed. "How many members are still in Twenty?" Last he'd heard, the gang was working with the president.

No answer.

He glanced at Raze. "Take the kids outside, would you?"

The girl buried her face in the boy's back.

Raze frowned. "You sure? I can handle these guys. I think it's my turn to shoot people."

Tace knew he couldn't be gentle at the moment, and those kids needed gentleness. "I can't do it."

"Ah." Raze tucked his gun in the back of his waist and strode close to the kids. "I'm Raze, and I have the weird name because I was named for my dad, Ryan, and my uncles, Albert, Zeke, and Elton. They were all good guys, and so am I. Do you two have anywhere safe to go?"

The boy turned and faced Raze squarely, which few adult men could do easily. "Yes. We live close. Can we go now?"

Raze hunkered down to meet the kid's eyes. "Just you two?"

"No." The boy's lip shook. "We have a whole bunch of uncles who all have guns." Ah, the poor little liar.

"I see." Raze rubbed his chin. "My friend here needs to have a discussion with these two guys in purple, and I don't think the little lady behind you should be here for that. You get me?"

The kid's eyes darkened. "Yeah," he whispered. "I get you." He turned and took the girl's hand. "Let's go outside, Tina."

The girl stood and nodded. "Then we should get back to our, um, uncles."

Tace's heart, what was left of it, broke even more. The two kids were totally alone, and it was a miracle they were still walking. "Tina, I'm Tace." He used his best Texan drawl. "What's your name, buddy?"

The boy looked him over, no doubt seeing yet another predator in a world gone to shit. "Rory Samuelson."

"Nice to meet you, Rory. I'd like to talk to you when I'm finished here, so if you'd stick around, I'd appreciate it. We don't hurt kids, and we know of a safe place for you and Tina if you're interested," Tace said.

The first gang member moved for his knife, and Tace kicked it out of his hand. "Go now, please."

Raze herded the kids out past all the straws.

Tace sighed. "Go for the gun next time."

The first guy winced and shook out his hand. "We were just going to have a little fun with them. Tell you what. You use the girl first and then leave her for us. It'll be a win-win."

Without even thinking about it, Tace shot him between the eyes. Blood blew through the air, and the guy fell back, more blood congealing around his head.

The other guy cried out and scooted away on his knees.

Tace stepped over the spatter and pressed his gun to the second gang member's head. He hadn't earned kill tats yet and looked about twenty years old. "You rape kids?"

"No," the guy whispered, his voice shaking. "I was just going along with Skip so he wouldn't kill me. I've only been a member of Twenty for a month. There wasn't anywhere else to go."

"How many members are there?" Tace asked, ignoring the smell of gunfire, blood, and death.

"I don't know—maybe about fifty? Everyone is kind of joining Twenty because they're the strongest gang and now they work for the Elite Force." The guy wiped his nose on his sleeve.

"Where's the Elite Force?" Tace asked.

The guy blinked away tears. "Up north at some old mansion the Parks Department owned. The president is there, and they're training Twenty members to be the front line of defense. We matter, man."

"Then why are you here, dickhead?" Tace asked.

The guy glanced at his fallen friend and blanched. "We're out in teams of two watching Vanguard and reporting back."

Damn it. The president was about to make another move against them—Tace could just feel it. "What kind of fire-power does the president have?"

"Dunno."

Probably the truth. The guy definitely wasn't in the know. "How many scouts are there watching Vanguard?"

"At least six teams of two. That's all I know." The guy's shoulders slumped. "If you're gonna kill me, just do it."

"I'm not." Tace wanted to, but he had to hold on to a small part of his humanity. "Though if I hear of you terrorizing any more little kids, I'm going to hunt you down and cut you apart piece by piece."

"I get it."

"Good." Tace stepped over the widening pool of blood and headed for the back door. The hair on the back of his neck rose, and he pivoted just in time to see the guy reach for his gun. Tace fired, and the bullet impacted the guy's temple. He dropped dead. "Thanks," Tace said, turning on his heel. Now he didn't have to worry about another rapist asshole out there.

Should he feel bad about killing the two? Probably, but truth be told, he felt relief.

He reached the outside and pushed open the door to find both kids sitting on the hood of the truck, the boy with his arm around the girl. Raze lounged against a pillar. "They won't get in."

Tace nodded.

"Did you kill those guys?" Tina's lips quivered when she asked the question.

"No," Tace lied easily. "I shot at them so they'd run away

and leave us alone." By the somber looks on the kids' faces, neither one of them believed him. "Are you two coming with us or not?"

Tina wiped tear tracks off her face.

Rory just stared at him, desperation in his light eyes.

Tace took them both in. "Listen, if we wanted to hurt you guys, we already could have, right?"

"This isn't a good place," Rory countered, "but maybe your lair is worse."

"Yeah." Tace rubbed his chin. The bottom line was that the kids were going with them, but there had to be a way to gain their cooperation instead of taking them by force. It would delay the scouting trip for hours, but they had to get the kids safely behind the fence. "You ever heard of Vanguard?"

Tina sucked in air and put her face into Rory's neck.

Tace sighed. "I take it you've heard bad stuff." It made sense that the president and the local gangs were talking them down to keep folks from seeking asylum. "Vanguard is a good place where nobody will hurt you."

"Oh yeah? Where'd you get the black eye?" Rory challenged, red infusing his pale skin.

"From his girlfriend," Raze said easily.

Tace cut him a look.

Rory's light eyebrows rose. "Your girlfriend hit you? Did you hit her, too?"

Tace scowled. Truth was, he had smacked her ass quite a bit. "No, I didn't hit her back. She was mad at me and she punched me, but she had some cause. We usually don't go around hitting each other, and we don't hit kids. Ever."

"Tace's woman can really fight," Raze said. "Her name is Sami, and she could train you, if you want."

Tina peeked around Rory at Raze. "Do you have a girlfriend?"

The deadly soldier blinked. "Um, well, yeah. I do."

Tace snorted. "You are so smooth."

Raze frowned. "The term 'girlfriend' is just so high school. But yeah, I'm with somebody, and her name is Vinnie. She's kind and soft . . . and works as a shrink. In fact, she's the smartest person I've ever met."

Tina nudged Rory. "They have a Vinnie and a Sami."

"So?" Rory asked, studying Tace with way too old eyes.

"A place with a Vinnie and a Sami can't be all bad, right?" Tina asked with perfect logic.

"We have other kids, and one is named Lena, but she doesn't talk," Tace said. Maybe they'd be enticed by the thought of other kids.

"Why not?" Rory asked, still glaring.

"We don't know," Tace said gently. "She seems happy, and she's always around, but she's never spoken a word. Maybe somebody her age could get her to talk."

Glass broke a block away, and both kids jumped.

Raze eyed the area. "We need to get out of here."

Tace nodded. "Please come with us. We'll make sure you stay safe."

Rory looked at Tina, who slowly nodded.

"All right." Tace looked up at the rapidly rising sun. "Let's get them home safely and then go scouting." They had to find explosives in order to infiltrate the Bunker. So far he hadn't had an attack of dizziness all day, but hell . . . the day was still young.

Chapter Twenty-One

*I never thought to find a man who'd want all of me,
much less demand it.*

—Sami Steel

Sami hustled downstairs wearing her favorite cargo pants
and black T-shirt with a knife strapped to her thigh. She'd
awoken alone in Tace's apartment, and the guy hadn't even
left a note.

All sorts of private places ached on her body, from her
butt to her core. Even her breasts were tender from the wild
night.

And wild it had been.

She shrugged off any sense of uneasiness and loped
across the soup kitchen to the infirmary. If Tace thought he
could just sneak out without talking to her, the man was in
for one hell of a surprise. They still needed to talk, damn it.

"Sami," a female voice called out.

Sami turned to see Barbara sitting at a wooden picnic
table. "Hey, Barb." Man, her face started to heat. She wandered over and filched a cookie and bit in. Peanut butter
filled her mouth, and she moaned.

Barbara grinned. "New cook. Nice, huh?"

"Yeah," Sami breathed. "So, um . . ."

Barbara's smile widened. "No need to explain. I heard you last night . . . who knew you were such a screamer?"

The heat turned to molten lava in Sami's cheeks. "Oh God."

Barbara snorted. "Yep. That's what you screamed."

Sami slapped her arm. "You're sure you are okay with it? I wouldn't do anything to hurt our friendship."

"It's a relief, to be honest." Barbara leaned toward her. "Derek and I are trying to make a go of it. He's just so solid, you know?"

Ah, they did make a good couple. Relief filled Sami and washed away the embarrassment. "Yeah, I do. I'm so happy for you." Happy for herself, too. She could stop feeling guilty. "I have to go, but we should have a girly poker game one of these nights with Lynne and Vinnie."

"I could use the money," Barbara joked. She glanced up and a pretty pink flushed over her face as she caught sight of Derek. "Hi."

The mechanic was about six feet tall and filled out his overalls well. He had blond hair and dark brown eyes, and right now, they were completely focused on Barbara. "Hi, beautiful." He leaned down and pressed a light kiss to her head.

Barbara breathed out.

Sami bit back a smile. They were just too cute. "Hi, Derek."

The man glanced up, surprise filling his face before he smoothed it out. "Oh, hi. How are you?"

Totally invisible to the man, which was kind of cool. "Great." Sami grinned. "You two have a great day."

Derek nodded and dropped into the seat next to Barbara.

Okay, so that was awesome. Those two were totally in love. Sami turned for the infirmary, her mind back on Tace. Why hadn't he waited to talk to her? Hurrying into the infirmary, she walked right into Jax Mercury.

He steadied her with hands on her biceps. "Slow down, would you?"

She stopped short. "Is Tace here?"

Jax pinned her with a hard look. "Good morning, Samantha."

Why did she feel like she was back in second grade and called to the principal's office when Jax used her full name? She planted both hands on her hips. "Good morning, Jax." That was his full name, damn it.

"I'm thinking we need to have a chat," Jax said, turning and striding past the former reception area. "After I check in on Damon."

Sami followed him, more than ready for a good old chat. She'd told the truth, she'd apologized, and now they all needed to get back to normal. Raze had lied, too, and now everyone had forgiven him. "What was up with Damon yesterday, anyway?" She hadn't expected the Merc to be so volatile after they'd patched him up.

Jax entered Damon's room and motioned Sami inside before closing the door.

The Mercenary soldier sat up in the bed, his nicely muscled torso bare save for the bandages. His dark skin was no longer pale, and his soft brown eyes were clear. "Morning."

Sami crossed her arms.

"How did I do?" Damon grinned.

"Awesome." Jax knuckle-bumped him.

Sami frowned. "Did I miss something?"

"Yeah. I'm undercover all of a sudden." Damon tugged at the bandage across his stomach.

Ah. "So you faked the whole fear of Scorpius in front of the Pure pastor," Sami said, putting the pieces together. " take it you're going to stay at Vanguard for a bit?"

"Have to," Damon said easily. "Now all I have to do is ge an invite to the church. They already sent pretty April t see if I'm interested, and I told her maybe but I wasn't sure, and she's reporting back."

Pretty April? Protectiveness rose in Sami for her new friend. "April's still vulnerable, Damon."

The former LAPD officer held up both hands. "Just friends. I swear." He smiled. "Told you there was no way you were LAPD."

"Shut up," Sami said easily. "I just met you, thus you don't get to be pissed at me."

"I, however, do," Jax said.

Sami winced. "You forgave Raze for lying to you."

Jax's light brown eyes flashed. "Raze and I beat the shit out of each other, twice, and then we made up. I hit him to hurt him."

Sami's head jerked up. "So let's go to the gym."

Jax paused. "No."

"Yes." She put both hands to her hips. "You've always treated me like one of the soldiers—like one of the guys. If we need to fight and bleed for you to forgive me, let's do it."

Jax studied her, his lip twisting. "I can't."

Fire and hurt washed through her. "What do you mean?"

He shuffled his feet. "I can't hit you to hurt you." His hand went up when she started to lambaste him. "I'm sorry, Sami. I know you fight better than most of us, and I know you're trained, and I know you're smarter than most soldiers." He shrugged. "I still can't hit you to hurt you. I kinda feel like you're my little sister."

At those words, those kind words, she lost her anger and burst into tears.

"Holy fuck no." Jax backed away, shaking his hands. "Don't do that. God, don't do that."

"You made her cry," Damon snapped.

"I'm . . . not . . . crying," she sobbed.

"Jesus." Jax moved in and put both arms around her,

patting her back like she was choking. Her ribs rattled. "It's okay. Um, let it out."

"I do trust you but I didn't at first and then I liked it here and didn't want you to kick me out when you learned the truth," she sobbed into his chest, soaking his shirt. "Now Tace hates me, and everyone hates me, and this is home, and I don't know what to do."

"Okay. You're forgiven." Jax smacked her back again. "It's all good. You're home. It's good."

"Make her stop crying, you asshole," Damon growled. "I'm not gonna work here if you make nice women cry."

"I'm trying," Jax snapped back, panic lowering his voice. "It's okay, Sami. I'll talk to Tace. If he doesn't forgive you, we'll just shoot him. I promise."

She sniffed against his chest. "I'm really sorry, Jax."

"You're forgiven." He lifted her away from him and gently wiped her cheeks. "We need you here. I can't run Vanguard without you."

She sniffled. "The Bunker is a bad place, Jax."

"Yeah, but you gave us the coordinates to save Tace, honey. You did that for him," Jax said gently.

"You should tell Tace that," Damon piped up.

"I will." Jax kept his voice soft. "You better now?"

She sniffed again and nodded. "Yeah. Do I look like I've been crying?"

"Yes. Your nose is all red and blotchy and kind of big all of a sudden." Jax rubbed his chin. "In fact, how do you feel about storming out of here in about one minute?" He glanced down at an old Timex on his wrist.

Sami had never been a pretty crier. "Sure. Why?"

"The good old Pastor King should be arriving at Vinnie's office in a minute. If he asks what upset you, how about you say something about Damon yelling at you about infection? Let's pour it on thick."

Sami nodded. "No problem. Where is Tace?"

"Tace and Raze went inner city to find explosives," Jax said, glancing again at his watch. "I'll go out the front, you wait one minute, and then storm out of here."

She gulped. "Okay."

Jax tweaked her hair and then slid out of the room, silently disappearing.

Damon cleared his throat. "You okay now?"

She nodded.

"It's understandable. Everything you did and said. If Tace doesn't understand and forgive you, then he's an idiot."

Sami smiled, but her lips still trembled. "For a Merc, you're not half bad, Damon."

"I do aim to please." He sobered. "April is really off limits?"

Sami shook her head. "I can't speak for her, but she's a former suburban soccer mom who's lost everyone, including her teenage daughter a couple of weeks ago. She married her first love at sixteen, and she lost him three months ago."

Damon winced. "Ah. Got it."

"Yet you're kinda hot, Winter. She might want to take the leap." Sami grinned when the former cop actually blushed. "You asshole," she yelled, turning on her heel and going through the door, slamming it loudly.

"What a complete dick." She kept in character, stomping through the infirmary and past Vinnie's office, where Pastor King hovered in the doorway. "Sorry."

Zachary glanced behind her. "Are you all right?"

Sami sighed and rubbed tears off her face. "I'm fine. That Damon Winter is an ungrateful dickhead, yelling about Scorpius and infection. We should've let the damn Merc soldier bleed out." Giving Vinnie a wave, she started down the hall.

"Sami?" Jax called from the front of the infirmary as if they hadn't seen each other all day.

"What?" Sami bellowed back.

Jax came into view. "There you are." He studied her face. "What's wrong?"

"Nothing." She pretended to hide her eyes.

"Sami?" Jax asked.

"Fine. Damon is a jerk. That's all." She hunched her shoulders.

Jax sighed. "He's requested asylum from the Mercenaries, and I'm considering it."

"Why?" Sami pretended to explode.

"He has intel we need, darlin'." Was Jax trying to sound patronizing for Zachary's sake? If so, he was doing a bang-up job of it. "I'll keep him away from you."

"Thanks," she gritted out.

Jax nodded magnanimously, amusement darkening his eyes. "No problem. For now, I'd like for you to sit in on the meetings with Vinnie and the Pure members. I want backup for her." He said the last with a hard look at Zachary.

The back door opened, and little Lena ran inside. She wore jeans short overalls with a bright pink shirt, and her long blond hair was back in two cute braids. She grabbed Sami's hand and tried to tug her toward the front area.

Sami paused. "Lena? What's going on?"

The girl dug in her heels and tried to drag Sami.

Vinnie got up from her chair and craned her neck. "Sami? Go with Lena and see what she wants. She's never engaged to this point, and I'm getting weird images from her. I mean, if I get images. I probably don't, you know. But—"

Sami nodded and cut her friend off before she babbled any more. "I'll be back in a minute." She glanced down to see a doll and a truck in Lena's arms. "We're going to play?"

The girl shook her head, frustration marring her pretty face.

"All right." Sami followed the girl out of the infirmary, through the soup kitchen, and into the vestibule. Sunlight leaked in through the windows, bringing the heat of early summer.

The girl stopped and stared at the closed glass doors.

Sami kept her hand and tried to focus. Tace, Raze, and two kids came into view in the parking area, all walking slowly toward the doors.

Lena hopped up and down, releasing Sami's hand.

Raze opened the doors, and the two kids, one boy and one girl, inched inside. They both looked at Lena.

Lena strode forward and handed the doll to the girl and the toy truck to the boy. She smiled.

The girl, a pretty black girl with dark eyes, clung to the boy's hand. The boy had blue eyes and almost white hair, and he kept a step ahead of the girl as if to shield her. They both accepted the gifts with small smiles.

"Are you Lena?" the girl asked.

Lena nodded vigorously.

"I'm Tina, and he's Rory. Is this a safe place?" Tina asked.

Lena nodded solemnly.

Rory's stance relaxed.

Sami's gaze flew up to Tace's face. He watched the kids impassively, but his eyes had darkened like they did when she knew he felt something. His feelings were still there . . . just deeper below the surface.

"Lena," called April Snyder from the far end of the soup kitchen. "I don't know how you get away so quickly." The pretty brunette jogged up and stopped short at seeing the other two kids. "Well, hello." She smiled and dropped to her haunches. "Who are you?"

"Tina and Rory," Sami answered. "I believe they're joining Vanguard?"

Tina looked at Rory, who didn't answer. Finally, Tina stepped forward, keeping a tight hold on the boy. "Yes. We are joining Vanguard."

Rory stepped up to her. "We stay together. Me and Tina. Together."

"Sure thing," April said, standing. "You can stay together

no matter what, but I need to know if either of you has had Scorpius."

"We both have," Rory said. "Before we found each other, we both had the fever and survived. But our families didn't."

April swallowed, her blue eyes almost glowing. "I promise you two can stay together for as long as you want, even if it's forever. I lost my family, too. All right. Are you hungry?"

Tina whimpered.

Rory shrugged. "We could eat."

God, the kid was tough.

April nodded. "Let's get you some soup, and then we'll find you a nice place to call home in Vanguard, all right?"

The kids nodded and waited for Lena to follow April before they fell into step.

Raze smiled at Sami and then headed for the infirmary, probably to see Vinnie.

Sami swallowed.

Tace's gaze ran over her face, and his entire body tightened before her eyes. "Have you been crying?"

She took a step back. "Well, I—"

"Crying?" Tace said, his voice sounding like gravel crunched beneath tires.

"I met with Jax, and—"

Jax hustled their way, a stack of papers in his hand. "Hey, Sami—"

"Goddamn it, Jax." Tace swung and nailed the Vanguard leader in the cheek with a wicked right cross.

Jax flew sideways and through the glass doors, sending shards in every direction.

"Tace!" Sami shoved past him to reach Jax, who was sitting up and shaking his head.

"What the hell?" Jax asked, yanking a piece of glass from his arm.

Tace stalked toward him. "You made her cry."

Sami jumped up and put her body between Tace and Jax before one of them went crazy. "Stop it. He didn't yell at me."

Jax shoved to his feet, and glass fell all around him. "She was crying about you, asshole."

For a guy with a temper, Jax seemed surprisingly all right with being thrown through a glass door. Sami looked from one to the other, her knees wobbling and her head aching. Her nose kind of hurt from crying, too.

Tace glared down at her. "You were crying because of me?"

She faltered. "No."

"Yes," Jax countered, stomping by them. "Clean this mess up, Justice. You're in charge of finding a replacement door. Sami, you go assist Vinnie, and Tace, you and Raze get back out there and find me explosives."

Tace reached out and ran a knuckle down Sami's swollen face. Her insides quivered.

Jax half turned. "You two have ten minutes to get the personal shit ironed out right now, or I'm shooting you both and leaving you for the Twenty gang to find." He kicked glass out of his way and disappeared inside, muttering about motherfuckers and glass doors.

Sami swallowed.

Tace breathed out and looked at the bloody glass on the ground. "So. Guess we should talk."

Chapter Twenty-Two

Love makes phenomenal soldiers act like morons.
I know . . . I did.

—Jax Mercury

Glass still tinkling down from his jeans, Jax leaned his head around Lynne's door. His woman sat muttering to herself while sketching out the Bunker. "If the labs are here, then supplies for the labs should be here and here." She made notations as she talked.

"Blue?" he asked.

She jerked and looked up, welcoming him with a smile. "Jax."

That smile kicked him in the chest every time. "Do you mind stitching me up?"

She jumped to her feet and was at his side in a second. "Oh my. What the hell?" She gently pulled his hand away from the bleeding wound on his upper arm. "Is that glass?"

He winced. "Yeah. I walked away like a badass, but the glass has to come out." It was starting to really hurt, but that just meant he was healing.

She yanked off her flowery shirt to press against his wound. The blue of her heart glowed through her plain white bra.

"Put that back on." He tried to pull away and make sure nobody was around.

She faltered. "Oh. My heart. Sometimes I forget the blue bothers people."

He didn't give a shit about the blue tone or if it bothered anybody. "No, your tits. Those are mine and mine only." He ushered her toward the one remaining examination room and shut the door. "I'm happy to prove it to you right now if you wish." He kept his voice low and direct.

She rolled her pretty green eyes. "Okay, tough guy. Sit on the table, and I'll get Tace. He's much better at stitching people up."

"Tace punched me through the glass door." Jax jumped onto the table.

Lynne paused. "Is he still breathing?"

"Yes," Jax sighed. "He thought I made Sami cry, and he reacted, which was probably a good thing so they can get their shit figured out. So I didn't kill him. See? I'm growing as a person."

Lynne hustled to the counter and yanked out surgical stuff that looked pointy and painful. "You really are." She returned with a syringe. "Can I give you a local?"

"No. Save it for when we really need it." He tugged off his shirt and barely kept from wincing as the material pulled against his wounds.

Lynne frowned but leaned in and picked glass out with a pair of huge tweezers.

He drew in a breath and centered himself, allowing the pain into his body. "I sent more drawings of Marcus out with scavengers and scouts earlier this morning, telling them to tack them to trees and leave them in various places."

Lynne bent her head closer to dig out a stubborn piece of glass. "That's good."

"I'm starting to think I'm just crazy." Jax kept still so she could do the job right. His enemy, the one he'd killed weeks ago, had hinted that his younger brother was still alive after Scorpius. Jax had held on to that one possibility with both hands, when it probably was just another lie in a world full of them. "Do you think I'm crazy?"

She lifted up and pressed a kiss to his mouth. "No. We all need hope."

Yeah, and it didn't hurt anything to send out drawings, now did it? He sucked in air when Lynne pressed the needle into his flesh.

"Please let me give you a local," she whispered.

"No." They needed to hoard what few drugs they had. What if one of the kids got hurt and needed a local? "I'm fine, baby. Just finish up, and then I'll show you how much I like your tits."

"You're impossible," she said, biting her lip as she continued stitching.

The door opened, and Tace poked his head in. "I'm sorry, Jax."

Jax glanced down to make sure Lynne's back was to Tace before answering. "I've been there, and I understand. Take care of it so neither of you gets dead during the next mission."

Tace nodded. "Sami went to provide backup for Vinnie, and I'm heading out with Raze to find explosives. I promise Sami and I will reach an understanding tonight, whatever that may be."

Jax lifted an eyebrow. So they were going to act like morons for a little while longer. He didn't have time for this shit. "I thought you were reaching said understanding *last* night when furniture was broken, somebody got spanked, and you ended up with a black eye."

Tace's head jerked back.

Jax smiled, finally feeling better about the entire situation. "The walls are thin, buddy."

Lynne slapped a bandage over Jax's stitches with a little more force than was necessary. "Jax. Geez."

He grabbed her arm before she could turn around. That bra concealed absolutely nothing. His mouth watered. "Go away, Tace."

The door shut with a soft click.

Lynne's mouth dropped open. "Are you joking?"

Jax hopped off the table, grasped her hip, and put her right back on it with his good arm. "Isn't the examination room one of those kinky fantasies people have?"

Her eyes widened, and that had to be horror filling them. "God, no. Definitely not. Ewww."

"What about you and me in a private room all by ourselves that happens to double as something else?" He tugged down the middle of her bra and dipped in to see her pretty pink nipples.

She slapped his hands without much force. "Jax. It's the middle of the day."

He paused and then looked at her, humor attacking him so quickly he threw back his head and laughed. The middle of the day? Seriously? God, he fuckin' loved her. "It's time to explore a little, Dr. Lynne Harmony."

"Explore?" she burst out. "Are you kidding me? We've explored nearly every possible way there is."

True. He flattened his good hand between her breasts and pushed down. She fought him, but without any leverage, she was soon flat on her back.

Finally. His day was looking up.

Sami slipped into Vinnie's office and looked around. Vinnie glanced up from her desk. "Zachary had to run back to his church to get records, but he should return any moment." She gestured toward the sitting area. "Let's chat."

Sami sighed and dropped into one of two seats. They'd let

Zachary take the sofa. The second Jax had started trusting Vinnie, he'd ordered all of his soldiers to get one-on-one time with the shrink to work on feelings and stuff. Sami had managed to avoid doing so up until now. "What do you want to chat about?"

Vinnie smiled and moved to take her seat, crossing her legs beneath a green pencil skirt.

"What's up with the skirts lately?" Sami asked. The post-apocalyptic world called for jeans or yoga pants, not fancy clothes.

"Raze found a bunch of skirts on a mission a few days ago, and he likes it when I wear them." Vinnie smoothed down the skirt. "Plus, I'm trying to be a shrink to people, so I figure looking the part is a good thing? Who knows."

Sami tapped her cargo pants. "All right."

Vinnie's eyes sparkled in a classic face. "How are you and Tace doing?"

"Considering I lied to him from day one? I'd have to say that we are not doing all that well," Sami said quietly. Although Tace had just put Jax through a glass door on her behalf, so that had to mean something.

"Yeah, well, men feel like fools when they've been lied to, but a good night of sex when they get their own back usually helps. It kinda sounded like that happened last night." Vinnie pushed long blond hair away from her cheeks. "Right?"

Heat blossomed into Sami's face. "You heard us?"

"Thin walls, sister." Vinnie leaned forward. "Tace looks like he'd be a champion in bed, you know? Is he?"

Sami choked. "Is a shrink supposed to ask that?"

"Hell if I know." Vinnie tapped her fingers on her bare knee. "I'm not really a shrink. So is he all hot and sexy?"

"Is Raze?" Sami shot back.

"Oh my, yes. Raze is over-the-top dominant, sweet, and sexy all at the same time. In fact—"

Sami held up a hand. "I work with the guy, Vinnie. Let's

leave it at that." Geez. Raze was a fellow soldier, for Pete's sake; she'd just wanted to throw Vinnie off balance. Since Vinnie was pretty much off balance anyway, clearly it had been a miscalculation. Although, settling in for girl talk filled Sami with a few warm fuzzies. She'd missed her sister, and Vinnie had a way of drawing her in.

"So. Tace in bed?" Vinnie asked.

Sami sighed. "Fine. He's very good in bed. Hot and sexy. A little scary last night, to be honest."

"Yet you enjoyed it." Vinnie lifted her eyebrows up and down.

"Yes." Sami frowned. "I shouldn't have, but I did, so life is just all sorts of screwed up."

"Eh." Vinnie reached for a pencil and pad of paper. "Sounds like you guys are getting back on track. What do you want from him, anyway?"

"I don't know."

"That's fair."

Sami eyed the small office. "I don't want a shrink, Vinnie."

"How about a friend?" Vinnie tapped her pencil end over end. "I like you, and we can be friends. Do girl talk and stuff."

"Isn't that what we were just doing?" Sami asked.

"Yep."

Sami nodded, and her throat clogged. "I'm scared, Vinnie. I'm scared we won't be able to find the enzyme for Tace and he'll die. Worse yet, I'm afraid that if I had spoken up earlier, we'd have that cure now and it's my fault it's too late." The words burst out of her.

Vinnie sighed. "I understand, but the second you realized what was wrong with Tace, you came clean. You sacrificed your safety here, your position here, the very minute you thought you could help him. That means something."

Sami let the words sink in, but her chest still ached. What if?

Vinnie stiffened, and then Pastor Zachary King strode into the room like he owned the entire building. His nose was swollen and his left eye purple from Tace's attack.

Vinnie smiled. "We're not finished talking, Sami. As you know, Jax would like a determination as to duty fitness, so we'll continue later." She sounded all official, which was probably a cover for Zach.

Sami played along and scowled. "I had not known that fact."

Vinnie smiled. "Yep." She looked up. "Zachary? Please take a seat on the sofa."

Zachary looked from Sami to Vinnie, each in her own chair. There was no doubt the sofa was not the power center of the room. Yet he moved by Vinnie and gracefully sat. "It was kind of you to meet with me, Doctor Wellington."

Oh, he was smooth.

"I'm so happy we have time to speak," Vinnie said easily. "Did you bring me a list of your church members?"

Zachary's lip twisted. "I did not. I do apologize, Doctor, but the church elders have decided that our list is private, just like it would have been in years past."

"The world has changed, Zach," Sami interjected.

Vinnie leaned forward, her face set in sympathetic lines. "Pastor King, surely you understand Jax's concern about people being coerced into joining or staying with your church. He has a duty to all of Vanguard, and those are Vanguard citizens. He must make sure they're all right."

Zachary nodded. "I do see his dilemma, but my hands are tied. If people don't want to be part of the Pure, then they're free to leave. That's all the assurance I can give today."

"Are you planning on leaving Vanguard?" Sami asked.

"We have not decided at this point. Best-case scenario would be for us to remain in place, safely behind Vanguard walls. I do understand this isn't a fair request." Zachary spread his hands out as if helpless.

Sami kicked back. "I have a list of your church members, Zachary."

He glanced her way. "Excuse me?"

"Oh, it took important time I could've spent elsewhere, but we've conducted housing checks on every Vanguard member, cross-checked those against intakes from the beginning, and we now know exactly who is living in the three Pure apartment buildings." Sami watched the pastor carefully. No flinch. He didn't care.

"Oh then." He smiled. "I guess the meeting is over."

"No. Are there any Pure members living outside those three apartments?" Sami asked.

He shrugged. "Maybe a couple, and definitely potential members are living outside our quarters, but not many."

"Good. So now we know." Vinnie made a notation in her book. "We'll need to schedule one-on-one appointments with each member to ensure they're willing participants, and then we can put all this to bed." She tore out a sheet of paper with times listed on it. "Have folks sign up."

He took the page. "I'll have all my men sign up today and bring the paper back later tonight."

Vinnie faltered. "That's a great start. Women and children sign up tomorrow?"

Sami's body tensed.

Zachary neatly folded the paper in two. "I'm sorry if I wasn't clear. Our women and children must be protected from Scorpius. Few of them are willing to leave the safety of our compound."

"They're the ones we're worried about, Zach," Sami said evenly.

"Pastor King or Zachary, please." He finally turned to face her directly. "As I hear it, you're no longer in the inner circle, so please mind your own business." He angled his head toward the door. "Your psychotic bodyguard isn't here to defend your honor this time."

She pushed to the edge of her chair, her chest heating. "Oh, Zach. If you think I need Tace around to kick your ass three ways to Sunday, you're sorely mistaken. I can make what Tace did to you look like a first date."

Vinnie pressed her lips together, and her eyes twinkled. She cleared her throat. "Pastor King, we need to interview every single member of the Pure. How can you make that happen?"

"I can't," he said.

"What are you afraid they'll tell us?" Sami asked, naturally countering Vinnie's respectful tone. Who said she couldn't be LAPD? Here she was already mastering good cop–bad cop. "You seem more scared of the truth than of Scorpius."

Vinnie leaned forward. "We can make provisions for their safety, and you know it."

His chin lowered, and he barely touched the shiny bruise beneath his eye. "Can you?"

"Yes, and you're the only one who can make these meetings happen, so please do so. Jax Mercury won't let kids or other vulnerable citizens leave without an interview, and as impressive as your forces may be, you won't win in a battle with him or the Vanguard soldiers. Especially since the Mercs are now our allies," Vinnie said gently. "Work with me, Pastor."

Sami kicked back. "You don't have a choice."

Chapter Twenty-Three

I think I've had worse ideas . . . maybe?

—Tace Justice

When he strode into the war rooms close to midnight, Tace was pleased to see Sami still included with the Vanguard soldiers as they sat around the conference table, all looking at a drawing of the Bunker.

Jax waited until he'd sat. "Before we get started, anybody want to hit Sami for lying?"

Tace stiffened.

Nobody moved. "All right. It's over, we've moved on, and Sami is forgiven. If there is any personal crap between any of you and Sami, get it taken care of within twenty-four hours, or I'm slicing you open like a trout." Jax fingered a bandage covering his upper arm.

Lynne opened a notebook. "I would like more information on Scorpius survivors' rejection of vitamin B."

Sami shook her head, lines fanning out from her eyes. "All I know is that some enzyme or medicine took care of it. The information is at the Bunker, as is the enzyme." She kept her gaze on Lynne, looking exhausted. Tace should've made sure she'd gotten some sleep the night before.

Lynne bit her lip. "How bad can it get?"

"The condition leads to death if not treated, which is why I've come forward," Sami said, her voice catching.

Tace's heart thumped twice. She'd exposed herself to save him. "I appreciate it."

She turned even paler. "I wish I knew more about the actual science, but that wasn't my job, and I didn't pay any attention. I'm sorry."

He wanted to reach for her hand, to touch her somehow, but she was all the way across the table. Next time he'd arrive early and sit closer to her.

"Moving on for now." Jax looked around. "Who's next?"

Vinnie leaned forward. "After meeting with Pastor Zachary, Sami and I have interviewed twenty of the Pure men, and they all fanatically want to stay with the Pure and follow Zach."

Sami nodded and gave a mock shudder. "Was kind of creepy, really."

Vinnie patted a notebook in front of her. "I think Zach sent his most ardent followers to meet with us first. We're still trying to figure out a way to meet with the women and children."

"It will happen," Jax said, his eyes hard.

"Agreed," Vinnie said softly.

Raze reached for her hand. "I want a soldier on Vinnie for every interview. If Sami is called somewhere else or is on a different mission, no interviews take place unless one of us is there."

"Understood," Jax said. "How was scouting?"

"It was a bust," Tace said, kicking back in his chair. His ankle ached from tripping over a pile of bodies earlier. "We went inner city and looked through all the home construction businesses we found in the phone book, and none of them had explosives left."

"Find anything?" Lynne asked.

"Some prescription drugs, canned food, toilet paper, tools, and gas," Raze said. "Wasn't a bad day, but no explosives."

"Shit. Maybe it's time to reach out to the Mercs," Jax said. "But from the list Sami put together, they have weapons and ammo . . . and no real explosives. That is if all the depots have the same resources."

Sami nodded. "Oh, if they had explosives like we need, Greyson would keep them close and in that depot I found. The Mercs are heavy in medicine but not explosives."

Tace winced. "I'd rather take the Bunker first and then call them in. There's a chance they'd cut us out if possible, and you know it. Right now we have the advantage because we're the only ones who know the location. That will probably change soon."

"Yeah." Jax turned and stared at the board. "Guns aren't enough to infiltrate and then defend ourselves."

Tace cocked his head to the side. "I have an idea, and it's crazy, but it's the only one I can think of."

Jax arched an eyebrow. "I'm intrigued."

"Our first option is to try to take explosives from the Mercs, but that creates an instant enemy, and we might not survive it," Tace murmured. "Plus, the Mercs are prepared and waiting for us to make a move after Sami and I scouted the place from within."

"I doubt they have the explosives we need," Jax said thoughtfully. "Sami is right. If Grey has the good stuff, at least some of it would've been in the centralized depot she saw. I'm guessing the Mercs don't have C4 or grenades."

"So the odd idea?" Lynne asked Tace.

Odd? It was fucking crazy. "There's only one group we know of that definitely has explosives," Tace said.

The room was quiet for a moment.

"Have you lost your mind?" Sami was the first to connect and react.

"Probably," Tace said. "But they won't be expecting an

attack. Hell, all we've done is hunker down and defend ourselves . . . unless they've forced our hand. Let's take the fight to the president and the Elite Force and acquire their explosives."

Jax stared at him, his mind obviously calculating the odds. "They won't be expecting it."

Raze nodded. "Downside is that they'll know it's us and they're bound to retaliate."

"Yes," Sami said, her brow furrowed. "And if they wait until we go take the Bunker, our forces will be split, leaving Vanguard vulnerable. We're pretty strong right now, even against the president, but that would change."

Vinnie cleared her throat. "We can't go in alone—not to fight the president and his force. What if we ally with the Mercs? I mean, tell them the plan to get the explosives, but later on when we are attacking, we don't let them know the location of the Bunker until we get there?"

"And risk a double cross at the location?" Raze countered.

"We have to trust somebody at some point," Lynne said quietly.

"No, we don't." Jax rubbed her shoulder to soften the point. "I'm just fine not trusting anybody but Vanguard. However, to infiltrate the Bunker and also protect Vanguard, we need to bring in the Mercenary soldiers. How do we do that and not give them an edge?"

"There's always blackmail," Raze muttered.

Jax snorted. "Speaking of which, it seems Greyson Storm has a thing for your sister. Think rationally, don't freak out, and let me know if there's a way to use that."

"There isn't," Raze said shortly.

"All righty then." Jax leaned back. "Let's keep Damon Winter here since he's in place to infiltrate the Pure with April Snyder, and maybe we can trade his safe return to

erc territory to gain some cooperation." Jax held up a
nd when Lynne started to argue. "We'll just hint at it—
thing overt."

"You're assuming Grey gives a crap about Damon," Raze
d.

Tace nodded. "I think he does. They seemed like friends
me, and Grey won't want one of the few people he seems
like killed by us."

"Okay. Send scouts to Merc territory under the cover of
rkness tonight and invite Greyson here for a meeting—
's see if he has the balls to enter Vanguard alone. We'll
him in on the plan to attack the president of the United
ates and take explosives—we can agree on some sort of
lit." Jax stood and started sticking papers over the draw-
gs of the Bunker. "We don't tell him about the Bunker or
y we want explosives."

"Let it slip that we want them for protection and to blow
that apartment building across the way that we've wanted
get rid of forever," Tace said. "We have to give him some
rt of explanation."

"Grey isn't stupid," Sami interjected. "But having explo-
ves would be good, and he can probably see Jax making a
ove like that. A crazy one."

Jax nodded. "Good. I like having them think I'm a wild
rd."

"You mean you're not?" Raze asked, his lip twitching.

"I may have mellowed a little," Jax said, his gaze on Lynne.

"Not even close," she countered, smiling.

Jax pushed back from the table. "All right. We meet
ain, all of us, when Greyson is here tomorrow morning, and
want Maureen present. Just to observe their interaction."

"There's nothing between Greyson Storm and my sister,"
aze said in a near growl.

"He sent her a letter, dude." Jax assisted Lynne to her

feet. "I just want to watch." He tilted his head toward Vinnie. "You keep an eye and profile him, Doc. Get me into his head."

Vinnie nodded. "No problem."

Tace stood. "Sami? I'll walk you up. We need to talk."

The room fell completely silent. What a bunch of busy-bodies.

Sami looked around, paled, and rushed to her feet. "Fine." She hustled by him, and her scent of wild orchids surrounded him, providing an odd sense of comfort and grounding him. Then it hit him. He could smell her scent. His sense of smell had come back.

He turned to follow her, his gaze straying to her fit ass in the cargo pants. Hopefully, he hadn't bruised her the previous night while making his point. She needed to be at full strength if they were actually dumb enough to attack the president and his Elite Force.

She stomped up the stairs and down the hallway, shoving open her door.

Damn it. He had to get her a new door and some sort of lock. "I guess we talk here."

She moved inside and dropped into the chair facing the sofa. "I have no idea what we have to say to each other."

Yeah, he got that. It was time to be completely honest even though he had no clue if he had feelings, much less what they were. Yet something about her called to him, and he grabbed on to it with both hands. "I want to make a go of it. Like Lynne and Jax. Raze and Vinnie."

Sami blinked. "I lied to you."

"Yeah, but I don't care." There were a whole lot of other words to add to that, but he couldn't find them. "You like me, you're attracted to me, and I'll try not to turn into sociopath."

"That's quite an offer." She flipped a braid over her shoulder. "There's something I didn't tell everyone."

He paused. More secrets? "What's that?"

She swallowed. "The dizziness from rejecting the B doesn't abate for a while, even after the cure. It might take some time."

Great. "Why didn't you tell them?"

She lifted a shoulder, vulnerability darkening her eyes. "I figured you could tell them if you want."

The little sweetheart. She was still protecting him. "It'd kill me if Jax benched me right now," he said.

Sami nodded. "I know."

"Thank you for not saying anything." If he still had a heart, and he probably did, the pretty soldier had just claimed it for her own. "I guess it's you and me, huh?"

"Yeah. Tell me if you're struggling, if you feel off, and we'll figure it out."

His leg shot out as if a doctor had tested his reflexes. He frowned. "I'm still obsessing about you."

"Who can blame you? I'm awesome in bed." She grinned.

He swayed. His knees buckled, and he went down.

Sami dove for him, turning him and helping him land on his back. "Tace?"

"That was sudden," he ground out, his vision turning black. Fire flicked up his spine and exploded at the base of his neck. "It's happening more often and I'm blacking out more quickly." He moaned, and his body started to convulse.

A fist pounded on the door, but he couldn't move.

"What?" Sami bellowed.

"Greyson and several Mercs just stormed the castle without waiting for an invite," Jax yelled back. "They came for Damon. I need you two downstairs and now."

Tace's head thumped against the floor, and Sami pressed hand to his forehead.

"We're naked but will be right down," Sami called. She aned down, her mouth at his ear. "You'll be okay, Tace.

I promise." The soft kiss to his ear was the best sensation he'd ever felt, even though his body was disintegrating rapidly.

Tace ignored Jax's glare as he and Sami returned to the war room at least ten minutes after Jax had pounded on the door. "Sorry we're late."

Sami adjusted her shirt. "You wanted us to make up."

Damn, she was kind. Acting like they'd been having wild sex instead of his having seizures that had left his legs still weak. Tace drew out a chair for her before dropping into his own.

His hands shook, so he kept them under the table.

Greyson Storm sat at the table with Damon Winter next to him. The Merc leader wore a pissed-off expression. "Somebody could've sent word that Damon was all right here."

Jax shrugged from the head of the table. "We figured you'd send a scout at some point, and no way was I putting one of my guys at risk to send you a Candygram."

Lynne sat next to him with Vinnie and Raze on that side of the table.

Ah. Somebody had made sure Raze and Greyson were too far apart to start throwing punches. Smart.

"Then we'll be going now," Greyson said.

Maureen Shadow crossed into the room, tying her long hair up in a band and covering a yawn. "You called for me, Jax?" She stopped short at seeing Greyson at the table.

Grey sat up straighter. "Maureen. How are you?"

"Greyson." She dropped her arms to her sides, her face flushing a lovely pink. "What's going on here?"

Grey turned toward Jax. "Are you willing to let Maureen work on food resources in our territory?"

"Whoa." Maureen held up a hand. "I make my own decisions, men."

Sami nodded vigorously.

"We're willing to consider an agreement between Vanguard and the Mercenaries to develop food resources, if you'll provide us with ten soldiers for a mission up north," Jax said easily. "That is, if Maureen agrees, of course."

"Of course," Greyson said, his gaze remaining on Maureen.

Raze scowled at his sister. "I don't like this."

"You don't have to," Maureen returned.

"What's the mission?" Greyson asked.

"No questions asked. We just need ten more guys to attack a holding up north and steal ammunition and explosives. Then we can discuss food development." Jax crossed his arms.

"I'm in," Damon said.

"No." Jax shook his head. "The second part of the deal is that Damon stays here, undercover, and works his way into the Pure group. You'll have to denounce Merc territory as unsafe. Temporarily."

Greyson frowned at Damon. "What have you gotten into?"

"An undercover operation," Damon said, grinning. "They did save my life."

"So you said," Greyson muttered, obviously concerned for his friend. Hell, the leader had come himself to find Damon even after Jax had threatened to shoot him if he took one step inside Vanguard territory. Grey studied Maureen and then Jax. "Damon said the president's men attacked him."

Jax nodded.

"I'm guessing you're planning the dumbest thing you've done so far and attacking the president and his Elite Force. That's the only way you'd ask for my help." Grey glanced at Damon. "If we do this, it's all-out war with the president."

Damon lost his smile. "Anybody know if the Brigade is with the Elite Force?"

Jax shook his head. "Last we heard, nobody quite knew

where the Brigade ended up." He reached out and ran a hand down Lynne's arm. "The leader, McDougall, is married to Lynne's best friend, so we're hoping they're safe somewhere."

Greyson glanced at Lynne. "All right."

Jax eyed the Merc leader. "So. You in or out?"

Greyson met his gaze. "We're in, so long as Maureen agrees to come back to Merc territory and work on food resources after we get back. I want her word as well as yours, and I decide when she's finished. Oh, and half of the explosives are ours."

Jax looked up. "Moe?"

"Agreed," she said, giving her brother a look and obviously avoiding Grey's contemplative gaze.

What was up with those two? Jax nodded. "We have a deal. Let's start planning—I want to attack after dark tomorrow night."

Chapter Twenty-Four

No risk, no reward . . . but shit. This is fuckin' crazy.

—Jax Mercury

Sami held tight to Jax's waist as he expertly maneuvered the dirt bike through rubble and pieces of glass, her mind on Tace in the truck a mile or so behind them. While she understood the need to separate them, she didn't like it. Not one bit. What if he had another episode?

Barbara was covering Tace, and he was along only because he'd freaked out at the thought of being left behind. If he was anybody else, Jax would've shot him.

They reached Lake Tahoe and skirted the southern end, stopping at the edge of the park. Sami jumped off the bike and helped Jax hide it in the trees. "The mansion is a good choice for defense," she whispered.

The moon shone down, highlighting the harsh angles of Jax's face. "The president isn't an idiot."

She nodded and drew a knife from her back pocket. They'd stopped to gather ten Merc soldiers, and combined with the twenty Vanguard fighters, there were thirty of them. The plan was to infiltrate from three angles, not counting the lake. "I came here once on a Girl Scout trip," she whispered.

Jax lifted his head. "You were a Girl Scout?"

"Till I got kicked out." She grinned.

He nodded. "I told everyone you were forgiven because I need unity on the mission."

Her stomach dropped. "Am I forgiven?"

"Yes, but don't ever lie to me again." Jax's expression was edged with somber determination.

"I won't." Of course, she was keeping the full extent of Tace's problems from Jax. She'd made her choice, and her first loyalty was to Tace Justice. Sure it had happened quickly, but that didn't change the way she felt. If anybody could understand that fact, it'd be Jax, because of his feelings for Lynne. "Thanks for letting me stay at Vanguard."

Jax checked the clip of his gun. "You're family, Sami. No matter what you do, that's the beginning and the end of it."

Sami paused and warmth infused her. "Ah, Jax."

He looked up. "That doesn't mean I won't ground your ass at base for life if you fuck up again."

Yeah, he kind of sounded like an older brother. "Right."

"Are you and Justice on the same page now?"

She breathed out. "Well, if you consider us both lost in the woods along a windy trail with alligators snapping at our heels, then yeah, we're on the same page."

Jax tucked the gun away and frowned. "What the hell does that mean?"

The man really didn't work with analogies, did he? "We're finding our way."

"Ah." Jax unsnapped a knife from his calf. "So long as it doesn't get in the way of the mission, take your time. There's no hurry, you know."

"Says the guy who claimed Lynne as his own within hours of her arriving at Vanguard," Sami murmured.

He grinned. "She's mine. Time wouldn't have changed that fact."

The air changed just a bit, and Tace came into view with Raze and Barbara. Sami's shoulders settled, and her focus narrowed. All right. They had been working together for over a month, and there was comfort to be found in that.

Even if they were going on a suicide mission.

Raze crouched and unfolded a map they'd dug up to lay on the dirt. "I say we search the outbuildings before hitting the mansion. Chances are we'll find plenty of explosives stored close to the mansion but not inside."

Jax nodded. "Agreed. Each team either has a map or a set of drawings to find the outbuildings." He glanced up at the waning moon. "We might even have cloud cover for a while. If anybody gets a bead on the president or VP Lake, take them out. No hesitation."

"No problem," Tace said easily.

Jax gave a hand motion. "Let's go."

They moved through the trees silently, reaching the first of several outbuildings. The scent of pine surrounded them. Jax pried open the door. Old inner tubes and life jackets filled the shack along with spiderwebs and rat droppings.

They moved on. Jax suddenly held up a hand, and they all stopped.

Two men came into view, patrolling and smoking cigarettes. Idiots.

Jax and Raze stepped behind them, using headlocks to knock both guys out without much effort. "Tie 'em up," Jax said, motioning for Raze to follow him. "We'll take the five buildings closest to the mansion, and you three take the lake. Tace, if you have a problem, get out of the way."

"Copy that," Tace said easily.

Barbara lifted her gun from the holster. "We'll be fine, Jax." Her blue eyes were narrowed and determined.

"Agreed," Sami said. Good. She could keep an eye on his attacks. She helped Tace drag the unconscious Elite soldiers back to the shack while Barbara kept point, her gun sweeping the area for threats. Using fishing line, they tied and then gagged the men, shoving them inside. A spider crawled across Sami's boot, and she shivered, kicking it away.

Toward the lake, Tace mouthed.

Sami ducked low and crept along an overgrown trail, heading closer to the mansion beside the lake. The water lapped against rocks, and somewhere in the distance, an owl hooted impatiently. Tace followed her with Barbara bringing up the rear. The brunette kept pace easily, her movements sure and smooth.

Sami enjoyed working with another woman. They'd have to scout together more, especially now that Barbara was with Derek and Sami didn't feel guilty about Tace.

They reached the next shack, and she yanked open the door. Water jugs were piled high. Man, they needed those. Not as badly as they needed explosives, but it was tempting to go back for the truck.

Barbara shook her head, and Sami sighed, carefully shutting the door.

A gun fired, arcing a red flare above the lake. The water glowed as if an inferno burned beneath the surface. Shrill and loud, an alarm suddenly pierced the night. Gunfire pattered, and an explosion ripped through the air, sending smoke and fire flying high.

"Shit," Tace said, running ahead of her toward the next shack. "Get your gun out."

Sami followed him, tucking her knife away and drawing out her weapon. There was no need for stealth, as the sound of guns and men fighting overtook everything else. Her heart pounded, and adrenaline shot through her veins, bringing the night into focus.

Barbara followed her, gun ready.

Three men rounded the curve ahead.

Tace shoved Sami out of the way and fired.

She rolled and came up firing, hitting one of the guys in

the leg. He cried out and dropped, shooting toward her at the same time. She scrambled behind a tree.

Three shots echoed, and then Tace dropped into a slide to land next to her.

Barbara took cover on the opposite side, carefully aiming and hitting one Elite soldier between the eyes.

Sami sent her a thumbs-up.

Barbara nodded, her jaw set. She crouched low, her gun aimed toward the threat.

"She's a great shot," Sami whispered.

Tace nodded. "One more of them to bring down."

Raze rounded the nearest tree. "The shack to the left about fifty yards from here has explosives. Go get the truck, and we'll defend the position."

Tace nodded and grabbed Sami's arm, jerking her to her feet. He motioned toward Barbara. "Run."

Raze fired toward the threat, and Barbara ran across the road, coming alongside Sami. "Let's go," she whispered.

Sami launched into a run, ducking debris falling from the sky. What the hell had blown up? Her breath panted out, and she ran faster, skirting a stand of trees to reach the bike. "Where's the truck?"

Tace turned left and ran down a dirt road, his stride easy and fast.

Sami ducked her head and increased her pace, turning the corner to find the truck hidden among some trees. Barbara stopped short on her heels, her breathing smooth. The former paralegal had been working out.

Two Elite soldiers barreled around the front of the truck, already firing.

Barbara yelled and tackled Sami to the ground. Tace partially turned and fired twice, hitting the soldiers center mass. He followed up with head shots, and the bodies thumped against the ground.

Sami struggled beneath Barbara. "Barb?" She shoved the

soldier off her, and Barbara rolled onto her back. Blood welled from Barbara's neck, and her eyes bugged out. Her mouth moved, but only a gurgle came out. "Tace!" Sami yelled, her breath heated.

Tace ran over and slid onto his knees, his hand going to Barbara's neck. He winced. "Hold on, Barb. You'll be okay."

The soldier's eyes softened.

Tace slipped a hand behind her neck to support her head.

Sami grabbed the woman's hand. "Can we sew her up?" Gunfire echoed behind them, and she partially ducked over Barbara. God, they had to save her. They couldn't lose Barb.

A slight smile curved Barbara's mouth. Blood spurted from the neck wound. "Vanguard," she whispered.

Tears filled Sami's eyes, and pain clawed through her gut. It was too late. There was no way to save the young woman. "Vanguard."

Barbara's eyes closed, and her body relaxed into death.

Sami sobbed out a cough. "Barb?"

Tace slowly lowered her to the ground. "She's gone, baby. The bullet went through her jugular and out her spine."

"Barbara?" Sami asked, patting the woman's chest. "It was so fast."

Tace nodded and stood, helping Sami up before lifting Barbara into the back of the truck and covering her with a blanket. "She was a good soldier."

"An even better friend," Sami murmured, her heart physically hurting like she'd been stabbed.

"We need to get back there." Tace moved away from the truck bed and then stopped short.

"What?" Sami swung around, gun out, looking for the threat.

Tace reached for the driver's door and fell forward, face first. His forehead hit the door, and the metal crunched inward. He slid all the way down.

Oh God. Sami rushed to him and tried to lift him up. "Tace!"

He was out cold and limp as a rag. She dropped him and yanked open the door. "Tace, wake up."

The man lay in a crumpled mass, his gun falling to the side.

She grabbed the gun and tossed it on the dash before reaching for his armpits. Man, he was heavy. She grunted and tried to pull him toward the truck, her arms protesting. Tace was solid muscle and as dead weight, she couldn't get him into the seat.

Panic and frustration had her looking wildly around. Could she leave him in the trees? What if they had to drive a different way to get out?

"Tace, wake up." She shook him.

Nothing. Man, he'd gone down fast this time. All right. Holding on to his shoulders, she scooted around and stepped into the truck, balancing on her knees on the seat. Using all her strength, she yanked him up and fell back while keeping a tight hold.

His big body banged against the passenger seat and door-frame, but his shoulders were above the seat.

Tears pricked her eyes, and sweat broke out on her chest. She banished the thought of Barbara's body from her mind—she'd grieve later. She pulled harder, finally getting his torso on the seat. Good.

She turned and jumped out the passenger-side door, trying to shove his legs and feet in. He half fell onto the floor, his head still on the seat. Holding her breath, she leaned over and felt his wrist. Pulse weak but there. Thank God.

No way could she get him buckled in.

She shut the door and ignited the engine. Carefully backing out, she tried to calm her racing heart and concentrate. If she didn't do this right, they'd both be dead.

So she drove along the dirt road and then punched the

gas, speeding up and yanking left to head toward the storage shack Raze had mentioned. There were several dirt roads. God, she hoped she'd found the right one.

The sky blazed orange and black from a burning fire. Had they blown up the mansion? Was it Greyson's men or had Vanguard soldiers done so?

She caught sight of a firefight up ahead and drove straight for it, swinging the ass end of the truck around at a storage unit.

Raze leaped from the unit and tossed boxes in the back of the truck. They were throwing explosives into the truck. What if one went off? Sami looked down at Tace, who hadn't moved.

Shit. She jumped from the truck where Jax and several Vanguard soldiers protected the shack from Elite soldiers advancing from the south. Merc soldiers guarded and fired from behind trees to the north. The lake was to the east.

She ran to help Raze.

"Where's Barbara?" he asked, muscles in his arms bulging as he carried two heavy boxes.

Sami swallowed and shook her head, pointing to the small blanketed form in the front of the truck bed.

Raze paused, his jaw ticking. His hands clenched. "Ah, shit."

Sami nodded, her chest aching like she'd been punched.

Raze's jaw hardened. "Rest in peace, sweetheart."

Tears pricked Sami's eyes again.

"Fall apart later, Sam. Mission now." He pointed to a bunch of crates. "Everything. Get it all."

The guy was right. Deal now, feel later. She bent her knees to grab a crate of what looked like C4. Maybe. She'd only seen the stuff on television. The box was heavy, and her back ached, but she hustled to the back of the truck and shoved it in, careful not to disturb Barbara's body.

"Where's Justice?" Raze asked over the gunfire.

"Out cold." Sami turned back for another crate.

A bullet impacted the shack above her head, and Raze knocked her inside with his shoulder. She stumbled and regained her balance, half hunched over.

"Stay in here and hand me boxes," he ordered, lifting two crates and heading back outside.

"No." She lifted a crate, and the top fell off. Her breath stopped cold. Grenades. She was holding a huge box of grenades, people were shooting at her, and there was a fire roaring out of control. Smoke filled the air.

Raze returned and caught sight of the grenades. "Perfect." He took the box and disappeared.

"If they hit the truck, everything will blow," Sami yelled, reaching for a stack of semiautomatic weapons.

"Yep." Raze returned, wiping blood off his forehead.

"Were you hit?" she asked, reaching for him.

"Scraped." Raze pivoted and put his body between her and the door. "I said to grab boxes."

"I don't work for you." If he was going to put himself in danger, so was she. Worse yet, Tace was defenseless in the front of the cab, and Barbara's body lay in the back. The woman deserved a burial.

Bullets sprayed through the right side of the shack, and Sami tackled Raze to the ground.

"Defend to the west," Raze bellowed, jumping up and in front of Sami.

More gunfire echoed, and somebody screamed in pain.

"Hurry," Sami said, scrambling to her feet. Her ears rang, and her head ached. Smoke was messing with her equilibrium, or maybe that was adrenaline.

Jax crashed through the door with two guys on him.

Sami leaped up and kicked one in the chin, throwing him back outside. She followed, going into training mode, using her feet to stop his advances, her father's lessons in her head. The guy was of medium build with angry blue eyes. His knife flashed, and she pivoted, bending his hand back until he dropped it.

She threw an elbow into his gut, went up into his chin, and punched him dead center in the temple. He fell hard.

"Nice," Raze said, throwing the second unconscious guy toward the lake. The man landed, rolled, bounced, and then smashed into a narrow pine tree.

"My dad was the best," she said, more than thankful for her odd upbringing.

"Wish I could've met him," Jax said, hauling three more crates outside.

"Sami." Raze bent at the waist to lift two long crates. "Grab the other end."

She hurried over and slipped her hands beneath the bottom crate, her mind on Tace. He should've gained consciousness by now. This was a bad sign.

"Where's Justice?" Jax ran back inside and tucked handguns into a backpack.

"Out cold," Raze said, leading the way with the crate.

"Is Barbara covering the road?" Jax asked.

Sami grabbed his arm. "No. She was hit and didn't make it. She's in the front of the truck bed."

Jax faltered, and his face lost all color. He drew in air, and fury lit his brown eyes. "Copy that."

Sami shivered. The Vanguard leader felt every death as if he'd caused it. "Barbara was a soldier, Jax. She knew the risks."

Jax didn't answer but tossed the backpack as well as what looked like grenade launchers and a couple of weird missile-looking things into the back of the truck by the boxes. Gunfire erupted all around them. "Sami, go now with the truck. We'll follow up."

She slammed the tailgate into place and hurried around the truck.

"Wait at rendezvous point B for thirty minutes," Jax

yelled, running toward the other end of the shack. "If we're not there, get to Vanguard."

"Avoid Mercenary territory," Raze bellowed, taking the other side.

Sami yanked open the driver's-side door just as pain exploded in her shoulder. Blood sprayed from her to coat the metal. Her vision wavered, her stomach rolled, and darkness fell.

Chapter Twenty-Five

Some men are destined for greatness, while others hunt it down and make it submit.

—President of the United States Bret Atherton

Tace awakened the second Sami fell, and his brain instantly kicked into gear. Gunfire roared all around them, and an explosion rocked the earth yards away. "Fuck." He plunged across the seat and grasped her arms, yanking her inside the cab. A quick glance into the truck bed confirmed they were carrying every sort of explosive imaginable as well as Barbara's body. "Double fuck."

He set Sami across the seat with her head in his lap and quickly twisted the ignition. Yanking the door shut, he punched the gas. "Sami?"

She didn't move, and blood covered the front of her shirt.

Bullets pinged into the side of the truck, and the back window shattered.

The rear end fishtailed, but he kept up the pressure, driving the vehicle between a series of trees and down the dirt road. His stomach hurt, and needles poked the back of his eyes, but he shoved the pain away. "Sami!"

Nothing.

How long had he been out? He drove faster and weeds scraped the truck. Wind and smoke billowed in through the shattered window, and glass cut down his neck. Where was everybody?

He tried to gather as much of Sami as possible in his lap to protect her from the glass, feeling her neck for a pulse. Good. Strong and steady.

Two four-wheelers barreled out of the forest, and shock took him for one instant as he recognized the president and vice president. They were joining in the fight? The VP was known to be a soldier, but the president usually hid behind shields.

No more, apparently.

Vice President Lake, his blue eyes sizzling, drew out an automatic weapon.

"Shit." Tace jerked the wheel and pressed his foot down as hard as he could, aiming straight for the asshole. The truck bumper clipped the four-wheeler and it spun out of control, tipping end over end, leaving Lake crumpled in a heap. One down.

The president fired a gun, and something exploded. The truck jumped into the air, and Tace fought to keep it straight. They landed hard, swerved, and skidded into a tree. They rocked, and glass sprayed down his back. Fuck. The president had shot out a tire. When had the bastard gotten so damn brave?

Tace jumped from the truck, his hand going for his gun . . . which wasn't there.

Atherton rolled to a stop, his gun pointed at Tace's head. "Tace Justice," he murmured, shoving designer sunglasses up his nose.

Tace took several deep breaths, searching around for backup. Where the hell were Raze and Jax? "You know my name."

"Oh, I'm getting extensive reports on all Vanguard members, though I hadn't expected this attack from you rebels." The president had light brown hair, blue eyes, and classic good looks. Since Scorpius, he'd filled out into lean muscle and apparently liked to engage in gun battles.

The firefight continued down the road.

"We like to keep our enemies on their toes," Tace returned, measuring the distance between them. He'd have to attack and cover Sami at the same time.

"You think Mercury will stop fighting if I return with a gun to your head?" Atherton asked.

Tace leaned back against the door to shut it. Maybe Atherton hadn't seen Sami. "No. Jax will shoot me before he'll let you use me as a bargaining chip."

"Yes, I would, too." Atherton craned his neck toward his fallen comrade. "Lake? You dead?"

The vice president didn't even groan.

"You should go check on him," Tace said, his trigger finger itching for a gun.

"I don't suppose you brought sweet Lynne Harmony or even Vinnie Wellington with you?" Atherton asked, leaning forward on his handle bars but keeping a steady aim with the gun.

"The two women you kidnapped and then lost?" Tace forced a smile. "Nope. You snooze, you lose."

"Hmmm. Well, I'll have to make do with the brunette in the truck. She still alive?" Atherton asked.

Shit. He'd seen Sami. "She had better be," Tace said evenly, his heart rate speeding up as he tried to control himself. Fear and rage attacked him with sharp blades, and he coughed out, his lungs heating. Raw and dangerous emotions darkened the edge of his vision. Not now. He couldn't have an attack now. "We're at a standstill, Atherton."

The president laughed and swung off his vehicle. "I like your style, Justice. Sorry I have to kill you." He set his stance and aimed.

In a burst of power, Tace dropped into a fast slide, feet out. The second he lost momentum, he rolled and leaped up, tackling the president across his four-wheeler. The gun went spinning through the air.

Atherton hit Tace in the throat and kneed him in the groin.

Pure agony detonated in Tace's balls. He grunted and punched the president in the nose.

"Tace?" Sami said, her voice weak.

He half turned to see her climbing from the truck, her expression disoriented.

"Sami." He shrugged off the president and looked frantically for the gun.

Atherton sliced at him with a knife. Where had the knife come from?

Tace jumped back, pain prickling his wrist.

Sami fell to the ground and slowly drew a gun from her boot with her good arm.

Atherton bellowed and jumped back on his vehicle, spinning it around and spraying dirt.

Sami wavered but lifted her arm.

Atherton barreled down the road.

Sami shot several times, her aim wide.

Tace gritted his teeth and ran for her, already yanking off his shirt to press against her wound. "How bad?"

"I don't know." Her head rested back on the dirty truck.

He lifted her, ignoring his bleeding wrist. "Keep pressure on it."

She winced and put her hand over the shirt, tears sliding down her pretty face.

He scooted her over and started the engine. "We're going as far as we can on the rim, and then we'll have to change vehicles or find a spare." Finding a spare was the better idea. "As soon as it's safe, I'll take a look at your wound. Just stay with me, okay?"

She turned, her face pale, blood dotting her neck. "Yes, Tace. I promise." Then she passed out again.

He set her head in his lap and punched the gas, wincing as the truck rocked and then slowly moved into action. There had been a series of park ranger trucks about two miles down the road. If he could get there without incident, he could change the tire and go find medical supplies for Sami.

He maneuvered around trees while reaching down to feel the pulse in her wrist. Steady and strong although a little slow. "You'll be okay, baby." He said the words to reassure them both. She had to be okay.

Sami held her shoulder, not sure if numbness was a good sign or not. But she'd stopped bleeding, so the injury couldn't be that bad. They'd driven for a while, and she had passed out for a bit, but now they were going through a small neighborhood south of Lake Tahoe. A handmade sign proclaimed an older home as a place to rent trucks.

"Perfect." Tace turned down a long driveway littered with rocks and foliage. Two beaten-up trucks were parked next to the rough siding on the house, and darkness showed from within. A large metal shop, probably bigger than the house, rose up in the back. He drove around the home, and the moon shone down, illuminating a big, empty back courtyard. Oil and gasoline stained the concrete. One lone truck was parked over by the shop and had jeans-clad legs hanging out. "Hold on." He jumped out and left the engine running.

She nodded.

He used a small penlight he always kept and ran for the truck, cautiously looking inside. He moved a little and then returned. "Old guy has been dead at least a month. No obvious injuries—probably Scorpius."

Sami winced and looked toward the house. "Might be bodies inside." She couldn't handle the smell right now—she just couldn't.

"Yeah." Tace reached over and patted her thigh. "I'll take care of it. We have to fix your shoulder. Stay here."

He turned and disappeared through the back door of the house.

Silence pounded outside the vehicle. The wind swirled newspapers, mail, and pine needles around the courtyard. When Tace returned and opened her door, she jumped.

"I think the guy lived alone. No bodies inside, and it doesn't look like he packed to leave." Tace reached past her to turn off the engine and then lifted her, carrying her into a small mudroom with an ancient washer and dryer. Men's work clothes hung from metal pegs, and the place smelled like musty dishcloths and cigar smoke. He continued into a living area with a worn chintz sofa and matching easy chair facing a boxy television with a dusty satellite dish controller on top.

"What about Barbara?" Sami asked.

Tace paused. "I made sure the body stayed covered, and it'll be better in the back of the truck."

Sami winced when he set her down on the sofa. Dust wafted up. "Remember the days of television?"

"Barely. Let me look." Tace gently pulled her hand away from her arm. "The bullet sliced you, darlin'." He pointed the penlight closer. "A couple of stitches should do it." He stood and noted a lantern on the floor, quickly igniting it. The room glowed a soft yellow. "I bet this guy had a first aid kit. If not in the house, then in the shop. Just hold on."

Sami nodded and leaned her head back to rest. The place felt empty and kind of sad, but maybe there was food in the kitchen. A bachelor ought to have tons of canned food. She should get her butt off the sofa and start scavenging, because they couldn't waste any opportunity. Yet the sofa was just so darn comfortable.

She thought of Barbara again, and her eyes welled.

"Eureka." Tace came back into the room with a kit and a prescription bottle. "Take one." He handed over a pill.

She shook her head, even though her right side ached.

"Take it, or I'll help you do it." Tace leaned in. "We're safe for a while here, and then we have to get on the road again. So you're going to take this very nice pain pill and let your body relax. Trust me."

Relaxing without pain? Man, she wanted to be all tough and defiant, but no pain for a few moments was just too tempting. She took the pill and swallowed the entire thing without gagging.

"Thank you." He set out the materials. "This is gonna hurt, and I'm sorry." Without waiting for her to comment, he lifted her shirt over her head. "Hold on."

She nodded and curled her fingers into the sofa.

Tace slipped the needle in, and pain rippled through her. "You okay?"

"Fine," she said, her teeth gritted. "It's not that bad."

He grinned. "You're tough, baby. You really are." He bent his head and continued, his movements sure and careful. Finally, he sat back and plastered antibacterial gel and a bandage over the wound. The minor surgery had hurt but not nearly as much as she'd expected. "All better," Tace murmured.

She smiled as the pain pill started taking effect. "I'm fine."

"Good." He tugged her forward to look at her back. "You have a couple of scrapes but nothing bad." He ran the pad of his finger along the VANGUARD tattoo across her left shoulder blade before sitting her back up. "If you're up to it, why don't you raid the kitchen while I go find a spare tire for the truck? I'd like to be on the road in an hour. We'll be in full light for most of the trip as it is." He frowned, and those blue eyes darkened. "I don't think we should stay put, especially since we have all the explosives. If the president regroups faster than we hoped, I'd rather be on the road than trapped here."

"Agreed." She pushed up from the sofa. The president would be looking for those explosives, and they needed to be safely behind Vanguard fences. "Go fix the tire." They both needed to deal with Barbara's death once they were safe.

He dropped a quick kiss to her forehead and then turned to go back through the kitchen.

She stilled and touched her head. Her silly heart jumped. Then she took the lantern and walked toward the red brick fireplace to the left. Framed pictures were stacked all over, showing the evolution of a family. Mom and Dad with three kids. Then grandkids. Then grandparents—just the two of them.

She reached for a pink funeral notice for Eugenia Flangston from nine years ago. Apparently, Mr. Flangston had been a bachelor for nine years. Sami rubbed her chest. Had he died alone in his truck?

She cleared her throat and moved toward the bathroom, finding toilet paper, lotions, and some over-the-counter medication that she put in a shower caddy. There were clothes still in the dresser in the bedroom, and a feminine vanity sat in the corner with perfume bottles still on top. Sami moved toward the vanity, feeling like a thief but curious. Who had Eugenia been?

Yarn and needles took up one drawer, while letters from Albert Flangston when he'd been in the service so long ago were stacked in another drawer and wrapped with a hair ribbon. Sami opened another drawer and gasped at a beautiful green rosary. She hadn't had one in so long. She picked it up, and the beads felt right in her hands.

"Tire is fixed. You find anything?" Tace asked from the doorway.

She jumped and turned, her shoulders hunching. "This."

Tace looked at the beads. "I'm sure she would've wanted somebody to have it, you know? Somebody to use it."

Sami nodded and slipped the rosary into her pocket. "Yeah. I would've wanted somebody to pray over mine, if I'd left it somewhere." She carefully put Albert's letters back into the drawer where they belonged. "I'll check the other bedroom."

"I'm going to go scout through the shop for anything, and I found a shotgun in the truck with the body. There was a full box of shells in the glovebox, too. Hit the kitchen after the other bedroom, would you?" Tace looked her over, nodded, and turned on his heel.

She breathed in the quiet room that had probably seen the Flangstons through decades. "I hope you're together now," she whispered into the silence. The time of houses and generations and tradition was past. Families like the Flangstons were in the past. Life was different now, but maybe someday there would be nice families raising kids in a house like this one again. She said a quick prayer for all of them and turned for the other bedroom.

The living needed supplies.

Chapter Twenty-Six

Sanity is for wimps.

—Dr. Vinnie Wellington

Sami's shoulder ached and her head pounded when they arrived back at Vanguard around three in the afternoon. The pain pill had definitely worn off. Raze and Jax ran outside the fence to reach them almost immediately.

"Status?" Jax barked, bruises along his jawline and down his neck.

Tace stretched from the truck and crossed to lift her out.

"I'm fine," she protested halfheartedly, wanting to snuggle into his neck and sleep for a month.

"Right. We had to stop to change the tire and then find supplies to stitch her up," Tace said, his wrist bandaged. "Then we took back roads to avoid detection, and now here we are."

The sun blasted down, and Sami tried unsuccessfully to swallow. "Did we lose any more soldiers besides Barbara?"

"We lost three total and the Mercs lost two," Raze said, yanking a tarp Tace had found off the weapons and explosives. "Several wounded in the infirmary."

"I'll see to them after I get Sami settled," Tace said, starting for the fence.

"I have inner-territory doctors with them. Right now I

need you in the war rooms to strategize our attack on the Bunker," Jax said, motioning for several men to fetch the explosives. "We go tomorrow night."

Sami nodded. "The president will be sending men to retaliate, Jax. We'll have to go before they can come up with a plan."

"We're done for the day, Jax. Sami and I will be in the war rooms first thing tomorrow morning to plan." Tace didn't wait for a response. "You guys get Barbara's body, and let us know when Derek wants the funeral."

Sami paused. "Oh, God. Derek. I should—"

"It's my job," Jax said from behind her. "I'll talk to him."

Sami snuggled into Tace's chest, allowing his strength to comfort her for the moment. She'd lost so many people, it was surprising it still hurt so much. Yet the mission continued on, and she had to think, damn it. She blew out warm air. "We'll need to leave late afternoon or early evening."

"Not we," Tace countered, striding toward the fence and going through the opening. "You're not coming to the Bunker."

She looked up at his strong jawline. "Yes, I am."

"You were shot a few hours ago," he said, crossing the parking lot and heading inside Vanguard, where cooler air brushed her face. Somebody had replaced the glass door with one covered in unicorn stickers.

Sami stiffened, and pain lanced down her arm. "You were stabbed."

"Not bad enough to need stitches," he said, climbing the stairs.

"I'm the only one who has been to the Bunker," Sami said, her eyelids closing for a moment. Man, her head hurt. What she wouldn't give for an ordinary little aspirin. "I'm going on the mission, Tace." From day one, she'd known deep down that she'd have to return at some point.

"You can give us the schematics tomorrow morning." Tace strode down the hallway and shoved open her door with his shoulder. "I keep forgetting you need a lock."

She shook her head, her stomach aching. "I'm a soldier in Vanguard, Tace." It was the first time in her life she really fit in and had found a calling. "You either get that or you don't." Not once had she asked him to be anybody other than who he was. Or rather, who he was becoming. Now she had to save him.

"You need to heal that shoulder."

"I'm the only one who can hack into the system and get the data we need," she said. "If the computers are still functional with generators, and I think they are, then I'm needed."

He paused and kicked the door shut. "I hadn't thought of that."

She leaned up and nuzzled beneath his jaw. "That's 'cause you think I'm a badass soldier. You should see me hack into a secured computer system."

He kicked off his boots, still holding her against his broad chest. "I've never considered computers sexy before right now." Without missing a beat, he strode across the room and sat on the bed. "I'm fighting the dual sides of myself."

She blinked. "That's awfully self-aware."

"I know, right?" He nuzzled along her ear.

She shivered. "Talk it out."

"All right. Part of me wants to see you in your glory hacking, I really do. The other half wants to tie you to the bed where you'll be safe until we get back." He sounded more thoughtful than determined at this point. "Both avenues hold merit for me."

"Ah." His hard thighs heated her butt, and she shifted to get more comfortable. Desire warmed through her, but she had to concentrate. "Not for nothin', but maybe you're the one who should sit this out." She braced for his temper.

"Yeah, I've thought about that."

"Geez, you're awfully reasonable all of a sudden," she whispered.

"Eh." He lifted a shoulder and nearly dislodged her. "I'm sure it's temporary. I'm feeling a momentary relief from all the damn emotions that keep taking me over. Guess I should try to be reasonable as long as I can."

There was the old Tace—or at least a semblance of him.

He cleared his throat. "With the people you studied— what was the progression of the illness?"

Her heart dropped. "It was quick, Tace. One day passing out, the next . . ."

"I figured." He sighed and kissed her forehead. "Each attack has been more sudden and worse than the last. But you saw this enzyme or whatever it was work?"

"Yeah. It was like an EpiPen for somebody suffering an allergic reaction. Very quick." She tried to reassure him. "We'll get the cure, shoot it into your ass, and you'll develop some sort of antibodies that'll make you stop rejecting the vitamin B concoction. I mean, I think. I saw it work but don't really know the science behind it." She should've paid more attention.

"My ass?" he asked.

"Yep. That's where they put it." She reached up to cup his jaw. "It'll be all right. I promise."

"Well then." He leaned down and captured her lips, warmth and promise in his kiss.

She moaned and opened for him, her tongue dueling with his. He turned and gently, so gently, placed her on the bed and removed her clothes. Her body rioted, and her brain short-circuited. "I don't want soft."

"You're injured." He swept both palms down her arms, avoiding her new stitches.

"We're always injured," she said, avoiding the bruises on his neck and the wrapping on his wrist. Oh, they had shit to deal with, but she needed to get lost for a while. Pain was constant and pleasure rare. Losing Barbara had left Sami's chest aching, and she needed to run away from death for the moment. "Please. Let's just forget reality for a short time."

He shucked his clothes, those dark eyes watching her the entire time. "Tomorrow is gonna be dangerous."

"Yeah," she said softly. Attacking the president was risky, while taking on the Bunker was downright insane. "Not all of us are going to make it back—we need to know that." But Tace had to survive. Taking the risk for him was worth it.

"You'll make it back," he murmured, leaning over her, his big body bracketed on his elbows. "I promise. No matter what, you'll get home safely."

"Home." She ran both hands through his hair, her body instantly primed and ready for him. "I feel like this is home." Finally.

He grinned and nipped her bottom lip, donning a condom and settling himself between her legs. His warmth soothed her, and his nearness ignited all sorts of tingles. "Don't get too attached to LA, sweetheart. We're gonna have to move and soon."

"I wasn't talking about the place," she murmured, vulnerability suddenly swamping her.

His head lifted just a bit. "You're home to me, too." With the soft words, he slowly entered her, filling her completely.

She breathed out, letting her body adjust. Tears pricked the back of her eyes. Loss had become a constant in the post-Scorpius world, but the idea of losing Tace Justice hurt somewhere deeper inside than she'd ever known. "Tace."

"It'll be all right." He repeated her words, kissing her, promise and hope in his kiss. And something else. Something concrete and just for her.

He started to move, and she dug her nails into his back, taking all he had to give. She climbed high, much more than her body engaged with him. Taken over by him. Heat flashed and uncoiled inside her. She arched and cried out his name, ripples of pure pleasure assailing her.

She came down with a soft whimper, and he shuddered against her, kissing her deep.

Finally, he lifted his head, those eyes dark and intent. "It's you and me, Sami. No matter what."

Tace lay on his back with Sami half sprawled on top of him, sleeping quietly, her body bare. She'd fought him, but he'd insisted she take another pain pill. He leaned over and traced the VANGUARD tattoo beneath her left shoulder. He'd tagged her with it over a month ago, and the lines were feminine and deadly, just like the woman herself. He'd nearly swallowed his tongue that first time she'd taken off her shirt.

Of course, he'd been whole then. Healthy and mentally stable. Or at least as mentally stable as was possible after most of the world had died.

His body ached for Barbara and for the life she could've had with Derek. Anger sizzled through him. There had been too many of the president's soldiers still standing, even though Tace had killed the one who'd shot Barbara.

Poor sweet Barbara with her kitten.

He wouldn't survive if he lost Sami. He knew that without question.

She lifted her head and blinked, her brown eyes soft. "Did you sleep?"

"Yes," he lied.

She stretched her neck. "How long was I out?"

"A few hours. It's not dawn yet. You should go back to sleep." He ran a hand down her hair, luxuriating in the softness.

Pink tinged her cheeks. "I'm on top of you."

His eyebrows rose, and his body temperature followed suit. "I've noticed that."

"How are you feeling?"

Crazy, obsessive, possessive, protective, determined, sad, angry . . . "Fine. I'm feeling healthy." But the attacks had stopped giving him any warning, so within seconds he could be out cold again. Yet he swept his hand down the curve of her back to her sweet butt. "I love your ass."

She grinned, the look all sauce. "Oh yeah?" Moving carefully, she rose to sit on his abs, her legs on either side of his waist. "You have a great butt, Texas. Do all Texans have butts like yours?"

He reached up to play with her breasts, and her nipples sharpened instantly. The woman was beyond responsive. "I never looked." His voice roughened, and his dick hardened. He tweaked both nipples just enough to add a bite of pain, and she gasped, pressing down on him. Yeah. He'd known she'd be a wildcat in bed. Now, if they could both just make it through the day without getting shot, stabbed, or bruised, maybe they could really play and have some fun. "You're beautiful, Sami."

She raised her butt up. "So are you."

"Wait." He reached for his jeans to grab a condom. "Any chance you found birth control pills in that bathroom?"

"No." She smiled. "Even if I had, one month wouldn't do it. It's condoms for us."

Yet what if he wanted to see a little guy with his eyes and her hair? Or her eyes and his hair? The idea that it might never be possible hit him like a sledgehammer to the gut.

She grasped the condom and ripped open the foil with her teeth. "You sure you're ready?"

He grabbed her ass and fought a grin. "Yeah."

"I'm not sure." She scooted down and licked the tip of his cock.

Jesus. He almost lifted off the entire bed from raw pleasure. "Sami."

"That's me." She grasped the base of his shaft and settled her mouth over him, pretty much killing him right then and here. The woman hummed, and he felt it in his balls. She played, taking him in her mouth, using her hands, until he was a sweating jumble of nerves.

"That's it." He grabbed her hair and tugged her mouth away from him. "Put on the condom."

She pouted. "I'm not done."

"Now." He growled it, unable to stop himself.

Triumph lifted her lips, and she slowly, way too slowly, rolled the rubber down over him.

He grasped her hips, careful of her injury, and rolled her onto her back.

She chuckled and opened her legs.

He plunged in with one hard stroke to the hilt.

She stiffened and then sighed, her arms going around his upper torso. "Tace." She leaned in and bit his shoulder.

Sparks of pleasure surrounded his dick along with impossibly wet and hot heat. He grasped her hip and started to move, shoving inside her, increasing the strength of his thrusts. Pillows fell to the floor. He pounded into her, hard and forceful, enjoying the bite of her nails in his skin. She gasped and her body tightened.

Oh yeah. She was there.

He altered the angle of his thrusts, hit her clit, and she clenched his dick so tight he saw stars. Waves pummeled through her body, transferred to his, and he shoved inside her and came hard.

They panted against each other, and he leaned back to kiss her, going deep.

Finally, he drew back.

Her pretty lips curved in a smile. "So *now* you kiss me."

He chuckled, and the perfectness of the moment shattered him. God, he couldn't lose her. They had to find the cure.

Chapter Twenty-Seven

*I always thought love would be sweetness and daisies . . .
not the abyss and raw need.*

—Sami Steel

The closer they drew to Century City, the more difficult it
became for Sami to breathe. They'd gone over the plan so
many times during the day that she had it memorized in full.
Yet now that the convoy had reached the nicer part of Los
Angeles, or what used to be the nicer part, a panic attack
threatened to steal her concentration.

They'd buried Barbara first thing in the morning, and
Tace had brought her kitten to Sami's room since Derek
ended up being allergic. The mechanic had wept during the
service.

So had Sami while clutching her rosary. How many
people had to die?

"Mission, baby," Tace murmured. "Focus on right now."

She nodded.

The Plaza building had thirty floors aboveground, so
there was no way to infiltrate via the roof. There had to be
escape tunnels built into the facility, but she had no idea
where they led to or from.

As assault plans went, they were operating in the dark.

Literally and figuratively. The idea of seeing Dr. Ramirez again, if he was still alive, made her want to throw up.

They parked and quickly exited the vehicle from behind a deserted and silent bank building that had at least fifty floors.

A team moved in from each direction, leaving getaway vehicles and medical supplies exactly three blocks from the target. If one escape route was blocked, they had three more chances.

Six Vanguard and Mercenary soldiers composed each team . . . a total of twenty-four people in all. It was the most either group could afford to lose.

Sami's group of six included Tace, Jax, Raze, Greyson, and Damon. Grey and Damon had gotten in a blowup about Damon's participating, but the ex-cop wouldn't be dissuaded. They'd left without letting the Pure church know he was part of the team. Hopefully.

"Remember the good old days with radio communications and earpieces?" Jax muttered to Raze.

"I'm still not talking to you," Raze countered, shoving a knife into his boot.

"You just did," Jax said.

Sami shimmied a bulletproof vest over her head and secured the Velcro. "Boys. Now isn't the time to fight, although I think Raze was correct." The soldier had insisted, rather loudly, that Jax needed to stay behind and lead Vanguard in case they didn't make it out.

Jax had disagreed—just as loudly.

"I'm a soldier, Raze. That ain't never gonna change," Jax said, glancing up at the waning moon and securing his own vest.

"If you get shot, I'm not hauling your ass out," Raze retorted.

"Ditto," Jax snapped.

"Knock it off." Sami carefully slipped a backpack ove

her arms, which held grenades and C4. The haul from the president's safe house had been scarily impressive. Good thing she was with people who were familiar with the weapons and explosives. She'd only seen such things on television and still wasn't sure of the official names for some of the devices.

Tace grabbed a rocket launcher and hefted it over one shoulder. Sweat dotted his forehead, and his pupils had dilated.

She moved toward him. "Are you okay?" she whispered while everyone else suited up.

He nodded.

She elbowed him in the gut and hit his vest. She winced. He glanced down. *Can't see out of my left eye,* he mouthed.

Shit. "Let me know if it gets bad enough you can't move," she whispered. While leaving him at the truck might be a safer move, if he had another attack, it might be his last. They needed the syringe for him and right now.

What if she couldn't find the right enzyme? What if the Bunker was out of the stuff? She shook off her fears and waited for the "go" sign.

Jax motioned for everyone to gather. "We have no idea how many soldiers they have or what kind of patrols they do. Keep an ear out . . . and if possible, knock out and secure instead of kill. Remember, these folks might think they're still working for the US government."

Sami shivered. "Some of the soldiers might not even be aware of the experiments. But who knows."

Greyson turned to Damon. "If it's you or them . . ."

"Copy that," Damon said. "Mercy is a luxury."

Sami swallowed. For two months she'd served as a soldier in the Vanguard territory, but she wasn't trained as a soldier. Not really. She could fight, and she could hack . . . and that was about it. Mercy was more than a luxury to her—it was a necessity. Even heading back into hell, she'd hold on to that. But if it came down to Tace or mercy, she'd choose Tace every time.

"Stay at my side," Tace ordered, his voice low and strong.

She glanced up.

He nodded. "I'm fine. Vision cleared."

Good. "The labs are on A-floor." She wiped a hand across her eyes. "If they're still secured, I'm sure the scientists have changed the passwords, so I'll need to hack before we can get to medicine or the cells." She'd tried to warn them about what they'd find in the cells if the scientists had found more test subjects after she'd let so many free, but words didn't do it. "Proceed with extreme caution if there are more experiments taking place."

"Affirmative," Jax said, eyeing his watch. "Go. Now."

She ducked and followed Raze around the skyscraper, hugging the building. Deserted luxury vehicles, even a couple of limos, were still parked at the curb. Glass littered the sidewalks from early looters, and wires from a smashed ATM spiraled out from the corner.

A couple of one hundred dollar bills still hung out of the machine.

She passed the useless money, keeping low, her body on full alert.

Raze stopped and held up a hand. The squad halted, guns out and ready. He made another hand gesture, lifting his head to listen. Then he held up two fingers and slid his gun into his vest, reaching for a knife.

Without making a sound, he turned the corner with Jax on his heels. Tace edged to the side in case he needed to set down the launcher.

Several grunts sounded.

Sami dodged behind Jax and stopped short at the sight of two Bunker soldiers out cold on the ground. They wore the blue fatigues she remembered, but she didn't recognize either of the men.

Raze searched the unconscious soldiers, securing three knives and four guns.

Then he gave the high sign, and they were on their way again.

They encountered two more soldiers and left them unconscious and tied up as well. Finally, they reached the Plaza building.

The windows reflected the moonlight, but still revealed the inside. The reception desk ran along the far northern wall, while a bank of elevators took up the entire south and west with a stairwell adjacent.

They just had to get to the stairwell and climb a few flights before trying to force open elevator doors.

The lobby had always been well guarded, so they planned to go in the back service door, hoping it wasn't too well secured.

"You escaped out the front door," Jax muttered, shaking his head.

Yeah, she knew exactly how lucky she'd been. "We created chaos and then ran. It was our only choice." There had been six of them who'd engineered the escape, and on the outside, they'd all gone their separate ways toward family and home. Two of the women had been soldiers she'd barely known, the other two lab techs, both male and one studying to become a doctor, as well as a female doctor who'd just started her residency.

Sami had wondered about them through the ensuing months. Had anybody survived?

Finally, the group reached the back service door to the building. Tace set down the rocket launcher, his face pale beneath the moonlight.

Jax tested the door. "Locked."

Sami nodded. Wasn't much of a surprise.

Raze studied the metal. "A crowbar won't do it."

"Explosives it is." Jax reached for his backpack. "Everyone get ready."

Tace kept an eye on the surroundings, instinctively putting his body between Sami and the alley. His vision had cleared, but the toes on his left foot had gone numb. Death had stopped scaring him a while ago, weeks ago really, but the idea of leaving her alone pierced him like a frozen blade.

Sami had a softness to her, a vulnerability, that very few people saw.

If he died, who'd protect her?

So he gritted his teeth and shoved down the weakness. Just a little while longer.

We'll find the enzyme, she mouthed, her gaze concerned.

He tried to nod, to give reassurance, but he seriously doubted they'd find anything. Even if the Bunker was still functional, how much enzyme could they really have? If only a small percentage of victims rejected vitamin B, why waste valuable resources and ingredients creating more of the enzyme?

Scorpius was what mattered, especially if it was true about no live births occurring once a woman was infected.

"Fire in the hole," Raze hissed.

They jogged around the corner, and Tace covered Sami.

A small explosion rocked the ground.

They ran forward, and Raze yanked open the door. Tace kept one arm around the launcher and the other extended out with his gun. The metal was familiar in his hand, and his aim steady as Greyson swept high and Jax went low.

"Go," Tace whispered.

Raze moved beyond him with Sami on his six, scouting. Quiet. All was quiet.

Tace followed with Damon.

They stood in a storage area with empty shelves. A series of dead computer screens took up one wall.

Jax motioned them forward and nudged a thin door open with his boot. He jerked back and held up three fingers.

Tace nodded and handed the launcher to Damon. The guy couldn't fight hand to hand with the stitches still in his gut unless absolutely necessary.

Damon took the launcher, his face taut.

Tace motioned for Jax to go in, and he followed, straight on. Raze went left.

Three Bunker soldiers pivoted, mouths agape.

Tace was on the middle guy before he could draw his weapon, punching his jaw, flipping him over, and choking him out. The man was thin but muscled and gave a good fight, but Tace managed a submission hold, and soon he went limp.

"They're not expecting company," Jax whispered, his voice echoing across the grand lobby where once hundreds of people had passed every day.

Tace nodded, looking toward the stairway as Greyson and Raze dragged the unconscious soldiers behind the desk and bound them tight.

Sami ran for a large door and waited for Tace before tugging it open and peering inside. She gave the all clear, and they ran inside, jogging up to the seventh floor. A radio crackled from the stairwell a few floors up, and Sami pulled open the door, peeking inside. She motioned them in.

Tace went in first with Greyson on his heels. Shiny chrome and glass sparkled from a dry wall fountain next to a steel sign that proclaimed the LITIGATION DEPARTMENT OF LAWESON AND GEORGE.

A wide counter ran the full wall with pictures of the Los Angeles landscape behind it.

Tace headed for the elevators, and Greyson tossed him a crowbar. The Bunker workers had all held magnetic keys to go beyond the first floor, and Sami had believed each elevator could access the underground facility. Hopefully, she was remembering that part right.

He grunted and used the crowbar, creating an inch of an opening. Raze stuck his fingers in one side, and between the two of them, they opened a gaping hole in the wall.

Dizziness slapped Tace up the side of his head, and he wavered, then regained control. The metal rungs attached to the walls led down to a hatch several floors below. A quick look up confirmed the elevators many floors up had stopped.

He said a quick prayer they'd stay that way.

Slinging his pack into place, he swung into the shaft and landed on the pseudo ladder. Stale air and the smell of metal surrounded him.

They climbed down easily, and Jax blew the hatch with a small amount of C4.

Then they dropped into hell.

White walls, the shiny kind, surrounded them. Men came running from two different directions, guns already firing.

An explosion rocked the walls from a different elevator shaft and then another. Good. Three of the teams had made it inside. The fourth squad was to scout the lobby and outlying areas for patrolling threats. If they failed, the whole mission might fail.

Tace pivoted and fired, hitting a blond male in the chest. The guy fell back, and his head thunked against the marble tiles.

The place smelled like bleach and rubber gloves. Raze took a man down hand-to-hand while Jax shot another. Sami kept up the rear, protecting Damon. If they ended up in a hand to hand contest, she would be front and center. But when it came to shooting, she was better utilized in close quarters.

An alarm blared through the facility, and red lights hanging from the ceiling began to spin.

"Shit," Greyson muttered, looking both ways down a wide corridor. Team Two dropped to the right, and Team Three to the left.

Jax gave the high signs for them to continue down to the other two levels. The current level spread out in two different directions, and they had to walk over bodies each way. "Greyson, Damon, and Raze, go north and then down to where Sami thought the command center was on level B. Sami, Tace, and I will go south to the computer labs and then down to the command center. Whoever gets there first, take it with no mercy." He glanced up at the lights. "Generators seem to be going strong, but let's hope most personnel have bunked down for the night."

With the order, everyone launched into motion. The center personnel weren't ready for an attack, but they were well armed, and now the alarms blared. The element of surprise had gotten the soldiers in; now fighting skills would come into play. They had to fight hard and fast. Otherwise they were dead.

Jax took the lead. Tace waited until Sami followed so he could cover her back. His energy, his focus, was on the woman and her safety. The need to protect her rose inside him so quickly his breath heated.

Emotions had returned in full force, perhaps with the adrenaline of the mission.

They passed a glass half wall, and a soldier barreled out from behind a closed door, already firing.

Jax took him down with a punch to the throat. Footsteps echoed behind them. The hallway extended about fifty yards. Jax pivoted. "Go find the labs and medical supplies. I'll cover here."

Tace nodded. Then his leg went numb. He dropped to the hard marble. Shit. No. Not now.

With a whoosh of sound, the world went black. He pitched forward, and he was pretty sure Sami screamed his name. Then his heart slowed, his chest compressed, and nothingness claimed him.

Chapter Twenty-Eight

Hell has white walls and a concrete floor.

—Sami Steel

"Tace!" Sami rushed to him and flipped him over, her hands shaking and her body going into overdrive. "He's out cold."

"Fuck." Jax reached down and hauled Tace over a shoulder with a loud grunt. "Get out of the main corridor," he yelled over the blaring alarm.

Sami burst down the hall toward the main lab, reaching it to yank open the door. Her heart beat frantically. God. He had to be all right. "This way."

Jax followed, grimacing under Tace's weight, his gun out and steady.

Two female lab techs scrambled out of the way, and Sami motioned them toward a closet she thought held cleaning supplies. "If you want out of here with us, hold tight," she said, easily locking them in. There were two massive doors, shut and locked, taking up the western wall. "The jail cells for experiments are through there."

Jax dropped Tace to the ground. "Cover the door," he ordered.

She did so, still looking around the medical lab. Machinery whirred on the counter, and seven refrigerators were lined up against the far wall, all humming softly. "They're still intact." Lynne Harmony would love to relocate to this lab. Then Sami dropped to one knee and leaned her ear over Tace's mouth. "Oh God. He's not breathing." She reached for his neck, her voice rising in pure panic. "No pulse."

"Damn it." Jax slid across the room on his knees. "I'll do CPR. Find the fuckin' enzyme."

She nodded and scrambled for the glass refrigerator doors, ripping one open. Vial after vial were lined up, some with blood, some with other liquids. She fumbled for one and read it. "IX208756." A quick glance at other vials confirmed the same thing. "They're labeled with numbers." She shoved the vials back and went for the next fridge—same thing. Almost in slow motion, she turned to see Jax furiously performing CPR and then breathing into Tace's lifeless body. "I don't know which one to use." They could accidentally inject him with smallpox or Ebola or even bleach. Who knew?

The door flew open, and Jax reacted, pulling his gun out.

"Wait!" Sami yelled.

Jax paused.

"Penelope?" Sami asked, her heart thundering as she took in the newcomer, a petite woman she'd once barely known.

The doctor nodded, her black hair flying, her dark eyes wide. She wore striped pajama bottoms with a pink cami, and her feet were bare. The doctor had been in bed. "Sami. What the hell?"

Sami coughed as Jax started CPR again. "I thought you got free." Penelope had been the doctor who'd planned the escape with Sami, having only arrived a week before Sami had come up with the escape plan. She'd had no idea what was going on at the Bunker and had just wanted to get home to her family.

Penelope shook her head. "They caught me three blocks out." She ran for the computer system. "We have to open the jail cells. I promised."

Jax grabbed her arm and yanked her down easily. "You know CPR?"

"She's a doctor," Sami confirmed, her heart aching. "Well, she had just finished medical school when Scorpius hit, so she's as good as a doctor these days." The woman hadn't had any practical experience when they'd met, but she probably did now.

"Good. Keep him alive, or I shoot you in the head." Jax shoved Penelope down toward Tace and rose for the door, his gun out. "Which one of those vials holds the vitamin B enzyme thing?"

Penelope shook her head. "I don't work in the research department. No clue." She started compressions on Tace's chest.

Jax cocked his gun and held it to her temple. "Get a clue."

She looked up, her black eyes clear. "I'm a medical doctor, kind of, and I patch soldiers up. The only time I'm on this floor is when I'm escorted into the labs to fix whatever damage these bastards have done." She turned back and blew into Tace's mouth, counting out compressions. "There's a computer bank right there, and Sami is the best at what she does." Penelope looked up. "There has to be a master code, right?"

"I don't know." Sami skidded toward the computers and flipped one on. It whirred to action, and something inside her eased. "It works." A real computer. The generators in the Bunker were phenomenal. For now, anyway.

Penelope stopped.

Jax turned and pointed his gun.

"I'll keep working on him, but you have to let me open the cells," Penelope said, her mouth pinched.

Sami winced and waited for the computer to boot up. "If I remember right, the experiments all wanted death."

"Not this time," Penelope said, focusing on Jax. "Deal?"

"Deal." Jax turned for the outside door, partially opened it, and fired.

A man screamed in pain from outside the lab.

"Get a move on, Sami," Jax ordered. "There are more soldiers coming."

A cursor blinked. Sami started typing in code. God, it was like coming home. Her fingers flew as she accessed private data, coming up against a firewall almost immediately. Lowering her chin, she started to tear it apart.

"He's breathing on his own," Penelope said from behind her. "But his vitals aren't good. No eye movements. He's slipping, Sami. If he drops into a coma, it's over."

"You know about the vitamin B rejections?" Jax asked tersely, his focus on the hallway outside.

"Yes. I read the data early in my time here, but I haven't treated a patient with it. In fact, I don't think we've had a patient with it since months ago," she said. "The lab techs would know more than I do about that side of the business."

"Fuck." Jax stomped over to the closet and ripped it open to face the women Sami had secured. "Either of you know what the numbers of the refrigerated vials mean?"

"No," a woman said, crying. "We just do the data collection and don't work with any of the samples."

"Great." Jax slammed the door.

A Bunker soldier shoved inside, shooting.

Sami half turned in time to see Jax shoot the guy between the eyes.

Penelope jumped up and rushed for the man. "You didn't have to kill him."

"He shot at us," Jax returned. "Get back to Tace."

Penelope glared and hurried back to the downed Vanguard soldier. "I take it you're Tace," she murmured, feeling his wrist. "Weak but there."

Sami turned back to hacking the system. "I'm sorry you didn't make it home, Penelope." The woman came from a huge Korean family north of Los Angeles and had been desperate to return to see if anybody had survived.

"Me too," the young woman said. "Guess you found family?"

"Yeah," Sami said, typing quickly. "Well, not my family, but I guess we created our own." Her voice clogged. She desperately needed Tace to survive, but she knew the odds. Were they about to lose another Vanguard soldier? She still missed Wyatt, but this would tear her apart. Tace, the former good old boy and the new dangerous soldier—both held her heart. "How did you get up to this floor?"

"Somebody blew the doors wide open," Penelope said. "I ran up the second I figured out what was going on."

"How many soldiers are stationed here?" Jax asked, peering outside to the hallway.

"I don't know. Maybe fifty?" Penelope answered.

Tace muttered something.

"Hold on, Tace," Sami called.

He fell silent again.

She added another code, and lists unfolded on the screen. "Eureka." She typed furiously, searching for anything to do with the vitamin B deficiency. Her breath caught, and explosions pummeled her abdomen. "Found it along with dosage. Third fridge—a yellow liquid labeled RTY78400." Jumping up so quickly her chair shot across the room, she ran for the third refrigerator.

Blue vials, red vials, even purple vials were inside. She scrambled through them, shoving aside a bunch of clear vials.

"Go easy," Penelope barked. "You have no idea what's in some of those."

"Do you?" Sami shot back.

"Yes. I've treated lab techs who've been infected by some of that stuff. They usually die," Penelope said.

Sami slowed down. "Okay." She gently moved aside a bunch of green beakers. "I'm not seeing yellow."

"They might have stopped producing it," Jax said. "We're hoping for leftovers at this point."

Leftovers. What if they found some but the contents were spoiled or past their effectiveness date? Sami dropped to her knees and reached to the very back of the bottom shelf. Yellow. Three yellow vials. Her hand shook, but she reached for them. "RTY78400," she murmured, reading one. No date was on the vial. What if it had gone bad and what was left would kill Tace?

She turned to see him unconscious again. Did she really have a choice? She fumbled through drawers until she found a packaged syringe and drew out the correct cc's from the vial. "Flip him over."

Penelope rapidly turned Tace and yanked down the right side of his jeans. "Here."

Sami handed over the syringe, and Penelope quickly injected Tace before turning him over.

The guy didn't move.

Sami patted his face. "Tace? Wake up." Her throat clogged. Nothing.

The alarm suddenly shut off.

Jax breathed out. "Either Raze has taken command of the control room, or we've lost enough men that the Bunker leaders no longer wanted the alarm."

A speaker crackled in the far right corner. "Attention, Bunker personnel. Stand down, and you'll be escorted to the cafeteria on level B. If you resist, or if you are armed when found by Vanguard soldiers, you will be killed immediately," Raze said over the loudspeaker.

Jax turned and nodded at Sami. "Looks like we're in control."

She shook Tace's shoulders. "Wake up, damn it." Tears pricked the backs of her eyes.

Penelope jumped up and typed quickly into Sami's screen. An image of a long corridor with metal doors came up on the screen. A man of about forty with salt-and-pepper hair ran in from a door at the far end, a gun in his hands and two Bunker soldiers behind him. "We have to open the cells," she screamed. "They'll kill everyone." She pointed to a keypad next to the overlarge doors. "I don't know the code." Panic rippled through her voice.

Jax turned, pointed, and fired at the keypad. Metal and keys rocketed out. The doors snicked. "Stay behind me."

Penelope yanked a gun from Tace's hip and jumped up. "Hurry. They'll kill Marcus."

Jax stopped cold. "Marcus?"

Penelope shoved by him and ran for the door, ripping it open. "There are only two men in the cells. We have to save them."

Sami felt Tace's pulse. Steady but not exactly strong. Yet she took her gun and followed Jax. Tace would be okay. He had to be.

"Marcus?" Jax launched himself into motion and shoved Penelope behind him, entering the long corridor, already firing. "Sami—hack the cell doors."

She nodded and turned back for the computers, going to town on the nearest one. A quick schematic brought up the cell door configuration, and she hurriedly found the codes. "Are you sure?" she yelled at Jax's retreating back.

"Yes," he bellowed in return.

She typed in the code to open the doors. Then, with a quick glance at Tace, she hustled after Jax and stopped short.

Three men faced them with guns—two soldiers in blue and the doctor.

"We seem to be at a standstill," Dr. Ramirez said. "Sami. How good to see you again."

"Leave and you live, Dr. Ramirez," Penelope said, her

voice shaking. God, he was still such a monster. Sami's legs went weak.

"Not a chance," Ramirez said. "There are more soldiers behind me."

A metal cell door was shoved open, and then all hell broke loose. A prisoner barreled out, and Ramirez turned to fire at him.

"No!" Penelope yelled, jumping in front of the guy. A bullet hit her bare shoulder, and blood sprayed.

The roar that came from the man filled the hallway and sent chills down Sami's back. She fired at Ramirez, who jumped behind the already-firing soldiers. Blood burst from Ramirez's white coat, and he stumbled behind the soldiers, fumbling for the door behind him.

The guy from the cell reached Penelope as she fell but didn't touch her.

"Marcus?" Jax's voice shook, and his gun lowered.

Sami fired at one of the soldiers, and he went down, his eyes wide in death. The other soldier turned and disappeared behind the doors with Ramirez.

Sami scanned the corridor. "We have to hurry. They're just getting backup." She looked at Marcus. Was it really Jax's brother?

The guy was the same size as Jax, with brownish green eyes, similar jaw structure, and the same nose. His chest was bare with raw cuts everywhere bleeding freely. A shadow covered his jaw, and anguish his face. "Penny?" he croaked, looking at the fallen doctor, not seeming to have heard Jax.

"Marcus." Jax seemed frozen or in shock. His mouth dropped open, and his gun hand lowered.

"Jax!" Penelope shoved to her feet, her shoulder aching. "We have to run."

Running footsteps echoed from the other side of the doors. A metal cell door opened, and another prisoner, this one with bandages across his shoulders, ran out and straight into Sami. Pain lanced down her arm, and she fell hard.

He grabbed her gun and backed up. Blood matted his blond hair, and scratches covered his blistered face. He appeared to be about forty, and the expression in his eyes was haunted to the point of madness.

"Wait. George. Stop," Penelope whispered, reaching out to him.

Marcus tried to step in front of her and fell to his knees. Blood poured off him to coat the cement floor.

George looked around with wild brown eyes. Scars marred his body where it was not bandaged. He lifted the gun to his chin.

"No!" Penelope yelled.

George looked at her, and peace settled over his face. He smiled. "Finally." He pulled the trigger. His brains splattered across the wall, and he fell in death, still smiling.

Penny jerked back.

The doors burst open.

"Retreat," Jax yelled, dragging Sami up with one arm while already shooting toward the doors, his gaze remaining on Marcus.

Penelope shoved her bleeding shoulder beneath Marcus's arm and tried to lift him.

"No!" he yelled, shaking to dislodge her. "You're not infected." His blood flowed all over her chest and the new bullet wound.

"Run, Marcus," she yelled, trying to drag the muscled man.

He took a look at the soldiers opening the door, half lifted her, and ran after Jax.

They reached the lab room and kept going.

Jax released Sami to lean down and haul Tace over his shoulder, while Sami ran over and unlocked the closet to let out the lab techs. They all ran into the corridor just as Raze, Damon, and three other soldiers hustled up.

"Soldiers coming—keep the computer room secure and take them out," Jax ordered, not pausing in his stride. "Where's the infirmary, and is it secured?"

"One floor down to the south, and affirmative," Raze said, yanking open the door to the computer lab. "Greyson has the control room secured in the center of floor B."

"Everyone move," Jax ordered, cutting a quick glance at his bleeding brother. "We need bandages."

Sami kept her gun out, scanning for threats while also trying to see any improvement in Tace, who hung raggedly over Jax's shoulder. What if she'd been too late?

Chapter Twenty-Nine

It's not death I fear . . . I'm just not ready to leave those who need me.

—Tace Justice

Tace blinked and sat up with a gasp. Sami sat next to him, his hand between her two smaller ones. "Tace?"

His body vibrated with the need to leap up and fight. "Status?" he tried to bark, but his voice came out hoarse.

"We're in the Bunker infirmary," Sami said, her eyes glistening. "The command center and all of floor B is secured, while we're still fighting on A and C."

Tace swallowed and shook his head, looking around. The infirmary had clean linens, antibacterial wipes, and actual rubber gloves. Compared to the infirmaries at Vanguard, the place was luxurious. "Jax?" The Vanguard leader covered the door, his back to the wall, and his focus on the bed next to Tace.

"We got you the injection. Feel any different?" Jax asked, lines cut into his face.

Tace blinked. "No dots in my vision." He turned to look at the bed next to him, where a small woman was busy patching up a guy with multiple knife wounds. She had long black hair and flawless mocha skin, and her movements were quick and economical.

Tace narrowed his gaze on the patient. There was something familiar about the guy.

"That's Marcus," Sami whispered. "Right, Jax?"

Jax wavered in place, his face unusually pale. "Yeah. That's my brother." He seemed almost in a daze.

Tace's eyebrows rose. Yeah—he did look a little like Jax. Where the hell had he come from? Marcus was broad across the chest, looked tall, and held himself perfectly still. Turmoil filled his eyes as he let the woman stitch a slice over his right pec.

"You let me infect you, Penny," Marcus rumbled, his voice raw.

Tace craned his neck to see a bandage over the woman's shoulder.

She finished the stitches and gently placed a bandage over the wound. "I told you I'd get you out. That's all that matters." Sweat dotted her forehead, and her hands shook a little.

Ah, shit. Tace pushed himself up in the bed, his arms feeling like he'd lifted weights for twenty hours straight. He was the only medic there. "Do you have vitamin B?"

The woman nodded and pointed toward a counter near Jax. "I had an injection yesterday."

"If you've been infected, you need another one now." Tace shifted his legs to the edge of the bed.

"I'll get it." Sami patted his shoulder and crossed the room to take out the B. She filled a syringe and paused when Marcus growled.

Tace stiffened, preparing to insert himself between Sami and the threat. There was no doubt Jax's brother was all threat.

"It's okay," Sami said calmly, handing the syringe to the woman. "Penelope can inject herself."

Marcus settled back down, his gaze scanning the room.

"Marcus?" Jax said, leaning forward like he was approaching a wild animal. Hope and fear sizzled in his eyes. "You remember me?"

Marcus looked him over, no expression on his hard face. "No."

Ah, shit. Tace looked at Marcus. "Are you a Mercenary?" Had they somehow missed Marcus before?

"No," Marcus said.

Jax shuffled in place as if unsure what to do next. Emotion swirled in his dark eyes.

Tace glanced at the small woman Marcus seemed to be protecting. "Marcus, are you a soldier here at the Bunker?"

Marcus stilled. Tension rolled from him in a swell of heat. "No."

Penelope reached out to touch him and then stopped. "Marcus was held in the cells." At her words, Marcus's face went blank.

Sami shook her head. "We let everyone out two months ago. Where were you before that?"

Marcus kept his gaze on Penelope and didn't answer.

"Marcus," Penelope said gently.

He didn't blink. "This wasn't my first Bunker."

"How many are there?" Jax asked.

"Dunno." Marcus said. "You infected?" he asked Penelope.

She nodded, her lips turning down. "I'm sorry. I think so."

"Told you to run. You promised," Marcus said so softly Tace could barely make out the words.

"I also promised to get you out of there." Penelope sagged against the wall.

Marcus stood and gently laid her down on the bed. "You'll be okay." Gun still in his hand, he sat on the edge between the woman and everyone else. "We'll move after the fever. Tomorrow."

Tace cut a look at Jax. If Marcus thought Jax would let

his younger brother loose again, he really didn't remember Jax at all.

Jax cleared his throat. "Slam? I'm your brother." His voice shook.

Marcus studied Jax but didn't speak. He had features similar to Jax's, but his were broader and somehow more rugged. His eyes held more green than brown, but his muscles were just as well defined as his brother's.

Tace exhaled. The strength returned to his legs, and his breathing smoothed out. He couldn't just sit there. "I'll go help Raze." He shoved to his feet.

Sami grabbed his arm. "You need to stay here. We don't even know if the injection worked."

"I know." He reached for a gun in his boot. "I guess we'll find out soon enough. If I go dark and pass out again, it didn't work." But he'd go down fighting. "For now, isn't there a computer center we need to secure? Just think of the data you could get there, Sami."

Her eyes glowed, and something settled deep inside him. There was his little hacker. So much of her made sense now, and he liked her even more than before. "I guess we could go make sure Raze has it all under control," she said, almost bouncing toward the door.

The gunfire had stopped, so either Raze was down, or the computer room was secured. Either way, they needed to find out. Tace took the lead, his vision incredibly clear. "Stay behind me, Sami."

"I can fight," she grumbled.

Yeah, but she still sucked at shooting. "If we go hand to hand, you can lead," he said.

Jax opened the door. "Yell if you need backup."

Tace nodded, dodging into the now-empty hallway. "Copy that." Just as he finished the last syllable, Raze strode out of the computer center, a man over his shoulder. "Looks like we have injured."

"I can handle it," Penelope said, pushing from the bed.

Marcus stepped back, effectively blocking her.

"Please," she whispered.

Without a word, he shifted to the side.

Tace shook his head. Here he thought he'd had problems. "Yell if you need me," he told Jax, hurrying toward Raze. "Status?"

"Entire floor is secure—several Bunker soldiers dead." Raze kept moving, his strides long and strong. "We're holding prisoners in the cafeteria on B for now and will need to make some decisions soon."

Tace motioned for Sami to follow him back into the computer room. "I guess we're on data collection for now." He'd cover both doors while his woman went to work, as long as his vision remained. He felt better but still weak in the limbs.

The fight had been bloody, and they'd surely lost a few. But was there a cure for Scorpius hidden somewhere in those computers?

A real cure? It was the first time he'd felt hope in so long that it took him several moments to recognize the feeling.

Hope.

Jax stood at the Bunker command center window, staring down a level at the sprawling cafeteria. White plastic chairs surrounded wooden tables all around with a long orange counter holding food. "That's all the people left standing?" he asked.

Greyson walked over from a wall of computers to stand next to him. "Yes. At least ten people escaped through an underground tunnel when we breached the facility—we'll know who once Sami hacks into these computers when she's finished with the medical ones."

"Nobody down there, not a person, knows the codes?" Jax asked, irritation clawing his skin.

"I don't think so." Greyson pointed to the door in the far wall of the command center that had now been cordoned off. "Once they started losing floors, they escaped from here. The top soldiers, doctors, and scientists all had escape plans and are probably halfway to another facility." He stared down at the people held below. "Not that we shouldn't interrogate every single person down there."

"Agreed." Jax studied the people. Twenty-five soldiers in blue uniforms, ten lab techs or scientists in lab coats, and another twenty people in off-duty comfortable clothes. "Fifty-five people here, ten escaped, thirty dead. That's only ninety-five personnel in a facility created to hold probably three hundred."

"Scorpius took two hundred, according to the lab tech I questioned," Greyson said. "I don't know how many down there are survivors, and how many haven't been infected."

"The doctor with my brother right now hadn't been," Jax said slowly. He'd left Marcus with the suffering doctor in the infirmary, posting three guards on the door.

"That's weird about your brother. You okay?" Greyson asked.

"Fine. Just glad he's alive." Jax's chest hurt and he wanted nothing more than to go hug his brother and force him to remember their childhood. But right now, he had other things to deal with. The last thing he needed to do was bond with Greyson Storm, since he was still considering taking Storm's resources. Plus, it was almost certain Raze was going to kill the guy at some point. "Anybody down there know of a cure for Scorpius?"

"I've only interrogated three lab techs so far, and I don't think anyone's found a cure for Scorpius. But one lab tech had plenty to say about a vitamin B inoculation that helps the body create its own B. Unfortunately, she deals with data and isn't a scientist."

Sami moved into the room, reams of paper in her hands.
"I've hacked through all the security in the medical computers
and have a couple of the guys collecting data. I had to use
an encryption program, so they'll collect it now and we'll have
to sift through it later. Frankly, somebody with a medical
background needs to translate half that stuff, anyway." She
looked around the command center and gave a low whistle.
"Nice."

Tace entered and covered the door.

"You okay?" Jax asked.

"So far," the medic said. "If I pass out again, then no. If
not . . . I'm back, baby."

Jax snorted.

"You okay, Jax?" Tace hissed out.

Jax sobered and gave the truth. "No."

Greyson pointed to a center console. "Sami, I tried to get
in and had absolutely no luck. Can you do it?"

"Sure. First I'll—" Sami started.

Jax held up a hand. "Get started, Steel. I don't want the
details." The last thing he wanted to worry about right now
was trying to understand how to hack anything when the hair
on the back of his neck was raised. "I need you to get into
the overall physical security of this place right away. Did
a warning go out to the other facilities when we breached this
one? What kind of forces might they send—what kind of
forces are out there—and who will be coming for us?"

Sami paused. "Coming for us? You think—"

Jax nodded. "Yeah. It'd help if we knew where the facili-
ies are and how long it'll take the assholes from here to get
here." This was his facility now, and he wasn't losing it.

What if there was a cure for Scorpius hidden in those
omputers?

The risk was worth it.

"Maybe we should get all civilians out of here?" Sami asked.

Jax turned to stare down at the people quietly sitting at tables awaiting their fate. "No. If an attack is coming, we need everyone here. The Bunker residents don't get to leave without us, if ever."

Greyson crossed his arms. "Agreed."

Jax partially turned. "We know that the president is looking for this place and that he obviously doesn't know about the many facilities. That begs the question—who does? Who or what is in charge of this shit show? Find me the answers, Sami." Hopefully, there was information listed somewhere. He hated being in the dark like this. "I have men searching floor C for the generators and storage—and who knows what else. Find an inventory list after the security shit, would you?"

Sami nodded and started typing, muttering to herself. Her fingers were so fast over the keys that the sound was almost rhythmic and soothing. Except for the fact that enemy soldiers were probably heading their way right now.

"Can you talk and type?" Jax asked.

"Yeah."

"Did you find anything in the medical computers that showed a cure for Scorpius?" Jax asked.

Sami shook her head. "I just decrypted the files and didn't have time to read. We need Lynne here."

Lynne would give her left leg to be in a working lab again, but no way in hell was she coming to the Bunker until Jax knew it was safe. "We'll take data back to her."

"Yep," Sami said.

"How about Marcus? Were there records of what they did to him?" Jax tried to keep his voice level, but a thread of heat wove through his words. When he found the doctor who'd harmed his brother, he'd rip the skin from their bones with his bare hands. "Sami?"

"I'm sure the records are there, but I didn't stop to rea

anything," she said, her typing speed increasing. "I need quiet for a moment, Jax. This is a tough layer."

"Copy that." Jax leaned closer to Greyson. "I have scouts looking for hidden rooms and other floors. Who says there are only three?"

Grey nodded. "Damon is leading a team doing the same thing. I think we've just touched the surface of this place, you know? Maybe Sami will find schematics, if there are any."

"If we don't get attacked first," Jax muttered.

"There is that." Greyson shook out his arms. "I need to do something. You want to scout or do you want to start questioning people?"

Jax looked at the Bunker residents below. Healthy and hardy . . . with good food. Some of them may have been prisoners, while others had chosen this life. There was only one way to find out. "Let's go start chatting one-on-one with these folks." He pointed to a door that must lead to the kitchen. "There are plenty of tools in there, I'm sure."

Greyson nodded, his jaw hardening. "Sounds like a plan."

Jax turned for the door. "Tace, you staying on point?"

"Yeah. I've got Sami's back so she can type away," Tace said, his Texan drawl back in full force.

It surprised Jax how much he'd missed that sound. Interesting. "All right. The second you have information, any information, get me, okay? Soon, Sami." He didn't want to pressure the young woman, but if well-armed forces were about to blow a hole in the side of the facility, he needed to know. Worse yet, what if there was another back door somewhere? They'd be sitting ducks. "Thanks."

Chapter Thirty

I can be this person. I know I can.

—Sami Steel

The sound of a printer running was almost foreign and instantly comforting. Sami fell right into typing code, Tace at her back, a screen at her front. If it were possible to feel a slight moment of contentment in this crazy world, she was almost there. Except the damn firewall was blocking her. She'd pared through several of the defensive layers and was already printing out personnel files and some communications between different facilities.

Yet there was something hidden . . . a file she couldn't quite reach.

Her instincts hummed, and the thrill of the chase poured through her.

"You're stunning in your element," Tace drawled from her left.

That drawl . . . that sexy twang. The sound slid right down through her, warming her in the cool room. "Stop flirting with me." She grinned.

"Can't help it. In fact, truth be told, you're always stunning." He probably sounded just like the scores of Texas lawmen in his family who'd come before him.

She'd wondered if he'd like the studious side of her—the real her. Guess she had her answer. She would've given anything to have kept digging through the medical records downstairs, but now that she'd unlocked the files, anybody could gather the data. "You'd better be cured of rejecting B, Justice."

"I'm hoping, darlin'." His voice was clear, as were his eyes. That had to mean he was cured. It just had to. The idea that the tough soldier, the brilliant medic, could be brought down so unexpectedly scared the hell out of her. Yet the man he'd become, the badass with the twang, kept her interest every day. He had to survive.

She typed faster. "There's something here."

"I'm sure." He turned and scanned down the hallway, his shoulders relaxing as he focused back on her. "Is this place just like you remember?"

"More people were here before," she said softly. "Then they had to go cover other Bunkers, and fewer people made it back."

"The air is secure here, right?" he asked. "Wait a minute. That doesn't matter. Scorpius is a bacteria, so air doesn't matter. But this place is secure, right?"

She paused. "Well, it was secure until we breached it. We've brought the bacteria with us into the facility."

"Shit. Be right back." Tace jogged out of the room and was gone at least five minutes before returning. "Jax and Greyson already had figured that out, so they're not touching anybody they're questioning. Or to be more accurate, they're threatening to bite anybody who doesn't cooperate."

"I guess people are cooperating," she muttered.

"Definitely."

She sighed and kept typing.

"Just take your time and work the problem," Tace said, standing at attention near the door.

"Are you still feeling obsessive?" she asked.

"I am."

She let her fingers fly and her brain work the problem, kind of zoning out a little. "Then you should stop fighting it so much. Maybe if you settle into it, you'll relax."

"Maybe. Sex helps."

Humor bubbled through her. "I'm here to help."

"You're a giver, Sami," he drawled.

She shivered at his sexy tone. "If we keep this facility, I'll probably need to stay here and keep working on the computers."

"Shouldn't you concentrate on what you're doing?" he asked, curiosity in his tone.

It probably did seem odd to somebody who didn't work the way she did. "My brain and fingers are working, and sometimes if I concentrate on something else, talk a little, magic happens." It sounded weird now that she tried to explain, yet she knew he wouldn't judge her. Not Tace.

"Odd, but okay—let's chat. If you want to stay here at the Bunker and work, if the place remains secure, then we'll stay here."

She blinked and kept typing. He'd said "we." The little word warmed her throughout, even though she'd wanted to sound so strong and sure of herself in this conversation. The Texan had the power to hurt her, and he was smart enough to know that fact. "Hmm."

He chuckled low. "You didn't think we'd live in different places, did you?"

She narrowed her gaze and ran code through her mind. Time to try something else. "Vanguard needs a medic, Tace. They need you." So did she. Man, she needed him at her back and in her heart. It was much easier to admit that truth to herself than out loud. She'd almost lost him and frankly still could, if the enzyme wasn't at full strength. Yet duty called her right here and right now—these computers a

the information locked inside them were what she could give
to Vanguard. To the people who'd taken her in and given
her a home. "You and I are needed in two different places."

"Then we'll split our time and be useful at both places.
But where you go, I go, baby." His voice roughened. "Unless
you don't agree?"

"I agree." Even though his tone said he would insist, she
already agreed. Maybe he needed reassurance just as badly
as she did. Although he was better at stating his feelings—
his wants and needs—much better than she was. Finally, a bad
boy who could stand on his own two feet, which was a first
for her. "Just wanted to make sure."

"Be sure, then," Tace murmured. "This is a weird time
to be discussing this, but when I told you it was you and me,
I meant it."

She couldn't imagine her day without him, and the idea
of sleeping alone for the rest of her life made her sad. Well,
sleeping without Tace pricked tears to her eyes. "I don't want
to give up being one of the soldiers." Her voice quavered.

"You don't have to, although you're the most valuable
computer person we have. Is it that you don't want to be out
of the inner circle, or is it that you want to keep scouting?"
he asked, his voice deep and so masculine.

She tried another set of codes, her mind working the
problems. Tace had zeroed in on her fears with impressive
accuracy. "Both, I guess."

"Then do both. Although I think the computer aspect will
take a lot of time for a while, and that still means you're in
the inner circle. Don't worry. Vanguard is family, Sami,"
Tace said.

"Yeah." She breathed in. Jax had said the same thing.
Finally, she'd found a place where she actually belonged—
all of her. She wished her family could see her and meet
Tace. Her dad would've liked Tace Justice, she was sure. The

dull ache of missing all of them would never go away, but the family she had built after Scorpius offered comfort.

Her breath quickened, and she focused on the screen. Ah, there it was. She leaned forward, rewriting code and creating a back door. Should've known—they'd used her original security measures with slight enhancements. "I can get into anything here." Yeah. Lazy bastards. Files began opening on-screen in rapid succession. She wanted to turn on the other screens, but conserving energy was still paramount.

Her eye caught a file, and she clicked a couple of keys.

Her fingers froze.

She blinked. Her chest seized. "Oh God."

Tace hurried toward her, lowering his chin. "What is that?"

She leaned over and typed rapidly, bringing up schematics and finally, a graphic of a digital clock, its big red numbers counting down. "It's a facility failsafe," she whispered, her hands shaking even as she typed. "Get Jax. Hurry."

Tace ran from the room.

She flipped through files and brought up a coded schematic file, taking several precious moments to go through the first back door she'd set up, almost surprised when she made it. They'd never realized she'd left herself a way back in. "Shit, shit, shit."

Tace ran back into the room with both Jax and Greyson on his heels. "What's up?"

She hit PRINT for one of the files, turning around. "There a failsafe in place that they set off before they escape Doctor Ramirez commanded the facility, and he used h codes to activate it."

Tace leaned in to look at the computer. "Everything w shut down?"

She gulped and shook her head wildly. "More than th The level below C, right under the room with the compu servers, is rigged with explosives, and in exactly fourteen minutes, the bomb will blow."

"Will it take out the entire building?" Jax asked, his jaw clenching.

She shrugged and typed quickly, bringing up the explosives list and bomb details. "I don't know anything about explosives."

Jax leaned in and blew out. "Grey—shit. This is beyond bad."

Grey leaned over her other shoulder, surrounding her with the scent of male and the sense of a whole lot of testosterone. "Holy shit," he said.

Sami partially turned. "Jax?"

The Vanguard leader leaned back, his eyes hardening. "That'll take out the entire city block. If we want to get clear, we have to do it right now." He winced. "Not sure we'll make it even if we go now. We'll have to evacuate everyone."

Tace reached for her shoulder.

"Wait," Sami said, looking back at the computer. "If the bomb was activated here via computer, why can't I deactivate it the same way?"

"No," Tace said, pulling on her chair so she rolled away from the keyboard.

Sami struggled against the move. "There's a chance we have a cure for Scorpius in this facility. Or a concoction so a patient's body can make its own vitamin B, removing the need for injections. Or even a way to protect pregnant women and ensure full-term pregnancies. If there's a possibility, we have to try, right?"

Tace shook his head, his jaw set rock-hard. "If you fail to deactivate it, there won't be enough time to get free of the blast area. I don't have Jax or Greyson's experience with explosives, but even I know that. Right?"

"Yeah," Jax said. "To get clear, we have to go now. Even then, it ain't gonna be pretty."

Sami dug deep and breathed out. "Get all the civilians and soldiers out that you can. I'm staying." She jerked the chair free and rolled back to the keyboard.

Chapter Thirty-One

*My daddy, his daddy, and his daddy were all Texas
Rangers. That means somethin'.*

—Tace Justice

"Have you fucking lost your mind?" Tace bellowed, reaching for his woman again. Here he was being all understanding and supportive of her career choices, and now she
wanted to hang out where a bomb was about to go off? "We
are running hard and fast for Vanguard."

She turned and slapped his hand—actually fucking
slapped him.

He lost his shit. Letting loose with a snarl that sounded
too much like Marvin the lion, he reached down and yanked
her ass from the chair, his temper nearly blowing off the
top of his head. Which was exactly why he didn't see her
punch to the throat coming. She nailed him and hard. He
dropped to his ass like a sack of bricks, still holding her
against his chest. His throat seized and his eyes stung.
"What?" he wheezed.

Her elbow impacted his cheekbone, and she spun around
to straddle him, smacking both hands to his ears.

Pain smashed through his skull. Oh, hell no. He shot his
arms up between hers, grabbed the back of her head, and
turned to flatten her ass to the concrete. He'd learned his

lesson well last time, so he used his groin to press her into the floor and his bigger hands to clasp her wrists above her head. She wiggled beneath him, bucking hard, using a string of swear words that had certainly never been thrown together so colorfully before. At about the third "fuck," she lapsed into rapid Spanish.

Finally, shooting poisonous darts from her dark eyes, she subsided beneath him.

Jax leaned over one side. "You guys about done?"

"Get the fucking trucks ready," Tace snapped. "We're going."

"No, we aren't," Sami countered, struggling again, her breasts rubbing against his chest. "I'm the only chance we have to stop the bomb, and you're wasting time. Get off me."

Greyson bent down at the other side. "Not for nothin', but if there's a chance to diffuse the bomb, how about we try it?"

Tace looked up and pinned the Merc leader with a hard stare.

Greyson held up both hands and backed away. "Your woman, your decision. I'll go have my men start clearing out the Bunker folks."

"Get my brother out of here," Jax ordered. "If you have to take that Bunker doctor, that Penelope woman, in order to motivate him, do it."

"Copy that," Greyson said, striding from the room.

Tace leaned down into Sami's face. "Here's what's going to happen, little hacker. We're going to get up and run like hell. Got it?"

Her bottom lip trembled. "You don't think I can do it?"

Ah hell. "I don't want to risk it," he said, his voice lowering.

She blinked. "I thought you saw me. The real me."

"I do." Every instinct he'd ever had screeched at him to get her the hell away from a block of skyscrapers about to explode. "I can't lose you."

"We need the resources here," she whispered. "The bomb was activated by computer—I can deactivate it."

Tace shook his head. "Too risky."

"Don't stop me," she said.

In that instant, that one little instant, he knew he'd lose her if he stopped her. Yet what else could he do? At least she'd be alive and hating him.

"Trust me," she whispered.

She was killing him. "Promise me you can do it," he said.

She blinked. Once and then twice. "I want to promise, but I said I'd never lie to you again. I can't promise I'll be able to turn it off, but I want to try. I *need* to try, Tace. Let me be who I'm supposed to be."

Who she was supposed to be was fucking alive and in his heart. In his life. He slowly stood up and pulled her to her feet. "All right."

Surprise and then gratitude glowed in her eyes. She ran for the chair and sat, her fingers already moving across the keyboard. "Get everyone out, and if the building doesn't explode, you can all come back in about fifteen minutes from now."

Tace nodded at Jax. "Go."

Sami partially turned, her fingers still working somehow. "You too, Tace."

"No." He crossed his arms.

She paled. "You have to go. I can't risk you."

He shook his head. "It's you and me. Remember?"

Tears filled her eyes. "Just in case this doesn't work, one of us has to go on. To remember the other one."

"Sorry, baby. I'm staying here with you. There's no life for me without you." He'd give her until five minutes left on the bomb, and then they'd try to outrun the explosion. Probably unsuccessfully, but at least they'd be together.

She looked over his shoulder. "Jax? Vanguard needs a medic. Please take Tace out of here."

Tace partially turned to face one of the few remaining men alive he'd die for. "Jax?"

Jax breathed out. "You're like a brother to me, Tace." He glanced around Tace at Sami. "If he took me away from Lynne, I'd never forgive him. I love you, Sami. You're the sister I never had. Get typing, because I ain't losing either of you." He clapped Tace on the arm. "I . . ."

Tace nodded. "Me too."

Jax's eyes darkened.

"Go, Jax. Get Marcus out of here and make sure Raze gets free. Doc Vinnie needs him, and he'll try to stay and find the bomb to strip. Get him clear," Tace said.

Jax took another look and then nodded, turning for the corridor.

Tace moved toward Sami, standing behind her chair and putting his hands on her shoulders. "I suggest you get typing, because you and I need to have a little discussion about you hitting me in the throat."

She gave a half chuckle, half sob, turning back to the keyboard. "That sounds like a threat."

"It is." He noted the clock in the corner of the screen. Ten minutes. She had five minutes, and then he was carrying her out of there whether she liked it or not.

"You should go," she whispered, leaning over the keyboard.

"You risked your life coming here to save mine," he said. "How could I do any less?"

She typed faster somehow. "I had to decipher the computers."

He nodded. "I have to reassure you that you can do this."

"I know I can do this," she snapped, her shoulders rigid.

Yet she didn't—not really. The little girl who'd tried to please her father by learning to fight so well, who'd tried to please asshole boyfriends by hacking so well . . . she didn't know she could just be. "I love you, Sami. Whether you're fighting, hacking, or just sitting on your butt daydreaming. Everything about you, that is just you, is inside me and always will be." He leaned down and pressed a kiss to the top of her head. "I trust you."

She shivered. "I love you, too." She sniffed. "It was wrong of me to ask Jax to knock you out and take you away from here. You can make your own decisions just like I can."

"We'll discuss retaliation for that later," he promised. Man, was she going to fight him at five minutes. Would he have to knock her out? No. This was Sami, and she was the best hacker around. "You can do it," he said, fully meaning the words. If it were possible, which he didn't know, then she could do it. *If* it could be done. He read the clock.

Nine minutes.

She started mumbling to herself, and he left her alone, just being present. Her fingers clacked keys, and she blurted out an expletive every few moments.

Eight minutes.

She kicked the drawer and dragged the keyboard closer to her chest, her gaze on the screen and not the keys.

Codes flashed across in red and blue so quickly he couldn't read them, but Sami kept typing. "Got rid of my other back door," she muttered. "Fucking dickhead of a bastard."

Seven minutes.

The woman had admitted the feat might be impossible. He had absolutely no clue what she was typing or doing, so he couldn't tell how close she was or if she was close at all. Hell. He'd had one of his sisters set up his e-mail account years ago and hadn't changed the password since. Wasn't sure he even knew how to do so. Not that he needed e-mail any longer. Memories of his family, of his little sisters, flashed through his mind. They would've loved Sami, and she would've enjoyed Texas and them. He focused on the screen.

Five minutes.

He stiffened. "Baby? Let's run for it."

"No." She shook her head and kept typing. "I'm close. Trust me. Please, Tace."

His eyes shut. If he dragged her out of there, he'd be saying he didn't believe her. His woman, the only one he'd ever love, had asked for trust. When the woman you loved asked for something so important, you gave it to her. He'd learned that from his daddy, who'd learned it from his, and so on. "All right." He grasped her shoulder to just hold on. If it was their last moment, he was going to be touching her when it all ended.

"Four minutes," she muttered, her body hunching. "Damn it."

He wished he'd made a move on her at the very beginning. They could've had a couple of months together instead of this short time. Yet he wouldn't trade what they'd had for anything.

More memories flashed through his mind—these of Sami. The first time he'd met her, she'd shaken his hand too tightly, trying to be one of the guys. He'd disarmed her with his drawl and a joke, and in that second, he'd seen the sweet girl inside. She'd trained him to street-fight, and when he'd surpassed her in strength, she'd glowed with pride.

The first time he'd made love to her, she'd sighed his name.

That sound. That one little sweet sound would stay with him through eternity. He opened his eyes.

Two minutes.

At the sight of the two, everything in him settled. All right. It was too late to run anyway. He wanted to hold her hand, but her fingers were flying, so he kept his grip on her shoulder. She mumbled, panic in the sound. He rubbed her, careful not to disturb her typing. Man, she was in the zone. Fast typing, rigid body, computer-term mumbling that might as well be a foreign language.

"Thank you for the last couple of weeks," he whispered.

She stiffened. "I want more of them." Flashes flew across the screen in different codes that made no sense.

"Me too," he said.

One minute.

He held on to her, thanking God in this last minute for giving such an incredible woman to him. For giving him the chance to really love and be loved. They hadn't had time to explore it, but they'd felt it.

Thirty seconds.

Would there be an afterlife? He'd always believed and he still did. He and Sami would get another chance together, and she'd meet his family. Yeah.

Twenty seconds.

She hit one more key.

The clock halted at eighteen seconds.

He stiffened. His head cocked, and his heart stopped. "Sami?"

She coughed and hesitantly lifted her fingers from the keyboard. "Um."

"Sami?" he asked again, his voice turning rough.

She turned. "I did it. We stopped the bomb." She lunged out of her chair and jumped.

He caught her, his mouth on hers as she wrapped her legs around his waist. She tasted of woman and something sweet—all Sami. He kissed her, going deep, putting every feeling he'd ever have into the kiss. Finally, he leaned back. "I knew you could do it."

Jax poked his head around the corner. "Jesus. Did you have to make it so close?"

Tace stilled. "What the hell are you doing here?"

Raze leaned around him. "We're a team. But still. Eighteen seconds? God, Sami. You gave me a heart attack."

Sami smiled, her lips trembling and tears filling her eyes. "You guys stayed."

"Yeah. We believe in you." Jax breathed out heavily. "All right. Everyone get back to work. We have people to interview, and we're all staying the night here. Then we'll come up with a plan for the next step." He glanced at them. "One more minute of kissing, I guess. Then back to work." The door shut behind him.

Tace grinned. "I guess we have a minute."

"We have more than that." She leaned in and settled her sweet mouth on his.

His legs trembled. Shit. His vision went dark. This time when he fell, he made sure to go backward so he wouldn't squish her.

The last sound he heard was her screaming his name.

He came to with Jax, Raze, and Sami all staring at him and Sami patting his face. "I'm fine." His voice sounded groggy.

Raze shook his head. "You're definitely not fine. I wonder if the enzyme has gone bad?"

"I don't know," Sami said, her voice thick with tears. "I'll get into the computer and figure it out. I promise."

Tace nodded as Jax hauled him to his feet. Yeah, a part of him had thought he'd been cured, but apparently it wasn't going to happen. He was gonna see those Texas ancestors of his sooner than he'd thought.

Chapter Thirty-Two

*I knew Tace Justice would break my heart, but not by
leaving. I didn't see this coming.*

—Sami Steel

Sami had worked on the medical computers all day, trying
to decipher the technical jargon and find out why Tace had
passed out again. Finally, both Tace and Jax had shooed her
from the room to work on the other computers, saying they
could read through the data but not hack into the remaining
cryptic files up in the command center.

Later in the evening, Sami glanced into the examination
room in the infirmary where they'd had to move Penelope
as she fought the fever. The young woman thrashed uncon-
trollably on the bed, and Marcus hadn't allowed anybody
close enough to secure her. He'd shackled her to the bed himself with restraints already in place for the newly infected.

He leaned against the wall, his chest still bare save for
multiple bandages and bruises. A gun was tucked into his
waistband, and a knife showed in his back pocket. His gaze
remained on Sami as a clear warning not to enter the room.
Man, he looked just like his brother.

Sami cleared her throat. "Penelope started working here
just a week before we escaped."

Marcus lifted his chin.

Sami nodded. "She didn't know a thing about the Bunker—only that she wanted to get free to find her family. The Bunker leaders wouldn't let her. She didn't know about the jail cells or the human experimentation going on."

"I know," Marcus said.

Sami swallowed. "I discovered the truth about the experiments, and the second I could, I opened the doors."

Marcus just stared at her.

"Your brother has been looking for you since he returned to the States. Jax is a good guy," Sami said. Was there any way to get through to the man?

Marcus blinked, and something burned in his eyes for the briefest of moments.

Sami retreated. Maybe it would be baby steps with Marcus. "How is Penelope doing?"

"She'll survive," Marcus said, turning his focus back to the doctor on the bed. "She has to." His voice was lower and rougher than Jax's.

Sami nodded, something in her wanting to ease the tortured pain in Jax's brother's eyes. "You and Penelope are together?"

Marcus frowned. "No."

"Oh." Sami blinked. "Okay." Boy, had she read that one wrong. What in the world was going on? Marcus was the most protective guard dog she'd ever met. "You don't owe me anything, but I'd consider it a favor if you'd at least talk to your brother. Jax has been frantic about finding you."

Marcus leaned his head back on the wall but kept her in his sights.

She cleared her throat when he didn't answer. "All righty, then. Good talk." Turning on her heel, she almost walked into Jax. "Your brother was talking my ear off."

Jax's upper lip curled. "Funny. Tace is waiting for you outside the infirmary. He's finished with the last field dressing, and I want you both to get some shut-eye before returning to work early tomorrow morning." He moved past her toward Penelope's room.

Sami fought the urge to salute. "Jax? I still have some files to decode, and they could be important." Something was nagging at her in one of the encrypted files, but she couldn't put her finger on it. She'd been working all day, and her eyes stung. "I haven't found the enzyme for Tace. He's okay now, but he might not be tomorrow."

"You can barely stand. Get some fuckin' sleep," Jax called back.

Sami bit her lip. They'd had a rough day, had almost died several times, and she could use a break. So she trooped outside and found Tace waiting, leaning against the wall, his eyes closed. His muscled arms were crossed, as were his ankles above his boots. Fatigue all but rolled off the medic. "Tace?"

Those stunning blue eyes opened and focused on her. "We're done for the day."

She nodded, her abdomen tingling. "Then I'm back to it bright and early."

"I have a surprise for you." He held out a hand.

Curiosity wandered right through her. "Oh yeah?" She slipped her palm against his, her heart aching. Why hadn't she been able to save him? "Maybe we should go back to the medical files and figure out why that enzyme didn't work."

"The last time I passed out, my heart kept beating." Tace shrugged. "It's an improvement."

"Right." She fell into step next to him. "I get that, but that's not uncommon, from what I read. The attacks vary in strength, and if you get one strong enough, that's it for you. I can't lose you now."

"You won't." He led her down the stairs at the end of the corridor and into a long hallway.

"Where are all the Bunker people?" she asked, nodding at a couple of Vanguard soldiers guarding the stairs.

Tace grinned. "They're all confined to quarters on C level, while we've taken control of all resources on A level and the quarters on B level. I found a nice room for us." His smile uncoiled a physical burn inside her.

"Your smile is my favorite sight," she said.

He blinked and stilled. "God, there's a part of you, a hidden sweet side, that owns my heart and soul."

She gaped, her chest aching like she'd been punched. "Man, you're good with the mushy words." All of her insides felt gooey and warm, and she would've rolled her eyes at herself if a mirror had been handy. Instead, she could only feel. "Tace—"

"No." He nudged open a blue doorway and led her inside a darkened room, pushing her against the wall. "For tonight, there are no worries—no fears—no pain. Just one night, you and me, dreaming big."

She blinked back tears. "I can do that." Her voice was thick, and she cleared it. "How big are we going to dream?"

"Close your eyes." His warm breath brushed her ear.

She trembled but did as he'd said. "All right. What now?"

He swept her up, pressing her head against his neck, moving to walk deeper into the darkness. "Keep them shut."

"Okay." She inhaled his masculine scent and nibbled up his jugular to lick beneath his jaw. Rough whiskers scratched her tongue, and she moved up, kissing his earlobe.

He sucked in air, and that powerful chest moved against her.

The world lightened a little behind her closed lids, and then he gently set her down. Her feet touched a thick rug, and she swayed, grasping his forearms for support. He lifted her shirt over her head and shoved her pants down, leaving her nude. Quick movements against her proved he was stripping as well.

She chuckled. "Can I open my eyes?"

"No." He moved away, and the swish of a shower came on.

Her eyelids flashed open, and she stared in wonder at a wide shower with steam rising. "Hot water?"

He chuckled, pulling her under the spray.

It was so hot and wonderful, she almost orgasmed right then. "Oh my God." She tilted her head back and let delicious heated water sluice over her. Tace moved in behind her, shutting the glass door, his big body pressing her into the spray. "It's heaven." How quickly she'd forgotten. She stepped back and wiped off her face, looking beyond the glass to a light blue energy-efficient light in the ceiling. "It's hot water—real hot water."

Tace nodded and stepped beneath the spray, groaning in pure pleasure. "To think we once took this for granted."

"I know." She moved into him, put her face against his wet chest, and held on with both hands around his waist. "Jax obviously doesn't know."

"Not yet. I'm sure the minute he does, he'll turn off the heat to save gas for the generators." Tace reached for a ledge on the stonelike tile and poured vanilla-scented shampoo into his hands. "Let's not talk about Jax while we're naked."

She laughed and turned around, her back to him. "That's a deal."

Tace lathered the fragrant soap through her hair, and she couldn't help but moan. Steam surrounded them, and his hands were magic. He rinsed her hair, washed his own, and then they took an inordinate amount of time washing each other head to toe.

Finally, Sami panted in rough need. "Tace."

He spread both hands over her breasts. "I'm takin' you in the shower, Sami. In the hot shower, just once for the memory. It'll probably be a cold shower next time."

"Now that would be a pity, although I love the sound of there being a next time and then another," she said, running her hand along his impressive length. His cock jumped against her hand, and she smiled, feeling the fun and power of Tace Justice. "Let's do this right, then."

He speared one hand in her hair and tilted her head back. "Now we talk about you asking Jax to knock me out and take me from you."

She smiled, desire ripping through her stronger than the hold on her head. "Want me to apologize?"

He leaned down and nipped her lip, sending shards of need zinging through her. "I was kinda hopin' to spank you again."

Humor and lightness bubbled up through her. "How about I spank you instead?"

"That ain't how it works." His drawl deepened, and he flipped her around, landing a playful slap on her butt.

She laughed out loud and tried to turn back around, only to have him hold her in place. "Tace."

"What?" He leaned over her, his mouth on her shoulder, his hand flattened across her entire abdomen. The sheer power and strength surrounding her came from pure maleness, and she took a precious moment to luxuriate in Tace Justice.

She leaned her head back against his chest, trusting him to keep her from falling. "I've never trusted a man like you, Tace. I mean, like this."

"This how?" he asked, running his palm up to her chest and then back down, playing between her thighs.

Her knees buckled, and he easily held her in place. "Completely," she whispered into the steam, her gaze on the damp tile. "You told me that you liked all of me. The soldier, the fighter, the hacker."

"And the woman. Definitely the sweet woman," he whispered against her ear, licking along the shell.

Her breath panted out, and she fought to concentrate. His talented fingers ran over her labia, tapping across her clit. She shook her head, and her vision fuzzed. "I like all of you, too."

"Yeah?" He drew the shell of her ear into his mouth.

She bit back a moan. "Yeah. The good ole boy, the Texas lawman, the guy who loved his mama."

"That's me." He tilted her head to the side and scraped his teeth down the side of her face to her jawline.

"That's part of you," she breathed. "I like the soldier, the man who'd kill in a second for me, just as much."

He paused, his lips at her jugular. "You do?"

"I love the darkness as much as the light," she whispered. "All of you—I want it all."

He opened the door and grabbed something off the nearest countertop. Something crinkled—a condom. He flipped her around, his hands rough as he lifted her, his face near hers. "Then take all of me." He bent his knees, pressed between her legs, and stood up, impaling her.

She gasped and grabbed onto his shoulders, holding tight. He filled her completely, all of him in all of her. Tears filled her eyes, but even through the haze, his blazing blue eyes claimed her.

Her breath panted out, and her body rioted, overtaken. Pain and pleasure melded together until she couldn't tell them apart and didn't want to give either up. Her nails dug into his skin, and he lowered his chin, all man. His hand spread across her ass, holding her in place, and he started to move. Deep and strong, he stroked inside her.

She cupped his jaw with one hand, the bristles scratching her skin. His hard face showed the rugged strength of his ancestors, those Texas settlers, and she could see the men who'd come before him. Who'd created him. She could see their power—their darkness and their light. Scorpius might have brought out part of his nature, but she'd bet everything the darkness had always been there. This male side of him that he'd tried to fight, that he'd tried to hide . . . was hers. "I love you," she murmured.

His eyes devoured her. "There's no going back, Sami."

"I don't want to go back." She held him tighter, feeling safe in his hands. He'd never drop her. "You said it. It's you and me. Forever."

He swelled even bigger inside her. "Hold on." Dropping to his knees, he kept her in place, partially bending over her.

She gasped as electricity uncoiled inside her. In this position, he could go so deep inside her she'd feel him forever. He held her neck and her butt, using his knees for leverage and hammering hard.

He buried his head in her hair, holding on, increasing the strength of his thrusts.

She closed her eyes, feeling him everywhere—inside her—all around her. Her world narrowed and expanded to only Tace Justice, and for a moment, a perfect slice of time, the world was right.

Then she exploded and screamed his name, the waves of raw pleasure ripping through her so completely she rode them for what seemed like forever and then ended on a sob.

He came against her, his powerful body shuddering.

Then he got up and kissed her so sweetly everything inside her settled.

The water pounded around them, while steam blanketed them. She blinked, allowing reality to return. God. She had to save him.

Chapter Thirty-Three

Even the blood of the warriors from times gone by eventually slowed and stopped. Damn it.

—Tace Justice

Sami inched her way to the command center, her body thrumming and her heart aching. The night had been spectacular, and the bed perfectly soft and new, but she could tell Tace's head hurt in the morning. His eyes were bloodshot, and his jaw tight in pain. He'd have another attack soon, and unless she found the right enzyme for him, he might not survive.

First she had orders to finish decrypting the files in the command center, and then she could return to the medical center. Tace had already headed to the infirmary to check on his patients.

So she cleared her mind and ignored the delicious tingles still taking over her body. Tace Justice knew how to spend time in a good bed. In a shower. On the floor. Hell, on a table. She grinned and tried to keep her face from flushing.

"You okay?" Raze asked from his guard position, a scowl marring his handsome face. With his "about to go into battle" expression, he looked every inch the Native American warrior he would've been in earlier times.

Sami paused. "Fine. You?"

"Just fine and dandy."

Ah. Sami tried to get rid of what must be a contented glow. Raze didn't like being away from Vinnie for any amount of time, and now that Sami had found amazing sex and romance, she actually understood why he was so cranky at the moment. "You'll be heading back to Vanguard soon."

"I'm not leaving until we fix Tace," the Vanguard soldier returned.

Sami paused, her chest filling. The Vanguard soldiers were family, and she belonged. They cared about Tace, too. "Raze." Tears filled her eyes.

Horror filled Raze's. "Stop that. Geez." He reached over and awkwardly patted her shoulder, nearly sending her into the wall. "It's okay. We'll cure him."

She sniffed and headed over to her rolling chair. "I'll go back to the medical files as soon as I decrypt the rest of these."

"Jax and I were up all night going through the medical files. We need to get them to Lynne or the doctors of Vanguard," Raze said.

Sami turned, her heart warming all over again. "All night?"

"Yeah, but we couldn't figure out some of the scientific formulas." His lip twisted. "I'm sorry."

"It's okay. We'll get it." They were fighting for Tace as hard as she was. That meant something. Heck, it meant everything. She turned on the computer and waited for it to boot up. "What about Penelope? How is she?"

Raze shook his head. "Not good. Still incoherent even though we plugged her full of B and morphine all night." He winced. "I guess it's fair to say that Marcus plugged her full of them. He wouldn't let us get close."

"Did he talk to Jax at all?"

"No. The only person he seems even remotely interested

in is Penelope. I have guards on him in case he tries to take her and run." Raze leaned back against the wall. "He's half-baked, Sami."

Sami nodded. "Yeah, but we've all been there at one time or another. Maybe he'll relax and come out of it at some point. Who knows what those doctors did to him in their experiments. It's amazing he's coherent at all—trust me. Doc Vinnie might be able to shrink his head."

"That man isn't getting within ten feet of Vinnie," Raze said. "Not a chance in hell."

Hmmm. Vinnie would probably be of a different opinion, but Sami had other things to worry about at the moment. The cursor flashed. "All right. Let's open this bitch up." She started typing.

"Can you get everything?" Raze asked.

"Yeah. When I worked here, I created a buffer overflow to give myself super-user status." She shrugged. "They upgraded a couple of times, or tried to anyway, but I created a backdoor." She smiled. "Old habits die hard, you know."

"So you have a backdoor to the server?"

"No. You want to watch that because a backdoor to the server might be removed during a system upgrade. I created the backdoor in the compiler." She warmed to her subject. "In fact—"

Raze lifted a hand. "It's fascinating. Really. But I need to scout the hallway and back." He turned on his heel.

Sami fought the urge to stick her tongue out at his retreating back. It *was* fascinating, damn it. She turned back and typed quickly, methodically going through a large amount of data she didn't recognize. A video suddenly blinked on camera. "Raze?" she called.

Raze returned with Jax on his heels.

"You hungry? There's great food down in the cafeteria."

Jax slipped a doughnut in front of her. "It's kind of fresh, even."

She typed in a couple of commands. A street camera went live outside of Merc territory in Santa Barbara. "They've been watching."

Jax leaned in. "Holy shit."

"Yeah. Not all the time because they don't have the resources. It's on a rotating schedule, but they can tune in anytime they want." She clicked a couple of keys, and the entrance to Vanguard territory came into view just as the guards were changing. She sucked in air. "Whoa."

Raze straightened and glanced around the pristine command center. "We're missing something."

"Huh?" Sami asked, leaning in to read the different files.

"There should be notes, maps, and even printouts of all the surveillance targets. No way was one guy just memorizing everything. Where is all the data?" Raze asked.

Sami stiffened. "Good point. Let's get a schematic for this Bunker before we access all the surveillance data." She switched screens and typed rapidly, accessing hidden files she hadn't had time to investigate yet. Maps poured onto the screen.

"Stop," Jax said, leaning over her shoulder.

It didn't just stop. She grabbed the mouse and clicked on the one she figured he wanted. A full schematic of the entire Bunker facility came up. She flipped it around on the screen. "There's the fourth level with the bombs and two additional storage areas." She'd already found that, but this schematic had more detail than the other one.

Jax pointed to a part of the screen. "That huge area is off this room." He moved toward the far side of the computer counter and tapped on the paneled wall. He turned and looked around. "All right. Find the secret button."

Sami let the men search the room while she pulled up

schematics on the rest of the facility. "Looks like there's a hidden lab off the medical computer room as well." Her fingers flew across the keyboard as she tried to measure the dimensions. "There isn't anything about how to access it, but there's a lot of energy hooked up to the lab." Was there a cure for Scorpius only hallways away? Was it possible?

Jax pulled her chair back and looked under the desk before pushing her back. "Where is it, damn it?"

"We could blow it," Raze said.

Jax nodded. "Blow it."

"I'll be right back." Raze pivoted and ran from the room.

"How's Justice today?" Jax asked, running his hand along the top of the wall and still searching.

Sami shook her head. "Not good. We have to figure out the right enzyme. Maybe it's in the hidden lab?"

"Probably." Jax's voice didn't exactly sound reassuring.

Raze returned with a backpack. "Out."

Sami jumped up and hustled into the hallway. Within thirty seconds, the Vanguard soldiers followed. Jax covered her for three heartbeats, and then an explosion rocked the floor.

They hurried back.

Sami blew out air and followed Jax through a gaping hole in the wall. A monstrous world map took up the very far wall with pins stuck in different places. File cabinets, rows and rows of them, lined each wall. Surveillance photos had been tacked to corkboards above them. Photos of Vanguard, the Mercenaries, the president's Elite Force, and many others she couldn't identify.

"The locations of the other Bunker facilities have to be here somewhere," Jax said, his voice hushed.

Raze nodded. "We have time to go through everything. Right now, let's get into the other hidden room. The lab."

"Yeah." Sami turned and ran from the room, all but barreling down the hallway and into the medical computer room.

"It's over there." She pointed to the one wall area that had enough room to serve as an entrance.

"Out," Jax said.

She huffed out a breath. "At some point, I want to learn the explosives part of this job."

"Later," Raze muttered, taking something from his pack.

She turned the corner and ran into Tace. "We're finding secret rooms."

"Really?" His cheek creased. "Sounds fun."

"Raze and Jax are setting up explosives." She studied him. Bloodshot eyes, stiff shoulders. "You're in pain."

"I'm fine." He tucked her into his chest and turned around as the other two Vanguard soldiers rounded the corner.

This explosive was quieter, and smoke billowed out.

Sami shoved the men aside and ran inside and through the hole. "Wow." An aquarium took up an entire wall of the massive lab and was filled with jellyfish swimming gracefully.

Tace came up behind her. "It's not surprising, considering Lynne's blue heart and the failed cure. There's something about vitamin B and the luminescent nature and ability to regenerate of the jellyfish." He pointed to another wall tank filled with squid. "And squid."

Counters were set throughout the room, and notations were on every available surface. File cabinets lined a side wall.

Sami turned to Jax. "We need Lynne here."

The Vanguard leader looked around and then nodded. "Yeah. All right. For now, go see what else is hidden in those computers."

Tace checked on the wounded again before grabbing two coffees from the cafeteria. Real coffee with real creamer. He wondered what the Bunker folks had planned to do in a year or so when supplies ran out. Was there an underground bunker somewhere filled with coffee, creamer, and dough-nuts? At this point, he'd believe anything.

His hand shook, and the toes on his left foot had gone numb. An episode was imminent, and his chest felt so heavy he wondered if his heart was fibrillating.

But he shoved the panic down and strode into the com-puter command center to find his little hacker hard at work and muttering to herself. "You need to eat something." He placed a coffee and what looked like mac and cheese in front of her.

She glanced down. "I love mac and cheese." She grabbed the carton and dug in with a spoon, humming softly as she ate.

He grinned and ran a hand over her hair. Loose and long, the waves fascinated him. "How's it going?"

She smiled up at him, her eyes concerned and the grin forced. "Great. I'm zeroing in on the other Bunker locations, I hope."

"Excellent." He sipped his coffee and enjoyed the moment with his woman. "What's that?"

"I was trying to determine the schedule for surveillance. They had cameras all over California, and they've been watching several groups on a rotating schedule." She brought up Vanguard. "Look. It's home."

"Interesting." He leaned in and pointed to the options. "Narrow in there, would you?"

"Sure." She typed several commands, and a camera focused on the rear corner of Vanguard territory. "Whoa. Who is that?"

Tace leaned over her shoulder. "Can you sharpen that?"

"Yeah." She sharpened the video until Joe Bentley, the organizational leader of the Pure, could be seen clearly speaking to somebody on the other side of the fence. "Let me zoom in on the other guy." She did so and gasped at seeing a soldier with a clear EL on his chest.

"Shit. Bentley was talking to one of the president's Elite Force? When was that?" Tace's heart began to drum.

Sami sucked in air. "About seven hours ago."

That was long enough to get back to the president and make a plan. "Can you bring up the Elite Force? Let's see the president's headquarters." Tace's instincts shifted into overdrive.

"Yeah." She clicked on it, and nothing happened. Setting down the mac and cheese, she typed furiously, and a bunch of code started to run. "The last check-in at his location was three hours ago. I think they take a snapshot every three days, but if they want to focus and watch for a while, they can manually do so. I mean, they could."

She brought up a series of video and then sat back. "Huh."

"So that's three hours ago."

"Yes."

Tace straightened as truck after truck exited the California forest, loaded with men and weapons. "Shit. Bentley told the Elite soldier that we were gone. He gave them our weaknesses." He rushed into the hidden war room where Jax and Raze were poring over documents. "We have a problem." They followed him back into the computer room. "Sami? Can you track the president's movements?"

She was already typing. "Yes. They headed south." She brought up two more cameras. "Oh God."

Tace leaned back. "Vanguard. They're going to try to take Vanguard." He'd figured they'd retaliate but not this quickly. Damn Joe Bentley and the Pure. His chest compressed, and his mind spun. "We didn't cripple them as badly as we'd hoped."

"We only took explosives and weapons from one outbuilding," Sami whispered.

Tace caught Raze as he barreled from the room. "Wait a minute. We need a plan."

"The plan is to get to Vanguard and stop the massacre," Jax snapped, striding past them, fury on his hard face. "We've left our people defenseless."

"No, we haven't." Tace sprang into a run behind his friends. "We left soldiers—both Vanguard and Mercs—guarding the civilians. We'll get there in time." Yet the president had a huge head start and an impressive array of firepower.

Sami ran behind him.

Jax reached Greyson outside the medical computer room. "Vanguard is under attack. I'm taking all my soldiers—you have to hold down the Bunker."

Grey nodded. "My men have it. I'm coming with you."

Jax paused. "No, but I appreciate the thought. We need the Bunker to remain secure in case forces are coming from other facilities. I'm leaving you vulnerable here, Grey."

The Mercenary leader clapped Jax on the shoulder. "Fine. We'll go into lockdown the second you leave. Let's get whatever explosives and weapons you'll need. You're gonna love the bulletproof vests I found." He nodded toward the far door. "We searched the parking garage adjacent to the building. In the bottom floor, there are two Humvees, fully armed and ready to go."

Tace coughed. "Awesome. Let's get them."

Sami ran in and grabbed a wild stack of papers. "I've been compiling these for Lynne." She hurried toward a fridge and grabbed one of the two remaining yellow vials. "Maybe she'll know what to do with this."

Tace's vision wavered. "Put it back—we need it cool, I'd bet."

She wavered.

"I'll make it back here, Sami. Trust me." Yet his entire left side was tingling.

She nodded and returned it to the fridge.

He reached for her hand. "Let's go protect our home."

Chapter Thirty-Four

President or not, he messed with the wrong men.

—Jax Mercury

The ride back to East Los Angeles was tense, fast, and nearly desperate. Tace kept point out the window while Jax drove like a lunatic, but Tace couldn't blame him. If Sami had been the target of an attack, he'd lose his mind, too. She sat next to him, alternating between making soothing sounds and wincing when Jax drove over instead of around debris.

They drove furiously down the 101, an interstate they'd avoided until now. Too many rogue gangs controlled areas of it, but Jax's orders to shoot anything that moved seemed to be working. They turned onto the quiet 405 with cars and trucks rotting and rusting on the sides.

The Humvee barreled through a series of crashed cars in the center lanes, tossing trucks aside like they were Tinkertoys. "We need more of these," Tace murmured.

"It's eating gas," Jax replied, his knuckles white on the steering wheel. "They've been retrofitted for city use, not like the ones we used in the desert. Anyway, they'll do for today."

Raze drove the other one, his recklessness matching Jax's "Ahead," Tace said to Jax.

Two black vans emblazoned with bright purple "20s"

blocked the middle of the freeway with a series of crashed cars on either side.

"Get down." Tace shoved Sami's head down and leaned out the window, waiting for a target. "Don't slow up."

"No problem." Jax pressed down hard on the gas.

Tace took aim and waited, the vision in his left eye fuzzing. Three men in purple ran around the far end of a van, automatic weapons already firing. He plugged one center mass, the second in the head, and then paused as Raze took out the third from his Humvee.

Tace slammed a hand over Sami's chest to hold her to the seat.

Jax plowed between the vans, sending them spinning in opposite directions. Metal crunched, and tires shredded. "I love this thing," he muttered.

Sami shoved Tace's arm off. "Watch the ribs."

"Sorry." He rubbed a hand over his eyes. His chest grew tight, and his balls hurt. He'd never figured that his balls would ache right before he died. Death was a heartless bitch. He snorted.

"What?" Sami asked.

That quickly, he lost the humor. "Nothing. I just like the Humvee." He took her hand with his free one, tracking the world outside. His eardrum popped, and he bit back a wince.

God had given him one more mission, and he'd use it to make sure Sami had a safe home when he left her. Blood trickled out of his right ear, and he casually wiped it away before she could see.

They made record time, and soon the nice brick on the side of the freeway turned to gang tags and graffiti.

Sami gasped, looking out the front window.

Tace turned. "Shit."

Smoke billowed from Vanguard territory in frightening yellow and black. "Fire. Something is on fire," Sami said, her voice full of panic.

It looked like the entire world was filled with smoke. "She's okay, Jax," Tace muttered. Lynne Harmony had to be all right.

Jax didn't answer. He leaned forward and sped up, careening off the freeway and down the exit ramp. A series of shopping carts filled with garbage were no match for the vehicle and flew up into the air to bounce harmlessly behind them.

They careened through abandoned neighborhoods and almost hit a pack of wild cats that scattered in record time. Finally, the protective perimeter of Vanguard came into view. The two Humvees would go in the front, while the other vehicles would crash through the rear. As a plan, it was fraught with problems, but it was too late to turn back.

Jax took the corner squarely.

"Holy hell," Sami breathed.

The Elite Force had blown a hole through the front Vanguard gate. The downed vans, trucks, and even the tires all burned bright with fire. "Did they use gasoline?" Jax hissed, swerving around a burning mass of metal.

An explosion blew out several windows on the second floor of headquarters, spraying glass down across the entire parking area. Jax drove around a truck to see the president's men behind their trucks, throwing grenades and firing rapidly. Vanguard soldiers fired back from the burning building, their bullets pinging off the trucks.

A quick glance toward the front headquarters door confirmed black uniforms. The Elite Force had breached the building.

"Start spraying," Jax ordered, gunning the vehicle toward the middle truck.

Tace took aim toward the soldiers behind the truck to the right. Men yelled as Jax plowed into them, and bodies flew up into the air. They impacted the truck with the sound of metal bashing metal. Tace rocked back in the seat and grabbed onto Sami before she could fly into the windshield. "Stay behind me." He opened the door, already firing. Bullets pinged against metal.

The other Humvee crashed into the third Elite truck, and blood sprayed through the air to mix with the smoke.

"Take back headquarters," Jax yelled, charging out of the Humvee.

"Damn it." Tace kept low and tried to cover both Sami and Jax. "Take cover, you asshole."

Jax ignored him, running full bore across the open parking lot.

Tace sprayed bullets to the left while Raze fired to the right. Sami took aim next to him and plugged a guy coming out of headquarters. "Nice shot, baby," he yelled through the smoke.

Bullets threw concrete up around them. "From the roof." Jesus. How had they gotten on the roof so quickly?

Raze rolled and came up on the other side of the door, his back to the brick. Blood flowed down his face from his forehead, but Tace couldn't determine the type of wound. The soldier nodded, lifted three fingers, and then counted down.

Tace's left knee shook.

He waited.

When Raze's last finger dropped, Sami yanked open the door. Tace went low, Jax went high, and Raze provided clean up. Sami moved behind them, rapidly firing toward the parking lot.

Tace shot an Elite soldier in the knee while sweeping his leg out and taking a second down. Raze and two men grappled over to the left, while Jax took the stairs three at a time.

Sami shut the door.

Bullets impacted the glass.

"Sami!" Tace grabbed her arm and yanked her away from the flying glass. She winced and clapped a hand over her shoulder. "I'm okay."

Raze kicked one of the soldiers across the room while slicing his knife into the second.

An Elite soldier jumped up, and Tace squeezed the trigger, hitting the bastard in the chest. He went down, dead before he hit the ground.

Sami gulped air and ran for the soup kitchen. "Clear," she yelled.

Raze hustled for the war rooms, quickly returning. "Clear." He ran for the stairs. "The quarters."

Tace followed him, keeping Sami at his six. Which room had exploded? He counted in his head. They reached the landing and turned to see Jax kicking down doors. Smoke billowed through the entire hallway. He kicked open the door to Raze's apartment and then leaped out of the way as bullets sprayed across the wall. "Blue?" he bellowed.

"Jax!" Lynne Harmony ran out, blood across her chest, gun in her hand. "Sorry."

Vinnie Wellington was right behind her, soot on her face and in her blond hair. "Raze." She barreled into his chest with a muffled sob.

The soldier held her tight and dropped his face into her neck. His body shuddered.

Jax held Lynne away from him while smoke swirled around. "How bad?"

Lynne shook her head and wiped at her collarbone. "Just glass. Hurts but isn't fatal."

Tace pointed up.

Jax nodded and set Lynne to the side. "Go inside Tace's place and barricade the door in case more grenades come from the other side. Both of you shoot anybody you don't know."

Tace's vision wavered.

Jax waited until the two doctors had followed his advice. "We need the roof."

"Yeah." Tace let Jax pass him and lead the way. "Sami?"

"I'm not staying here," she hissed through the smoke.

His chest compressed, and his left arm hurt. Was he having a heart attack? God, it felt like it. He tucked his arm against his abs and followed Raze to the landing and up the stairs, where they kicked open the door.

The firefight was in full force with the president's soldiers shooting down from every angle.

"No mercy," Jax said, dropping his chin.

"It's way too late for mercy," Tace said, ducking as debris rained down. More explosions sounded from several blocks away at the rear entrance to the territory. God, there were kids and pregnant women near that area. For now, they had to neutralize the most immediate threat. "I've got north." He pivoted and crept toward the soldiers.

One soldier turned, and Tace shot, taking him down. Then the world exploded around them. He grabbed Sami and shoved her against a metal air duct, firing wildly.

Jax shot two men. His eyes widened, and he clutched his chest, dropping to his knees.

Raze sprayed the other side of the roof, and three of the Elite soldiers fell over the edge.

"Jax!" Tace yelled. "Sami, cover." He ducked low and crisscrossed to his friend, grabbing Jax's shoulder and yanking him across the rough rocks on the roof. He got him behind the duct work and yanked open his shirt. Thank God. He'd been wearing his vest.

Jax coughed and sat up. "Fuck."

Sami screamed.

Tace pivoted to see a broad Elite soldier dragging her to the north corner, a gun held to her temple. His legs weakened, and he dropped to one knee.

Jax rolled to the side and up, yanking his arm. "You okay?"

"Yeah." Tace stood and wavered, lowering his chin to focus.

Sami's eyes were wide, and blood slid down her neck. Had she been hit?

The soldier, a tall black guy with scars down his face, kept moving backward.

"Where does he think he's going?" Tace muttered, stalking him, his chest all but exploding in pain. The roof was now cleared except for the five of them. "Let her go, and we won't kill you," he called out.

The guy didn't respond but moved with a definite purpose. Not his first firefight on a roof, apparently.

Sami struggled against him, but he held her tight, the gun steady.

Tace held up his hand, signaling her to keep still.

Her gaze stayed on him, her body relaxing.

Good. She was a hell of a fighter, and if the guy would just move the gun, she could get free. But the soldier kept the barrel tight against her temple.

Trembles cascaded down Tace's legs, and his vision fuzzed. Not now. God, not now. He shook his head, continuing his advance.

"Stop," the soldier said, his dark eyes promising death.

"Where are you going to go?" Raze asked reasonably, as the others spread out to flank him.

As if in answer, an odd whirring sound pierced the chaos. Oh, Tace knew the sound, but it was so unexpected, it took him a moment to understand what it was. The helicopter, a Super Huey, banked a hard right and aimed for them. "What the hell?" he breathed.

Four massive blades competed with the whirring rotors, dropping the beast. A faded MARINE logo still showed on the tail boom. He squinted and could make out the president in the copilot seat and Vice President Lake piloting the craft. A soldier leaned out and pointed a M249 Squad Automatic Weapon at them.

Jax grabbed him and tackled him behind the ducts. "Shit."

Tace's gut cramped, and fear competed with the attack his heart kept fighting. "Sami," he whispered.

Raze crouched. "I can take out the shooter, but the guy with Sami has her angled just right."

Tace set his feet. "The second he gets her in the chopper, take out the guy with the gun."

Raze paused. "You sure?"

"Yeah." Pain shot through his chest, and he winced, grabbing it. "I don't have much time anyway." Adrenaline pumped through his veins. "Tell her I love her if I don't get the chance."

"You will," Jax said, taking aim. "I'll go for the president."

"One of you has to be below me," Tace grunted, sweat starting to roll down his face.

The soldier holding Sami backed toward the gaping opening in the Yankee. The bird hovered down, almost gracefully, at the edge of the building. Sami's eyes widened, and she started to struggle. The guy stepped back and lifted her, following her inside the helicopter. The movements were almost too smooth to be real.

"Now!" Tace bellowed.

Keeping his head low, he ran hard and fast across the roof.

A shot whizzed by his ear. The soldier with the M249 SAW widened his eyes, and his chest burst open in blood. He pitched forward and bounced twice on the roof.

Tace leaped the last few feet, hitting the Elite soldier

holding Sami head-on. The gun went off. He punched the guy in the face, grabbed his shoulders, and threw him out of the helicopter. The guy's head hit the edge of the roof with a sickening thud, and he plummeted to the alley below.

A bullet pierced the front window, and the president yelled in pain.

The helicopter hitched and then banked. Shit. Tace only had a second. He turned to see Sami's face white with shock and blood flowing down her cheek. No time. He swept her up and looked down. Too far to jump. So he kissed her fast, bunched his legs, and tossed her at the only men he trusted in the world.

Jax caught her and fell back into Raze, who'd braced his legs already. The three fell into a heap.

Raze rolled and came up firing toward the front of the helicopter.

"Shit," Lake bellowed.

"I'm hit," the president wheezed.

The helicopter banked and rolled, swinging wildly and dropping closer to the roof.

Tace saw his chance and jumped, almost hitting the roof. He was off a foot, and his hands slapped the edge.

A strong hand banded around his wrist, and he hung for a moment, grabbing the ledge with his free hand.

Gunfire erupted above him, and the helicopter swung a hard left, smoke pouring from the back. Jax leaned over, and he used his other hand to secure the hold around Tace's wrist. Tace grabbed the ledge and crab-walked up as Jax pulled. He slipped over the edge and dropped to his knees, gasping for air. "Sami?"

She rushed for him. "Are you crazy?" she yelled.

"I love you." He could feel the energy leaving his body. "You okay?" He tried to reach up to her bleeding head, but his arm wouldn't work.

Tears filled her eyes.

A crash sounded in the distance, and he turned, seeing smoke billow up. "Helicopter?"

"Yeah," Raze said, satisfaction in his voice. He leaned in. "You okay?"

"Sami?" Tace asked. "Your head?"

She wiped blood from her forehead. "Just a scratch. Let's get off the roof."

Good plan. "Love—" His heart seized, and his lungs collapsed. Blackness caught him, and the last thing he saw was her pretty face. It wasn't a bad way to die.

Chapter Thirty-Five

I had to almost die to learn what it was to really live.

—Sami Steel

Sami screamed and reached for Tace. His eyes shut, and his color turned an alarming gray. "Tace."

"Downstairs." Raze reached down and grunted while hauling Tace over his shoulder. "Cover, Jax."

Jax provided cover, but except for some random gunfire from the southern end of Vanguard, the world had quieted to the crackle of fire and raining of debris. "I think it's over."

Raze nodded and ran inside the building and down the stairs. "Get Lynne and Vinnie." He kept going, rushing through the vestibule and through the soup kitchen, his gun sweeping. They reached the infirmary, and he set Tace down on a bed, ripping open his shirt. "He's not breathing."

Sami's legs almost gave out, but she rushed forward and breathed into his mouth.

Raze waited and then pressed his hands over Tace's chest, counting out beats, his face a hard line of concentration.

Lynne and Vinnie ran into the room, Jax covering their backs.

Tears clogged Sami's throat. "He's not breathing." Raze paused, and she breathed into his mouth before Raze started again. "We brought printouts, but they're in the Humvee outside."

Lynne rushed forward and lifted his eyelids. "Not good. Tell me everything. Jax said you found the enzyme."

"I think so." Sami's legs gave out.

Vinnie grabbed her and shoved her into a chair, taking over the breathing with Tace.

Lynne's blue heart glowed through her shirt. "Tell me more, Sami. What did it look like?"

Tears poured down Sami's face, but she didn't care. Tace wasn't regaining consciousness. "It was yellow. I found the right vials according to the data, and when I injected him, he did get better."

Lynne dropped down to face her. "You injected him?"

Sami nodded. "Yes. I filled a syringe and injected him, and he got better for a little while. Then he started having attacks again."

Lynne leaned back, biting her lip. "It's an enzyme that works like a counteragent for an allergy." Her eyes widened. "Oh God. I know what to do. We have to get back to the Bunker and get the enzyme."

Sami sucked in air. Hope tried to take hold. She yanked a vial out of her pocket. "He said not to bring it, but I did anyway."

Lynne grabbed the vial and looked at the yellow liquid. She stood and ran to the counter, frantically removing syringes. "Where's the B? Damn it. Where's the B in here?" She fumbled through the cabinets and tugged out a vial of the vitamin B concoction. Her shoulders straightened, and she quickly filled two syringes.

"What are you doing?" Raze asked, stopping his compressions.

Lynne squirted a little liquid from one of the vials. "The enzyme needs the harmful agent, in this case the vitamin B, in order to bind. He needs both injections." She paused. "Probably."

Sami stood and grabbed Tace's hand. "He's still not breathing. We have to try."

Lynne swallowed. "If I'm wrong, then injecting him again with the vitamin B concoction will kill him."

Sami clutched her stomach and almost bent over from the pain and fear.

"There's no other choice," Jax said from the doorway, his expression harsh.

"Sami?" Lynne asked.

Sami sucked deep, saying a quick prayer to all those old Texas Rangers hopefully watching over him. "It's his only chance. Turn him over."

Raze half lifted Tace, and Sami yanked down part of his jeans. Lynne quickly injected him, emptying both syringes.

They all leaned back and held their breath.

Nothing.

Tace didn't move.

"Damn it." Raze settled his hands over Tace's chest again and continued performing CPR.

Sami slapped her hand against her mouth to keep from crying out. "It didn't work."

Vinnie tipped back his head, waited, and then breathed to fill his lungs. Raze continued the chest compressions.

Sami stumbled back and into the chair, holding Tace's hand. "Wake up, please." She lowered her head to his knuckles. The man had jumped into a damn helicopter to save her. He couldn't leave her now.

Tension rolled through the room on the heels of desperation as Raze and Vinnie continued to work together, not even pausing once. Nobody was willing to let him go.

Sami started to cry in earnest, clutching his hand, praying to every god that ever existed.

Lynne sat beside her and slid an arm over her shoulders while Jax covered the doorway, unable to leave.

Tace meant so much to every member of Vanguard, but especially to this small group that had become family.

Sami had no idea how long they sat there, but her heart hurt so badly she wondered if she'd survive. This just couldn't happen. She lunged forward and shot her face beneath his neck, her mouth at his ear. "Please wake up, Tace. I—need you. So much. Don't leave me." Her voice broke at the end. Then she dissolved into sobs so hard that Lynne had to help her back into the chair.

Raze slowed the compressions. "Damn it, Justice. Wake the fuck up." He smacked Tace's chest.

Sami stood. "Yeah. Wake up. I love you." If she yelled, maybe he'd come back. She grabbed his shoulders and started to shake him as violently as she could.

Lynne grabbed her arms and tried to pull her back, but Sami fought fiercely.

Tace partially sat up with a hard wheeze. "What the hell?"

Sami burst toward him, cupping his jaw. "Tace?"

His eyes opened and focused. "Did Raze just break my ribs?" He coughed.

"You're okay." Sami leaned down and kissed him all over the face, laughing and crying at the same time, her heart swelling. "You're all right."

He breathed out. "What happened?"

She smiled through the tears. "My love saved you."

He blinked.

"Well, maybe it was the enzyme." She laughed out loud, crawling over him to land by his side and curl right in. "I brought the enzyme, and Lynne figured it out. You're alive."

He stretched his arms and then ran a finger along the cut near her temple. "Are you all right?"

"I'm perfect." She buried her face in his arm, smelling

man. "You jumped into a helicopter to save me." She lifted up. "You're a hero."

Jax snorted from the doorway. "Jesus. Everyone get back to work. We need to assess damage." He lifted a hand. "Justice? You scared the shit out of me, so you have to stay there for the night and let the doctors watch you."

Were those tears in the Vanguard leader's eyes? Sami sniffled.

Raze backed away, his light blue eyes full of emotion. "Sorry about the ribs. You're kind of a pansy."

Tace rubbed his chest. "I'm fine. You hit like a member of the Elite Force."

Raze grinned. "Oh, you'll pay for that. Later."

Tace played with Sami's hair and pressed a soft kiss to her head. "I have a later. Who knew?"

Chapter Thirty-Six

I'll love you from this life to the next . . . and back again.

—Tace Justice

Tace finished moving the rest of his stuff into Sami's quarters, admitting silently to himself that her place was much nicer than his. Oh, he'd groused enough that she'd kissed him quiet, but maybe she just wanted to kiss. His woman liked to kiss, and since the day before, she hadn't taken a moment for granted.

Their kitten slept peacefully on the countertop as a reminder of the soldier who'd been their friend. They'd give the little guy a good home.

Sami leaned against him from behind and snuggled her face into his back. "How are you feeling?"

"Fine." He turned and pulled her closer, inhaling her fresh scent. "I think I'm cured." He felt great, actually. It had only been twenty-four hours since Lynne had shot him up with the enzyme and B concoction, but he felt stronger somehow. "We only have a few minutes until we get back to work, and I wanted to talk to you really quickly."

She breathed out and ran her hands over his chest. "What about?"

"You and me."

She paused and looked up, her pretty eyes sparkling. "What about us?"

He breathed out slowly. Vanguard had been damaged, and they'd lost twenty soldiers in the attack. Their primary goal was to build the defenses back up as well as deal with the Pure church. Then they could branch out and find those other Bunkers. But Sami had work to do as well. "I've talked to Jax, and the plan is to stay here a week to work, then go to the Bunker for a week. We'll have to alternate." There was plenty for him to do at the Bunker as well. "If that works for you."

"So long as we're together, I'm fine with any plan," she murmured.

"Good." He brushed her hair back from her face, frowning at the red scratch along her forehead. "I was so scared when he had you with a gun to your head."

"I know." She leaned up on her toes to kiss his mouth. "We're both fine now."

Yeah. They were. Scouts had already found the wrecked helicopter, but neither the president nor the vice president had been in it. However, by the pools of blood they'd found, at least one of the men should be dead. "We're staying here to fix Vanguard, but at some point, we'll need to go north."

"One thing at a time. For now, let's just relax and heal a little."

That was a damn good plan. He could do this right. He had to. So he took her hands and dropped to one knee.

Her mouth gaped open. "What are you doing?"

"I've never loved anybody like I love you, because you're my heart, Samantha Steel." He let his drawl free, feeling his family all around him for the first time in way too long. "Marry me."

She blinked. "I, ah, I."

He grinned. "Try again."

"Yes," she breathed. "Okay. I mean, yes."

He stood and kissed her, taking her mouth and vowing to himself that she'd never want for anything. The woman would never doubt him or herself, for that matter. He might be darker than before, deadlier, but he could love deeper, too. He'd make sure of it.

Finally, he leaned back. "I love you."

She smiled. "I love you more."

That was truly impossible, and now he had years to prove it to her. So he leaned down and kissed her again, putting every promise he'd ever make into that one act. While he still missed his family and wished they could know Sami, something told him, deep down, that they knew.

And they were finally at peace.

In the worst of times, he and Sami had found love, and he was never letting go.

Read on for a taste of Rebecca Zanetti's
next Realm Enforcers novel,

WICKED KISS!

So far, the magical world of Ireland pretty much sucked eggs. Her dreams of rolling hills, rugged men, and wild adventures had given way to facts that tilted her universe, spun it around, and spiked it headfirst into the ground.

The world held too many secrets.

Tori Monzelle leaned her shoulders against the cold metal wall of the van and tried to blink through the blindfold turning the interior dark. Nothing. The carpet in the rear of the van smelled fresh and new, but she sat on the floor, her knees drawn up, and her hands tied behind her back.

The sounds of drizzling rain and honking horns filtered inside, while two men breathed from the front seats. She hadn't recognized either one of them when they'd arrived at the penthouse just an hour before. For an entire week, she'd been held hostage in various luxurious locales after having been kidnapped from Seattle.

Had it only been a week since she'd learned the world wasn't as she'd thought?

Witches, vampires, and demons existed. As in *really existed.*

They were just different species from humans, apparently. So far she'd seen witches create fireballs and throw them, and she'd met a demon who'd shown her his fangs. She had to go on faith that vampires really existed, but at this point, why not believe?

She cleared her throat. "Listen, jackasses. I'm about done with this entire kidnapping scenario." It had to be the oddest kidnapping of all time, with her being flown across the globe and then put up in zillion-dollar penthouses for a week. "I promise not to tell anybody that supernatural beings exist. Just let me go."

A snort came from the front seat. "Supernatural," one of the men muttered.

Her chest heated. "All right, so you think you're natural. Then how about I refrain from announcing that your species even exists?"

Another snort.

What a dick. Fine. "Are you witches, demons, or vampires?" If she had to guess, they were witches.

No answer.

The van swerved, and she knocked her head against the side. "Damn it." It was time to get free. "Let me go, you morons. This is international kidnapping." Did witches care about international laws? Her shoulders shook, and a welcome anger soared through her.

The van jerked.

"What the hell?" one of the guys snapped.

They tilted.

Something sputtered. The engine?

An explosion rocked the day, and the van spun. Her temple smacked the metal, and she rolled to the other side across the carpet. Breath swooshed from her lungs. Pain pounded in her head, and she blinked behind the blindfold.

The van stopped cold, and she rolled toward the front, her legs scrambling. Her forehead brushed the carpet, and she shook her head, dislodging the blindfold.

Doors opened, and grunts sounded. Men fighting. Punches being thrown.

The back doors opened, and light flooded inside.

She turned just as hands manacled her ankles and dragged her toward the street. Kicking out, she struggled furiously, her eyes adjusting and focusing on this new threat. A ski mask completely covered the guy's head, leaving only his eyes and mouth revealed. With the light behind him, she couldn't even make out the color of his irises.

His strong grip didn't relent, and he easily pulled her toward the edge, dropping her legs toward the ground.

She threw a shoulder into his rock-hard abs and stood. He was at least a foot taller than she and definitely cut hard.

Everything in her screamed to get the hell out of the area and make a run for it. She was smart, she was tough, and she could handle the situation. No time to think. Tori leaped up and shot a quick kick to his face. While he was tall and fit, he probably wasn't expecting a fight.

He snagged her ankle an inch from his jaw, thus preventing the impact. Using her momentum to pull her forward, he manacled his other hand behind her thigh and lifted, tossing her over his shoulder in one incredibly smooth motion.

Her rib cage slammed into solid muscle, knocking the wind from her lungs.

One firm hand clamped across her thighs, and he turned, moving into a jog. The sound of men fighting behind them had her lifting her head to see more men in ski masks battling the two guys from the van.

Then her captor turned a corner and ran through an alley, easily holding her in place.

"Let me go," she gasped, pulling on the restraints holding her hands. Cobblestones flew by below, while cool air brushed across her skin. Rain continued to patter down, matting her hair to her face.

He didn't answer and took two more turns, finally ending

up next to a shiny black motorcycle in yet another alley. Her hair swooshed as he ducked his shoulder and planted her on her feet. Firm hands flipped her around, and something sliced through her bindings.

Blood rushed into her wrists, and she winced, pivoting back around. "Who are you?" She slid one foot slightly back in an attack position.

He reached out and tugged the blindfold completely off her head before ripping off his ski mask.

Adam Dunne stood before her, legs braced, no expression on his hard face. Rain dripped from his thick black hair, and irritation glittered in his spectacular green eyes. That expression seemed to live on him. He was some sort of brilliant scientist, definitely a brainiac, and he always appeared annoyed.

She blinked twice. "Adam?"

He crossed his arms. "It has been nearly impossible to find you."

His deep voice shot right through her to land in very private places. Then the angry tone caught her. She slammed her hands against her hips. "And that's my fault? Your stupid people, the fucking witches, *kidnapped* me."

Witches. Holy crap. Adam Dunne was a witch. Sure, she'd figured that out a week ago, but with him standing right in front of her, she had to face reality.

The man looked like a badass vigilante and not some brilliant otherworldly being. For the rescue, he'd worn a black T-shirt, ripped jeans, and motorcycle boots. Definitely not his usual pressed slacks and button-down silk shirt.

His sizzling green eyes darkened. "I have about an hour to get you to a plane and out of this country, so you'll be quiet, *for once*, and you'll follow orders."

She pressed her lips together. No matter how badly she wanted to punch him in the face, she wanted to get out of the country even more. "Fine."

He lifted an eyebrow. "We're getting on the bike, heading to the airport, and then you're flying to Seattle. You don't know who rescued you, and you haven't seen me in weeks."

She swallowed. "How much trouble are you in if we get caught?"

He turned and grabbed a helmet off the bike. "Treason and death sentence."

Everything in her softened. He'd risked his life for her. Sure, his brother was dating her sister, but even so. "Thank you."

He turned and shoved the helmet at her. "Don't thank me. Just do what I tell you."

Man, what a jerk. Nearly biting through her tongue to keep from lashing out, she shoved the helmet on her head.

He did the same and swung a leg over the bike, holding out a hand to help her.

She ignored him and levered herself over the bike and into place, anger flowing through her. Why did he have to be such a dick? She'd wanted to thank him, that's all.

He ignited the engine. It sputtered. He stiffened and tried again.

Hell. She closed her eyes and tried to calm her temper. They had to get out of there. *Work, bike. Damn it, work.* The more she tried to concentrate, the more irritated she became.

He twisted the throttle again, and this time, nothing happened.

Damn it. Why the hell did this always happen to her? What was wrong with her? "It won't work. If it's broken, it won't work." She tugged off the helmet and slid off the bike.

He turned toward her. "The bike ran just fine an hour ago."

She shrugged, her face heating. No way was she telling him about her oddity. "I know the sound of an engine that's not coming back to life, and so do you."

He frowned and tried the bike again. Nothing. "All right."

He swung his leg over and stood, reaching for a buzzing cell phone and pushing the SPEAKER button. "I have a problem," he said.

"The woman has been tagged," came an urgent male voice. "There's a tracker, and you have about five minutes until the Guard gets there." Keys clacking echoed across the line. "Get rid of the tag and find safety. I'll be in touch with new coordinates as soon as I can." The line went dead.

Adam surveyed her from head to toe, reaching for her shirt.

She slapped at his hands. "What are you doing?"

He sighed. "Your clothing has been tagged, and I don't know where. Strip, baby."

Baby? Did he just call her *baby*? Wait a minute. "Strip?"

"Now." A muscle ticked in his powerful jaw. "Our tags are minute and could be anywhere on you—even lightly threaded in the material." He dug both hands through her hair, tugging just enough to flood her with unwelcome tingles. "Not in your hair."

"I am not stripping," she said through clenched teeth, her body doing a full tremble.

He lowered his head until his nose almost touched hers. "Take everything off, or I'll do it for you."

She blinked.

He gave a barely perceptible eye roll and turned around, pulling off his T-shirt. "Drop the clothes and put this on. It'll cover you for the time being."

Muscles rippled in his back.

Her mouth went dry.

"Now, Victoria. We have to hurry."

The urgency in his voice got through to her. She shucked her clothes, kicking off her socks and shoes, shivering in the light rain. The second her jeans hit the ground, she reached for his shirt and tugged it over her head. The soft material fell beneath her thighs and surrounded her with the scent of male.

He turned around, and yep. His bare chest was even more spectacular than his back. "Everything off? Bra and panties?"

Did Adam Dunne just use the word *panties*? A slightly hysterical giggle bubbled up from her abdomen, and she shoved it ruthlessly down. "Yes."

"Good." He took her hand. "Sorry about the bare feet, but we'll get you replacement clothes soon. For now, we have to run."

A car screeched to a stop outside the alley.

"Bullocks. They're here," he muttered, launching into a run down the alley. "Hurry, and don't look back."

Panic seized her, and she held firm to his hand, her bare feet slapping hard cobblestones.

A fireball careened past her, smashing into the brick building above her and raining down debris. She screamed.

Adam stopped and shoved her behind him, dark blue plasma forming down his arms as he pivoted to fight.

She gulped in air and peered around him as three men, each forming a different color plasma ball, all stalked toward them from the street.

"Run, Victoria," Adam ordered.